SHADOWS OF SOMETHING REAL

by

Sophia Kell Hagin

2013

SHADOWS OF SOMETHING REAL

ISBN 10: 1-60282-889-X
ISBN 13: 978-1-60282-889-6

This Trade Paperback Original Is Published By
Bold Strokes Books, Inc.
P.O. Box 249
Valley Falls, NY 12185

First Edition: July 2013

CREDITS
EDITOR: CINDY CRESAP
PRODUCTION DESIGN: SUSAN RAMUNDO
COVER DESIGN BY SHERI (GRAPHICARTIST2020@HOTMAIL.COM)

Dedication

For Susan, always for Susan

All around the house is the jet-black night;
It stares through the window-pane;
It crawls in the corners, hiding from the light,
And it moves with the moving flame.

Now my little heart goes a-beating like a drum,
With the breath of the Bogies in my hair;
And all around the candle the crooked shadows come,
And go marching along up the stair.

The shadow of the balusters, the shadow of the lamp,
The shadow of the child that goes to bed—
All the wicked shadows coming tramp, tramp, tramp,
With the black night overhead.

—Robert Louis Stevenson
Shadow March
from *Penny Whistles*
(*A Child's Garden of Verses*)
1885

CHAPTER ONE
WHERE AND WHEN

Z ero three hundred, Lieutenant. Wake up and smell the sulfur."
Jamie Gwynmorgan roused to a hand jostling her shoulder,
the insistent pungence of mangrove swamp, and a bead of sweat teasing
her temple as it trickled toward her ear. Even before she could open
her eyes, the jagged electric dread sparked again in her gut and ripped
lower, deeper, until it jolted her clit and incited another frenzied urge to
thrash, howl, claw her way to escape.

But there would be no escape. And no bitching and squirming about
it either. She might forever think of herself as Corporal Gwynmorgan,
but she'd forsaken that and agreed to it all—the stuff about true faith
and allegiance, about how "this Officer is to observe and follow such
orders and directives, from time to time, as may be given…"

Long ago, such orders and directives had consigned her to the
sweltering island, the unending mission, the life she'd be risking yet
again. She clenched her jaw, and the clench quickly spread to every
muscle in her body, claiming her arms, her shoulders, her abs and
legs and glutes, especially her glutes, until the ache of it squelched
her compulsion to run or scream or sob. And then…*One more breath,
Corporal.*

Just one more breath of this muggy, buggy, foul air, and then she'd
open her eyes, swing herself out of her hammock, and—

Wait! The hand on her shoulder, the swamp-stench, the cloying
humidity had all vanished. Her stomach tumbled, left behind while the
rest of her levitated into dizzy realization: *That's wrong. I'm not there
anymore.*

Where, then? When?

Trapped behind eyelids that refused to open, an acidic bubble of
nausea rising to her throat, she bent low, curling toward the green of
ferns and sagging palms. All around her, bullets shredded the blameless
fronds, pop-crack-whining nearer, nearer—but it wouldn't hurt for
long, right? *Wrong, that's wrong…*

"Just a target," whispered a voice too much like her own. Stretched flat on her belly, she heard only the scant rustle of her body worming into position as she squinted through a rifle scope, unable to prevent its reticled crosshairs from slipping down, down from the man's head to his torso, unable to keep time from slowing, dilating the span between exhale and inhale into a stillness that impelled but one infinitesimal motion: Her finger's tiny tug on the rifle's trigger. "Just a target," the voice repeated. *No, that's wrong…*

Now silence. She saw a small child—yes, a girl child—and the silence gave way to the sounds of her own frantic, bleated remorse as the child scampered away from her into a devouring darkness.

She wanted to follow, but the live wire terror in her gut, her clit, immobilized her in the bright, cruel cone of a spotlight. Helpless, she watched her own hunched shadow tremble while she struggled to stand, naked and filthy and cringing, bloody wrists and ankles hobbled by heavy manacles. "I don't know," she rasped, "I can't remember…"

That's when she heard it: The Bastard's laugh—shrill, corrosive, contemptuous. And close by, too close by. "My turn now," he grated in his strange accent.

No, please, not again.

The Bastard's metal-on-metal laugh scraped along the seams of a language she didn't recognize. *Uh dee yapizz dahmah terayno.* She tried anyway to make sense of the sounds—*uh dee yapizz dahmah…* But his excoriating sneer had receded into the blackness enclosing her prison of light, the blackness that always hid him.

Jamie held her breath and listened.

Where is he?

She listened and heard…nothing.

Where am I?

It had been so easy once to wake up already knowing where and when. But not anymore. How many times had she opened her eyes to scam upon hoax upon hoodwink, layer after layer of delusion about having left the Palawan, about Alby sober and sensible, about the little girl who wanted to hold her hand?

What if the child could never reach for her? What if Alby had been too shit-faced to bail from that burning car? What if what if *what if* getting out of the Palawan had been just another pathetic, desperate dream?

This could be Saint Eh Mo's. And Shoo Juh's interrogators could be standing centimeters away with their electrified batons, avid for her first waking flutter.

Listen...for the spitting buzz of the current dancing between the baton's electrodes—that nanosecond of warning before her body would explode into a havoc of excruciating spasms. She must tamp down the fever-red horror always simmering low in her belly, threatening panic. She must lay utterly motionless and...*listen listen*—

Thump. Thump-thump.

Her eyes snapped wide and she bucked half-upright, legs scrabbling to get beneath her as she registered the white-yellow light and gray-yellow shadows splayed across a ceiling above her. Confounded, she let her feet slip out from under her and thudded flat on her back breathless, her frenzied heartbeat thundering in her ears.

"My god, Jamie, are you all right?"

A woman appeared above Jamie's feet, trim and graceful in the smoothly draped contours of cream-colored trousers and jacket, her sandy, white-streaked hair gleaming in sunlight.

Dawn's early light. Around here this time of year, that'd be zero six hundred hours, give or take.

Ah. Jamie gulped air. *Here.*

At Great Hill. Tuesday, August something...August twenty-seven, right? Almost four years since Alby died, ten thousand miles and twelve time zones from the Palawan. And still five whole months to go. Right?

"Sorry. Guess I lost my balance." Jamie gazed up at Lynn Hillinger's worried frown and, heart rate daring to calm a bit, attempted a smile; Lynn hadn't yet morphed into the glacial, menacingly elegant Shoo Juh, who was uncontestably the scariest woman Jamie had ever encountered. *If she smiles back, she's real and I've got it right.*

"Jamie," said Lynn, bending forward, shaking her head, her short, bobbed hair whiter now as it cast toward her cheekbones. "Why are you sleeping on the floor?"

"Uh—" *The floor*...In the room of Lynn's house that everyone called "Jamie's room" as if it had belonged to her for all her nineteen years, not just sheltered her like a rescued puppy for twenty-seven going on twenty-eight days. Jamie sucked in more air. How the hell did she end up on the floor? Assuming the floor was real, assuming Lynn was real.

Pleeease smile at me.

Lynn bent closer. "Are you sure you're okay?"

"Yeah." Jamie hiked herself up on one elbow, then the other, and wiggled her toes. "All the parts still seem to be attached."

A bemused version of Lynn's famous grin creased her handsome face, lit her clear gray eyes, and for a second, as she straightened up, she looked twenty-five years old instead of forty-five.

Oh, thank god.

Jamie hummed with a high-frequency wave of gratitude while Lynn's head shifted back and forth again. But Lynn's smile stuck around, like maybe it knew how important it was. Every time Jamie saw that smile, a nourishing melt of comfort and something almost like optimism flowed through her.

Even so, she wondered: Why would Lynn be dressed for a power lunch at 0600? Why would Lynn be dressed at all at 0600 during this last week of what was supposed to be a vacation? Keeping her eyes on Lynn's smile, Jamie started to lift herself off the floor.

"What's up? Why're you—"

Jamie froze; she tried not to groan aloud, but she couldn't stop the wince. A stupid mistake, forgetting like that and trying to stand as if nothing had happened. She let her backside retreat to the cotton throw rug where she'd been sleeping in the narrow space between bed and wall. This would need thinking about.

"Easy does it, kiddo." Leaning quickly forward, hand extended, Lynn examined Jamie, her smile abandoned as her eyes searched out the scars unhidden by Jamie's boxers-and-tanktop sleepwear—as if inspecting those surface slices and dices might tell her how fared the innards' regenerative stem cell treatments.

The docs had said that First Lieutenant Gwynmorgan had good odds for a full recovery, eventually, minus only a uterus and a centimeter or two of intestine. Even so, the scars rankled Lynn. Her eyes gave it away by narrowing for a nanosecond at each one she spotted, just like they had every time they'd looked for the last—

How long had it been?

Sixty-five days—or has it been sixty-six, maybe sixty-seven?

Jamie didn't remember squat about a bunch of those days. For a long while, she floundered for where and when and, later, how: How the hell could she still be alive?

Yet what she did recall included Lynn. And kept including Lynn— because Lynn didn't leave. Then came the part Jamie remembered with a kind of hushed reverence: How after the hospital with its interminable surgeries and injections and scans and more surgeries, Lynn had insisted she come to Great Hill to heal instead of shipping out to the nearest Marine Corps lame-and-halt battalion to perfect her pushups and supervise the emptying of garbage cans.

Why Lynn did all that—why *truly*—and how she got her spirited tribe to go along with it was a mystery Jamie pondered more and more now that the daze of debilitation had begun to lift a little and it was possible to take a dump without almost passing out from the cramps.

"Ready?" asked Lynn, positioning herself on Jamie's right side, one hand steady at Jamie's shoulder, the other clasping Jamie's forearm.

While Jamie pushed, Lynn pulled, emitting a small grunt as Jamie rose to stand half a foot over her.

"Thank you." Jamie smiled; maybe it was a good sign that her body had simply forgotten how injured it was.

But as Lynn reached up to ruffle Jamie's hair, a new tension tightened her face—a tip-off that sent a phalanx of tiny icicles blitzing along Jamie's spine. *Something's happened.*

"I didn't realize your hair's so dark," Lynn said, and Jamie heard her procrastination. "Or that it curls when it's given a chance. Nice effect with those baby blues of yours." Lynn allowed the moment, and her hand, to linger before she spoke again. "I have to go to DC today."

Jamie studied Lynn's face. "Washington? I thought the Senate was in recess 'til next week." What else had Lynn embedded in this beginning of the Great Hill good-bye ritual, that oh-so-conscientious protocol that intimated the household had barely withstood some never-mentioned past travail?

"Our people in Paris—"

"At the truce negotiations." The imperishable dread smoldering deep in Jamie's gut flared into her chest, down her legs.

"Yes. They've hammered out an agreement. Finally. I'm due at a briefing in a few hours."

Clumsily, Jamie sat on the bed. "Does this mean it's over?"

"God, I hope so."

Ever since she grasped that the fight for Palawan hadn't finished her, Jamie tried to leave behind what she'd seen on those little Philippine islands, what she'd done there. What had been done to her.

Of course, she failed. No one had yet invented a stem cell treatment to fix the way combat fucked up your head—so the Palawan had become a hyper-real monster of recursion that cornered her into exhausted sleep every night and besieged her awake every morning, haunting guiltless sounds and smells, taunting from the vague edges of her peripheral vision. Haunts within haunts, taunts within taunts, her very own fractal pattern of fear and revulsion, ever more malignant and unpredictable.

And now the fight was actually over?

It had taken almost a year of one endless Palawan day after another to scour away the last of that rah-rah shit about "winning" and those pipe dreams about when the conflict might cease. Only a single raw realization remained: The struggle to live and keep her people alive would take all she had until it killed her. And kill her it did. Sixty-five days ago—or was it sixty-six days ago, sixty-seven days ago, forever ago?

That she once more breathed Massachusetts air was a perverse coincidence of ordnance trajectory and advanced casevac technology.

Caprice again, that masturbating goddess of vagaries, coin flips, and flukes.

Goddamn. It's over.

Two years of the Palawan's blood and blackness and fear-stink. Over. Those seven months at the prurient mercy of Shoo Juh and The Bastard in the POW camp where Lynn found her—the place its prisoners called Saint Eh Mo's, foreigner-garbled Mandarin for "evil demon." Over. What had defined her so much more than growing up with a junkie mother like Alby ever could. Over.

Without the Palawan, site of her aberrant journey from almost-virgin baby dyke to accomplished shooter of many enemies and at least one innocent, from lance corporal to first lieutenant to flailed hong mao, what was she? *Over.* As in over a cliff, as in death warmed over. As in turn over a new leaf.

Why doesn't it feel over?

"You're going down there in person? Not telebriefing?" This wasn't what Jamie wanted to say, but she could find no words for what she wanted to say.

"It's foregone, really," said Lynn. "All except the blustering. But it's been decided by people other than me that we can't have a record of any kind. No lenses, no sensors, no comlinks. No chance of eavesdropping or somebody's chat texts getting leaked to the media. So we're meeting at the SCIF in the Hart Building."

"The skiff?"

"Sensitive Compartmented Information Facility. Four-factor secure access, level-eight surveillance resistance—the whole schuten-geschmeer, as my grandmother used to say."

Jamie nodded. She'd heard of SCIFs, certainly. All the very important people who decided on the fate of fodder had SCIFs. She waited for the rest of Lynn's good-bye.

Instead, Lynn sat, too. "Before I go, I'd like to show you something." *No. Don't.* But, once decided, Lynn wasn't easy to dissuade; Jamie didn't bother trying, but she wanted to keep her shoulders—and her voice—from slumping. Endurance in body can distract the mind. "Okay."

Lynn tapped her wristcom, which woke up the room's videoscreen. She tapped again and the videoscreen displayed a satellite view of the South China Sea. At the top left of the screen, the bulge of Shoo Juh's China loomed ominously. At the bottom right dribbled a skimpy, bumpy forward-slash of an island accompanied by tiny splotches of land at its top and bottom. The Palawan.

Jamie preferred to keep her eyes on Lynn rather than the screen. She hadn't seen any Palawan imagery for more than nine months; the sight of it sent another harsh tremor nipping along her vertebrae. "I thought you said level-eight surveillance resistance."

"Not to worry. We're level-eight-plus here."

"In the house." Jamie gave the room a swift, skeptical scan. "This house."

"House. Garages. Offices. Because of Callithump. It's one of five outfits authorized by the government to do level-eight technical surveillance countermeasure consulting and development. All Callithump's senior people have level-eight-plus at home."

"Callithump" meant Lynn's company, of course. Never taken public, closely held, worth billions thanks to its breakout security and telepresence technologies. Several years ago, shortly before her eleventh-hour leap into a run for the Senate, Lynn had turned over the reins to Dana, the hard-driving daughter of her partner Rebecca; as far as Jamie could glean, what wealth Lynn hadn't given away she'd stashed in treasury bonds and she didn't have anything to do with Callithump anymore. But Great Hill certainly did.

Four generations resided under its capacious, smart-solar-tiled roofs. Lynn and Rebecca shared the place with not only Lynn's teenage daughter, Robin, and Rebecca's mother, Mary, but also with Dana and Dana's partner, Lily, who had recently become both Callithump's chief technology officer and the mother of Evelyn, a four-month-old baby girl endowed with a police-siren wail. After twenty-eight days among them, Jamie hadn't yet figured out what made them choose to live together. Definitely not financial necessity. Nor was it one of those twisty, emo-neurotic loops that snare some families into sticking close so they can spend their lives chomping on each other. No, this crew got along pretty well, and Jamie liked how they watched one anothers' backs—and how she was never sure who was boss.

"Lynn," she said, "I don't have that sort of security clearance, remember?"

"Oh, I expect you can be trusted. I'll be home by Thursday night, I think, which gives us plenty of time to plan for Sunday. So—"

"Sunday?"

"The cookout. We may have to deal with some additional media interest."

"Oh. Yeah." So far, Jamie had managed to dodge several dinner parties and hoped to evade the annual Great Hill Labor Day weekend cookout, too; she wanted nothing to do with the 200 people who'd spend the afternoon snarfing hamburgers and swilling beer on the south meadow. "I thought I could just stay in here. There's this online course I've been wanting to start."

Lynn's face had clouded so completely that Jamie suspected her words hadn't registered at all. "Tough to tell what the media will pounce on," Lynn said absently. "Mmm...they do love coincidence. If they get wind of the truce agreement this afternoon, they just might focus on the dates rather than you."

"Me? Why me?"

"Every war has its icons, at least until it fades into obscurity. You've become one of this war's icons, I'm afraid. That video of you—" Lynn's eyebrows hiked when Jamie shook her head. "You haven't looked at *any* of the coverage?"

"Once, last week—a GNN piece from early July. Couldn't bring myself to actually read it. And the video—saw the first frame and didn't stick around. Only reason I got that far was because a guy at the Corps's Public Affairs office passed on some interview requests—along with links to earlier stories and a list of stuff I'm not supposed to talk about." Jamie stretched and rotated her suddenly taut shoulders. "Got me wondering whether the face apps can recognize me from what's out there."

"Not easily, I'd say, especially if you wear shaded eyewraps and maybe a full-brimmed hat. And avoid closeup photo ops, of course. The media glow fades pretty quickly—a few days or a week after the headlines move on. It's the chasers you have to worry about. The obsessives who've decided to make you their hobby. Of course, they have to know where to look. The longer you're out of sight, the quicker they move on, too."

"Whole thing creeps me out. How the hell do you do it?"

"Oh, it's not so bad. But it does take some practice. Security helps, too."

"Uh-uh. Not going there. I'm ignoring those interview requests."

"Chances are there'll be others."

"I'll damn well ignore them, too."

"At least you're beyond their reach here on the property. But whoever you might talk to out there, I'd appreciate you pretending we didn't have this conversation."

"Sure. I'm wicked good at playing dumb."

A pensive smile on her face, Lynn tousled Jamie's hair again. "I just didn't like the idea of you finding out about the truce agreement from over-hyped headlines. I wanted you to hear about it from me—" She halted, thrown off-balance, Jamie suspected, by the pitch and roll of her own Palawan memories and the toll her decision to venture there took on Robin and Rebecca, on everyone at Great Hill. Lynn cleared her throat and tilted her head toward the videoscreen. "See the red shading?"

"Let me guess. It's what The Powers That Be want to hand over to the Zhong."

"I wouldn't say 'want to,' but, yes, this shows the gist of the agreement."

"So the enemy gets Half Moon Shoal."

"Sadly, yes again. And we're not calling them 'the enemy' anymore. Or 'Zhong', for that matter."

"Half Moon Shoal is eighty klicks from the Palawan." Jamie wished none of it mattered to her, but she couldn't keep the shadow from her voice. "That's only fifty miles, Lynn."

"The Chinese have already been there for decades."

"But this'll make it legal, won't it? The precedent they want."

Jamie turned away from the screen and stared out an open window at the vertical-axis wind turbines visible through the trees rising behind the house. "Our three pirouetting minarets," Mary liked to joke whenever the wind topped ten miles an hour. Most mornings, Jamie found herself gazing at the turbines; from the pair of north-facing windows in her room she could just make out the movement of their sinuous blades, which usually mesmerized her—but not this time.

"People died to prevent that," she whispered. *People killed.* She refused to count the lives she'd obliterated during Operation Palawan Liberation. Now numbers reeled by her mind's eye, random and reckless like in a slot machine, threatening to match up into truth revealed as they climbed higher. How many dead by her hand so that the Zhong would end up with Half Moon Shoal and unchallenged sovereignty over a third of the world's known fossil fuel deposits?

No. Jamie twitched her head back and forth, trying to shake away the thought. *Don't.*

"The Chinese will withdraw from all Philippine territory immediately, including that airbase they've just finished building on Bugsuk Island," said Lynn as if she were apologizing, and then her apology buzzed on with details about withdrawal, reconciliation, monitoring, enforcing. "And after a couple of years, the tourists'll start to come back."

"Great," Jamie said. "Like it never even happened." For a nanosecond, gravity let her go; a hand seemed to press itself against the inside of her skull and lift her upward. *Fuck it. It's over. Over.*

"We were lucky to—" Lynn drew in a deep breath and took hold of Jamie's hands, which quivered just slightly most of the time these days.

To get out alive. To make any deal at all. Jamie refrained from saying it aloud, from saying anything about the now infamous attempt to sabotage the truce negotiations by kidnapping Lynn's Zhong counterpart, which had sparked an equally infamous, game-changing chain reaction: The Zhong decision to retaliate by holding Lynn at Saint Eh Mo's, Shoo Juh's inexplicable aid so essential to their escape, and the daring, deadly escape itself.

Jamie didn't like talking or even thinking about any of it because every time she did, she faced an onslaught of phantasms as mindfucking as any nightmare. Yet none of it added up—not Shoo Juh's help, not the official story about some previously unknown anti-truce splinter group kidnapping the Zhong official, nor his liberation by a Marine special ops team the day after Lynn and the Saint Eh Mo's POWs were rescued. She flashed on the moment nearly three months ago when she and the other prisoners first heard that the truce talks had been suspended, that Lynn would not be allowed to leave Saint Eh Mo's. She'd known right then something huge had happened, that escape was very likely the only way they would survive. But the Why of it all? She had no clue then. None of them did, not even Lynn. Only weeks later, flat on her back in a hospital bed, did she hear the official Why, once she could stay lucid long enough to be debriefed and comprehend the answers to her questions.

Trouble was, too many of the answers made no sense, and nobody seemed to give a damn. Never mind that the whole thing had the foul stench of boomeranging bullshit that only she and Lynn seemed unable to get out of their nostrils. The message from Jamie's debriefers was crystal clear: Forget about it.

Because fuck it, it's over.

Sighing, Lynn gently rubbed the raggedy crater-scars on Jamie's palms, souvenirs from Saint Eh Mo's. "It's their backyard, Jamie. We've made the best deal we could."

"Yeah." Jamie kept her eyes on the turbines and managed to blink away the semi-transparent image of Shoo Juh's face hovering at the window. The morning's humid haze had begun to give way to blue sky, and the smell of the sea occasionally wafted through the open windows of her room on a mercurial southeasterly breeze off Massachusetts Bay. Her head hurt as she waited for Lynn to finish saying good-bye.

But Lynn didn't release her hands. "Maybe now your nightmares will begin to ease up."

Jamie gaped. *How the hell—*

"You cried out. Night before last," Lynn said, reading her thought. "Don't you remember? Mary heard you from across the hall, and Dana and Lily—"

"Dana and Lily, too? Oh christ. Their room's gotta be ten meters down the hall." Jamie scowled at the wind turbines. "I should—"

"You should not."

"—go back to—"

"No."

"Jeezus, Lynn, I'm waking everyone up at night—"

"Actually, you didn't wake anyone. Dana and Lily were already up with the baby. Fact is, you have no hope of competing with Evvie. And Mary was just up." Lynn's eyes narrowed. "You really don't remember?"

"What? What'd I do?"

"Lily came in, to make sure you were okay. She said you woke up before she even got to the foot of your bed. You looked right at her, mumbled 'gé xià,' and went back to sleep."

"I don't remember any of that." But Jamie had begun to remember those words. *Guh shyah*, she'd pronounced them, always reluctantly, never often enough or obsequiously enough to satisfy Shoo Juh.

Lynn watched her own fingers stroke the scars on Jamie's hands. "I get them, too."

"You?" Jamie stared at Lynn. "*You* have nightmares?"

"I'd never been shot at before." Lynn's smile seemed fragile, almost timid. "Never had to literally run for my life before. I keep dreaming about not making it to the helicopter, about falling and…and getting shot."

Say something. Say yeah, me too. Or try not to think about it. Something…But Jamie only nodded.

"Does it burn?" Lynn whispered.

"Sometimes," Jamie whispered back, turning away from Lynn. *And sometimes it's like a sledgehammer whacking you in the gut, and sometimes a bomb explodes in your chest, and sometimes you can hear yourself splattering…*

"Oh god, Jamie, I'm sorry," Lynn said, her voice faltering as she reached to touch Jamie's cheek. "I'm so sorry."

"Yeah." Jamie's eyes closed beneath the touch, so familiar, so soothing. "It's okay." And it was. As always, something deep inside her yielded and, exhaling, she went just a little limp, like a whelp picked up by the scruff of its neck by its mother. These moments beneath Lynn's touch were the only times anymore when she could let her eyes close for longer than a few seconds without seeing flashes of something that made her recoil.

"Rebecca thinks we're both exhibiting suppression and avoidance behaviors, that we need to talk more about what happened, how it's affected our lives," said Lynn quietly, her hand slipping from Jamie's cheek.

A burst of humid red heat encircled Jamie's head like a steaming blindfold as her eyes snapped open. *What the fuck does whoop-de-doo*

Dr. Westbrook know, anyway? She gritted her teeth to keep the thought to herself.

"God, it's so hard," Lynn continued, her head drooping. "Every instinct I have tells me I got screwed over there and that everyone else at Saint Eh Mo's got stuck on what was supposed to be my ride straight to hell. I have my theories, but I still don't know the how of it, and I can't prove anything. So most of the time I'm pissed past description. The rest of the time, I just want Reb to crawl into bed with me and hold me so I can start to feel safe again. And every time I start talking about it, I end up in a rant."

"I'm supposed to talk, too." Jamie wiped a film of sweat from her eyelids and tried to ignore the canopy of Palawan jungle her hypervigilant senses kept insisting had closed in around her. "Part of the recovery program."

"Your behavioral therapy group."

"Yeah, well…guess I'm not ready yet."

"We each have to find our own way, don't we? 'By untaught sallies of the spirit.'"

"Sallies? As in 'sally forth'?" Jamie grimaced—and confessed. "My ass gets sallied right back to Saint Eh Mo's and those interrogators just about every time I close my eyes."

"Which is exactly why you have to turn around and fight your way out."

Sighing, Jamie rolled her shoulders. *Not sure I got a whole lot of fight left anymore.* "Sounds like you're putting on your game face, Senator."

"I suppose I am." Lynn straightened, then stood. For an instant, just before she leaned over to place a delicate kiss on Jamie's forehead, she looked as tired and afraid as she had when she was running for her life through Palawan's jungle-covered mountains.

Jamie grabbed her hand, searched her eyes. "Anytime I can help—"

"I know." Lynn smiled. A pale smile. "Thank you."

And Jamie recognized what wasn't in Lynn's voice or her eyes or her hand's reassuring squeeze. She'd already steeled herself and wouldn't be asking anyone for anything.

CHAPTER TWO
IN CASE THERE WAS ANY DOUBT

*F*ucking leg. Fucking cane. Jamie wanted to get down the front stairs the way a scout/sniper should: *Without making a fucking sound.* But between her leg and the cane she still needed, anyone in Great Hill's large basement gym couldn't help but hear her coming.

At 0700 on a Tuesday, at least that would likely be only Lily.

Jamie didn't tense out around Lily Sabellius the way she did around Rebecca or Dana, who shared not only the same strong-boned faces, curly saffron hair, and squinty-eyed skepticism—they also had the same way of looking into you without unmasking themselves. Jamie wasn't at all sure either Rebecca or Dana liked her, or maybe it was just that they hadn't decided yet and weren't about to let their faces give anything away.

By comparison, Lily *showed* in her face. Lily seemed unveiled, which made it easy to relax and enjoy the graceful sculpture of her cheekbones, the smooth, subtle texture of her caramel skin, and the special gentleness in her glittering golden eyes—eyes that hadn't ever shown the flashes of pity or taxed patience that Jamie sometimes glimpsed in Rebecca and Dana.

At 0700 on Tuesday, August 27, Jamie held her breath, rounded the corner. And exhaled. The gym was empty.

Leg, ab, and upper body routines came first. Then the treadmill, during which she counted each step of her left foot. Counting helped; one to somewhere around forty or fifty—or however long she could keep it up until the phantasms invaded again. Trying to shimmy them out of her head, she'd stare at the view beyond the solar glass curving over the lap pool at the far end of the gym. And while she watched the oaks and pines backlit by hazy sky and peeks of sea, she'd push herself to go faster and start the count afresh.

The first time she got on the treadmill, Lynn or Dana or somebody had clicked up music—fast, sexy, aggressive music that made the phantasms writhe from pallid semi-transparency to color-saturated, crimson-edged 3-D. And it got worse, much worse, when she closed her eyes. That's when she heard things under the music's rhythm and bass—the crack of a .416-caliber round exploding out of the chamber of her rifle, the grinding of a heavy cell door dragged open, the choppy dissonance of a Cantonese insult, the ominous thud of Zhong boots...

But she just wasn't strong enough or steady enough to work up a sweat walking the trails on the property, much less run them like she wanted to. So she found chunks of time when she could do the treadmill alone, without music. She had only three rules: Don't stop counting, don't close your eyes, don't step off 'til your lungs can broil butter and your legs scream for salvation.

One-two-three-fo—

"Jamie!" Mary's dismayed voice reverberated through the large space. "For god's sake, you look awful!"

"I'm...fine." Jamie checked the time. It surprised her. Almost a whole hour had passed. And she'd unintentionally escalated from a brisk walk to a jog.

"I could hear you wheezing from the top of the back stairs," Mary said. Small, elderly thin, long white hair gathered at the base of her neck and set off by a plain black tunic shirt, Mary stood especially erect as she placed herself directly in front of the treadmill's console. She usually offered Jamie a benevolent smile that crinkled around warm blue-green eyes. Grim-faced this time, however, Mary seemed to Jamie bravely defiant of her own fear, an old woman staring down a feral beast. "You're trembling all over and in obvious discomfort," she persisted. "Please get off that thing."

Jamie gawked at her. *Oh my god, is she afraid of me?* "Mary—"

"Please, Jamie."

Quite abruptly, Jamie couldn't do anything right. Her fingers fumbled at the console as they tried to press the OFF button, and her feet tangled when she stepped from the machine. "I'm sorry," she panted, and had to clutch the treadmill's handrail to steady herself. "I didn't mean to—I never wanted to—to—"

She couldn't finish. She stood before Mary slightly dizzy, head bowed, tremulous fingers tentatively clasping each other.

Mary's hand gentled onto Jamie's arm. "Time to ice, don't you think?" she asked. Rhetorically, it turned out; she gestured toward the large mat table near the lap pool. "You lie down. I'll get the ice wraps. Two, isn't it?" She didn't wait for Jamie's reply before heading off to the basement's kitchenette. "I couldn't avoid noticing," she said as she went. "Lately you've been coming upstairs from these workouts of yours looking more and more like—" Mary had disappeared around a corner, but Jamie imagined her shaking her head. "Like you've just lost a very nasty fight."

"No," Jamie called to her, "it's not like that."

"Well then, tell me why you always exercise alone. And why you always go straight back to your room using the front stairs. The back stairs are much closer. You're traversing three sides of a square—" Mary reappeared carrying a tray loaded with ice wraps and two large glasses of water. "Instead of just the fourth side. Since the fourth side can be seen from the family room and the kitchen, I'm guessing you don't want anyone to notice the state you're in."

"I can handle it." The words lurched out rougher and angrier than Jamie intended.

"You've been spending more and more time down here, but nothing like today," Mary said, apparently oblivious of the edge in Jamie's voice. "I was worried."

"I've only got five months left and it took me 'til today—just now—to walk the treadmill without using the handrails."

"You weren't walking. You were running. With a limp, I might add."

"Well, more like a lumbering jog."

But I'm ready. Gotta be twenty or thirty klicks of trails in the woods around this place. And I'm finally ready for them. How soon might she learn them all?

And how soon might she climb the hill behind the house—Great Hill itself near where the turbines stood—and where a cloudless night would show its stars unencumbered by lights from the house and the village beyond, where she might find a spot to sit and look at the stars, talk to the stars, find in the stars the old comfort and some sorely needed new hope? Jamie arranged the ice wraps extra slowly, to avoid watching Mary watch her. "I'm okay, Mary. Really."

"Here." Mary put one of the water glasses in Jamie's hand, then sat near a corner of the mat table with the other. "I'll seem less irritating if you hydrate."

"You're not irritating."

"And you're a terrible liar. Humor me. Drink."

Quashing a smile, Jamie downed the glass, lay back, and kept her eyes on the fitful summer sway of the trees beyond the solar glass.

"Lynn talked to you this morning before she left, yes?" Mary asked just before the moment succumbed to gravity. "Told you what's going on?"

"Yeah." *Please just leave me be…*

"Good. Just making sure." Mary didn't move and a second jilted moment floundered by. "At least things should be quiet for another day or two," she said. "So I'll leave you to finish up then."

Jamie swung her head toward Mary, who'd begun to walk away. "What happens after a day or two?"

"Oh, that's just my semi-educated guess. I could have it all wrong."

"What? Have what all wrong?"

Mary turned around. "I'm sorry. I was talking about what'll happen when word of the truce agreement gets out. Lynn's been very visibly in the crux of this for a long time. So unless by some miracle there's no leak and no announcement until next week when she's back in Washington, I expect we'll have reporters hovering at the main gatehouse. Perhaps a drone or two buzzing around or even a helicopter flyby—if one of the media hotshots decides to focus on Lynn's role. You know, then and now."

"Then and now?"

"It's been a year, remember—almost to the day, in fact—since the first try failed."

"I don't know what you mean."

"The truce talks last year. In Singapore."

"I, uh, must've been, uh, busy. I never heard a fu—" Jamie managed to bite off her preferred obscenity. "Don't recall hearing about them."

"Really?" Mary returned to the mat table and sat down. "I assumed you'd have been—what's the term? Briefed."

"Maybe I was. I don't know...can't remember." Jamie shrugged. "Once upon a time, I used to wonder when there'd be talks. You said they happened last August? That first time, I mean."

"Actually, they started a year ago July, failed in late August."

"Failed? Why?" *July...Wasn't last July that forever slog along the mid-coast, doing those pointless scout-and-search pings into the mountains? Yeah, yeah, and it went right through most of August, until...*

"It all revolved around nine twenty-two," said Mary. "The Chinese had drawn a line through Palawan at latitude nine degrees, twenty-two minutes, and acknowledging that line was the starting point of the talks. When our people crossed over it, the Chinese called the talks a fraud and walked out." Mary sipped her glass of water. "Lynn was furious. She was a member of our negotiating team then, and they'd pretty much worked out a preliminary agreement that would've had the Chinese eventually withdrawing. Just like now—or at least quite a lot like now. But the Pentagon got the president to okay one last surge, supposedly to give us better leverage in the talks..."

*Until...*Jamie lurched upright on the mat, one hand spread across the fire erupting deep in her gut. Until Narra. In the middle of what they'd been told would be The Last Big Push South. She struggled for breath. How the hell could she ever forget what happened in Narra on, on—*Jeezus, it was on August twenty-seventh.*

"Jamie?" Mary moved closer, reached out a hand. "Are you—"

"Ahh—" Jamie heaved, "wahh." She blinked at the view before her, but a bass drum pounded in her ears, and the edges of her vision dimmed to black as her world condensed around a rifle scope lens suddenly splattered arterial-red. "Please..." *A whole year ago. Awa would be seven years old now...*Before her sprawled a child's body with a bloody stump where the head had been until a .416-caliber round from her sniper rifle collided with it.

"Jamie. Open your eyes."

"So damn tired...couldn't catch my zone anymore..."

"It's over now, Jamie. Open your eyes. That's right, open your eyes."

"Over," Jamie said breathlessly as Mary's hand stroked her back. "Yeah. Over." She squinched Mary's anxious face into focus and slowly, slowly, the red remains of Awa faded into flat grays that warped the filmy membrane sheathing her vision, her memory, her sleep, her reality like a caul. "Sorry," she said a little too loudly after a little too long.

"Awa was the little girl who—"

"Yes," Jamie clipped. *So Lynn's talked about it with them. Not just Rebecca. All of them.* She meant to stand up and get away from Mary as fast as possible, but the sound of Awa's name spoken by another human being glued her to the mat table.

"That must be very painful."

"Y-yeah."

"I'm so sorry. For both of you."

Mary didn't say anything else. She just sat next to Jamie and gently ran her hand up and down Jamie's back while they both gazed at the trees beyond the solar glass. After a while, Jamie looked at her and Mary answered with a soft smile—and for an instant, just one, Jamie thought she might weep.

Oh.

What if Mary wasn't afraid *of* her? What if Mary was afraid *for* her? Jamie couldn't decide which was worse.

❖

August 27 and appointments with docs and therapists would wreck yet another afternoon. But what about the two-plus hours before she had to leave for the hospital? Until last week, Mary took an hour or so in the mornings to play the grand piano downstairs in the family room. Whenever Mary played, Jamie stopped reading to tiptoe to the door of her room, open it, and let Mary's music float up the back stairs to soothe her as she sat on the floor just inside the doorway.

Lately, though, Mary's mornings had been occupied by the vegetable garden, so Jamie tried to stick with her self-imposed "assignment"—generally some screed about architecture or engineering. Yet nothing—not even the soothing effect of playing Tetris—seemed to fend off August 27's itchy, prickling unease.

"Maybe just a short walk," she mumbled, grabbing her wristcom and eyewraps. "To check out that trail up to the turbines."

❖

Oh, for the body she used to be, the one that ran without effort, feet light on the earth, mind dancing ahead to show her the way. *Run!* her mind prodded. *Run run run!* But the wounds had long since separated her thinking from her doing.

So Jamie had to walk, and by the time her impatient mind expected her to be halfway to the turbines, she had merely stepped off the front porch of the house and crossed the broad, pebbled driveway to the far side of the second garage.

She turned to look back at the house and recalled the first time Lynn referred to the place as Great Hill. Still in a military hospital, probably still muddled from all the pharma, she thought it was a joke. But no, Great Hill turned out to be eminently real. All 172 acres of it—or 650 acres if you included the surrounding conservation preserves owned and maintained by the family but open to the public.

"This is where you live?" Jamie had asked Lynn in bleary amazement the day she arrived. Before her stood a cedar-shingled New England saltbox that had sprouted a series of additions, its successive sections of roof cresting over each other in their reach for the sun. Its scale rivaled houses in those certain Cape Cod neighborhoods where kids like her from the crappy side of Hyannis quickly got shooed away.

Which could explain why everything about the place seemed so familiar, why a voice in her head kept repeating *I've been here before*.

No way, of course. She hadn't been there before, not ever. Even so, she nodded with recognition at how the place snugged into the south side of the wooded granite hill, preferring shelter from the north wind to the brag of perching on the very top of its namesake. She already knew, somehow, that if you stepped rightward and a little downslope toward the meadow stretching across the south side of the place, you'd see amidst the stretches of roof a center section with four stories of south-facing windows. Before the front door ever opened, Jamie knew a long, spacious foyer awaited, expected the banquet-sized dining room on the left, the videowalled study on the right. Lynn led her to an elevator tucked near the unobtrusive front stairs, just where she anticipated it, and brought her to a second floor bedroom she could have sworn she'd already lived in. That first night at Great Hill was the first night she slept the night through in at least two years.

Jamie smiled at the house. She liked hanging out there, liked how the family part of the people who lived there—sitting down together to eat dinner or watching a movie or just talking with each other in a hallway—was simply available for her to join, or not. They let her know—dinner's at 1930, more or less, it'll be a comedy for the movie this Thursday night, the new batch of brownies has walnuts in it—but the information came without expectations or questioning glances, just a friendly, laid-back greeting, the invitation implicit.

Above all, Great Hill was comfortable—and it was nothing if not secure.

On how many Great Hill security center monitors might she be appearing right now as she stood there gazing back at the house? Several, no doubt, though locating the camera lenses and hyperspectral sensors would require a multifunction detector. Jamie shook her head; she didn't much like being surveilled—not by military satellites and drones monitoring missions, not by the network of expressway and transport center imaging sensor clusters stretching from sea to shining sea, not even by Great Hill's well-intentioned protectors.

Vowing to upgrade her eyewraps ASAP to include the best detector and signal jamming gear she could find, Jamie turned toward the 400-meter-long footpath up to the wind turbines before the security people might decide she was behaving oddly. They could watch just about every step she took if they chose to, since sensors were sprinkled all over the Great Hill property; all she could do was ignore them and keep moving. On another day, with the right tools, she'd make a game of dodging Great Hill's cams.

On this day, however, she remained a gimp with a cane. Anyway, maybe having an invisible babysitter wasn't such a bad thing, because although she moved along pretty well, the path was little used, minimally tended, and soon became both deeply shaded and sporadically rugged as it snaked between jutting granite outcrops, low shrubs, and wind-stunted trees. Jamie had to take it slowly, artlessly, too dependent on the cane. *I'll be better tomorrow—when this is my first workout of the day, not my second.*

Eventually, the path intersected with a rough but drivable maintenance road, and shortly she came to a sunny clearing on the far side of the hilltop where three masts, each encased in a concrete deck, rose out of granite to convex northwestward and exploit the prevailing winds of winter. Atop each mast, a pair of ribbon-like blades spiraled about eight or nine meters high into a sleek, metallic-blue double helix that blossomed above the stubby oaks and pines nearby, sometimes in a flurry of motion like a figure skater's scratch spin, sometimes with come-hither sensuality, sometimes in statuesque stillness.

Breathless, her right leg aching, Jamie pressed a hand against the stitch in her chest, eased down onto an undulant mound of worn rock, and watched the blades decelerate, abandoned by the light breeze.

Now, her back against smooth, sun-warmed granite at last, Jamie gazed upward—and yes, there it was: Intense and vibrant and alive, the same blue sky she saw in the Palawan as she bled out. The same lustrous blue that took her into a where and when beyond time and space and caring, took her to Safe, where *everything* was beautiful. Even her harrowing pain and plundered hope were beautiful. But she got pulled back, away from the blue, away from Safe and beautiful, back to the imprisonment of existing.

Now, again, for a blink of an eye she sensed it as she exhaled—the world turning upside down so she'd fall silently, gently into the blue.

Then it was gone.

She closed her eyes, her protesting "Pleeeease" whispering out of her—until another whisper interrupted her. Imagining an almost imperceptible swish of leaves brushed aside, the way an unseen enemy might were he bent on sneaking close enough to slit her throat, her eyes instinctively opened and flicked toward the sound.

Nothing.

She sat up and three-sixtied the hilltop around her, then stood and did it again.

Zilch except for the turbines, which now reveled in a strengthening breeze.

In case there was any doubt that I'm fucking crazy.

She picked up a golf-ball-sized stone and side-armed it in the direction of the swishing leaves before tramping over to the nearest mast, which emitted a light, smooth, machine hum—the nearly frictionless workings of maglev-guided parts feeding an inverter. From above her came the temperamental whoosh and whir of air in eager motion. Stepping onto the concrete deck, she placed the flat of her palm on the mast. The vibration of it thrummed through her arm into the center of her chest, up her neck, along her jaw, and seemed to disperse inside her head—a slow, low, allaying lullaby of *oh-oh-oh-verrr oh-oh-oh-verrr*...

Only when a gull screeched high above her did Jamie realize her eyes had long since closed again and she'd dropped to her haunches, her back pressed to the turbine's mast. Almost half an hour had passed—without any ghosts, without any echoes. She never once tried to count anything, never once imagined falling into the blue.

CHAPTER THREE
MUCH TO LEARN

Jamie took her time descending the footpath, keeping her eyes mostly on the ground just in front of her and leaning heavily on the cane. Even so, she twice lost her footing and ended up on her rump. The second time, she began to swear vividly—until the sight before her shut her up and had her scrambling off her backside and off the footpath into an adrenaline-drenched crouch, her left hand autonomically signaling her squaddies to do likewise while her right hand prepped to fire the rifle that wasn't there.

Squinting, she sucked air. *Sure as hell* looks *like a hide.* Like somebody had embellished a well-shaded, gnarled scrub oak off to her right with branches gathered from other trees. To provide camouflage. Not for the first time since that last battle in the Palawan, Jamie wished she really did have a weapon in her hands.

Her eyes raked the woods around her as she listened for the anomalies of human presence. But she saw nothing, heard nothing. *Maybe it's just a trick of the light.* She gazed at the "hide" again, wondering how come she hadn't noticed it on her way up the path. *Yeah, must be a trick of the light.*

She rose slowly, berating herself for the raucous boom-booming of her heart, for yet another nosedive out of time and place. *No squaddies, fool. This is Great Hill, August twenty-seven. And you don't need a goddamn weapon.*

Yet when she stepped back onto the footpath and looked again, the same sting of fear and hypervigilance needled up her spine and seared through her chest. *It friggin' looks like a friggin' hide!* More precisely, the beginnings of a hide. Built for one, and recently. Or so it seemed.

Seeking evidence one way or the other, she moved through a tangle of underbrush to the spot some three or four meters west of the footpath and elevated a couple of meters above it. Now she felt even less sure. The fresh-green branches that bunched around one side of the scrub oak hadn't been cut; they'd been torn.

Wind might've brought them down, swirled them around, but, shit, a good scout knows how to make it look natural. A good scout wouldn't cut; she'd tear, rip. Jamie studied the space around the scrub oak and spotted a furrow through the wild grass and dead oak leaves. *Heading west, too, away from the house, ideal for a quick exit, but it's plenty subtle enough to be an animal path.*

She squatted behind the concealing greenery and found a natural seat in the contour of the ground, yet saw no sign of anyone having used it. She sat and played the scout. *What do I see from here? What can I target?*

Answer: About a hundred meters of the main driveway, from the garages to the curve around the granite mound sitting southwest of the house. And about 200 meters of the west driveway, too—the driveway Lynn usually used. Plus any activity around the front of the house, and even some of the south meadow. Oh, and the footpath up to the wind turbines.

Nice high spot for monitoring who comes, who goes, what the security people are doing. Good for taking out a senator or a CEO or anyone who doesn't sneak in or out via the east driveway.

Jamie didn't move. Because she couldn't decide: *How fucking crazy am I?*

Eventually, one of the doors of the second garage slid open; a car backed out and halted ten or so meters from the front door. The man who emerged from the driver's side wore the Great Hill security staff "uniform"—khaki pants and white polo shirt with the Great Hill Conservation Preserve logo on the chest and left sleeve.

Jamie glanced at the lower right corner of her eyewraps' shadowscreen: 1221 hours. First appointment in thirty-nine minutes. "Shit, my ride," she hissed, clambering to her feet and squinting to see who'd been assigned to drive her to the hospital.

Good, it's Fitzgerald. Her favorite among the security people. She called to him as she reached the bottom of the path. "Give me five, Fitz. I'll be right back."

"Oh." He pivoted, clearly startled to find her behind him. "Sure thing, Lieutenant."

She didn't take time to ask him yet again to just please call her Jamie. She'd barely have time for the requisite good-byes.

Because Great Hill good-byes involved more than chirping "See ya" from a doorway before you took off. That might have been the very best Alby ever managed, generally on the heels of a sheepish promise to never repeat her latest pharma-induced fiasco. But at Great Hill, that sort of thing wouldn't do at all.

At Great Hill, you took a moment to look someone in the eye, and maybe even—if it was Lynn or possibly sometimes Mary—you'd ante up a hug or a diffident kiss on the cheek as you told her that you're leaving, where you're going, when you'd be back, and that you hoped her time without you around would go well. And you really meant it. In response, the good-bye-ee gave you a small chunk of genuinely undivided attention as she wished *you* good things and affirmed when she'd next see you. The protocol, which Lynn's tribe never failed to follow, fascinated Jamie all the more because she'd immediately been included in it as though she'd lived at Great Hill all her life.

Thus, she had a couple of chances to say something about the hide she'd seen or imagined, imagined or seen. The first chance came when she went to the offices above the garages, where she found Dana and Lily sitting head to head in whispered conversation as Evvie snoozed nearby. But when they both looked up at her, Jamie realized she'd never line up the necessary words without sounding like a wingnut.

She might have done better a few minutes later in the vegetable garden where Mary and Kizzy the cook were digging up root vegetables—but they'd just been joined by "Mary's gentleman friend" Edgar, who had walked up from his place in the village. Jamie imagined trying to explain what she'd seen, imagined Edgar eager to examine it for himself, imagined his kind, drawn-out "*In*-ter-esting…" as he privately concluded that she'd well and truly lost it while Mary looked on sympathetically and Kizzy studiously ignored all three of them.

Nah, I'll wait and go up there later. Look with fresh eyes. Because how the hell, really, could somebody have built a hide—a hide!—forty frigging meters from the house?

"Hey, Fitz?" she asked as she got in the car a few minutes later. "Ever take the footpath up to the wind turbines?"

"Once in a while. It's part of one of the loops we do. Y'know, at irregular intervals. Captain Travis don't want us bein' predictable."

Jamie knew that Eileen Travis—ET to everyone in the house— had turned down Dana's offer to oversee Callithump's protective services unit so she could remain head of Great Hill security, a job that also included protecting Lynn. ET had solid credentials—stints in Army intelligence and force protection—and a fervent loyalty to Lynn Hillinger. ET was among the reasons Lynn believed Great Hill to be one of the safest places on the planet. Jamie wanted to believe that, too.

"Ever see anybody up there?" she decided to asked anyway. "Or signs of anybody?"

Fitzgerald had just begun to steer the car down the main driveway, but his head swiveled to face her. "You mean on the path, close to the house?" When Jamie nodded, he answered with a quick, "No." A frown formed on his face by the time the car had traveled a hundred meters. "Lieutenant, did *you* see somebody on the path? That's something I should report right now."

"Nope. Not a soul. But I could've sworn—" Jamie shook her head, shuffled her shoulders. "I dunno. I thought this spot near the path looked kinda like a hide. Guess I got myself stuck in the jungle way too damn long, huh?"

"Yeah," Fitzgerald said, his voice warm with understanding and camaraderie. "But you showed those SOBs good, Lieutenant. And you're home now. That's sure as hell the last laugh, ain't it? I'll check out that footpath, though. Soon as I get back from dropping you off, Lieutenant."

"I'd appreciate that, Fitz. Thanks. And just please call me Jamie, okay?"

❖

Well, three out of four ain't bad, right?

Unpleasantly needle-intensive pre-checkup tests. Okay. A grueling hour of physical therapy. Okay, albeit barely. Telecheckup with an out-to-lunch new doc down in Quantico. Okay.

But that final group behavioral therapy session…

The shrink, who always sat in the same chair and wanted everyone on at least one anti-depressant, followed a routine that evoked all of the pointless monotony but none of the rhythmic satisfaction of close-order drilling. Only the fact that he'd called her Corporal the first time he saw her redeemed him, fleetingly. He apologized, blaming the hard-to-read form on his comlink tablet, but soon enough Jamie suspected it was his one moment of true, useful insight, never to be repeated.

"Bring up your PTSD checklists, please," he droned, tapping his tablet. "Read through the problems and tick off how you're feeling about each one. No second thoughts. Stick to your gut feelings right now, then kick your update over to me, just like always."

Just like always, so as not to jeopardize this experimental effort to balance the expendability of the individual combat-fuckee with the military's overriding commitment to good order, discipline, and mission accomplishment. Just like always, seventeen problems to be ranked according to how much each one bugged you, from Not At All to Extremely Bothered.

Finger poised beneath the shadowscreen projected in front of her by the comlink embedded in her eyewraps, Jamie read through the list with which she was far too well acquainted. *Physical reactions such as sweating, accelerated heartbeat, or difficulty breathing when something reminds you of a stressful military experience...repeated disturbing memories, thoughts, or images...happening again, as if you were reliving it...jumpy or easily startled...super-alert or watchful... cut off from others...feeling irritable...*

Seventeen problems that were none of anybody's damn business.

The shrink glanced at his tablet, then looked at her. "Jamie, I don't have your update."

This time, like every other time, she'd avoided thinking about the session before she had to. Each one so far had left her with a sour, unpleasant taste and a rumbling unease. Probably because the shrink wanted video records of them "describing"—which to Jamie meant reliving—their "trauma." She'd escaped his spotlight for seven sessions, thanks first to the Weeper and then to two guys whose bawdy mania had spellbound the shrink and his videocam for the last four sessions. But all of them had left now, and their absence meant the shrink would seek new targets. She watched him fiddle with his videocam, getting ready.

Fuck. My turn today. I can tell by the way he's eyeing me. Fuck. He'd love to hear about the hide, wouldn't he?

She'd endured seven of these sessions, and now, if she wanted him to sign off on the behavioral evaluation form she needed to return to active duty, this time she'd have to ante up more than the usual abstract one-liners that had sufficed so far. This time she must feed him "case material" that he and his videocam could chew on and regurgitate into some research document. And whatever she said, she'd have to endure the others' stares, some skittish, some pissed, some pitying, while the shrink pitched those oh-so-rational psycho-platitudes crafted to explain away the instincts clawing at the underside of her skin. Plus, she better damn well spit a line or two of his bullshit back at him, preferably with an appreciative, slightly wide-eyed I've-seen-the-light nod.

How about a lurid fiction of hypersexual binging? Or, what the hell, blurt the truth about the depth of her dread of anything remotely resembling sexual arousal. Maybe a snarly rant about her ripening hypothesis that the fight in the Palawan so dearly paid for by grunts like her had been just another high-margin racket concocted by a cabal of shadowy autocrats.

Session eight. Almost done. She could mutter minimally about the first time she lost a buddy in this latest, greatest Battle to Defend Freedom and Democracy. If she scrunched hard against the image in her brain of his terrified dead face, she might be able to steer between chill detachment and rage and heartache, and the shrink would find it all prosaic and boring enough to seek richer pickings in one of the others. She pulled her eyes from the checklist to gird herself—and caught glimpse of a teensy little gotcha smile on the shrink's self-satisfied face...

So right then it roared awake again, that wild, brawling *No!* living in some cave inside her. Ignoring the shrink, Jamie did a quick comlink search on "untaught sallies of the spirit." The source was long and dense, Ralph Waldo Emerson in 1836, and it stilled Jamie's fingers. "There remains much to learn...it is not to be learned by any addition or subtraction or other comparison of known quantities, but is arrived at by untaught sallies of the spirit, by a continual self-recovery, and by entire humility...A dream may lead us deeper into the secret of nature than a hundred concerted experiments."

"It's over," Jamie said to the shrink, silently promising herself not to go back and look for the hide, not to ask Fitzgerald about it, or ET. She would not cringe into counting anymore ever and she would masturbate, by god, or die trying. She deleted the PTSD checklist from her comlink, pushed herself from her chair, and walked out of the room.

"Where's Rebecca?" Jamie asked ninety minutes later, trying to keep her fatigue from showing as she neared the blond-ponytailed teenager sprawled on a chair in the small, reassuring-beige lobby, fingers lightly flicking away at what Jamie guessed was a shadowscreen game console. "Am I early?"

"Nope, you're right on time. But a guy just came in with a couple of four-inch construction nails in his neck, and there's been a six-car pileup at the rotary down the street," Robin Hillinger said a little too brightly, fingers going slack. "So she won't get done for a while. But we don't have to wait for her." Robin bounced to her feet. "I can drive us home on my learner's permit since you'd be in the car."

No Rebecca? A tiny shiver skipped across Jamie's shoulders. She'd decided she wouldn't lie to Rebecca, but she sure as hell didn't want to endure a lecture about the consequences of not completing the required eight outpatient behavioral therapy sessions. Not on this day.

Apparently, Robin understood. "Might not be a pardon, but at least it's a stay," she said, two fingers extravagantly dangling the keychain. "Don't worry, Puck's already clicked over my authentication to the car."

Puck—Robin's nickname for Rebecca. In Jamie's view, the only thing faintly puckish about Rebecca Westbrook was how her curly red hair refused to go the least bit gray even though she'd reached her fifties. Hard-nosed like her daughter Dana, and just as smart and imperturbable, Rebecca never seemed to get tired, and somewhere around the time Lynn decided Jamie should come to Great Hill, she appointed herself Jamie's unofficial medical guardian.

"All right," said Jamie. "Let's go."

"And no autodrive, okay? I mean, I gotta do it myself to learn, right?"

"Yeah, okay."

"Cool." Robin's familiar grin widened as she departed the lobby.

A moment later, both their comlinks signaled the same message from Pilar, ET's deputy:

MEDIA @ MAIN GATE

USE EAST DRIVE

"God," Jamie muttered through a sigh, "I'll be glad when this day is over."

CHAPTER FOUR

CAKEWALK

From the screened porch off the family room, Jamie watched caterers scurry in and out of two huge tents on the newly mowed south meadow while a small band stuttered toward a tune and ET's battalion of security people in white polo shirts began to disperse after her final briefing.

"Hey, not fair." Robin had appeared in the closest doorway dressed in torn cut-offs and a halter top. "You look like you're part of the security staff."

"I like to think of it as a happy coincidence." Jamie pulled a hand from the pocket of her khaki cargo pants to run a finger along the placket of her white shirt. "Besides, this here's not a polo shirt. I'm told it's a bush shirt. So there."

Robin squinted at the band. "It used to be *real* friends, y'know? Maybe thirty or forty people—from Mum and Puck's lesbo-party days and some from Callithump and the hospital, neighbors from around the old house. And Springer was still fun—not all wound up like she is now from being Mum's chief of staff. Lots of kids. Lots of laughing. We'd play hide-and-seek and capture the flag until it got too dark, and then jam ourselves into the house for ice cream and cake, and Puck and Dana would set off a few fireworks. But now—now it's just another campaign event. Every year there's fewer people I know and more of those creepy fake smiles. Christ, I wish I could just go over to Sam's house." Robin exhaled heavily. "I-I'm—" Her voice cracked. "I'm not sure I can do this cakewalk anymore."

"Tell her."

"What?"

"You could try telling your mother how you really feel." Jamie said it just a bit too loudly, because behind Robin, Lynn had crossed the family room and now stood six feet away on the porch door threshold. "Hell, she's not gonna disown you."

"Oh god," Robin murmured, "she'll be so disappointed." Lynn stepped back into the family room, out of Jamie's line of sight.

"But you know she won't love you any less." Beginning a retreat, Jamie gave Robin's shoulder a reassuring squeeze. "And this way you give her a chance not to disappoint you."

Once back in her room, however, Jamie couldn't concentrate on anything. She clicked up the physics textbook she'd downloaded only to click it off a moment later, unable to read. Nor could she work it up for Tetris or backgammon or a movie.

And she sure as hell wouldn't be trying to turn herself on again. Not after that debacle a couple of nights earlier when she still foolishly believed she could make it happen with merely touch, determination, and slow, steady four-count belly breathing—no fantasies required.

Stupid, *stupid*. She should've anticipated the sudden, involuntary pulse of imagination and memory, should've realized that even the faintest light of what once aroused her—a woman's caress of her quivering inner thigh, sweet breath stirring low along her neck with its promise of a kiss, the rise and fall of breasts inviting her nearer—any of it, all of it would succumb forever to the profound gravitational force of Shoo Juh's infinitely dense, dimensionless black hole. She'd veered away just in time and didn't fall asleep until the first glint of dawn shone at the windows of her room.

The wind turbines. Jamie paced around the bed for half an hour before she convinced herself that, yes, she *could* reach the turbines without attracting anyone's notice. After all, the guests were supposed to remain outside on the broad meadow south of the house; nobody'd have any interest in wandering the rough, wooded granite mound north of the house.

But for a few security people near the doors and the caterers in the kitchen, the place should be empty. Jamie decided her best escape route would take her down the second-floor hall to the front stairs nestled next to Lynn's tiny office, across the foyer, through the kitchen and the small serving pantry, then into the breezeway and out the door at the rear of the first garage, well away from visitors' eyes.

She planned to move quickly, quietly. And she did—until she reached the kitchen.

A glossy blonde leaning on a nearby counter broke away from conversation with one of the caterers to block Jamie's route. "Well, hello," she said, *finally*, her tone insinuated. "You must be Lieutenant Gwynmorgan."

She was perhaps the most well-tended person Jamie had ever seen. Sassy smile showing off flawless, glow-in-the-dark teeth. Full, flowing hair not *too* blond, highlighted in just the right places.

Porcelain-perfect skin so much like Shoo Juh's that Jamie shuddered. Cultivated eyebrows, chiseled cheekbones, suave voice, million-dollar jeans smoothed over sculpted hips, million-dollar T-shirt caressing come-hither breasts. And the eyes of a predator.

"I'm sorry, ma'am, the hosts are asking their guests to—"

"You *are* Lieutenant Gwynmorgan, aren't you?" The woman stepped closer to slink her gaze down Jamie's body and back up again before she presented her elegant right hand. "I'm Vivian Velty."

Jamie met her now-expectant gaze—after all, didn't *everyone* recognize Vivian Velty?—but played dumb and assumed the position of attention, shoulders squared, chin tucked. "Please, ma'am, the hosts are—"

"Of course, Lieutenant. My apologies." Smile unwavering, Vivian Velty withdrew her hand and retreated a half step. "Allow me to offer my congratulations before I leave. By every account I've heard, it's well deserved."

"Ma'am—"

"I understand Senator Hillinger will be reading the citation at the ceremony."

"What ceremony?"

A corner of Vivian Velty's plush mouth twitched victory. "The ceremony at the White House during which you will be awarded the Medal of Honor, Lieutenant. By the president. I'd like very much to talk with you about that and—"

"Stay the fuck away from me."

Stomach corkscrewing, Jamie about-faced and barreled back into the foyer and right out the front door, determined to find Lynn. So Lynn would assure her it was a lie. So Lynn would swear that Vivian Velty— or whoever the creature in the kitchen might really be—had made it all up.

When she reached the edge of the south meadow, the energy of clustered people jabbering and jostling hit her like rough surf at an oceanside beach, the waves breaking over her as she waded through them, struggling to maintain balance and momentum while she searched for Lynn.

What if it's true? What if General Embry put in for the Blue Max anyway, even though I told him—I damn well told him!—I wouldn't accept it? Nah, Lynn would've said something, right? Right? Ten meters ahead of her she spotted Rebecca on the far side of a thick clutch of guests. She elbowed people aside to get close enough to be heard, then interrupted the man speaking to Rebecca and demanded, "Where's Lynn?"

Rebecca glowered at her. "Excuse m—"

"Where. Is. *Lynn?*" Jamie yelled.

"What's wrong?"

"*Where?*"

"Jamie—"

"Goddammit, Rebecca!"

Rebecca grabbed Jamie's shoulders. "Calm down. I don't know where she—"

Jamie swung out of Rebecca's grasp to continue her search, but she had trouble seeing clearly, trouble pulling in a full breath. The watery forms of people just in front of her shunted sideways, avoiding her erratic tack, and from behind her came Rebecca's voice, distinct above the babble all around her, calling her name. But she didn't stop. *Lynn would've said something...*

Then a laugh—shrill, corrosive, contemptuous—pierced the chatter, pierced her outrage. It came from close by, too close by. *Here? How could he possibly be here?*

Jamie halted, frantically wiping her eyes on her sleeve as she spun around to search him out, the memory of Shoo Juh's words resurrecting like a ghost out of a grave. "Your organization serves many masters," Shoo Juh had snarled at him. *Because he's a damn mercenary! Jeezus, mercs can slither in anywhere. He could be working for one of the guests...*

Jamie pivoted again, searching, searching. But she searched in vain, because the sound had faded, because she had no idea what he looked like. *Because he could be anybody, anybody at all.* A moment later, she startled at the touch of Rebecca's hand on her shoulder.

"Did you hear that?" Jamie rasped. "That laugh? You heard it, right?"

"Jamie," said Rebecca, staring at her hard, "what's going on?"

"He's here. The Bastard's *here*. You heard him, didn't you?"

"Come on. Let's go back up to—"

"Oh god, Rebecca, please tell me you heard him."

"Hon, lots of people are talking and laughing."

For a few seconds, all the sounds around Jamie went small and hollow and distant, like when you've stood too close to a blaring loudspeaker for too long and after you step away you can hardly hear anything. She had to remind herself to breathe. *It's better this way, right? Better that he's my phantasm instead of being real, because if he was real, he'd be here to hurt them.*

She let Rebecca steer her off the south meadow as far as the driveway. "I'm okay now," she said when she sensed pebbles crunching beneath her feet. "A-And I didn't mean to act like such an asshole—"

"I know." Rebecca's face creased into its typical forbearing smile, but softer, less thin-lipped than usual. "I'll look around for Lynn and send her in to talk with you."

Jamie shook her head. The time had come for a strategic withdrawal. "No, she's busy. And I'm okay now. It can wait 'til later."

"Are you sure?"

"Yeah, I am. I think I'll just take a walk up to the turbines."

Rebecca squinted from beneath furrowed eyebrows, studying Jamie carefully. At last, she nodded. "All right. Please be careful. And drink some water first. You look a little dehydrated."

"I will. Thanks." Jamie reached tentatively for Rebecca's forearm, not quite touching it. "Rebecca? I-I'm really sorry."

"I know you are." Rebecca's slight smile may even have been genuine.

CHAPTER FIVE

EQUILIBRIUM

So which was worse? The unrelenting apparitions of The Bastard? The possibility that the same general who shoved an officer's commission down her throat now wanted to shove a Blue Max up her ass? Or Vivian Velty's porcelain smirk?

Hunkered on the concrete deck of one of the wind turbines, Jamie scowled at the GNN main page filling most of her eyewraps' shadowscreen. "Not just about being the great media messenger, is it?" she muttered at the image she found there. "You get off big time on watching what the message does to the sucker you deliver it to."

She fingered the baseball-sized chunk of granite she'd picked up near the crest of Great Hill, then stood and heaved it northward, away from the house. "God, I wish I'd never accepted that fucking commi—" The sound of someone approaching behind her snuffed her words and stuttered her heartbeat. She almost lost her balance as she whirled, ready to defend herself.

"Just me, kiddo," puffed Lynn. "Whew. Haven't walked this way in a while. Too long a while, obviously." She spent a few seconds looking around and catching her breath before she sat and motioned Jamie to join her. "Congratulations. You put Vivian Velty so far off her game that she told me what she said to you." Winking, Lynn bumped her shoulder into Jamie's. "Heh. And what you said back." Then she shook her head. "I want you to know I haven't heard anything about a Medal of Honor for you or anyone else, but I'll send Springer snooping and keep you apprised, okay?"

Jamie nodded. "I'm sorry for embarrassing you and Rebecca down there." She pulled her knees tight to her chest and wrapped her arms around them. "And for making you feel like you had to drag up here and talk to me."

"Hey, shit happens. Should've had Springer keep a closer eye on Vivian. Didn't pay enough attention to her once I knew Robin wouldn't be here." Lynn bumped Jamie's shoulder again. "Thanks for that, by the way. It's, uh, kind of scary how much space Robin needs now…"

"Well, I was winging it." Jamie shrugged. "When Robin starts talking, it's hard not to see things her way. Gets that from her mother, I think."

Lynn smiled, and for a moment they sat side-by-side in silence. "Who's The Bastard?" Lynn asked finally.

"He—" But Jamie's gut had seized. She gulped air. "He interrogated me. At Saint Eh Mo's. Shoo Juh called him lee-eh huaw—bastard—and he didn't hassle her about it, so that's my name for him. He—" Jamie held up her hands and nodded toward their teardrop scars. "I think he did this."

"You *think?*"

"I don't actually remember it. But I—there was this interrogation. The last one, and he was there, with Shoo Juh, and I recognized…Not his face, I never saw his face. I knew his voice, that accent, the way he laughed and taunted me, his presence. I had this sense, an overwhelming sense that he nailed my hands to…something. A table maybe."

"And he's here? Now?"

"I thought I heard him. Laughing. And I figure…the way Shoo Juh talked to him, I figure he's a merc, and they show up everywhere, work for all kinds of people and companies a-and—" Jamie flexed and stretched her hands. "But then…then he was gone."

"So it could've been—"

"I hallucinated. It was a flashback."

"It could've been someone else who sounded like him. And you'd been primed for it because you'd just dealt with Vivian."

Jamie shrugged.

"You do realize," Lynn said, "there's a fifty-fifty chance one of Vivian's boys at the Pentagon yanked her chain."

"So I have hope. Good."

"If they offer it, you'll turn it down, won't you?"

"Yep."

Lynn twice started to speak but halted. "I had the impression," she said at last, "that you plan to stay in the Marine Corps. That you wanted to make a career of it."

Jamie pulled her eyes from Lynn's gaze. "Might as well stick with what I'm good at."

"You do understand that the promotion process for commissioned officers is quite competitive, and quite political."

"Yeah, I've noticed."

"Have you talked with—I forget what they're called in the Marines—the career counseling people?"

"Uh-uh," Jamie said, rubbing her hands together to quell their tiny tremor. "Not yet." *No point if I can't pass the fitness and marksmanship tests. Which is gonna take a while. Hell, I barely made it up here without the goddamn cane. And god only knows when my hands will stop shaking.*

"I can't imagine how Ben Embry pulled off promoting you the way he did. It's unheard of."

"Didn't make me any friends."

"You're wrong about that. I, for one, am deeply grateful, because no one else at Saint Eh Mo's could've led us out of there and back to our own people. But you might find things a bit problematic now. The Marine Corps has no protocol at all for, um..."

"Everyone called us coyotes. Like mustangs—y'know, enlisted to officer—except we got *all* our training on-the-job. Primary qualification was not being dead yet."

Lynn squinted at something in the distance. A controlled cringe, Jamie thought. *Because she doesn't want it to be true, but she knows damn well it is.*

"For the Marine Corps," Lynn said after a pause, "it'll be entirely about getting you, uh, coyotes aligned with the existing promotion process. Mostly you'll need to catch up educationally, which means college—"

"I've started taking courses online. Well, one course. But it's worth a few college credits."

"That's good. Shows dedication to self-improvement. But awards count for a lot—especially awards for valor. For the sake of your career, you probably should take all you can get."

"No."

"Jamie, that doesn't make sense." Lynn couldn't keep the exasperation from her voice, but Jamie gave her points for trying. "You already have—what is it?—two Silver Stars, two Navy Crosses, god knows how many Purple H—"

"One Navy Cross. I declined the other one."

"Well, actually, that day Ben came to see you in the hospital and told you about it, he brought it with him. His staff had tweaked some of the protocol—planned a whole ceremony at your bedside and had quite a collection of big shots waiting down the hall to make their entrance. Something about the Secretary of the Navy being unavailable that day, which meant Ben had the ceremony all to himself. After you passed out, he pinned it on your pillow at the hospital before he left."

"*What?*" Jamie yelped. "I said I didn't want it!"

"I know. He told me. But he decided not to believe you— described you as muddled from your wounds and your medications, which was conveniently reinforced by you fading out on him more or less mid-sentence. He did realize his minions had picked the wrong time for ceremonies and official photo ops, though it wouldn't surprise me if he's got a pic of you unconscious in your hospital bed with him attaching the Navy Cross to the pillow a few inches from your head."

Jamie gaped at Lynn; after she'd mustered the strength to line up the words "I," "respectfully," and "decline," she buried all thoughts of medals. "What happened to it?"

"It's in a rather nicely carved wooden box in the safe in my office. With the rest of your medals."

"You—kept it?"

"Of course I kept it. And when your stuff from Palawan showed up, well…" Lynn's smile seemed a little penitent. "You were sound asleep and the seabag smelled awfully musty, so Reb and I went through it to pull out anything that couldn't be washed. We found your medals and ribbons and such scattered at the bottom, so we gathered them up, put them in a box, and I locked the box in my safe, where it's waiting for you."

"Nope. Finders keepers." Jamie shifted her eyes to the southern horizon where sea met sky. "They're all yours."

"Jamie, listen to me." Lynn leaned a little forward until Jamie met her gaze. "For most of the educational opportunities you'll need to stay in the Marine Corps, you have to be selected by a panel that bases its decisions on your fitness report. And all the details on your fitness report are boiled down to a number, just one number. Maybe you'll get away with coming up short on those behavioral therapy sessions, but turning down the Medal of Honor *will* hurt you."

"Guess I better hope it doesn't come to that."

Jamie decided to ignore the worry in Lynn's god-I-hope-so-too glance.

She decided then to ignore all kinds of other stuff as well. Her anger at Ben Embry. The way Lynn's unflagging generosity revealed how very much she needed the kindness of these people at Great Hill whom in truth she barely knew—because she had no real friends and never did, not ever once in her life. Most of all, she decided to ignore the vague sense of hopelessness that loomed before her like a fog bank, inscrutable, disorienting, creeping in to envelop her.

But she couldn't ignore how real The Bastard's laugh had sounded out there on the south meadow. Lynn's tribe was downright magnanimous about it, eloquently convincing themselves that, yes, certainly, what Jamie heard was true, actual in the world. Somebody had indeed laughed—just *not* The Bastard. They conducted a Monday morning breakfast table debate about the likeliest candidate and which of the guests had the most obnoxious cackle. Jamie couldn't help but smile at their dead-on mimicry as she watched for the moment when she could inconspicuously withdraw to her room.

Yet she kept on hearing The Bastard's laugh. In her sleep, in her waking, too, he brayed just behind her left ear, closer than ever. *Uh dee yapizz dahmah terayno.* Sometimes, she jumped when she heard it. Sometimes, for a nanosecond, the ground shifted beneath her feet.

Soon after the cookout, Great Hill shifted, too, transforming from the comparative relaxation of August's pseudo-vacation to the back-to-school, back-to-work September bustle, little of which actually happened in the house.

Robin had returned to prep school with a breezy, over-the-shoulder adios. Lynn left early on Monday mornings for Washington, taking Springer and ET with her and not returning until Thursday evenings. Rebecca added hours at the hospital—to evade the loneliness of Lynn's absence, Jamie suspected. Dana was also gone a lot, piloting an experimental light jet to autumn conferences on various continents. "Practically the only one in the whole freaking company who has to go to meetings *in person*," groused Lily, who usually disappeared into the workspace over the second garage before 0800 hours, baby Evvie in tow, and didn't reappear until at least 1800 hours.

The house seemed becalmed, which Jamie found somewhat disconcerting, especially since it happened at the same time that she no longer blearily slipped into those involuntary afternoon snoozes that had claimed her all through her first month at Great Hill.

At least Mary remained, as did Kizzy the cook and "the girls," as Mary called the cheerful young women who managed and maintained the house itself—three sisters unfortunately named Fannie, Florrie, and Flossie. Fannie embodied gentle patience as she supervised Florrie and Flossie, the shy Down Syndrome twins preoccupied with the achievement of cleaning and laundry perfection.

Without quite realizing it at first, Jamie began to leave the door to her room ajar during the day. When Mary played the piano, she ventured out to sit close by on the back stairs, mesmerized; between pieces they'd chat and she learned to recognize a few Bach preludes and the Moonlight Sonata and a Chopin nocturne that transformed her melancholy into something poignant and beautiful. Sometimes Edgar would come by to hang out with Mary, and she'd join them for a little while out on the screened porch or at the breakfast table while they drank tea and she drank Kizzy's lemonade.

A week slid into two, then three. Lynn reported nothing about a Blue Max and Jamie gained both strength and the beginnings of a faith that Vivian Velty had got it wrong. Then came Wednesday, September 25, and a message from Lynn appeared in the lower right corner of Jamie's eyewraps shadowscreen:

JUST HEARD——YOUR MOH RECOMMENDATION IS FOR REAL
APPROVED AN HOUR AGO BY DECORATIONS BOARD
WILL FACECALL YOU ±9 PM TONIGHT

After reading Lynn's message twice, all the wordless, swirling inevitability of Jamie's future splattered before her—revealed in her own vomit floating in the toilet bowl she knelt over, as if instead of hurling her lunch she'd handed the dregs of a cup of tea to an especially canny fortune-teller. *Read it and weep.*

Lifting her head, she fixed her eyes straight ahead and tried to quell her stomach. But the palaver in her head couldn't persuade her to calm down and ignore the suddenly sovereign *NO!* that threatened to turn her inside out—any more than the saliva seeping out of her mouth could protect her throat from the sour burn of stomach acid. Jamie spat saliva and refusal into the toilet, stumbled unsteadily to her feet, and left the house without speaking to anyone.

With little awareness of where she was and no notion at all of where she was going, she marched eastward along Great Hill's trails and then veered into woods just starting to sport their autumn color. Her head throbbed, a spasm of alarm knifed across her chest, and one thought ruled her, blinding her to time and place and purpose: *I told him no, I said no and he fucking did it anyway. I don't care if he's a fucking general. He had no right! I told him no—*

Only when the horn of a passing truck squawked at her did she realize she'd reached an intersection at edge of the village center well below Great Hill's expansive acres. For a moment, she contemplated turning around and going back. *To do what? Let Lynn talk me into it? Act all fine and dandy tonight when I'm introduced to Lily's sister? Christ, why'd the woman have to pick tonight to come back from where-the-fuck-ever, anyway?*

So Jamie walked on, choosing one street, then another that took her toward the glistening harbor and the stores and shops occupying what once had been the houses of old Yankee Manchester. Behind her, some guy whose path had shadowed hers for the last 300 meters switched direction like he'd forgotten something, and he hurried into an antediluvian grocery store across the street. *Okay, so I am just being paranoid.* Ahead of her, two middle-aged women emerged in a hurry from a little café. "We'll just have time to buy our tickets at the station and get the discount," one said to the other; neither of them noticed her, much less recognized her.

Jamie followed them into an unassuming yellow clapboard building next to the grocery store, bought what they bought, then stood a few meters from them on a simple blacktopped platform behind the building to await the train already rumbling toward the station. When the train stopped, she followed the women aboard and hunkered into a seat in the last row of the nearly empty last car.

❖

What am I gonna do? What am I gonna do?

The question colluded with the rhythms of the moving train. But Jamie had no answers, only a frenetic clawing in her belly, in her clit. She counted the number of seats in the car, the number of people in the seats, calculated the percent of seats occupied—and gave it up, because counting and calculating didn't help. She fiddled with her eyewraps, put on the khaki boonie hat stuffed in a pocket of the denim jacket she'd grabbed when she left the house, then took the hat off, put it on again—all distractions that lasted only seconds. She squirmed where she sat, yet no position granted any relief.

Finally, she whacked the side of her head hard into the window frame once, twice, a third time, so her head would hurt enough to counterbalance the furious fire in her gut and blot out thought. Thereafter, her head against the jouncing window, she stared at intermittent views of Massachusetts Bay, then careworn Beverly Center and Salem, until her eyes closed.

"It isn't over, hong mao." Shoo Juh's unblemished, crimson-edged face had commandeered the black undersides of Jamie's eyelids and, smiling icy anticipation, bore down on her slowly, menacingly—

"No!" The sound of her own voice jolted Jamie awake and opened her eyes to a view out the train window of decayed neighborhoods succumbing to concrete, steel, tar, and garbage—the gritty, grimy industrial necessities of the city just ahead. And the lacerating inferno in her gut raged stronger than ever.

What am I gonna do? Forehead pressed to the window, Jamie curled up on the seat, seized her crotch, and squeezed as she watched the train roll into Boston over bridges and under expressway overpasses, past old red brick railway structures and wayward clumps of defiant weeds and derelict piles of dirt and sand and stone. By the time the train shuffled to a stop alongside a gray North Station platform, Jamie stood fidgeting at the door, desperate to keep moving, keep moving, keep moving...

CHAPTER SIX
HAIL SWEET REPOSE

The kink in Jamie's intestines that was supposed to be healed twinged, silencing the incessant question, and she realized she didn't know where she was. She needed a few minutes to find out the old-fashioned way, by walking to the nearest street corner: Commonwealth Avenue and Dartmouth Street—the Back Bay. *Christ, I'm walking in circles.*

Not necessarily a bad thing. Comm Ave's grassy, tree-lined mall appealed to her, as did its blocks of old townhouses. She made herself slow down some to study the ornate features of a gutted brownstone just as the clamor of construction ebbed and a couple of the crew emerged full of jaunty talk about going for a beer. Then, somewhere in the building, a power drill sputtered.

When the drill went full bore, Jamie freaked. She tried to run as it buzzed louder. But she couldn't move anything but her eyes, and her eyes saw only the drill bit whirring closer as a finger revved the tool's threat and The Bastard's chill, shrill, grating laugh mocked her. It would take a long time, he jeered, death in slow motion, and he laughed again. She tried to keep herself from imagining how it was going to feel to die this way, with a fully torqued drill bit goring, gouging one millimeter after another through her eye and into her screaming brain.

The blare of the automobile's horn saved her from the drill. She gaped at the driver blankly at first, then apologetically when she grasped that she *had* run from the drill—all the way down Comm Ave through several intersections, across the entirety of the Public Garden, and into the middle of impatient rush hour traffic on Charles Street. The driver was red-faced and swearing wildly, having almost hit her. Several other vehicles quickly joined in, honking at her while she lurched across two more lanes of traffic into the refuge of the Boston Common.

There she wandered, breathless, bewildered, and afraid. Because either her mind was betraying her, hallucinating her into insanity, or she had blundered into the shrapnel of something heretofore unremembered. Jamie shuddered, desperate to think about something else. Anything else.

At the entrance to the Central Burying Ground in a corner of the Common, she halted. No one else was there, and despite the jam of vehicles nearby, the old slate headstones seemed to offer quiet palliation, so she ventured in and soon came upon what had once been a triple-arched stone marking the remains of three children. Only two arches with their primitive angel carvings survived. She discerned on the eroded surface a verse and hoarsely read it aloud.

"Hail sweet repose now shall we rest
"No more with sickness be distressed
"Here from all sorrow find release
"Our souls shall dwell in endless peace"

Jamie sat down cross-legged a few feet away, exhaled, and read the verse again and again; even though she didn't believe in souls, she needed to believe in release. Only the arrival of another visitor—a guy who walked in slowly, like maybe he'd recognized her and might try to strike up a conversation if he got near enough—drove her away.

That's when she started thinking about leaving. Leaving Great Hill. Leaving the Corps. *Maybe I should just jack everything and go and keep on going.*

❖

"ID please," said a big woman in black jeans and a tit-hugging red tech-knit top.

Shit. Jamie had forgotten about the age thing; it had never mattered in the Palawan dives where she occasionally found herself. She pulled out her military ID anyway and handed it over, expecting to be turned away.

"Mmm." The woman studied the card for several seconds and then returned it with a nod that bore no hint she recognized Jamie. "New in the neighborhood?"

"Yep."

"No cover charge for members of our armed forces. Welcome to Demeter, Lieutenant."

"Thanks—'preciate it."

Jamie had found the place by accident when she spotted a couple of dykes opening its green-and-gold door to go in. She could have checked out the local dyke bar options on her comlink, of course, but that would have meant switching it on, and switching it on would have meant she might see the message-received icon hovering in the lower right corner on her eyewraps' shadowscreen. And no, she just couldn't deal with that. Not yet. So her comlink—eyewraps and wristband alike—stayed shut down and packed away in her jacket pocket, zipper unequivocally closed. Thus, she didn't know the time, but the sun had set quite a while ago, she was plenty tired and plenty hungry—and she'd noticed a menu posted next to Demeter's door.

A brief wave of déjà vu buffeted her as she took in the three rooms, all in a row, all large, spare, and dimly lit. Tiny lights densely adorned the high ceilings without providing much illumination. A long, u-shaped bar dominated the first space, restrooms and kitchen behind it. The middle space contained bistro tables and chairs; heavy double doors separated the third area—the dance floor—from the rest, but the doors had been flung open and Jamie saw that it was empty but for a small sound booth, a laserball poking out of the ceiling, and one entwined couple. A narrow, elbow-height shelf lined every wall space not requisitioned for a more important use. The music was low-down sexy and, as always, too loud.

Jamie chose a spot at the back of the bar, near the hallway leading to the toilets, and ordered a hamburger, fries, and seltzer water.

"Got the time?" she asked when the bartender brought her food.

"'Bout nine thirty, amiga. Fun'll start in an hour or so."

She ate slowly, watching women enter singly, in pairs, in cliques, and tried not to think about the nine o'clock call she hadn't taken. It should have been easier, considering she'd never been in the company of so many dykes in her life. About the time she finished eating, a woman with hungry eyes sidled up to a neighboring barstool, but soon decamped. Jamie moved to a more shadowed barstool and ordered another seltzer water.

After a second and a third woman approached and retreated, Jamie realized that whatever game this was, she had no clue how to play it and didn't want to learn. She ordered a third seltzer water, then a fourth, and figured she'd sit there watching all the dykes until the place closed. She wished she could sit there until...*Until it's over*.

"It will never be over, hong mao."

Suddenly engulfed in pitch-black, Jamie shuddered; experience had taught her what the sneering malice in Shoo Juh's tone portended, and she girded for the blow. It would strike across her shoulder blades maybe, or her buttocks, delivering a convulsion of fire and pain and chaotic neon-red streaks bolting through the blackness toward her. And her helpless scream would be answered by The Bastard's scraping, scouring laugh.

Don't make a fucking sound.

"Hey there! Hey! *Hey!*"

Don't make a fucking sound.

"Take it easy now!"

She couldn't tell where the ground was. Someone on the other side of the heavy pitch-black held her shoulders. She tried to raise her head, but her chin kept dropping to her chest, pulling on the muscles along the back of her neck. *Don't make a fucking sound...*

Finally, the blackness faded into churning gray fog and, feature by feature, a face emerged from it. *Not Shoo Juh.* Jamie clutched the edge of the bar and pushed her feet against the floor. *That's not Shoo Juh.*

"You okay, sport?" The woman was about thirty, square-faced but not square-jawed, sandy blond hair cropped close, robustly butch in denim and leather, probably military.

"Sorry," Jamie muttered. "Guess I got a little dizzy."

Cautiously, the woman let go of Jamie's shoulders, but her concerned eyes stuck to Jamie's for a long moment before they flicked to a group wending between people and bistro tables toward the doors to the dance floor and the thumping music beyond. "Hmph," she snorted contemptuously. "That's fatuous enough to make anybody dizzy."

There were six of them, a small pageant adorned in assorted blacks and a variety of chains. One wore handcuffs and skintight leather pants exposing her naked backside; when the chain attached to her studded leather collar went taut in the gloved hand of her gaunt, expressionless companion, she halted abruptly and bowed her head. Then a third woman approached and slapped the handcuffed women's bare flesh so hard that the sound could be heard over the din of people and music.

Jamie nearly slid off the stool again. She had to grab the edge of the bar with both hands this time, nauseous and gasping, struggling to hold on to where she was. She peered at the wood grain of the bar top, not daring to shut her eyes and find Shoo Juh waiting for her.

"Army or Marine Corps?" the woman asked placidly.

"Corps," Jamie replied, thankful for the woman's willingness to feign normalcy.

"Mmm. Likewise." The woman smiled. "Been out for three years." Clearly wanting more than a polite nod, she settled onto the barstool next to Jamie's.

Okay, okay, I do owe you for keeping my ass from landing on the floor. "What're you doing now?" Jamie asked just before her silence had a chance to get awkward.

"School. For criminal justice. To be a cop, or corrections." The woman fisted and raised her right hand for the usual post-pandemic touch-free dap. "Name's Stacy."

Responding with the same gesture, Jamie stopped her knuckles' forward motion a couple of centimeters from Stacy's. "I'm Jamie. Thanks for, uh, keeping me upright."

"Anytime." Stacy had tacked a smile on her face that seemed uncomfortable, like it would rather be somewhere else, and she fiddled nervously with a small medallion on a stretch cord around her neck. "Can I get you a drink? Something a little stronger maybe?"

Jamie's spine prickled a warning that she attributed to Stacy's gaze lingering too long on her blemished hands, which gripped her glass of seltzer water. She wanted to thrust her hands out of sight, but she forced herself to keep hold of the glass. "No, thanks. I'm good."

Stacy ordered a beer and took a long swig. "You been in combat, too, huh?" she said, no longer looking at Jamie, no longer smiling. "That fight with the chinks in the Philippines?"

Resisting the urge to get up and leave the bar, Jamie nodded slightly at the far wall. *Do…not…ask…me…anything.*

"Yeah," Stacy said, gazing down the neck of her beer bottle. "Yeah." She finished her beer with a second long swig and ordered another. "Mine was that crap along the Mexican border. Five years ago now." She pulled aside her shirt to allow a glimpse of a raggedy scar eight or ten centimeters below her left collarbone. "Almost bought it."

Once more, Jamie nodded, this time looking at Stacy. *Okay, long as she's doing the talking, that's okay.*

"It gets better," Stacy said. "Y'know, up here." She tapped her head.

"Does it? When?"

"When you figure out how to slap the itch instead of scratch it." Stacy sipped her beer almost delicately. "Like the relief you get when you smack a mosquito bite. Long as you smack it *hard.*"

"Say what?"

"Can't get away from it, right?" Stacy turned to squint at Jamie. "Nightmares about all of your finer moments over there, like some auto-replay you can't click off. Flashbacks that slam you as soon as you let yourself relax. Something always sneaking up on you—" Stacy extended her arm, snapped her fingers sharply just beyond the edge of Jamie's peripheral vision—and it worked. Jamie jumped. "Yeah, like that, Lieutenant—a bogeyman. All in your head." Stacy shrugged and turned back to her beer. "Let that itch get infected and you end up with a real nasty wound. The kind that never heals."

Jamie shook her head. "No way am I taking that pharma the shrink gave me. No way."

"Pharma? Who said anything about pharma?" Stacy laughed. "Hell, that shit'll turn you into a sixty-four dollar zombie. With a wound that never heals."

"So I'm supposed to *talk* to him? How the hell will that help? He's a bobble head, for chrissake."

"I said *slap* the itch, not whine about it to a pretentious dweeb."

"And what exactly does slapping do?"

"It purges the shit outta you, that's what. Cleans out the germs—all the guilt, the fear, the haunts." Stacy stretched her shoulders casually, as if she was mildly bored.

"Release," said Jamie.

"Yeah, okay—release. Won't work if you can't handle the sting, though. Disinfecting a wound stings plenty, so you need discipline to see it through. Marine Corps discipline and commitment and perseverance. 'Cuz the mission fails and your infection gets a whole lot worse if you can't obey orders."

"Orders? What orders?"

"Whaddaya think—it just *happens?* You gotta do whatever you're damn well told by whoever helps you get your release." Stacy snorted as she looked Jamie up and down. "'Course, you can always head on back to your bobble head shrink and obey *his* orders." She glanced at her wristcom. "Shit, it's late," she said—and dismounted the barstool. "I gotta go. Need a ride anywhere?"

"I—" Jamie grabbed a breath and stood, too; she couldn't let Stacy leave yet. "How'd *you* do it?"

"Do what?"

"Release. Find release."

Stacy grinned. "With the help of a good woman. She taught me a lot before she moved on."

"Yeah…" Jamie dropped her gaze to Stacy's black engineer boots. She couldn't think, couldn't move.

"So, you want a ride?" When Jamie didn't respond, Stacy murmured, "Okay, guess I'll see you around." Her boots began an about-face toward the exit, then halted. "Or, uh, do you want me to pass on what I've learned?"

"I…dunno."

"I don't mind, but here's the deal: You do whatever I say whenever I say. You can take your leave anytime you want, but if you do that before *I* want, we're done, 'cuz I do *not* waste my time playing pamper-the-wimp games. Understand?"

Stacy's tone took Jamie by surprise. It had transmuted so fast from barroom casual to the impatient, imperious growl of a drill instructor's command voice that she nearly leapt to attention hollering "Ma'am-yes-MA'AM!" But actually she didn't understand, not really. So she told the truth. "It's not getting better. It's getting worse."

Gaze threatening to harden into a glare, Stacy stood as tall as Jamie but bigger-boned—a formidable presence. "I'm going. Now."

As Stacy turned away, Shoo Juh's voice resounded in Jamie's head. *It will never be over, hong mao.* "Okay," Jamie said, quickly stepping into Stacy's path.

Stacy stopped again. "Okay what?"

"It's, uh…it's a deal. I wanna do it."

"Tonight. Starting now."

Now? Jamie forgot to breathe.

"Now or not at all," Stacy said. "I don't make frigging appointments."

Counting the accelerating backbeats of her heart, Jamie inhaled, exhaled. *All right*, she told herself on the fourth backbeat. "All right," she said aloud on the fifth.

"From this moment on, you obey my commands. Without question. Without hesitation. Agreed?"

"Yes."

Stacy reached out, wordlessly demanding an old-fashioned handshake—the kind that signified trust so deep that you willingly exposed yourself to another's potentially deadly pathogens. Jamie gave Stacy her hand, tensing it to counter a crushing grip.

"On me," Stacy ordered, then right-faced and marched toward Demeter's green and gold front door.

❖

Stacy's front door was blood red. Number 55 on some tree-lined street in some diligently middle class, you-can-hear-a-pin-drop neighborhood on a hill overlooking the city. Northwest about ten klicks, Jamie estimated as she eyed Boston's distant lights, sharp beneath a clear, moonless sky. Not so far, really. Knowing this made it easier for her to enter the simple cape that was Stacy's house. *I go anytime I want. That's the deal.*

Once inside, Jamie glanced around a scrupulously impersonal living room, stopping to listen.

"Relax. I live alone. Nobody here but you and me," said Stacy, signaling Jamie to follow her into a hallway between the living room and the kitchen.

"I…gotta pee."

Stacy didn't hide her irritation as she pointed to a door off the hallway. "Keep it quick."

Sitting on the toilet in the unaccessorized lavatory, Jamie listened some more and heard only the sounds of Stacy opening and closing a refrigerator while the off-and-on whisper in her head tried one more time. *Maybe this isn't a very good idea.* But her whisper had no chance—not versus the nebulous, inexpressible, almost electric need trilling through her.

A moment later, Jamie followed Stacy across the hall, down basement stairs, and through a room with a vintage mechanical pinball machine and a raggedy sofa to the threshold of another room, this one windowless. Lit by a single bare bulb, the space was dominated by an impressive cable crossover machine, nicer than the one in Great Hill's gym. The machine's crossbeam spanned more than three meters; at each end stood a weight stack with at least thirty ten-pound plates that could be hooked to a cable system terminating at an adjustable pulley housing fastened to a stirrup-shaped handgrip. The machine stood on a large rubber mat covering most of the concrete floor, an assortment of grips, bars, and straps scattered at its periphery.

A small music system occupied a stool in the corner where the room's two concrete walls joined. The other two walls were plasterboarded only on the outside; the insides and the ceiling, too, were unfinished but rock wool-insulated and covered with clear plastic sheeting stapled to the studs and joists. Little sound would escape this space once the room's only door was shut.

When Jamie saw a large slide bolt on the door, her heartbeat kicked into double time and enabled the whisper in her head to achieve full voice, but only until she fingered the strike plate and realized how loose it was, loose enough to give way with a moderate shove. *Okay, that's okay.* Besides, a few feet from the workout room she'd spotted another door leading outside and had stolen a couple seconds to peer through its glass and take in features of the backyard beyond, ghostly in the scant light emanating from the upstairs windows. *No bulkhead, six or so steps up to the yard, raised deck maybe three meters away, thick bushes around it.* The door would be easy to open, too. *Just a simple, old-style deadbolt between me and going anytime I want, anytime I want.*

"Hey! In here," Stacy barked, and after a bracing inhale, Jamie obeyed. "Strip off," Stacy said as she moved the music system from the stool to the floor. "Put your stuff here."

Again Jamie obeyed, carefully removing and folding her clothes to make a neat pile on the stool—jacket first, then boots placed on the floor next to the stool, socks stuffed in the boots, finally adding shirt, jeans, underwear, and boonie hat to the pile. With narrowed eyes, Stacy watched from a couple of meters away. Naked, unsure, the fiery claw in her belly slashing lower, deeper, Jamie faced Stacy and shifted her left heel to meet her right, turning out her feet on either side of an imaginary center line to form a thirty-degree angle while she lifted her chest and pulled in her chin. She had automatically assumed the position of attention, thumbs rubbing her thighs in unconscious search of her pants seams, eyes fixing straight ahead. *Now,* her whisper begged. *Go now. Just grab everything off that stool and...*

Stacy circled, silencing the whisper; her eyes skimmed Jamie's body before shifting to the cable crossover machine. "Ever use one of these?"

"Yes."

"Good." With a speed and finesse born of habit, Stacy adjusted the machine, positioning the two pulley housings several inches above Jamie's head. "We'll start with high crossover curls."

Stepping toward the nearest pulley housing, Jamie reached for the handgrip.

"No," said Stacy, leaning over to scoop a couple of padded ankle straps off the rubber mat. "I want you to use a special technique— designed to encourage discipline and commitment and perseverance." She snap-linked an ankle strap to one handgrip, then the other. "Move to the middle between the pulleys."

Oh. Jamie didn't budge.

Hands on her hips, Stacy shook her head. "Running out of nerve, are we, Lieutenant?"

"I—"

"Give me a fucking break. We both know why you're here."

Jamie lowered her head and stared at the floor. *I'm here because—*

"Because you can't stand what happens when you close your eyes," Stacy snarled. "And this is the only way you get any relief."

Jamie raised her eyes to meet Stacy's. "Release. I want release."

For four quickening heartbeats, then five, then six, Stacy's eyes did not blink. "Move to the middle between the damn pulleys," she said with flat, deadly calm.

Somehow, Stacy's eyes, Stacy's commands had become the default, that which must be decided against. But Jamie couldn't decide. Deciding required willpower, and hers had been used up by the Palawan. She had no willpower left. So she obeyed.

"Face the concrete wall and extend your arms, palms up."

Jamie glanced at the pile of clothes on the stool off to her right. It seemed far away. Too far away. So she obeyed.

"Here." Stacy yanked the handgrip attached to the pulley on Jamie's right. "It's only twenty pounds. Hold it steady, slight bend at your elbow."

Jamie took the handgrip and Stacy snugged the ankle strap dangling from it around her wrist. A moment later, she also held the handgrip attached to the left pulley, and a moment after that, her left wrist was swathed in an ankle strap.

Then Stacy moved the weight stack pins lower, adding weight to both cable systems. "Thirty pounds now," she said, standing akimbo in front of Jamie. "Show me twelve reps."

Almost kinda normal. Except for being buck naked god knows where in a stranger's soundproofed basement, arms spread-eagled, wrists tethered. Except for not being at all sure how the hell to get untethered without help. Exhaling, Jamie pulled the handgrips toward her shoulders, bending her elbows, then straightening her arms. Twelve times.

"Forty pounds," Stacy said after readjusting the pins and returning to her spot a few feet in front of Jamie. "Twelve reps."

Jamie obeyed. When Stacy upped the weight to fifty pounds, Jamie had to brace her feet and her recovering left shoulder complained, but she managed a set—just.

Once more, Stacy shifted the pins. "Sixty pounds," she said, this time stepping behind Jamie, who turned to follow her motion. "Hey, don't look at me. Eyes front and do a set of twelve reps."

A new reluctance quivered up Jamie's legs and infused her chest. Not because Stacy had thoroughly fatigued her, not even because she gave a damn that doing reps at sixty pounds would surely screw up her shoulder—if she could do them at all. No, it was the expanse of bare concrete wall in front of her, uninterrupted now that Stacy had left her to face it alone. She didn't like its brutal gray impermeability, its rough, raw indifference—

"Waiting for a sign from some god?" Malignity tinged Stacy's words. "Twelve fucking reps. Now."

Jamie did not obey. Instead, she squeezed her eyes tight to shut out the concrete wall—and found Shoo Juh's flawless, arrogant face waiting for her, coolly avid in the pitch-black behind her eyelids. "I own you, hong mao," Shoo Juh purred, coming nearer to examine her nakedness.

"No!" Jamie pulled hard on the straps restraining her wrists and kicked at Shoo Juh with one foot, then the other. But the weight at the end of the straps held her in place.

Shoo Juh's steely leer closed in. "And I do so enjoy owning you."

"*No!*"

"You want this," a voice crooned softly, sounding as much like Stacy as Shoo Juh. "You need this."

One more time, Jamie yanked on the straps around her wrists. For a second or two, the weights responded. Jamie's yell turned into a moan as the effort extracted the last of her strength, and she sagged in defeat, the weights dropping with a dull clank. "You fucking bitch," she rasped at Shoo Juh's insouciant sneer. "What're you waiting for?"

Anticipation lit Shoo Juh's face at the very nanosecond a nasty slap stung Jamie's backside and a hand slithered onto her throat, choking her yelp and inducing her eyes to pop open.

"Apologize," Stacy growled from behind her, and the grip on Jamie's throat tightened.

"What?" Jamie croaked.

"No one calls me a fucking bitch."

The hand departed Jamie's throat, and precisely one breath later—the breath intended for her protesting "Hey! Enough!"—she got slapped again, a loud crack of a blow delivered from farther away and with enough savagery that her protest disintegrated to a grunt.

"*Jeezus*, Stacy!" Jamie gasped. "Sto—*ahh!*"

Stacy had hit her again. "I'll show you who's the fucking bitch!" Stacy roared.

And the blows kept coming. And coming. Onto her back, onto her bum, onto her thighs. She bawled at Stacy to stop, but that only seemed to inspire Stacy to hit her harder, faster. A belt, Jamie knew from experience. *Least it's not the buckle end.*

She tried to count the hits. *Six, seven, eight…*If each hit had a number, then she might hold its pain separate, discrete, unable to foment the conspiracy that pain so desired. *Eleven, twelve, goddamn, goddamn…*Her legs began to buckle; her hold on the handgrips slackened, and the straps around her wrists bore nearly the full weight of her body as she slumped forward, arms stretched hard, knees slipping slowly to the mat. Already, she'd failed; already, the familiar molten impulse seethed. There was no stopping it, just like there was no stopping Stacy's rage. It rolled through her, willful and incorrigible, and she writhed as its simmer intensified. The blows kept coming and, consumed in their fire, Jamie came, too.

When the concrete wall in front of her began to waver and dim, she heard Shoo Juh's whisper in her ear. "I told you, hong mao. It will never be over."

Chapter Seven

Slapdab

The darkness, sudden and almost complete, did what pain and self-disgust could not: It hurled Jamie out of stupor and into the mother of all adrenaline rushes.

In the time it took her eyes to blink, she knew where she was, what a spectacularly asinine thing she'd done, and that Stacy hadn't finished with her yet. Otherwise she wouldn't still be on her knees, hanging by her wrists from a cable crossover machine. And Stacy wouldn't have switched off the light.

"Okay, Garrett, I got her good and ready for him...Nah, she's out fucking cold. How long before he gets—" Then the door shut, obscuring Stacy's side of the comlink conversation and deepening the room's darkness, now mitigated only by an inch of sallow illumination at the bottom of the doorway. An instant later came the distinctive sound of the slide bolt slotting into the strike plate; Stacy had locked the door.

Him? What the fuck! HIM?

Panic exploded across Jamie's chest, scorched her throat, and launched her erratically to her feet. This sent the weights attached to the cable systems on either side of her thudding dully as they dropped onto the weight stacks, and she froze. Did Stacy hear that?

Jamie ceased breathing and counted. Three seconds, four seconds passed. Seven seconds. Then she heard muffled footfalls through the stud wall on her left as Stacy climbed the basement stairs. But her relief lasted only as long as it took a tumble of questions to scare the bejeezus out of her while she floundered for the handgrips to which her wrists were bound.

How do I get out of these straps before Stacy comes back? Are my clothes still on that stool? Will I really be able to shove the door open? Without Stacy hearing? What if I trip security lights when I get to the backyard—if I get to the backyard? How much time before Stacy comes back? How much time?

Grips in hand, Jamie pulled, but they didn't move. *C'mon, fool, you gotta let your weight do the work. And use your legs.*

So down she went, a slow-motion descent onto her aggrieved buttocks, pain blasting across her back from her shoulders to her hamstrings. This would be the price. Hoping it would be the only price, she swung her right leg upward over the right cable and shifted as much weight as possible onto it. By the time the cable furrowed into the arch of her right foot, then along her calf and the inside of her thigh, tears filled her eyes and trickled down her face. *Pull now, dammit! Pull!*

On the second attempt, she got her right wrist close enough to her face for her teeth to rip open the Velcro-secured strap circling it. Then, shifting her legs underneath her, she rose, angling her weight rightward. This strained her left shoulder cruelly as the weights on that side of the machine lifted, but it was the only way she could ease down the weights on the right side without Stacy hearing. At least her eyes had adjusted to the darkness and she could see, barely, when the six ten-pound plates seated softly atop the rest of the weight stack. Carefully, she let go the right handgrip to grab the left one and, with both hands, ease down those weights, too.

And now, while Jamie freed her left wrist, her mind darted ahead, scouting, anticipating.

Listen first—count it one two three. No sound on the stairs. *Still have time.*

Clothes? She found them on the stool folded precisely as she'd left them, boots nearby on the floor. By the time she'd hugged her stuff to her chest and turned toward the door, she'd decided on the fastest, quietest way to force the lock on the first door and get through the second door to the outside.

Listen, keep listening, right hand turns the knob, left shoulder low against the door, legs brace for an up-angle shove, not too hard so the strike plate doesn't bang to the floor. Keep listening, look right first after the door's open, 'cuz if the bitch is coming it'll be from the right, then look left, and if she isn't on my ass yet, close the door, quick and quiet, so the seconds she uses up checking inside the room give me that much more distance. Take three long steps to the outside door, turn the deadbolt, open the door, close the door, up those steps and into the shadows around that raised deck ay-sap, ay-sap, and run, keep running...

❖

Have I really got what I'm gonna need for this? She pushed against both her doubt and the door with her aching, quivering left shoulder;

and the door mutely submitted to just one shove. Jamie inhaled and kept going.

She had turned the deadbolt on the outside door and gotten as far as urging it ajar when she heard someone at the top of the basement stairs. Her heartbeat went rabid and her hands trembled violently, but the footsteps were in no hurry. *Bitch hasn't noticed anything yet.* A cramp in Jamie's solar plexus shimmied apart and fluttered down her legs. *Still got five seconds.*

It was enough to escape the house. Just. Clutching her clothes and boots to her chest, she reached the far side of the backyard's raised deck before she dove between the dense bushes skirting it to elude Stacy's flashlight beam. She curled tightly, fetally around her bundle of clothing, back smarting as it made contact with the deck's lattice trim, mouth buried in the cloth of her shirt while she gulped air, tried not to hyperventilate—and figured she was doomed. All Stacy needed to find her was a cursory sweep of the yard using the infrared viewmode now common on so many civilian comlink eyewraps.

"Fuck!" Stacy fumed, waving the flashlight erratically while she scrambled up the steps from the basement door to the yard. "*Fuck!*" Only the backs of her legs and her feet were visible from Jamie's hiding place as she stood about three meters away and swung the flashlight beam in a wide arc across the rear of the yard. "Fuckfuck*fuck!*"

Waiting for Stacy to turn around and spot her, Jamie began to plan how she'd attempt to fight. *Kicks to the lower legs first, fast as possible*...But Stacy didn't turn; the flashlight beam ceased its search to form a small pool of light that bobbed on the ground near feet that still pointed away from her. For an eternal nanosecond, Jamie waited, body clenched, breathing paralyzed.

"Garrett?" Stacy sounded both riled and a little tentative. "She's gone..."

Omigod, a comcall. Jamie exhaled into her shirt.

"As in she's not here anymore...I don't know how. I was upstairs...For as long as it takes to nuke a bag of popcorn and pee, like I told you I was gonna—Of course I locked the damn door." Stacy stomped a foot on the grass. "*Yes*, she was unfuckingconscious...Hey, I did exactly what you wanted, and I stretched it as far as it'll go without committing a fucking felony...Oh yeah? Well, screw him and the dick he rode in on. I didn't sign up to kidnap somebody, for chrissake, so you can just tell him his pizda skedaddled while he was taking his sweet time waltzing over here...What?...*Look* for her? How?...No, I didn't even see a damn comlink to bug, and anyway you said *not* to search her stuff...My eyewraps are fried, remember? So how the hell do I—... Fine, Garrett, *fine*, whatever you fucking say."

Stacy gave the flashlight one more haphazard swing around the rear of the yard, then marched toward the house muttering, "Oh sure, why would I wanna get any sleep tonight..." A second later, the basement door slammed and Jamie started to shiver uncontrollably.

Get up, get up, get outta here now. But Jamie couldn't stop shivering, couldn't move. Not until she heard the aggressive rumble of Stacy's sporty car engine starting up. She crawled halfway out of her hiding place then and hastily scanned the yard to choose a direction. *There.* She ran for a hedge along the boundary of the yard farthest from the fading sound of Stacy's departing vehicle, jumped a waist-high fence behind the hedge, and, crouching breathless behind a neighbor's screened porch, began donning her clothes.

The clothes hurt. They gave new meaning to the phrase "slash and burn" and brought a chastening perspective to the notion of just jack everything and go and keep on going.

Stifling a groan as she leaned down to tie her boots, Jamie flashed on the time she actually did just go and keep on going. Nine years old and fed up with Alby's shit and Meg's latest thrashing, she decided to walk to California—and promptly marched east instead of west. The Harwich cops retrieved her fourteen hours and ten miles later. And although her one night in the custody of scowling, irritated strangers wearing guns and black uniforms added up to merely a glimpse, she saw enough. Alby might've been a hopeless addict eternally unable to break away from hustling for Meg's police sergeant husband, but Alby loved her, Alby hugged her and cried like a baby after talking the Harwich shift commander out of consigning her to The System.

Never let them put you in The System, Alby said ever afterward. That's bouncing from the frying pan slapdab into the fire, Alby said. Slapdab.

Now, like then, all Jamie could think about was recovering what she'd so recklessly renounced: Safe. And yes, yes, it was only for a while Safe, done and gone at the end of next January. *But it sure as shit beats this.*

Jamie stood stiffly upright, sore, exhausted, grateful for the moonless night. She silently thanked whatever town this was for its decision to reduce light pollution and energy costs by dimming its streetlights. And she thanked this neighbor's large oak, which cast the heavy, darkness-bestowing shadow where she now hid and contemplated how to get back to Safe.

Must be pretty tough to find someone fool enough to take a flying leap into that bitch's fire. No wonder they're looking for me. She pulled her boonie hat low over her forehead. *Means anyone I see out here is suspect.* Then she patted her jacket where she'd stowed her wristcom and eyewraps. Still there.

But taking either one online would broadcast her ID and location to anybody with a mobile spoof comsite tuned to pick up comlink activity in the area. If Stacy or this Garrett guy or "Him" had something like that, say, in a car, then they could ante up a few bucks to one of a gazillion hacker groups and get near real-time access to the notoriously insecure communications network subscriber databases. Then it was just a matter of filtering for IDs associated with "Jamie," and in seconds they'd nail her exact location.

Probably just being paranoid.

She snapped on her wristcom and adjusted her eyewraps. One quick click would initiate its uplink, a second click and she'd have help on the way—even if it was only a taxi. Her finger hovered—until that distinctive cold sting nipped up her back. *No. Don't chance it.*

For a moment, Jamie rested her head against the tree and thought about curling up right there and going to sleep. Just for an hour or so. The notion vanished as soon as it formed, however, because the headlights of a car turning the corner about forty meters away almost caught her.

Heart booming in her chest, she moved with the tree's shifting shadow as the car's headlights swept slowly by—much too slowly. The car took its time turning the corner and then crept along the street. It didn't sound like Stacy's car, but Jamie didn't dare peek from behind the tree to see, because somebody in it using infrared viewmode on a decent pair of eyewraps just might pick up the heat signature of her head as she peeked.

Shit. I gotta get outta here.

At least she'd bought a comlink with decent built-in computing functionality, so she already had what she needed most without having to go online. No GPS, of course, but a searchable indexed hybrid map, so she could navigate, and a civilian video-infrared detector built into her eyewraps. Not as good as what the Corps could supply, but even its rudimentary ability would help her avoid notice while she worked her way on foot through kilometer after kilometer of unfamiliar streets. Jamie clicked her comlink offline, placed the compass readout, map, and a virtual joystick-keyboard combo to manipulate it into the lower left corner of her eyewraps' shadowscreen, and noted the time.

0231 hours. She'd have to appear normal as she moved though the empty streets—in case some insomniac glancing out a window should notice her, or if she encountered a lens or a sensor she couldn't dodge. But she'd need to scramble quickly out of sight whenever a car or a pedestrian came along.

She stepped from the shadows hiding her and, defying pain and an incalculable weariness, began quick-timing toward the distant glow of the city.

❖

That's it. I'm never fucking ever moving again. One more time, she'd stumbled and fallen to her hands and knees, setting off a whole new firestorm across her backside where Stacy's whacks had landed.

Heckled by the irony of her predicament, Jamie stared at the Indian grass bent beneath her hands. How does one moment's compulsive turn-on twist so easily into another moment's unalloyed agony? And how might she lower herself the rest of the way to the ground without making the pain worse?

But no, no, the nag who'd latched on to her somewhere back there was having none of it. Get. Up. Get up get up get up.

This did not inspire her to move.

Then the nag pointed out how close she'd already gotten. Look, look, it's right there.

Even the brief glance upward hurt; she bothered only because she didn't want to believe the nag. Which was pretty dumb after all this time, since the nag hadn't yet been wrong. Jamie lowered her head, sighed, and started crawling. Right hand, left knee, left hand, right knee…until she bumped her head.

"Ow!"

Almost there, insisted the nag.

She crawled some more, upward now and onto the concrete deck. Her fingers, then her palm, touched the wind turbine's mast, and at last, at last, its hypnotic vibration hummed through her. Shivering, her back to the sun just recently risen, Jamie curled up at the mast's base and let her eyes close as the turbine's *oh-oh-oh-verrr* filled her chest.

❖

"You were right."

A woman's voice, which Jamie did and didn't recognize. It came from behind her, full of surprise but resonantly gentle, and whatever it was about the voice that seemed familiar didn't quite sync with whatever it was about the voice that seemed new and undiscovered.

So the woman's words produced a kind of doppelganger effect, like maybe they'd cloned themselves as they were spoken and the copy had almost overtaken the original. Jamie reacted to both, unsure of which was which. *Stacy got me; that's not Stacy.* She waited, confused and hurting enough, tired and cold enough to stay tight in her fetal curl and leave her eyes closed until the nag scolded her to look. The nag, however, remained silent.

"I've found her."

The voice was nearer and the doppelganger effect had faded. *Uh-uh, not Stacy.* A swirl of curiosity lured Jamie's eyes open; she saw a shadow move against the pitted gray curve of the turbine's concrete mast and quickly acquire dimension. Legs. Blurry blue legs bending at the knees.

And then Jamie saw her. She leaned in close, her narrowed dark eyes quizzical. Jamie blinked slowly, expecting her to disappear. But she didn't, and as her gaze explored Jamie's face, her expression transformed. She touched Jamie's forehead. "Oh baby," she said softly, the sorrow in her voice echoing the compassion in her eyes, "what *happened* to you?"

Low, low in Jamie's belly, a fierce, relentless grip loosened, releasing a high-frequency tremor that swept her body. She wanted to tell this woman everything. Every moment of every day, from the first time she saw Alby getting ass-fucked by Meg's husband all the way to the last time the pain of Stacy's strap mutated into the cruel arousal she so despised—and so needed. Somewhere close by lurked a sentence, a single sentence that would say it all.

"T-Tried to—to—"

Jamie groaned. The words for her everything had abandoned her.

But the woman nodded and her eyes, those eyes that had been so unfathomably velvet-opaque a mere second ago, suddenly blazed. "You're trying to get home, aren't you?" And then she took off her hoodie and wrapped its comfort around Jamie's head and shoulders.

Chapter Eight
More Than That

Jamie dreamed of sweat and the stench of fear and piss. And a power drill revving. "Uh dee yapizz dahmah terayno," jeered The Bastard as the drill revved faster, louder, syncopating with the cadence of his incomprehensible words as she shuddered awake suddenly and completely into pulsating, stiff wretchedness. She didn't dare open her eyes—the enduring instinct of the wary prisoner. Sprawled on her belly, she remembered being cold and was glad of the warmth around her now; a scent she recognized gave hint that she lay on the bed in "her" room at Great Hill.

And then she opened her eyes and remembered the rest. She thought she remembered just about everything, which made her want to cry, to run. *Gotta go, gotta go now.*

So she started to push off the bed—right into pain searing across her shoulders, then down her back to her glutes and hamstrings. She persevered anyway and made it as far as lifting herself a few inches onto her elbows and knees before her body rebelled, collapsing nauseous and moaning nose first.

"Do you need to get up?"

Jeezus! The wary prisoner had neglected the simple duty of surveying her environment to see who else might be in it—and there was little in the world she hated more than being surprised by someone right bloody next to her when she thought she was alone. Jamie flung her eyes toward the source of the voice but saw only the bedspread's familiar folds.

"Let me help you." A hand brushed her cheek, then alighted on her arm. "Careful now."

"Mary?"

"The one and only. I bet you really, really need to pee, don't you?"

Oh yeah.

With improbable strength, Mary helped her ease off the bed, supported her doddering shuffle to the bathroom, balanced her as she straddled over the toilet she could not bear to sit on, and then helped her back to the bed and covered her with a fleece blanket. By the end of this difficult, humiliating exercise, Jamie had achieved a state of everlasting cringe. Having to lie there naked was the least of it.

"Oh god, Mary, I'm sorry." Jamie burrowed her face into the mattress, trying to move her arms higher so she could hide behind her hands. She managed only to paw unproductively at the bedspread. "I'm so sorry. I'll get outta here as soon as I can."

"None of us want you to leave, Jamie," Mary said serenely.

Jamie couldn't look at her. "How can you want me to stay? I'm s-so fu—" She broke off when sounds of piano playing floated up from the family room—Who? Because at Great Hill only Mary played the piano. And of all Mary's usual pieces, the transcendent Bach prelude that somebody else now played had become Jamie's favorite. This time its simple chord progressions carried a poignance she'd never heard before. Neither she nor Mary spoke until the pianist finished both the prelude and the fugue that followed it.

"Who?" Jamie asked it aloud this time as another prelude began.

"Oh, that's Lily's sister—Adele," Mary said, smiling broadly. "How fortunate for us that she loves to play our piano. And that she likes to practice with the *Well-Tempered Clavier*. Maybe she'll play the whole thing."

Adele. "She's the one who…"

"Yes. And none too soon. You were borderline hypothermic. Among other things."

Her name is Adele. "Could you thank her for me?"

"She'll be around for a few days. Staying down the hall in Evvie's room. So you'll be able to thank her yourself."

Jamie flinched, shook her head. "Gotta leave, soon as I can."

"No, Jamie, don't say that."

"I-I'm too fucked up to stay here anymore."

"Since that's how you feel, it'd be irresponsible of us to abide you leaving." Mary ruffled Jamie's hair. "Besides, you're in no shape to go anywhere." Into Jamie's limited field of view came Mary's hand holding a water bottle with a flip-straw angled toward her. "How about some water? Doctor's orders."

It tasted wicked good. It gave her some strength. She polished off half the bottle and had just relinquished the straw when footsteps approached from somewhere behind Mary's hand. Fast, firm footsteps. *Dana or Rebecca?* Jamie wondered.

"Here, Gram, let me take that."

Jamie had never heard Dana Westbrook sound so brusque.

"Dana," warned Mary as Dana's hand persuaded the bottle from Mary's, "she's not in any condition—"

"I won't bite," Dana said, and then leaned in close to Jamie, her gaze unyielding. "When did you get back here? Onto the property, I mean."

"Uh—"

"As precise as you can remember, Jamie."

"Seven hundred hours, maybe a little later. Not sure. Wasn't moving very fast." Jamie noticed the shades in her room had been drawn shut, but daylight glowed dimly against them. "W-What time is it now?"

Dana ignored her question. "How'd you get to the turbines?"

"I—" Sensing some sort of emergency, Jamie sacrificed her back to hike up on her elbows for a better view of Dana. "Walked." Dana nodded expectantly, clearly wanting details. "Uh, from the east, from town. The train. I came in, uh, not up the driveway. Animal path, farther south—"

"Can you show me?"

"I-I think so."

"Good." Dana pushed off the bed and began to turn away.

"Not *now*, Dana," said Mary, her exasperation obvious.

Dana spun back toward her grandmother and planted her hands firmly on her hips as she opened her mouth to object—until Mary, head lowered, gave her a look. Dana's hands lifted in reluctant acquiescence, then slapped against her jeaned thighs. "Okay. *Okay.*"

"What happened?" Jamie asked, stomach suddenly roiling. "What'd I do?"

"You got all the way to the turbines without triggering one single alert, that's what. And you didn't show up on any of the surveillance monitors. We've got you leaving yesterday afternoon, but nothing shows you coming back. Zip until you arrive at the wind turbines. Something is very, very wrong."

"Dana," a new voice called from the doorway. It was ET. "Can I have a word?"

Half-turned toward ET, Dana paused to point a finger at Jamie. "As soon as you can. I want you to retrace it with ET and me. Every single step you took."

"Yes, ma'am," Jamie replied automatically, distracted by the realization that ET standing in the doorway to her room meant Lynn must also be somewhere nearby.

But it was Rebecca who showed up next; her voice joining the subdued conversation in the hall that now included Lily and a happily babbling Evvie as well as Dana and ET. Mary met Rebecca at the doorway and they whispered briefly before Mary joined the confab in the hall and Rebecca entered Jamie's room, her arrival eerily coinciding with the first resolute chords of another Bach prelude.

"Let's see how you're doing," she said, whisking the blanket off Jamie. A long moment passed before she spoke again. "Do you want something for the pain?"

"Uh-uh."

"We've nailed the dosage, Jamie. You won't hallucinate again. And no needles. It's a tab."

"No pharma. Please."

"Mmm," Rebecca replied with studious neutrality. "I'm going to put a lighter blanket over you, then apply ice sheets. One on each thigh, one across your buttocks, one on your back. Ready?"

Jamie nudged her head down, up, down, and held her breath. Plenty cold, the ice sheets were heavier than she expected; they burned before they began to soothe.

"By the way," said Rebecca, her voice as chilled as the ice sheets, "Lynn blew off a face-to-face today with the head of the House Armed Services Committee and came home late last night instead— because nobody had a clue where the hell you were. So right now she's wrangling with the Honorable Mr. Warrick by comlink. When she's done, she'll tear-ass up here, since she's still worried sick about you." Rebecca's weight lifted off the bed and her footsteps retreated toward the doorway. "I've left you half a tab on the bedside table. In case you change your mind about what to do with pain."

Jamie heard the door to her room close. She was alone. The hall had already fallen silent; she assumed those who'd gathered there had gone elsewhere, probably to the kitchen, but Adele continued to play Bach, subtler and smoother than Mary ever did.

Rebecca's words echoed and the now-muffled piano offered requiem-like sympathy before finishing with a final hopeful chord. Jamie's solitude seemed as heavy and cold as the ice sheets. She missed the denizens of Great Hill and the way they treated her like she belonged there even when she pissed them off. She slipped into sleep missing them all.

❖

The dream had started without her, but there she was anyway, running from the house through dark woods, Mary and Rebecca and Robin alongside her, pursued into the night by unseen enemies, and Mary fell, then Rebecca fell, and she couldn't see them or see Robin.

But she could hear The Bastard's harsh, fraying laugh. "Uh deeya pizz dahmah terayno,"

"It's okay to decline the Blue Max, Jamie," Lynn said softly even before Jamie quite understood that she'd woken, that her sensation of endless falling lingered from the dream's hoax, that nobody was falling, that she still lay belly down, naked under a blanket and close to helpless. *Mary's okay, Rebecca's okay...*

Lynn stood next to the bed. "You don't have to stay in the Marine Corps, either."

"What?" Jamie realized someone had removed the ice sheets. She pushed off the mattress. "What time is it?"

"Take it easy, kiddo. It's a few minutes before two."

"Friday."

"It's Thursday."

Still Thursday. Saint Eh Mo's had been like this; a Saint Eh Mo's minute consumed hours, a Saint Eh Mo's day took a lifetime. Trying not to wince, Jamie pushed herself higher. "I didn't mean to—I just—I can't—I gotta go."

"Where? Go where?"

"Dunno." Jamie sank back to the mattress, angled her face away from Lynn.

"Oh god, kiddo, what am I going to do with you?"

"Find a deep, dark hole and throw me in."

"I'd say you're in a deep, dark hole right now." The mattress yielded as Lynn settled on it.

"I should—" Jamie rubbed her face back and forth against the bedspread. "Just go."

"So that's what you were doing yesterday? Going?" Lynn seemed to wait for a reply, but Jamie didn't have one. "Why'd you come back?" Lynn asked.

"I—" *Somewhere safe...*It had been instinctive, her return, mindless and primal—and so goddamn stupid. Grabbing the bedspread in fisted hands, Jamie growled futility and failure and frustration through gritted teeth. *Shit. I'm losing it.* "I warned you. Told you I was fucked up."

"Jamie, sweetie..." Lynn gentled, "I don't want you to leave. None of us want you to leave."

"You don't know me. You'd want me outta here if—"

"Jamie—"

"You don't understand." Jamie squeezed her eyes shut; if she saw Lynn's face, she'd never get it said. "I-I needed...this." She gestured awkwardly to her back. "Walked right into it pretending to myself that

I didn't know what would happen. But I knew, and I let her—. 'Cuz I-I need pain and fear and threat just to…just to feel like I'm still alive…"

"It's all right," soothed Lynn.

"No. It's not." Jamie forced herself to look at Lynn. "I needed her to beat the crap outta me. I needed to come like that, like in Saint Eh Mo's. Understand? That's what happened with Shoo Juh in Saint Eh Mo's."

Lynn's eyes had filled with tears and stillness; her mouth opened to speak, then shut again. "And it's still happening," she finally whispered, and Jamie knew she'd swung into problem-solving mode—analysis, then choose the best solution.

"Can't seem to escape it. Not this time."

"But yesterday wasn't only about Saint Eh Mo's, was it?" Lynn asked. "Maybe it was also about Awa. And about having to go back to war, because there's always a war somewhere. Wasn't it about hating yourself for what you did and hating yourself even more when you're told you'll get a medal for having done it?"

"Yeah, okay, it *was* about all that. And I'm fucked up from it. I'm fucking you up because of it, too. And it's not going away now that I'm hanging here in the Magic Queendom where everything's always beautiful." Jamie pushed herself up again, into the pain slicing across her backside, then turned to peer head on at Lynn—just as Mary walked in with a tray of food and drink. Mary's presence didn't stop her, though; it egged her on. She even raised her voice. "It's getting worse. And hell, why shouldn't it get worse? I killed people—lots of people. I plotted how I'd execute them and then I did it—deliberately aimed at their heads and blew their heads right off. Over and over and over. And you know what? For a long time, I thought that was just fine." She pushed harder into the pain, inviting it. "So now why shouldn't it hurt like hell and warp the bejeezus outta me? Like a frigging righteous punishment. I deserve that way more than a Blue Max."

Lynn's face had paled. Her hand splayed across her diaphragm. "No," she wheezed.

But Mary calmly set down the tray on the small desk near the bed. "Then what?" she asked, unperturbed, her eyes benevolent. "You suffer the pain, the pain subsides—and how do you feel afterward?"

Avoiding Mary's eyes, Jamie crumpled slightly toward the mattress. "I feel like—this. Disgusting. Like—"

"Like you'll have to start the search for pain all over again," Mary suggested.

A rushing sound filled Jamie's ears, invisible fingers pressed into her temples, and for a nanosecond, she was back with Alby in the battered little cottage where she'd grown up. Maybe she nodded; certainly her head trembled from the pressure against her temples.

"So it's a craving, then," Mary said as if she were describing the weather. "A craving for a pain fix. Not so different than being addicted to pharma."

Jamie peered at Mary, then at Lynn. "Omigod," she whispered as images of her mother swept across her mind's eye: Alby all doped up and oblivious to anything but the high, Alby slobbering and pathetic and, yes, disgusting.

"You don't have to be addicted to this any more than you have to be addicted to pharma," said Mary. "You can change what's happening to you, the way you feel about yourself."

"How? Tell me how."

"You can start by talking—"

"*NO!*"

Mary refused to give up, however. "It might seem counterintuitive, but talking about what hurts can make it hurt less."

"Talking about it makes it real all over again. Once was more than enough."

"Have you ever been wrong about anything, Jamie?" Mary asked the way she might if she'd misplaced her reading glasses and wondered if anyone had noticed them lying around. "Have you ever seen a person or a situation one way only to change your mind later?"

Jamie didn't bother to hide her annoyance. She wanted the conversation to end, so she clammed up and scowled at the bedspread.

"I see," Mary persisted, and Jamie could hear the smile in her voice. "You're always right, then. You've achieved perfection and it's never possible that you're not right."

"No, of course not!" Jamie turned her head too fast, sending a swath of fire down her back. "You're screwing with me!"

"Only a little." Mary winked. "So are you saying that you *can* be wrong?"

"Yeah, sure, I can be wrong."

"And during the time that you're wrong, you wouldn't actually *know* you're wrong, would you?"

"No…" Jamie's anger softened into dawning comprehension. In her peripheral vision, she noticed Lynn, too, beginning to smile. "Guess I wouldn't."

"Not until you got more reliable information, perhaps from someone with a better perspective on the situation than you're able to have." Mary leaned against the desk now, her eyebrows lifting convivially. "Isn't that what your commanders sometimes asked you to do when you were a scout/sniper? To get a good look at what they couldn't see for themselves?"

"Yeah." Jamie snorted, shaking her head. "And now you're gonna ask me if they believed what their snipes reported, right?"

"Bingo."

"And the answer is yes, mostly."

"And that's because scout/snipers have the kind of training and experience commanders find reliable and trustworthy, yes?"

"Okay, so maybe somewhere out there somebody has whatever the hell it takes to see what I can't." Jamie exhaled heavily. "But I'm *not* talking to a shrink."

Mary didn't skip a beat. "It doesn't always take a shrink to see—"

"What? See what?" The instant it burst out of her mouth, Jamie regretted it. She wanted to bitch that Mary had set a neat little word trap, that this was all monumental bullshit and let's stop right now.

But Mary didn't stop—she sprang the trap Jamie saw coming but fell for anyway. "Maybe you went off and got yourself beat up for the same reason you think you should leave us," Mary said, her gaze unblinking. "Because doing those things is actually less scary and less painful for you than talking. Which begs the question: What is it that you don't want to say—and don't want to hear? Especially given what you've said already."

Stomach corkscrewing like a wet towel being wrung dry, Jamie struggled not to yell out the *fuck you fuck you fuck you* rampaging in her head.

"Something to think about," Mary said in her no-big-deal way that so effectively kept Jamie off-balance. "When you're ready." She picked up a glass from the tray and joined Lynn at the edge of the bed. "In the meantime, here you go," she said affably, tilting the straw toward Jamie. "Kizzy just made a fresh batch."

Lemonade. The sight of it, the smell of it subverted Jamie's anger; they would leave her be, thank god. But they wanted her comfortable, too, and she had doubts about that. Didn't drinking the lemonade signify a betrayal of her duty?

Chin tucked, one eyebrow arching, Mary leveled her gaze at Jamie and inched the glass closer. "Come on now."

Jamie recognized the Look. *You sly old woman. You know.* And right then, for the first time, Jamie knew, too—knew that she believed she had a duty to grieve for the lives she'd destroyed by continually replaying the Palawan's horrors, by enduring not merely pain but punishment.

"Think of it as R and R," Mary said softly. "You're off duty now."

Off duty. Jamie let her forehead rest on the mattress as the possibility washed over her. "Yeah. Off duty." She lifted her head and took a long sip of lemonade.

"Good girl," said Mary. "Now how about a nice smoked ham and cheddar sandwich and that veggie-potato salad you like?"

"'Kay. Thanks."

"Lynnie, reach over and hand me the tray, will you?" Lynn did, and Mary arranged plate, lemonade glass, fork, and napkin a foot from Jamie's nose. The sandwich, on thick slices of Kizzy's homemade honey wheat bread, had been cut into quarters easily managed by someone who'd be eating it flat on her belly.

Mary briefly examined her arrangement, gave it a tiny head dip of approval, and stood. "You can have a good life, Jamie," she said as she moved toward the bedroom door. "You can live in peace without shame or guilt. It starts with understanding the difference between grief that honors what you've lost and grief that can't bear to let go, even when holding on requires pain and fear. No amount of grief or pain or fear will alter what happened. You cannot affect it, no matter how much you suffer. The way out isn't back. It's forward, where you *can* affect what happens, and where you can live in ways that honor those for whom you grieve."

"I, uh," Jamie said after a moment, even though Mary had already left, "never thought about it like that."

Lynn chuckled. "Yeah. That's her specialty."

Gingerly, Jamie hiked herself up, shifted some weight onto her left hip and left elbow, then reached for a section of the sandwich. *You can live in ways that honor those for whom you grieve.* She would have to go with some grace this time—with well-worded explanations and thank-yous wrapped in a classic, extended Great Hill good-bye. And she'd have to do it soon, soon, before going would hurt too much, before giving up Lynn and the rest of them could create an agony of emptiness. *Maybe they can do six months, but I can't.*

She offered a piece of the sandwich to Lynn, who declined with a small smile and leaned back against the headboard, watching her. Normally, she would have chafed and squirmed under such scrutiny, but this time she let Lynn's presence embrace her. It would all be over soon enough. Too soon. She ate the first quarter of the sandwich as well as a couple of forkfuls of salad before Lynn leaned forward and said, "Please don't leave."

Jamie put down the sandwich. Suddenly, eating it didn't seem right, even though hunger goaded her stomach, and the question she'd hesitated so long to ask spewed out of her. "Why'd you bring me home with you?"

Lynn went rigid. For several seconds, she frowned at her hands, which lay folded in her lap, and her intertwined fingers tightened around each other. Unable to imagine what would tense out Lynn so profoundly, Jamie tensed, too.

"I—" Lynn began in a hoarse almost-whisper, then shook her head. She pulled in a breath before raising her eyes to Jamie's. "That first time in Saint Eh Mo's when I looked up and saw you standing there, saw the condition you were in, I decided right then I had to do something more than—than just what I was supposed to do. I thought I had the clout to ensure you'd be treated better."

"That's why you stayed."

"Yes."

"I-I knew that."

"But when it all went south…Oh god, I was scared shitless and I knew you were my best shot at getting out of there alive. And I played you." Lynn raised her hands to her face and rubbed her cheeks. "You were so hungry for someone to see you, to care about you. Not your skill or your rank or your cleverness. You. And I played that because I was afraid. I fed morsels to your hunger. All I had to do was be kind and listen to you for a couple of minutes."

"I thought—" Jamie tried to breathe, but her gut had seized. She shouldn't say it. God oh god, she shouldn't say anything. But the words wouldn't be stopped. "I thought it was more than that."

"Yes, it is. Maybe it wouldn't be—if you'd acted like I thought you would." Lynn exhaled, half sigh, half groan, and lifted her eyes to the ceiling. "If you'd acted like just about anyone else on the planet, then I'd have shrugged it off. Once we'd gotten back to our people, I'd have given you a big hug and profuse thanks and added you to my Christmas card list—and kept on going." Tears streaked Lynn's face; she didn't attempt to hold them back or wipe them away. Her voice quivered. "But you didn't act like anyone else. You died for me."

"No," Jamie protested. "I only did my duty—"

"Oh, I'm not fooled," said Lynn in a tone swirling with sorrow and resignation—and wonder. "Your duty didn't require you to ask for volunteers to stay up on that ridge. You and I both know the rescue team should've been enough."

"Yeah, but it wasn't."

"You didn't know that 'til later. All of us were being rescued. *All of us* should have boarded that helicopter, but you wanted a team on the ridge—"

"Out of an abundance of caution."

"*Only* because I was there. Look me in the eye," Lynn said, her gaze fixing on Jamie, "and tell me, honestly tell me I've got it wrong."

But Lynn had called it. Jamie hunched her shoulders, sending streaks of fire across her back.

"And after you climbed back onto the ridge to help the guys you sent up there," Lynn went on almost breathlessly, "I saw it, Jamie. We'd landed by then and I'd blustered my way into the Combat Operations Center, and there you were on the satcam screens, and—" Lynn's chest heaved tremulously as she inhaled. "I saw what happened. I saw the light go out of your eyes…"

No. "Mmmmm," Jamie lowed, her eyes closing. *Don't…*

"And I begged you not to die, oh god, I begged. And they got to you fast, miraculously fast, and all the time they worked on you I begged you, don't die, and I told you I'd be there for you, I would try to give you some small measure of what you gave me if you'd just please please not die."

Jamie pushed the tray aside and inched closer to Lynn. "You don't owe me anything."

"Oh, sweetie, yes, I do. Because I love you. And because I know you love me." Lynn curled toward Jamie and kissed the top of her head. "What you gave me was so much more than what your duty required."

"You stayed at Saint Eh Mo's when you should've left. That was way more than your duty, Lynn."

"Let me tell you the difference between that and what *you* did. I stayed at Saint Eh Mo's because I overestimated the power I had, miscalculated the position I was in, and didn't anticipate becoming a political pawn. If I'd understood my actual circumstances, I'd never have gone to Saint Eh Mo's in the first place. But you—" Lynn kissed the top of Jamie's head again. "You knew exactly the situation you were in. You did it to give me better odds, and you expected to die there. Am I wrong?"

Jamie frowned at the bedspread.

"Am I wrong?" Lynn repeated.

"No."

"So it seems to me the least you can let *me* give *you* is a sandwich. Okay?"

Weightless, a little lightheaded as she continued to study the bedspread, Jamie drew in a breath. "'Kay," she whispered.

"And say you won't leave."

"That's a whole lot more than a sandwich."

"Please, Jamie."

"I'll have to go someday."

"But not before your convalescent leave is over."

"I don't know if—" Jamie closed her eyes. "What if I get, like, too attached? I-I might want to *never* go, and that's—You guys'll decide you've had enough of me and my fuckups, and then...it'd be—"

"Shh, Jamie." Lynn stroked her hair.

"It'd be so awful."

"Risk it."

"What?" Jamie's eyes flared open and darted to Lynn's calm, serious face.

"There are many things you can never get from me, that I can never get from you. But we can honor the connection we forged, we can share trust and loyalty. We can choose to be there for each other."

Jamie stared at Lynn while in her head a thousand tiny voices chaotically jabbered their fear, their doubt, their longing.

Slowly, slowly, Lynn's face creased into the smile Jamie found so nourishing, and something sparked in Lynn's eyes that Jamie hadn't seen before, as though a veil had been swept aside. "Risk it, sweetie," Lynn said. "That's what love is about."

CHAPTER NINE
RIGHT HERE IN RIVER CITY

Y es. That was it. The way I came in."
    "You're sure?" repeated Dana.

"Pretty sure—ninety-eight percent," Jamie said. "And you got my track, right?"

"Oh yeah."

The two of them stood a few meters east of the wind turbines, and Jamie could no longer deny it: She felt like shit, even though she'd slept plenty as Thursday blurred into Friday. Restored enough by Saturday morning to be itchily restless, she'd needed to move, stretch, even strain her body. So when Dana suggested she retrace her steps across the property "before anyone else finds out what we're up to," Jamie quickly agreed.

Now, more than anything, she wanted to sit down. Which would hurt like hell, of course. So she tried to hang tough and listen to Dana's comlink conversation with ET, who had watched her progress across the east side of the property on the videoscreens in the security center. But her ability to pay attention was succumbing to fatigue and discomfort.

"...only one other sensor cluster," ET's voice crackled out of the pocketcom Dana held. "That's incredible."

"Set it up side-by-side with the logs from last Thursday," said Dana with edgy eagerness. "We'll be there shortly."

"What'd ET say?" Jamie asked.

Dana's eyes bored into her. "You traveled twelve hundred yards from the southeast edge of the property near Forster Road to this spot, and the only sensors that picked you up are right over there." Dana pointed to one of the turbine masts behind her. "You sussed out blind spots in at least six locations that have full-spectrum, three-sixty coverage, including where you crossed the east driveway. Fuck, Jamie. How the hell did you do that?"

"Jeez, that's way more luck than *I've* ever had before." Jamie removed her eyewraps. "Guess maybe the detector I added to these helped more than I realized."

"May I?" asked Dana, and Jamie handed over the eyewraps. "This is discount store crap," Dana grumbled after looking through them for a second. "Wouldn't detect a damn stoplight."

"Yeah, well, I don't have my Marine-issue gear anymore. Discount store crap," Jamie lamented, "was the best I could do."

"Luck and a shit detector. I don't believe it."

"Considering I was sore as hell and had no countermeasures, I shouldn't have done anywhere near that well. Pretty weird."

"Jeezus. Why'd you even bother? With all the stealth, I mean."

"I just—" Jamie lowered her head and addressed her feet. "Wanted to get back without attracting a bunch of attention."

"Jeezus," Dana muttered again, turning to begin a hurried trek down to the security center in the second garage. Jamie followed, slipping farther and farther behind as they walked—the price of averting a stumble. By the time she traversed the security center's compact operations room, where Fitzgerald nervously monitored a large array of consoles and videoscreens, and opened the door to ET's office, the conversation there between Dana, ET, and Pilar, the deputy security chief, had already shifted into a problem-solving shorthand. Unable to sit or even lean against a wall, she held on to a chair back and listened.

The sensors on which Jamie should have appeared had gone out of position in a way that created a surveillance-free path through the east side of the property; ET displayed it on one of the screens in her office while her face cemented into a grimace. She'd already remotely readjusted the sensor clusters, but she had plenty of questions about how they could have been moved. Maybe it had happened naturally— the wind or squirrels or birds or some combination—but ET clearly didn't believe it. Especially since seven sensor clusters had gone out of whack—and the integrated surveillance system software neither logged nor corrected the changes.

"So it *was* weird," mumbled Jamie. "What's going on?"

"If we're lucky," Dana said, "all we've got is accident converging with a doozy of a programming glitch."

"And if we're unlucky, we could be looking at infiltration and sabotage," added Pilar. "It's possible to do it remotely. A bot, maybe."

Dana nodded. "Been tried before."

"But never successfully." ET glared at her closed office door, her thought transparent: Great Hill's sophisticated security systems offered no security at all if one of her handpicked, exhaustively vetted staffers had been compromised. "Goddammit, we can't be sure it wasn't done right here in River City."

Jamie recognized the fierce composure emanating from all three women: Calm under fire. The kind of calm that comes only from experience under fire. They talked on, these veterans of some private war she knew nothing of, discussing forensics and fixes, vulnerabilities and prevention. They were on the lookout now, reviewing scenarios, revising strategy, trying to figure out who they could trust. Clinging to the chair, Jamie attempted to absorb their words and implications—but the room had begun to blur and her arms, then her legs refused to stop trembling. *Shit*, she thought as blackness encroached on her peripheral vision, *I'm going down.*

So Jamie ended her Saturday where she began it—in her room, belly flopped on her bed. She oscillated in and out of murky, paralyzing nightmares about Great Hill under attack from which the distant sounds of a piano sometimes rescued her.

Chapter Ten
You Gotta Wanna

G lad to see you're feeling better."

A woman's voice, resonant and warm, which shouldn't have been there, freaking close behind her on the trail like that. Instantly, instinctively, Jamie spun into the warrior stance so well taught her by the Marine Corps—feet shoulder-width apart, left foot leading, elbows tucked, fingers curling into her palms as her hands leapt out front of her lowered chin, ready to protect her head.

"Whoa!"

Jamie registered her eyes first. Dark, lively eyes gleaming beneath ebullient, equally dark eyebrows—Adele Sabellius's eyes, no doubt about it. The kindest eyes Jamie had ever seen, except for in a dream once. So kind, so *interested* that Jamie froze. And forgot to breathe.

"I promise I'm unarmed." Adele half-stepped back, her own palms raised toward Jamie in mock surrender while one side of her playful mouth twitched into an almost-smile that already danced in her eyes.

She stood a few inches shorter than Jamie, sleek and supple and leggy in gray jersey workout pants and MIT-logo hoodie. Several inches of sable hair, dense and pin-straight, swung buoyantly around elegant cheekbones and cascaded in layers to the base of her long neck, setting off a sublimely sculpted jaw and a richly Mediterranean complexion. Her face, which didn't resemble her sister's at all, had flushed from running, but she wasn't winded—and how the hell could she even be there, just three meters away?

"Uh…" Jamie straightened up, dropped her arms. "Sorry," she offered clumsily. "Didn't hear you." *And shit—shit!—it's not supposed to happen like this. Not the very first time we get to really speak to each other…*

"Ah, well—the wind. Rustling the leaves." Adele glanced at her feet, then did a self-mocking little two-step. "And maybe my shifty new shoes."

"Yeah." Now Jamie dropped her head. *I'm not supposed to act like this, like some hopped up psycho…*

Yet it was ridiculous that Adele had snuck up on her. Not merely unfunny. Unnerving. There was little wind to speak of; nothing rustled. It shouldn't have been possible. Not for an untrained civilian cantering along a woodland trail strewn with crunchy dead oak leaves and pine needles—not even for a graceful, light-footed civilian. But Jamie had blanked, slipped right out of time and space into…nothing. No haunts or flashbacks, no worries or yearnings. Not even intent. Nothing. She needed a moment to recall why she'd left the house. *It's Sunday. It's been three days. This shouldn't be happening to me.*

"So…" Adele ventured a couple of steps toward Jamie, whose eyes had become glued to Adele's shifty new shoes. "You're doing okay?"

Jamie startled at Adele's movement, at the suddenly insistent twist low in her belly that had already transformed into an impetuous clitoral pulse. "Y-Yeah." She wagged her head, trying to shake away Shoo Juh's shadows mustering on her right, then her left, and forced herself to meet Adele's gaze.

"Thankyouforhelpingme," she burbled before her eyes skittered off to reconnoiter a nearby oak. Because yes, now she was sure: Adele was stunning. *Breathe in…two…three…four…*Clearing her throat, she looked back at Adele, who had somehow managed to keep a straight face. Jamie knew she couldn't banish Shoo Juh's shadows, but at least she could attempt to defy them; she could try, try to look past them like you look through a veil, then corral the words she'd say to Adele and let them loose one…by…one. "The other day at the turbines."

Her gaze scurried back down to the refuge of Adele's shoes, but that only provoked her to imagine Adele gently smiling at her with those riveting, numinous eyes—and now there could be no denying how the force Adele exuded reverberated through her. Twice more, Jamie had to command herself to breathe. "And. Thank you. F-For playing the piano. I—my room's right at the top of the stairs. Best seat in the house." Jamie snatched a peek at Adele's face, where the smile she'd imagined waited for her. "Sorry. You know that, of course. I just—it helps, the way you play…"

"Thank you." Adele kicked a small stone off the trail into the woods—almost shyly, Jamie thought as she squinted through Shoo Juh's veil, pulsing now to the ineffable rhythm of Adele Sabellius. "So, uh, you're going this way?" Adele asked rhetorically, pointing in the direction Jamie had been walking. "Mind some company?"

Jamie's pulse accelerated again, and, incredibly, Shoo Juh's shadows seemed to diminish. "I'd welcome it."

And they began walking eastward side by side.

"Lily tells me you're a marine," said Adele after a moment.

"Yep. She told me you work for the International Red Cross."

"Yep." Adele had precisely imitated Jamie's locution—a tease that flickered impishly in her eyes. "Volunteered one summer while I was in college and got hooked. Been able to come by paying gigs for over two years now. Just back from my fourth field assignment."

"Like it?"

"Yeah, mostly. This last time I was a shelter/disaster management delegate, which involved more of the engineering work I'm trained for. A scramble, like always, since I went in with about a third of the field experience they prefer, but they were desperate. Anyway, I kind of get off on that, and I've learned a lot. Made some good friends, too."

"And yet?" Jamie crooked her head to view Adele's face. "I did hear an 'and yet,' didn't I?"

"Mmm, well…" Adele sounded surprised; for several steps, she examined Jamie with narrowed eyes. "You heard two 'and yets,' I suppose. What I do helps improve things for individual people, and on a pretty impressive scale. Dozens of people. Hundreds sometimes. I like that. It's very gratifying, even though it's mentally and physically grueling. *And yet*, we're dealing with the same shit again and again, and a lot of it's preventable. Our efforts aren't as proactive as they ought to be. I want to focus on how to achieve what I like to call sustainable resilience. Or maybe it should be resilient sustainability. Anyway, I'm tempted to try something more analytic, more focused on the long term."

"And yet," Jamie prompted her.

"*And yet*, I know I'll miss that first responder rush, and I worry that I'll just be trading one set of frustrations for another. One set of bureaucrats and politicians and pathological creeps for another. I dunno. I've even thought about going back to school. I probably shouldn't decide anything for a while. This last assignment was a bitch." Adele leaned down to pick up an acorn, which she examined as though it held the answer she sought. "So what about you?"

"Sorry?"

"Do you like being a marine?"

Jamie shoved her hands in her jeans pockets, her eyes at the ground in front of her, and kept walking, which caused Adele to lean into her field of view, eyebrows raised and questioning.

"I'm good at it, I guess," Jamie said at last. "Got promoted six times in about a year and a half, but, hey, they were hysterically, insanely desperate. You know that adage about how everyone in a hierarchy rises to their level of incompetence?"

"Oh, right. The Peter Principle."

"That's me. And it happened in record time. It shouldn't even be possible in the Marine Corps."

"But do you like it?"

"I've learned a lot. It got me out of state custody, probably saved me from ending up in prison."

"And you've made a difference. You saved lives—"

Jamie's head swiveled to face Adele full on. "Who told you that?" she snapped—and immediately regretted it

Adele's eyes went wide, but to Jamie's relief she didn't flinch. "Oh, let's see—Lily, Dana, Rebecca, Lynn, all the media outlets in the northern hemisphere."

"Don't believe everything you hear." It had to be said; Jamie found herself needing to be starkly honest with this woman, but she tried to say it softly. "Whatever difference I made was way more bad than good."

She walked on, expecting Adele to hang back, prelude to departure. But Adele stayed with her step for step. *Another chance. I've got another chance.* "Lily said you've just come back from, uh…"

"Croatia."

"An earthquake, Lily said."

"Mmm hmm. Followed two weeks later by the second hundred-year flood in five years. Place is a mess."

"But you're not going back?"

"No." Adele's voice hardened. "My contract's finished and I really need a break."

Jamie skimmed Adele's profile, Adele's gait; everything about her had tautened just slightly. "What happened?"

"I dunno. I—" Adele shrugged. "Dumb stuff."

Jamie stared; she recognized the undertow that seemed to be claiming Adele and it surprised her. "For what it's worth," she offered, "dumb stuff is my specialty."

Adele stared back, her eyes shadowed, and Jamie knew she was deciding. After a few seconds, she looked away, and some steps later began to talk to the trail beneath her feet. "There was this so-called residential youth treatment center near the Sava River. Young ones, ages of ten to fourteen or so, locked down. Wasn't flooded, but the quake did some damage, so we inspected all the buildings. And that main building, the kids, the way the staff was so edgy and cold and impatient, the way sounds bounced off the walls, even the chairs in the offices—god, *everything* reminded me of…" Hand suddenly splayed across her lower ribs, she stopped. "Damn."

"Try breathing in from your diaphragm, through your nose," Jamie said quietly. "Slow count to four…"

Adele nodded and finished a cycle of classic four-count belly breathing—in, hold, out, hold. "Thank you."

"Phantasms."

"Yes, I suppose they are."

"Mmm, my other specialty. Wanna talk about it?"

It took several meters and a deep, preparatory inhale before Adele spoke. "I walked into that main building and wham! Thirteen years just evaporated and I was back in the quarantine facility where they declared me an EIRP subject. It was like getting sucked through a wormhole. Repeatedly, because we were billeted across the street for the last two weeks I was there. Made it bloody hard to keep my head on straight."

"EIRP…you mean the Emergency Immunization Research Program? The pandemic?"

"Yes." Adele started walking faster. "A few days after my eleventh birthday, my parents died. They were among the first American victims. They got sick really fast—from symptom-free to respirators in a single day. It all happened while I was at school. My father got them to the hospital sometime in the morning. I was pulled out of class just after lunch and quarantined that same afternoon. I never saw them again."

"How long? I mean, you survived the Program?"

"No, I was saved from the Program. By Lily and her moms—Luce and Biz. They came and got me out of there after sixteen days."

"I didn't think anyone ever got released from the Program once they were put in it."

"I wasn't released."

"Jeezus, you escaped? Like a prison break?"

Adele snickered—a sardonic almost-laugh. "It was Los Angeles, at the beginning of the whole thing. The EIRP plan had been developed, but implementing it—well, they were screwing that up to a fare-thee-well, thank god. They put me with a bunch of other kids in a converted warehouse near the port, and before they took everything away and locked me up in quarantine, I managed to call Lily."

"So you didn't get sick—which is how you ended up an EIRP subject, right?"

"Yeah, I passed their 'test,'" said Adele dryly. "Six days in a big room with eight other kids. Seven of them got sick. Two of us stayed healthy, though, which made us ideal EIRP subjects." Adele kicked a stone leftward ten or twelve meters off the inside of her right shoe; a soccer forward, Jamie guessed, and more dangerous than she looked if you pissed her off. "After that, I got put into a room by myself, no contact with anyone. A toilet in the corner, food on a sealed tray slid through a sealed hatch in the wall, a videoscreen that showed nothing but old cartoons, and once in a while, a guy on the screen who asked questions but never answered any. He said I'd be going to a new school where my parents would meet up with me once they got better, just had to wait a few days."

"You didn't know then that they'd died?"

"No." Faint echoes of muffled shock inflected Adele's voice, and her eyes stared across thirteen years at the moment resurrected. "Not 'til Lily told me. Later. But I—" She breathed in, out, in, deeply, from her diaphragm. "When I was with the others, we overheard them talking about how the first kid who got sick had died. So I figured all the others who got sick died, too. Then later, in that room alone, I waited to get sick, and I started wondering what it would feel like to die. And there was this instant—like when you get pushed and you fall farther than you expect to…And I realized my mother was dead and that there was no such thing as hanging around somewhere after you die, because death doesn't let anyone cheat. I knew my father was dead, too, and they were both gone from the world. Just gone."

So matter-of-fact; Adele had downshifted into something like detachment, sad but accepting as her eyes pulled away from that long-ago moment. Jamie found it difficult to speak much above a whisper. "H-How'd you get out?"

"Luck. Perseverance. Cleverness." Adele sighed. "Luck mostly. Lily said she was coming to get me, and she did, with Luce and Biz. I assumed she'd hop on a plane, like always when she visited in the summer, and I thought she'd be there in a few hours to whisk me away. The mind of an eleven-year-old, y'know?"

"Had commercial air travel been halted already?"

"Don't know. Wouldn't have worked anyway, since getting me out of there made us all fugitives. Lily was only eighteen, and Luce and Biz weren't about to let her try it alone. So they came by car—all three of them all the way to Los Angeles."

"From the Cape? I remember Lily saying she grew up near me…"

"The Outer Cape. Truro."

"God, that's—"

"It was almost four thousand miles. They had to avoid huge chunks of the interstates because there were checkpoints going up even then. Took them ten days of driving. They even switched cars somewhere in Ohio, then again in Colorado."

Jamie nodded appreciatively. "Just to be safe."

"Yeah, exactly." Adele's voice lightened some. "And the day after I'd given up hope, there was Biz in a wig, pretending to be this bitchy CDC researcher come to take me to some special new facility. They'd done their homework, so they had Biz's act down cold—she dropped the right names, blustered about the right protocols, brought along the right biohazard suits, arrived all full of self-importance and hurry-hurry waving this fake ID at lunchtime when the people in charge weren't around."

"Jeezus, plenty of cleverness and perseverance there. Not to mention raw nerve."

Adele shrugged. "Luck mattered more. Luck that Luce knew somebody to ask about where in LA they were stashing kids who might qualify as EIRP subjects—and about those names and protocols to mention and where to find biohazard suits and what a valid ID might look like. Luck that the security guy that morning was new and so clueless he didn't realize Biz's ID authenticated oddly because it was vectoring Lily's code-injection hack, which spoofed the authorization for Biz to enter the facility and take me out. Luck that the Program was still so backasswards that I hadn't been moved yet. Luck that we were able to dodge all those checkpoints on the way home and that Biz was so good at sweet-talking us through the ones we couldn't avoid. Luck that I wasn't a carrier and none of us ever got sick."

Quiet settled on them then; even the woods hushed, as though respecting a request for a moment of silence. What was it about the quiet that granted Jamie such clarity? She sensed its final flourish just before it evaporated, just before she should reach for Adele…*three*… *two*…*one*…Calm, unhesitating, she brushed her fingers along Adele's forearm. "I'm sorry you lost your mom and dad."

"Yeah." Adele's eyes glistened too brightly, but she managed a small smile. "Me too."

"I'm also wicked glad you were so lucky."

Slowly, Adele lifted and lowered her head in assent. "I'm the luckiest person I've ever known. More than half of the people in the Program died—and that's just the people they'll admit to. It'd be much worse if they included the undocumented—the illegal immigrants and homeless and missing."

"Thank you for telling me about what happened to you."

Adele examined Jamie's face as though she was looking for something. "I don't talk about it much. Can't remember the last time…"

"You haven't told Lily about the place in Croatia?"

"Uh-uh. She's got enough going on with the baby and that crazy job. But I'm glad you, uh, noticed. Thanks for taking it on."

"I know how hard it is to talk about—" Now came Jamie's turn to pull in a deep breath. "About stuff like that."

"And is 'stuff like that' the reason you still haven't told me whether or not you like being a marine?"

Jamie had to smile. "An example of that Sabellius perseverance, I presume?"

"You're stalling."

"It doesn't matter if I like it or not."

"Nope. Still stalling." Adele cast her gaze into the woods; once more, she was deciding. "What about friends?" she asked. "In the Marines, I mean."

It took Jamie a long minute to respond. "I'm not sure I know what friends are, really. There were these stretches—months, a year or more—where I spent every minute with the same people, and we cared about each other, took lunatic risks for each other, would've died for each other without even thinking about it. I don't miss what it was like day-to-day. Most of the time I was either bored as hell or mad as hell or terrified as hell. But I miss caring about those people in such an immediate, present-tense way. You get hooked on that kind of connection, on the rush of risking so much and coming out the other end together. Those of us who *did* come out the other end. And then everyone scatters. They leave the Corps or they're off to new duty stations. And it's done. They're gone and god knows if you'll ever see any of them again."

"Yeah," said Adele sympathetically. "You end up having to start all over with the next assignment—figuring out who you can trust, how you'll fit in a new team, finding buddies. I know *that* routine."

"I'm having a hard time working it up for the next one."

"Can you leave?"

"They own me for another two years, so short-term, no. Long-term, yes. But it seems like they want me to stay. Means I might have to accept a medal, though, and I made a promise not to do that. If I break my promise and accept it and let them parade me around and make me into a live recruitment poster, then they'll educate me, give me a chance to get all the credentials an officer's supposed to have. After that, I can probably do the kinds of jobs where I don't kill people, I just order others to kill people. But if I reject a career commitment—" Jamie lowered her head and stopped talking.

"Then what happens?"

"I don't know, actually. I worry that I'll have to pull a trigger again, and I—" Jamie hunched her shoulders, even though the motion hurt some, and shook her head. "God, it's ironic. I thought the Marine Corps would keep me from doing the kind of shit that'd land me in prison, and when I qualified to train as a scout/sniper, I figured it meant I'd finally be able to protect myself, have some control. But I ended up doing exactly the kind of shit that puts civilians in prison, and I have no control over anything."

"Doesn't sound like you want to stay in."

"I'm not any good for anything else."

"Really?" Quiet incredulity laced Adele's tone. "I find that hard to believe."

"I'm ignorant and uneducated—"

Adele snorted. "I know about ignorant. You're not ignorant."

"You've got—let's see if I remember what Lily said—a bachelor's degree, double major in geology and civil engineering, and a master's degree in environmental resource management, right? That's a whole other planet." Jamie moved her eyes away from Adele. "My mother was a prostitute and a hopeless addict. Burned herself up in a car on her way to trading sex for some pharma. I'm a high school dropout with a GED, and the only talent I have is nailing targets at two thousand meters with bullets bigger than your index finger."

"I hear you have a talent for keeping your head in a crisis, for smart decisions, for leadership, for living up to the trust people have in you."

Jamie halted. "My name is Jamie. Who the hell are *you* talking about?"

"I'm talking about the woman who led thirty-odd escaping POWs to safety across a jungle-covered mountain range—despite being chased by half of a Chinese-backed guerilla army," Adele declared resolutely. "The woman my incredibly impressive sister describes like you descended from Mount Olympus—"

Jamie spun on her heel, turning her back on Adele's words. "Oh for chrissake…"

But Adele raised her hand to Jamie's face, and even before her fingers made contact, their energy set Jamie ablaze. "I'm talking about the woman I found last Thursday morning who was in such awful pain," said Adele as her hand delicately, irresistibly drew Jamie back around to face her. "And in such desperate need—" Adele's fingertips softly traced Jamie's jawline. "Of being touched."

Jamie didn't move. Not one muscle. Yet every synapse exhilarated. She had gone electric, and the heat of it throbbed in her temples, stilled her breathing; it quivered across her chest, up and down her legs, lubricating the crackling hunger she figured she'd never experience again. The infinity in Adele's dark eyes took her, and time twirled and unfurled, speeding up and slowing down all at once until Adele's charged fingertips slid away—was it reluctantly? Was it? And Jamie ached from the silent, writhing *plee-eease* so forlorn of ever finding words for itself. *Say something, say something right now or she'll—*

"W-What'll you play this afternoon?"

"Ah, sorry. I'm leaving this afternoon."

"Oh." A stinging heat flared into Jamie's belly, into her chest, into her throat and threatened to fill her eyes with tears. No, you can't leave yet, she wanted to say, I haven't seen you play yet, I need to see you play. Already, she had imagined it—Adele's fingers commanding the keys with their magical dance, Adele's face in fervent concentration. But her chance had come and gone—she'd spent it in a fit of brutish pique at the wrong end of Stacy's strap. Three days and four nights of Adele Sabellius forever lost to her. And now—

Now she knew she should say something casual, breezy, something great-to-meet-you-maybe-I'll-see-you-around. But she had no strength for it. Jamie blinked at the trail in front of her. "Where do you go from here?" she finally managed to ask.

"Home to Luce and Biz's. It'll be HQ 'til I decide what comes next."

"Oh."

"Seems like we have that in common."

"What?"

"Needing to figure out what comes next. It can be difficult when you're really good at something you don't like."

"You said you mostly like what you do."

"Yep." One of Adele's eyebrows arched as she smiled and resumed walking along the trail, which now began a gradual loop back toward the house, toward her departure.

Jamie fell in beside her. "You mean me."

"When you feel hopelessly trapped, it's hard to understand you have choice." Adele's eyes transformed as she spoke from lush, light-absorbing deep brown to glinting obsidian, and Jamie wondered what else had happened to her thirteen years ago. "Getting swept along, believing you're out of options, doing nothing—those are all decisions you make, even when you're not aware of making them."

"Since, by definition, every decision has at least one alternative, grim though it may be."

"Sounds like the voice of experience."

"Mmm. But I—I made decisions that I didn't expect to..."

"To survive," Adele said quietly. "You did survive, though."

"Yeah..."

"You feel like a ghost in your own life, huh?"

Jamie gaped. "Yes."

"It gets better."

"Promise?"

"No," said Adele. "You gotta wanna."

They talked all the way back to the house.

Jamie asked about what it was like to live in hiding for two years as an EIRP fugitive, and Adele described nightmares, getting used to a new name, the solitude of hiding and surreptitious homeschooling, how devoutly she carried out the daily rituals of remembrance so she might endure the deep ache in her chest that was all she had left of her mother and father.

Adele asked about the teardrop scars on Jamie's hands, frowning at them as Jamie faced the shards of memory without blenching and told Adele about The Bastard. It was far easier than she expected; no pouncing phantasms, no color-saturated replays—only a few washed-out Palawan postcards as she simply let go the words and watched Adele absorb them and accept them without question or judgment or stipulation. Someday, if they ever saw each other again, ever talked again, maybe she'd tell Adele about Shoo Juh. About Awa.

When the time came, Adele kissed her good-bye, a soft, quick kiss on her cheek that trailed a faint, warm, honey scent. Jamie wanted to believe Adele's kiss lingered for an effervescent half-life that might mean something, but she pushed the notion away. Adele was the lucky one, not her.

CHAPTER ELEVEN
NOT A BAD IDEA

*F*uck*!*"
The curse trumpeted up the back stairway about an hour after Adele had left for the Cape with Lily, Dana, and Evvie—followed a nanosecond later by a resounding metal-and-glass crash. In her room, trying in vain not to think about Adele, Jamie tensed. She recognized Lynn's voice but had never heard it sound anything like that.

Another "*Fuck,*" louder and more guttural than the first, brought Jamie charging out of her room, down the stairs, and into the kitchen.

Lynn stood there alone, red-faced, hands fisted and on their way to pummeling a countertop. A couple of meters away, pieces of a pocketcom lay scattered on the floor amidst fragments of glass. Growling unintelligibly, Lynn struck the counter twice, then bent over until her forehead met her hands.

"What happened?" Jamie implored.

"That son of a bitch," Lynn muttered between clamped teeth.

"Who?"

"Richard Lambert." Lynn pushed herself off the counter. "As fucking usual."

Jamie had heard the name before but couldn't place it. "Who's Richard Lambert?"

"He's president, chairman, and majority owner of Fletcher, Dunn, and Lambert. Almost put Callithump out of business in the early days. He plays dirty even when he doesn't have to. For the sheer fun of it. And he's hated my guts for about twenty years now, so he plays especially dirty with me."

"Fletcher, Dunn—you mean FDL?"

"Yes."

"They were in the Palawan. They're mercs."

"Oh, please. We can't call them mercenaries. That's much too provocative," said Lynn, her tone ripe with uncharacteristic sarcasm.

"This is about your bill, huh? The, uh—"

"The about-to-be-relegated-to-the-dung-heap Federal Military and Security Contract Control Act."

"What happened? It passed the Senate *and* the House. And you said the president agreed to sign it."

"What the House passed isn't quite the same as what the Senate passed, so the bills went to a conference committee for reconciliation. And Lambert has blackmailed, bought, and/or squeezed enough committee members—three, to be precise—to keep that from happening. Nothing will be reported out of conference before the end of the session next Friday. Which means it's dead."

"Blackmailed, bought, and…"

"Squeezed."

"How do you know?"

"He told me."

Jamie peered at the pocketcom remains on the floor. "You talked to him? Just now?"

"Oh yeah."

"Did you record it?" Jamie scanned the floor for the device's small datacard. "Maybe we could—"

Lynn shook her head. "Anyway, it was all gloating metaphors and euphemisms. And a pinch of implied threat for good measure. But the upshot—"

"He threatened you?" Jamie gripped the edge of the counter. "How did he threaten you?"

"Oh, the usual. Vague, designed to keep you glancing over your shoulder." Lynn's voice deepened mockingly. "Might be wise to take a break from those foreign junkets full of your good works, *Senator*. After all, so many reelection pitfalls lay in wait for naïve first-term politicians who neglect the home front, *Senator*.' Christ, I hate the way he says 'senator.'"

A prickly chill dappled Jamie's spine; she didn't like the sound of Richard Lambert either. "Can you reintroduce your bill when the next Congressional session starts?"

"Yes." Lynn slumped over the counter again. "And I will. But god knows what the Congress will look like in thirty-seven days after the mid-term elections. The gun belt is spending plenty to get enough no votes into office. We've just lost our best shot."

"I'm sorry."

"You and me both, kiddo. It could drive a woman to drink."

"But it won't." Springer Knox had materialized in the doorway. "It'll inspire a vigorous, carefully targeted campaign for a new version of the bill. Starting tomorrow."

"How *do* you do that?" asked Lynn, turning around to face her.

Springer tossed her head, flicking pale hair out her eyes. "I follow through on shameless arm-twisting if I don't hear about what matters at least as soon as you do."

"Ah," said Lynn, "so Ken Warrick's chief of staff is—"

"In my damn pocket. The guy really needs someone to talk to. And after his boss's latest stunt, he's job hunting."

Lynn's eyebrows lifted in surprise. "Is he?"

Springer relayed the darkly comic tale of a bourbon-soused Warrick succumbing to Lambert's leggy blond operative—who recorded every slurred word of the House Armed Services Committee chairman's loquacious brag about using top-secret surveillance programs to spy on enemies and friends alike.

"So, uh, this Warrick dude is one of the three people on your bill's conference committee that Lambert got to?" asked Jamie.

"Mmm. Clearly via blackmail in Ken's case," Lynn replied as Springer strode to the counter and plunked down a piece of paper in front of her.

"Way I see it," Springer said, "we exchange your vote against the Cuban economic and technical cooperation trade agreement for support from the people on this list."

Lynn glanced at the paper and shook her head. "Except I'm voting *for* the Cuban trade agreement. No, we're better off working Everett Harris's posse. Though to get *them*, as well as the non-Floridians on your list here, we'll have to cut deals with several gun belt CEOs."

Springer's face scrunched. "So which of our big three do we sacrifice? Contract size thresholds, transparency and conflict-of-interest requirements, or the accountability clauses?"

Shoulders hiking into a shrug, Lynn's gaze shifted to the expansive window above one of the kitchen sinks. "If we give in on contract size," she said, "we'll get pretty much everything else we want, since everyone'll be able to just rewrite contracts to come in below the threshold. We'll save face, too. But the legislation won't be worth the space it takes on a tablet screen."

"Too bad," Jamie said; her knuckles had whitened as her hold on the counter edge tightened. "Because the current rules have way too many workarounds. So the mercs keep growing their experienced, highly-trained private armies and their extremely well-connected private intel networks. And then rent 'em to the highest bidder. Corporations exploiting the so-called developing world. Backwoods warlords. Pick a side, any side."

With Lynn and Springer staring at her, she released the counter and bent down to pick up pieces of glass and pocketcom. "I'm not *quite* as dumb as I look, y'know."

"Obviously." Springer's voice, dry as a bone in the desert.

"Anyway, when it comes to intel—" Jamie glanced up from the floor. "Sorry."

"Oh no." Springer waved a hand extravagantly. "Please continue."

Jamie figured Springer was mocking her, so she kept gathering up pocketcom shards. But what the hell…"To really cut off some of the workarounds your legislation's after means tracking intelligence gathering activity all the way down the ranks. But there are only so many rules and guidelines you can impose on dynamic situations like combat. We've got plenty now. Down at the grunt level, sometimes the intel recordkeeping is shitty because it's a pain in the ass, added steps that distract from mission execution. Whatever you want from the grunts, you better derive it from what they're already doing, like mission commo streams or company-level intelligence cells. It's a no-brainer, but don't count on it getting implemented unless you get pretty granular with the regs you mandate. Anyway, assuming your ultimate goal is to improve intel quality and security, I'm not sure it'd help all that much."

"Why not?" asked Springer, her impatience apparent.

Jamie rose and set the pocketcom debris on the counter in front of Lynn, who watched her with an unreadable expression. "Hey, I'm not saying it's bad to require more detail about sources and develop better ways to credential it, assess its value. With enough data, you might even be able to suss out patterns that point to who's zoomin' who. But…" She shrugged.

"Go on," said Lynn.

"The real problem is, well, conflicts of interest. That infects everything, from the junior people brown-nosing for a promotion to the senior people sidling up to corporations for the best job they can land after they retire. Then there are the contractors always sniffing for loopholes and shortcuts, the honchos happy to help them. It's how the beast really works. The inevitable cheat that's become part of the structure."

"Mmm," Lynn murmured. "Like insider trading on Wall Street. It'll always go on. Best you can do is close some loopholes, tighten your rules occasionally. So you catch the worst of them and the rest tamp it down for a while."

"Yeah." Jamie started to sift through the pocketcom debris. "Better than nothing—aha, gotcha." Jamie plucked a thin, centimeter-square piece from the pile, examined it, then retrieved a second piece. "Don't seem damaged." She offered them to Lynn one at a time. "Comcard. Datacard. Pretty resilient, these things. Maybe Lily or Dana can test them for you when they get back from the Cape."

"Thank you," Lynn said, pulling her eyes from Jamie's to squint at the small square now in the palm of her hand. "That's not a bad idea."

"Yeah," echoed Springer, extracting her own pocketcom from her jeans. "I'll go over our early drafts and start a rough reframing tonight, get the DC crew ready to rumble by tomorrow morning. We'll need it *before* the conference, yes?" Springer began to bounce on the balls of her feet. "So everyone's chattering away about it by then. We should start seeding by—"

"Slow down." Lynn rested a hand on Springer's shoulder. "First order of business is a few sit-downs with, let's see, some trustworthy data analysis and information governance people—"

Springer stopped bouncing and frowned. "IT people?"

"Jamie's right," said Lynn. "The heart of this lies in recordkeeping. We'll develop new specs—damn stringent ones—about what every ops record must include, how it must be preserved. We'll require compliance in every military and security activity, operation, and contract, no matter how small, no matter what euphemistic name somebody dreams up for it. We'll mandate new apps to accomplish this—quick, easy, automatic upchain red-flagging when something's missing or inconsistent. And we'll include changes to the National Security Court Act so our opposition has something to chew on. Bottom line, though, we make sure everyone involved in any operation remains inexorably linked to it—and to the real possibility that they may someday be called upon to justify their actions." Lynn looked at Jamie. "That should slam the door on a few workarounds."

Springer now assumed what to Jamie looked suspiciously like the position of attention. "I'm on it."

"And no leaks, Springer," said Lynn. "None. Zero. Once we nail our approach, we'll back out the dates so we can pop this right before the conference. A Sunday brunch here, I think, with food to die for, and early enough so they can all wend their way up north in time for those welcoming late afternoon cocktails before the first dinner speech."

"Yes, ma'am," Springer answered. "The Hail Mary pass it is, then."

"Fourth down, long yardage, and running out of time, so yes, a Hail Mary pass," growled Lynn. "Because we put together a modest little bill that got neutered in committee, but okay, it was a first step, a key precedent to build on. And then…" Again Lynn looked at Jamie, who wondered if those were tears in her eyes or just a trick of the light.

"The Palawan," Jamie whispered.

"Yes," said Lynn. "The Palawan. Where, supposedly, I'd been taken hostage and was about to be beheaded. Quite convenient for any number of people, who saw their chance to kill the bill entirely. But we survived, didn't we, kiddo?"

Jamie nodded; the chill along her spine had returned. *Why's Lynn bringing up the Palawan? It's travelogue. Unless...Oh. She's talking herself into it. Into going to war.*

"And I came back with the edge we needed to pass the bill in both chambers without neutering because I made a deal: I'd let what happened in Palawan, at Saint Eh Mo's stay below the radar in exchange for passage of the original bill. The best the reprobates could do was stall by getting Warrick to diddle a few minor differences into the House version."

Lynn stiff-armed the counter and lowered her shaking head. "And that's where I messed up. That was the sign I didn't pay enough attention to."

"You were exhausted," said Springer. "You needed a break."

"I let them get the edge *they* needed—the chance to send in Lambert and his dirty tricks goons at the last minute." Lynn sounded tired. But she pushed off the counter and met Jamie's gaze, then Springer's. "So screw modest. This time we go for broke with the bill I should've introduced in the first place. And yes—" Lynn raised her hands, anticipating Springer's reply. "I expect all hell will break loose. Good. I *want* all hell to break loose. If we play it well enough, we can turn the security aspects of the bill into exactly the distraction we need to get the important parts passed."

"A diversion," Jamie said.

Lynn nodded.

Springer looked hard at Lynn. "So you're really going to try taking it the whole way."

"I damn well am." One hand on her hip, a finger of the other hand massaging her lower lip, Lynn began to pace. "And we'll make sure this new bill dominates conversation at the conference, the damn Congressional cloakrooms, the chattering class's cocktail parties—and shows up on every videoscreen in the country until it damn well passes or I'm damn well voted out of office. I've got two years left, and in those two years we will take the initiative on this and keep the initiative so we can manage perceptions and maintain control of the terms of the debate. We've got the technology to track every hiccup of every citizen. It's time we used it to track every hiccup of every federal agency and contractor."

Springer resumed tapping on her pocketcom, but abruptly halted mid-tap and studied Jamie. "You don't like private military contractors much, do you?" she asked.

"Not my favorite species," Jamie said, bending down again to pick up the last of the pocketcom debris. "Too much merc intel is shit, for one thing, and—"

"Absolutely not!" barked Lynn from the far side of the counter.

"She's bloody perfect," Springer protested. "Straight from the trenches. Smart. Articulate. She could—"

"Off limits, Springer," Lynn said, her voice razor-edged.

Jamie stood. "Um, excuse me," she ventured as she deposited bits of shattered pocketcom in an under-counter trash can. "Could you tell me what you're talking about?"

"If you're willing—" Springer began.

Lynn slapped her hand on the counter. "Goddammit, Springer," she yelled. "I said *off limits!*"

For a few seconds, silence hung between all three of them while Lynn glared at Springer, who stood petrified in place.

"We are not going there," Lynn finally said, her eyes still on Springer, her voice very quiet. "Do you understand?"

Eyes lowered, Springer moved her head stiffly, minimally up, then down, and she didn't appear to be breathing.

"Thank you," said Lynn.

Jamie broke into what she feared would become another silence. "I should leave…"

"No, kiddo," Lynn said quickly. "We're fine." She reached for Springer's arm to lightly stroke it, and Springer exhaled—exhaled relief, Jamie thought—then smiled tenuously.

"So, you want the new version of the bill ready before this conference," Jamie asked, "And you're gonna show it to, um, who exactly?"

Lynn glanced at Springer—deferring, Jamie realized, so Springer could regain her balance, which she did with an explanation that soon blossomed into classic Springer-sardonic: The annual Bretton Woods International Security Conference seven weeks hence, some twelve days after the midterm elections, would attract the nation's defense establishment elite. Precisely the government, industry, and think tank pooh bahs whose support the bill needed—and who were likeliest to oppose it.

"We'll time it," said Springer, "so that a select pooh bah subset finds out about the new bill the day the conference starts."

"That's the Sunday brunch that'll happen here?" asked Jamie.

"Yes, exactly. By inviting them here, we're indicating that we think they're important." Springer winked. "Proper care and feeding of supersize egos like these guys have can be useful. If we do it right, the whole direction and tone of the talk about the new bill will be set here on that Sunday. We'll up-play some parts, downplay others. We want our opponents on the defensive from the start. So they won't be making arguments, they'll be cornered into having to come up with counter-arguments. Weak, unconvincing counter-arguments. A small but powerful distinction—especially if we seed the media properly."

"You mean get positive media coverage—" Jamie stopped herself when she saw Springer's expression. "No, you mean *set up* positive media coverage from the start. In tandem with your Sunday brunch. And the conference."

"Heh heh." But Springer wasn't laughing. She was deadly serious. "It takes a lot of work. The right interviews with the right people at the right moment. Impeccable timing. Finding all the ways to motivate all kinds of people to keep their mouths shut until we're ready."

"And skill," said Jamie, looking at Lynn and imagining her engaging in conversations that would end up on millions of screens, played and replayed for every nuance, every misstep. "In the strategies of persuasion…"

"Oh yeah," Springer agreed, "and we'll work every one of those strategies—especially liking and reciprocity. If we manage all that *and* the gods are smiling, the pooh bahs will be permanently stuck in catch-up mode by the time they come back from those post-conference bacchanals like the one Lambert always throws down in Chatham. And then—"

"Bacchanals? You mean like orgies?"

"Yep. Every year for who knows how long. The wives pass on Bretton Woods."

"You're talking about Chatham on Cape Cod?" Jamie nearly giggled. "Orgies in Chatham, where the ladies adorn themselves in teensy flower prints and the men wear elastic-waist seersucker pants and it's been like that for a hundred years."

"Ever seen some of those manses down there? Lambert's got a doozy sitting on a bluff overlooking a private golf course on one side and a deep-water cove on the other. Heliport a few hundred yards away."

"Must've missed that neighborhood."

"A little chilly in November, but there's plenty of off-season privacy and each bedroom comes with its own Montenegrin 'hostess.' Half a dozen other industry guys do the same thing. The après-Bretton Woods lost weekends are infamous. They fuck and get drunk and divide up the planet among themselves. All face-to-face and secret handshakes. Then they go home to Thanksgiving dinner with their families."

"Count me in," Jamie said. "That's what you were talking about before, right? That maybe I could help at the brunch? As, uh…well, as an example of why the current rules and procedures are inadequate, right?" Jamie found herself standing a little taller; it felt good to have a mission.

Springer's head moved side to side almost imperceptibly, but it was Lynn who spoke. "No, Jamie," she said gently. "No. They'll work hard to drag you off point. Poke at you with all kinds of questions about how many kills you have, about Saint Eh Mo's. If that doesn't rattle you sufficiently, they'll find ways to trick you into violating the DoD directives or even Article Eighty-eight."

"Lynn, if I was—" Jamie gulped. Once more, Adele miraged in her mind's eye. *No euphemisms, dammit.* "If I was normal, if I was un-fucked up and you didn't have to worry about scraping me off the ceiling, could it help if I was there? Or if not the brunch, 'cuz okay, after the first fifteen seconds I'd just be like, y'know, like an idiot savant taking up space, I could talk to a media person. Hey! I could talk to Vivian Velty. She already said she wants to—"

"Jamie, no—" Lynn began.

"Tell me honestly, please," Jamie said. "Could it help?"

Lynn exhaled loudly. "That's irrelevant—"

"I can just describe it," Jamie said, and the words tumbled out of her faster and faster. "I'll just tell her what it was like. No politics, just what it was like—how you never stop sweating and it's always hard to breathe, the way leeches try to go up your nose when you're belly crawling through swamps hoping you don't meet a crocodile face-to face. When the conversation turns to the use of intelligence provided by private military contractors, I'll say how in my experience it often was unreliable and sometimes it got people killed for no good reason. I can describe details without using names or mentioning a place. And if the conversation rolls around to what went down at Saint Eh Mo's, I-I'll—"

Jamie had to remind herself that the red-stained darkness bleeding into her peripheral vision was a phantasm, only a Palawan phantasm, and she could will it away. *Breathe in…two…three…four…* "I'll describe how Shoo Juh doubted The Bastard because he was a merc. I-I'll quote what Shoo Juh said to him. I can quote it verbatim, because I was a witness and it's branded onto my brain. 'Your organization serves many masters. Perhaps some of its loyalties are in conflict with others.' And—" Jamie closed her eyes. *Uh dee yapizz dahmah terayno,* echoed The Bastard's scraping-metal snarl.

"Jamie." Lynn's voice, then Lynn's hand, warm on hers, and Jamie opened her eyes to Lynn's face etched with worry, maybe even remorse. "The perspective you've added to this conversation is genuinely valuable, and I thank you for it. But that's it, kiddo. That's the boundary. Your offer is brave and generous and I deeply appreciate it, but it's not why you're here. I don't want you sucked into my crap. I believe it would harm you much more than it would help me." Lynn tossed Springer a daggered glance. "This is supposed to be a refuge. A safe place for you where you can begin to heal."

"It is. Oh god, Lynn, it's the most wonderful place I've ever been in my whole life." Jamie blinked through tears. "That's why I can do it." The phantasm had retreated; Jamie wondered if her tears had washed it away. "I'm strong enough and I want to help you get that bill passed. The mercs are dangerous. Right now there's not nearly enough to stop them from playing all sides at once."

A weary, almost sad smile briefly swept Lynn's face. "When did you read the bill?"

"Couple weeks ago," Jamie said.

"Mmm. Since it's all I've been able to talk about for way too long." Somehow, Lynn was nodding and shaking her head all at once. "I'm sorry for that. I do tend to get preoccupied."

"Well, I figured it must be important, so—" Jamie halted when she saw Mary coming into the kitchen the same way Springer had, Rebecca right behind her carrying several bright orange pumpkins.

"Uh-oh," said Mary, her eyes skipping from Lynn's face to the pocketcom remains.

Rebecca placed pumpkins on the counter. "Bad news," she said when she got a look at Lynn's face. She took up Lynn's hand in hers and eased Lynn toward her. As they slipped dancelike into a full, rhythmic embrace without ever looking away from each other, she added, "About the bill, huh?"

Lynn ran her fingers through Rebecca's hair, her eyes locked with Rebecca's, then she sighed, long and slow, a sigh that Jamie realized carried a language of its own shared only by the two of them.

Rebecca's face responded with a kaleidoscope of concern, sympathy, determination. For the first time, Jamie saw Rebecca unmasked, her face lighting with the smile she reserved for Lynn alone; the lines around her mouth and eyes transformed her, and suddenly, Jamie understood her power to soothe Lynn, to give Lynn strength and stamina.

"I have to say, Reb, you look just beautiful," Lynn said, her own smile blossoming. She kissed Rebecca once, then again. "Pumpkin picking suits you."

"*You* suit me," said Rebecca, returning Lynn's kiss. "You always have."

CHAPTER TWELVE
REBUTTABLE PRESUMPTIONS

Enemies. For a week, Jamie's dreams ran red with enemies. Seen and unseen, lone and in conspiracies vast and voracious. In her dreams, she did all the right things and flailed ineffectually anyway as new enemies mingled with The Bastard and Shoo Juh, plotting, attacking, killing.

Always, the dreams cheated, as dreams do. She hollered orders that went unheard, her finger couldn't pull her rifle's calcified trigger, she ran endlessly without ever getting anywhere.

Always, her enemies won, and with each dream their victories cut closer, destroying more and more of what mattered to her—who mattered to her.

Always, she woke drenched in sweat and fear and frustration, her heart slamming hysterically against her chest wall as the dream receded and she repeated the names of those the dream had taken from her... *Lynn is still alive...Adele is still alive...*

One morning, Jamie woke beneath a dream shadow that slowly silhouetted into a high-relief recall of one particular Palawan mission briefing. It stood out, even at the time, because of the new FDL contractor's self-satisfied, Charles-in-charge expression as he watched the regiment's command staff brief its junior officers about "the last big push south"—the mission that brought her to the rooftop a hundred meters from that school playground in Narra where her bullet ended Awa's life.

FDL. Don't know shit about FDL. Time to change that.

The company kept a very low profile, but in between workouts and studying physics and, yes, daydreaming about Adele, Jamie gathered what she could from public sources. And found it wasn't nearly enough; she needed to know more.

But who to ask? Great Hill was in a state of suspended animation: Lynn and Springer involved with an ever-changing parade of experts, ET engrossed in another security system "glitch," Rebecca pulling twelve-hour shifts at the hospital, Dana and Lily caught up in Callithump strategic planning for the coming year, Robin avoiding the house and the politics her mother brought to it—"for the duration," she announced when she left for school, which initially meant until the election, but now meant until at least Thanksgiving because of "all the crap with that mohumbug bill."

This left Mary. "I could attempt a guess," she said on the bright October afternoon of Brunch Day Minus Thirty-Nine as she finished a Chopin nocturne. Then she glanced up at Jamie, perched on the stairs as always, listening. "But why don't you just come down here and tell me what's bothering you."

"Am I that obvious?"

Mary smiled.

"FDL," Jamie said.

"Ah, yes. The current Richard Lambert battle."

"How many have there been?"

"Four major ones. Skirmishes beyond count."

"Why?"

"Rather a long story." Mary rose from the piano bench. "It'll require tea and lemonade. Come on."

A few minutes later, they settled at the long, rough-hewn breakfast table with beverages and a small plate of Kizzy's fresh-baked cookies. "Lynn came to Boston right out of college," Mary began. "She worked for a company called XTech, which developed security software, and when she'd been there for about three years, it was bought by FDL. It took Richard Lambert about a month to notice Lynn, invite her to lunch, and tell her, quite crudely, that if she wanted to keep her job, she'd better be prepared to bed down with him right after the entree. She was involved with Rebecca then, and he knew it. Lynn always said that made dominating her all the more appealing to him. She also said he really expected her to do it."

Jamie chuckled. "No way."

Mary nodded. "She quit on the spot. Never went back to the office."

"So that was the first Richard Lambert battle."

"More like the opening barrage," said Mary. "And maybe the way Lynn responded wouldn't have so thoroughly infuriated him if that had been all there was to it."

"What happened?"

"You know that Callithump was founded by three people, all from XTech."

Jamie shook her head. "No, I didn't."

"Lynn and her friends Brennan and Claudia. Lynn was the youngest, worked in marketing at XTech, but she took the time to understand the company's technology. The other two were classic introverted techies. Ironically, it was Lynn who thought up the idea on which they built Callithump. Brennan and Claudia ran with it, did the technical heavy lifting, and later Lynn did the selling. When Lynn quit XTech, so did Brennan and Claudia. In fact, there was quite an exodus. Lambert blamed Lynn, among others, and actually called her to say he intended to badmouth her every chance he got."

"Jeezus."

"Indeed. Fortunately, she wasn't job hunting. Nine or ten months after they left XTech, Lynn, Brennan, and Claudia launched Callithump. They pulled in some good contracts and were doing well enough to hire a handful of people, including a few who'd been at XTech." Mary paused for a sip of tea and a sigh. "A year later, Lambert ambushed them."

"How?"

"He approached one of the former XTech people they'd hired and bribed the man to steal Callithump source code. An outdated version, but Lambert used it anyway to compete with Callithump. He gave it a huge marketing budget and used FDL's government contacts to make sure federal requests for proposals were worded so that only FDL's software would meet the requirements."

"The first battle."

"Oh, yes. And it was brutal."

"That's what Lynn meant when she mentioned he almost put Callithump out of business."

"He managed to shut Callithump out of federal contracts for years. Callithump really did have a better product, a better service, though, and Lynn's a good saleswoman—so Callithump got by on commercial deals as well as state and local government contracts."

"So Callithump won," said Jamie. "Lynn won."

"Well, they fought off a much larger, stronger adversary. So, yes, I suppose they won."

"That sounds...ominous."

"Everything seemed fine at the time. Callithump did well, especially on the commercial side. Some accounts that had been lost to FDL even came back. After three years or so, nobody was thinking about Richard Lambert anymore, and Lynn, Brennan, and Claudia decided the moment to sell Callithump had arrived."

"Sell it?" Jamie put down her lemonade. "Why?"

"From the start, they regarded Callithump as a niche player that gets acquired by a technology behemoth and assimilated into a much broader, more sweeping infrastructure. As they saw it, their great accomplishment was that they'd fielded a couple of successful offerings through self-financing, without having to turn to any venture capital people, and their plan was to sell Callithump and move on. For Lynn, that meant taking time off to have a baby before she turned thirty."

"Robin." Jamie paused. "But they *didn't* sell Callithump."

"No, they didn't. Not for lack of trying, though. Which brings us to the second battle. It was a tough economy then, but they found a buyer and signed some preliminary paperwork. And Lynn—well, Lynn was three months pregnant when FDL swooped in and acquired the company that was going to acquire Callithump. Lambert wanted the Callithump acquisition to go through, but he dropped the offer price. Substantially."

"Ka-boom," said Jamie sympathetically.

"Oh god, yes." Mary's head wagged slowly back and forth. "I have to say, Lynn lost it. I've never seen her so angry. Not before. Not since—not even after coming back from that awful island where she found you."

"Did Lambert know she was pregnant?"

Mary shrugged. "Lynn certainly thought so. She was convinced he was exploiting that to underpay for Callithump. She scrambled to find another buyer. She wanted to be a full-time mother until her baby went off to school. But no buyers. So she and Brennan and Claudia had a choice: Take Lambert's very low offer or—"

"Or keep Callithump and somehow try to grow it themselves," said Jamie.

"And that, as all the world knows, is what they did."

"But no full-time motherhood."

"Exactly."

"Lambert must've figured he won," Jamie said as she left the table to replenish their tea and lemonade, "since Callithump never got sold."

"I expect that's true. He understood that without another idea, Callithump would wither away in the face of competition from much larger competitors, including FDL." Satisfaction permeated Mary's voice; Jamie returned to find her eyes gleaming almost mischievously. "But they *had* found another idea. Which is to say, Dana had."

"Dana? She must've been a kid then."

"She was twelve at the very beginning of Callithump, and completely enthralled with watching Lynn, Brennan, and Claudia create a company in our kitchen." Mary smiled at the recollection. "They couldn't get rid of her, so after a while they stopped trying and sent her scurrying around on errands. As the months passed, she started helping them in more sophisticated ways, and finally with aspects of the software itself. Even after Callithump had a whole floor of an office building, our kitchen table was still where Lynn, Brennan, and Claudia would plan and brainstorm. Of course, Dana was always there, too, and one day she presented an idea of her own, a way to make high-end telepresence truly mainstream."

"And the rest is history."

"Yes," Mary said. "The pandemic. Billions of people all over the world enduring wave after wave of social distancing and self-quarantine for almost three years. Callithump expanded wildly, bought and built infrastructure galore—processor farms, communications backbones, satellites, research labs. It became one of the behemoths."

"Thus endeth the second battle," Jamie said with relish. "That's a great story. But didn't you say four battles with Richard Lambert?"

"Number three happened during the pandemic. You know that Springer was—"

"An EIRP fugitive. Like Adele."

Eyebrows elevating, Mary's head bobbed slowly, a smile forming as she spoke. "So Adele told you…"

"You seem surprised."

"I'm pleased. Quite pleased."

Jamie decided not to ask why. She reached for a cookie instead. "Robin mentioned that Springer hid here…"

"With us, yes," said Mary, who also eyed the cookies. "Not in this house, though. It wasn't built 'til afterward. Back then, we lived over on Preston Place—in the white cape at the end of what's now the west driveway."

"Where ET lives?"

"Mmm hmm." Mary picked up a cookie. "During the second autumn, in the middle of one of the pandemic waves on the east coast, FDL contractors working for the Department of Justice showed up on our doorstep. They'd been granted public health police powers and they used those powers to harass us. Searches. Threats. Certainly we'd have been arrested if they'd found Springer."

Jamie stopped munching on her cookie. "Shit."

"That's precisely what I thought at the time."

"They never found Springer?"

"No. Even though they came three times. As public health police, they had to maintain the pretense of looking for EIRP fugitives, but it was obvious they were much more interested in harassment and intimidation. And that last time, all they cared about was what was on our comlinks. By then, though, Lynn had discerned the foul stench of Lambert and used a prototype of an app Dana had developed that conceals data—"

"You mean the Hider app? The one that camouflages whatever's on your comlink that you don't want anyone to know about?"

"A predecessor to Hider, actually."

"Wow. I had no idea Dana created that."

"Oh yes, it's Dana's. She'd started working on getting her pilot certificate, but the pandemic put that on hold, and she was bored. She and Lynn also planted covert videocams in every room of the house, plus one that covered the driveway. The FDL people were videoed from the moment they came onto the property until they drove away."

"So the whole incident got recorded."

"Yes, indeedy. Video *and* audio. Afterward, Lynn sent copies to someone at the Department of Justice—and to Vivian Velty. A scandal was born and the EIRP finally began to come under public scrutiny."

"Vivian Velty? Is she that, uh—"

"Old?" Mary chuckled. "Yes. Though she was just getting started then."

"So Lynn gave her the story that launched her career."

"Lynn helped, certainly. I think, though, that Vivian would've got where she is regardless."

"So that was the third battle. Number four…" Jamie tapped her fingers on the breakfast table—one, two, three, four. "Lynn's Senate run. Gotta be."

Mary nodded, but she didn't smile. "It was nasty. Very nasty."

"But he failed."

"And made a damn fool of himself in the process. Yet…"

"Yeah. Someone else got the blame."

"When Richard Lambert's involved, that's what tends to happen."

Day after day, Jamie couldn't keep herself from two near-obsessions: Whether Adele would respond to a message and counting the number of days until The Brunch.

Each morning, she composed a note to Adele, promptly trashed it, wrote another in the afternoon, and trashed that one, too. Sometimes, just before lights out, she tried a third time, but those efforts always got deleted after only a few lines. Little wonder:

HI ADELE…
~~JUST WANTED TO SAY~~ I WANT TO SEE YOU AGAIN
~~MAYBE WE COULD~~ SOON
TODAY
RIGHT NOW
PLEASE
I CAN'T STOP THINKING ABOUT YOU
IT'S STARTING TO HURT

Ah, no, no, no—a confession too far, and from who?

From whom, dammit.

A scruffy street stray Lynn brought in out of the rain, that's whommm.

And posing what any rational ops planner would call Serious And Critical Levels Of Risk*: Anything—everything—from* Degradation To Efficient Use Of Assets *all the way to* Causing Death.

No, she'd have to try for controls that would either eliminate the hazard or reduce the risks. The Physics I course was a start. When she finished it, she'd sign herself up for a second college course—proof of risk mitigation—and then send Adele a message. Only then.

Meanwhile, work on Lynn's new bill had gone into what everyone in the house called High Gear. This meant Don't Bug Lynn For The Duration.

When she wasn't studying or working out, Jamie tried hovering—especially at the breakfast table and in the front hall near the wide double doors to the study, now perpetually closed because the study and the little office next to it had become the only places at Great Hill where Lynn discussed either the new bill or The Brunch. But hovering got Jamie nowhere. Nor did her carefully contrived reminders, always concluding with "I want to help." Inevitably, Lynn found a gently adroit way to change the subject.

Springer took it a step further; she actually avoided Jamie, dodging eye contact as she sprinted in and out of the constant stream of meetings in the study. So when she marched into Jamie's room late on Brunch Day Minus Thirty-Four toting a small briefcase, Jamie's stomach backflipped. *Lynn's decided to let me—*

But Springer raised her hand, palm outward. "Don't wind up. This is unofficial."

"What does that m—"

"No questions. No expectations. No frigging talking about it later."

"So she hasn't—"

"What part of 'unofficial' do you find so difficult to grasp?"

"Fine. Unofficial. And…"

"We've pretty much nailed the guest list. Only eight of them will matter, assuming all eight accept. And that's assuming a lot. The other five are on our side."

"So just thirteen?" asked Jamie. "I figured there'd be—more."

"It'll be sit-down. The dining room table maxes at sixteen, but really only fourteen if the idea is to keep everyone comfortable enough to stick around for a bit. Which means one seat's still open. Capiche?"

"Oh." *Breathe in…two…three…four…*

"She won't talk about it and I'll be headless if I bring it up again. But there's no reason I can't give you a look at—" Springer rummaged in her briefcase and pulled out a tablet. "This. Background on our potential cast of characters and a few of their buddies."

"Encrypted?" Jamie asked.

"You bet your buppy."

"So you need bio-authentication stuff. Retinal, yes?"

"And fingerprint."

From her briefcase, Springer produced a pocketcom dedicated to the task and completed the scan and transfer process so efficiently that Jamie wondered how often she did it.

"One document on here. Don't attempt to copy it, move it, send it—everything'll fry if you do," she said. "It'll open to fingerprint scan, then retinal scan, then the username and password you just chose. In that order."

"Always offline."

"Oh yeah. It's set for Active Your Eyes Only, narrow-view, and it'll self-destruct upon tampering, so don't fuck up your authentication, don't wear comlink eyewraps, and don't let another set of retinas look at it. I'll sleep better if you keep it in this room." Springer opened a bedside drawer, put the tablet there, and shut it firmly before turning toward the door. "And don't forget—" She turned back to Jamie and placed her index finger across her lips.

"Not taking *any* chances, are we, Chief?"

Later, when Jamie clicked up the tablet, she understood why.

"Rebuttable Presumptions For Background Only, Do Not Promulgate" scrolled continuously across the top of each tablet screen as Springer's document detailed the adventures of four defense contractor CEOs, two trade group lobbyists, two senators, a congressman, and a former secretary of defense who now headed the think tank that sponsored the Bretton Woods conference. A mere glimpse revealed enough dirt, even if only half of it was half-true, to put several of them in prison for decades.

Yet it was the two who seemed the least egregious who riveted Jamie's attention.

Former Secretary of Defense Rafael Vicario, a Florida native now executive director of the independent, very well-heeled Institute for Strategic Studies, stood at the center of swirling rumors about what Springer's document referred to as a ginger group, a term Jamie had to look up.

ginger group *(noun):* A group within a party, association, etc, that seeks to alter policies, practices, or office-holders; from "gingering"—forcing a stick of peeled ginger root into a horse's anus "to make him lively and carry his tail well."

Vicario's ginger group had succeeded in keeping both its name and its membership list secret, but its mandate had been implicitly revealed by Vicario himself in a series of speeches: The Future of Civilization depended on the proper provisioning and protection of the world's essential commodities in the face of rising conflict and deteriorating Rule Of Law.

The ginger group's members were rumored to include CEOs and an ex-general or six, and they were said to share what Springer's document described as a "mildly apocalyptic" view of the next several decades. Those whose well-being depended on Vicario's version of the Rule Of Law would be at increasing risk unless they intervened "in time" wherever their interests were threatened. This, of course, would require Leadership, something which the ginger group and Vicario, who saw himself as kingmaker rather than king, were keen to provide.

And then there was Jonathan Armstrong Archer, CEO of Walker-Monroe, Incorporated, the nation's second-largest defense contractor. According to Springer's document, Vicario disliked Archer, who had publicly referred to him as "a cheap politician."

Archer, by contrast, was entirely corporate—and hanging on to his job by a thread. After all, Walker-Monroe interests in the Palawan had been badly singed by the conflict there. Its merc subsidiary, Columbia Aegis, had produced unreliable, reputation-wrecking intel and analysis that cost several Defense Department contract renewals. And its natural resources subsidiary, Inseque, lost a half-dozen Philippine licenses for South China Sea oil and gas exploration and extraction to an upstart outfit called Mundus Energy.

A long paragraph described how Mundus bested Inseque: Several months after Inseque's platforms were grabbed by enemy insurgents, they were retaken by Marine special ops units, and within days, the Philippine government refused to renew Inseque's platform licenses, instead granting them to Mundus, which by happy coincidence had made a deal to sell all its South China Sea oil and gas to the U.S. Defense Department for use by the Joint Pacific Command.

The paragraph ended with a couple of final notes Jamie couldn't stop thinking about. The first one described how, two years before the situation in Palawan escalated into open conflict, Mundus CEO Oscar Zanella hired FDL to provide risk assessment and operations security. The second note tagged a photo of Archer with the president and the chairman of the Joint Chiefs of Staff taken at Archer's Wyoming ranch some four months after Inseque lost its Philippine licenses—and a few weeks before the Last Big Push South wrecked the truce talks in Singapore.

Jamie inspected Archer's image, one arm resting casually on the president's shoulder. With his graying hair and chilly almost-smile, he remained patrician handsome at sixty. Had he talked the president and the top brass at the Pentagon into one more Palawan assault to keep the conflict alive long enough to restore Inseque's clout in the South China Sea?

If so, his gambit failed. Miserably. In thirty years of success evolving into unchallenged dominance, Archer had never endured anything close to the humiliating setbacks that plagued him in the Palawan. And Richard Lambert's FDL had helped his competitor best him. No wonder Lynn put Archer at the top of her guest list.

But he was a prick, obsessed with bottom-line profit and planet-altering power. Far more powerful than Richard Lambert, and, Jamie thought, far more dangerous. Happy to slit your throat for an extra nickel.

"Shit, Lynn," Jamie muttered. "You gotta be careful, really careful with this guy." She read on and on, devouring every word, every videoclip, past midnight, past 0100, until the tablet screens raced forward of their own accord, faster and faster, the scrolled warning atop each screen smudging incomprehensibly just before her eyes reached it.

Hey, look at that. I bet I'm dreaming…

CHAPTER THIRTEEN
SOMETHING NOT QUITE RIGHT

Thick paper textbook straddled across her legs, the next Physics I module clicked up on her eyewraps' shadowscreen, Jamie had just squiggled into studying position on her bed when Springer strode in and pulled open the bedside drawer.

"Where is it?"

Jamie peered over the top of her eyewraps. "Been only four days. How do you know I've even read it?"

Springer snorted. "You're a scout/sniper. You've read it—all of it—at least three times. Odds are you have most of it committed to memory."

"I'd like to go over it again at least once."

"Uh-uh. Time's up. Where'd you put it?"

"Why do you want it back after only—"

"You're kidding, right?" Springer stared at Jamie, her eyes slitting. "That stuff's incendiary as hell."

Jamie sighed. "Doesn't look good, huh?"

"What?"

"The fourteenth seat. Occupied by me."

Much the way Alby used to after a failed attempt at sneaking off with the grocery money to buy smack or oxy, Springer's eyes swung to the ceiling before her head drooped and she slouched onto the edge of the bed. "As *you've* already pointed out," she said crabbily, "when it comes to getting the new bill passed, you'd be most valuable in a high-profile interview with someone like Vivian Velty, who could help you make a hell of a powerful emotional argument—"

"It's more than just emotional," objected Jamie. "It's—"

"It's emotional unless you can point to evidence that current policy and practices have triggered wrongdoing—or at least conflicts of interest—which have caused serious harm, like geopolitical catastrophe or mission failure or unwarranted loss of life. And you can't. All you can do is express an opinion about dicey command leadership. Necessary maybe, and suggestive if you do it right, but far from sufficient without corroboration."

"I can repeat what Shoo Juh said to The Bastard."

"Yeah? Something you heard while you were getting slapped around? After months of brutal interrogation and physical deprivation and isolation? A snatch of inconclusive conversation between two people who shall remain forever unidentified because you don't know their names? And, oh by the way, you never even got a glimpse of the man who's supposed to make your point about the problems with inadequately monitored private contractors?" Springer's icy blue eyes softened. "All they gotta do is say your Bastard isn't real, Jamie. That, heroics notwithstanding, you hallucinated the whole thing. And you can't refute them."

Springer had stated the obvious, right down to the zing about heroics. Jamie felt the space between her shoulders deflate; no wonder Lynn had so unequivocally resisted her so-called "help."

"Then why—" Jamie stopped herself. *Breathe in…two…three… four…* "Why'd you ever even bring it up?"

"Because until yesterday—" Springer shrugged as if to fend off a pestering insect and started again. "You could've embodied a sympathetic and therefore very persuasive example of the consequences of bad policy. In the right context, that has the potential to put enormous pressure on the opposition. Maybe even a critical mass of pressure if you pulled off a good interview. Your value at the brunch is chiefly as a reminder of that potential."

"Dangling the threat, you mean."

"Yep. And if it were up to me, I'd see how much of a threat we can really make of you. I'd at least put you through your paces in front of the cameras once or twice. But even if the cameras adore you, it's still a crapshoot at best. Hell, everyone has camera candy, and odds are theirs will rival ours. What we really need is a one-two punch, which we almost had—" Springer shook her head. "But almost doesn't cut it."

"Two punches." Jamie peered at her. "If I'm potentially one punch, who's the other?"

"We were so close," Springer confided to the floor, then turned toward Jamie and extended a hand, fingers wiggling come hither. "Anyway, ante up."

"Not 'til you ante up about—"

Springer groaned dramatically. "Just give me the fucking tablet."

"You first."

Springer rubbed her face with both hands. "God, I suppose I asked for this." She turned to face Jamie full on. "We—that is, *I*—heard about something from one of the Intelligence Committee staff guys. And if it had worked out, it would've been our other punch—possibly a knockout punch. Certainly enough to get the people obstructing the investigations to duck and swerve. Only it didn't work out, so we won't be able to get them to recognize the link between what happened to Lynn and what happened to Chen Dongfeng."

"Lynn's counterpart on the Red Cross team that visited the Chinese and insurgent prisoners while Lynn was at Saint Eh Mo's—" Jamie closed her eyes and saw Lynn in rumpled linen striding across the prison yard, Lynn turning to whisk an inconspicuous nod toward the prisoners herded to the far side of the yard, Lynn risking so much more than any of them could have then imagined...

"Jamie?" asked Springer, her voice low. "Are you okay?"

"Mmm, I remember Lynn saying that since she pushed hard for those Red Cross visits, she ought to have the guts to—how'd she put it?" Jamie looked out the window at the wind turbines. "'Do the actual heavy lifting.'" She forced her gaze back to Springer. "So what happened to this Chen guy?"

Springer blinked surprise. "Are you serious?"

"I mean what *really* happened to him." Jamie let her eyes veer back to the turbines. "Just fill me in, okay?" *And stop frigging staring at me.*

"Ah, hell. Sorry." Springer's weight shifted on the bed. "I figured when you got debriefed, they told you—"

"Vague generalities. Bullshit about a splinter group nobody ever heard of. And I was, uh...I don't remember much."

"You must've seen at least some of the media coverage."

"Nope."

"None at all."

"Nope."

Springer sighed. "From the top, then. Chen was kidnapped near El Nido on his way to the airport from the last facility he was scheduled to visit. His convoy had to detour around a couple road washouts and got attacked on some dirt path about two miles from where it was supposed to be. The armored vehicle he'd been riding in was obliterated by automatic weapons fire and a rocket grenade. Next morning, the Chinese announced they were 'recessing' the truce talks, which was also the day—"

"June eighth. Saturday. The day they wouldn't let Lynn leave Saint Eh Mo's. I know that part." Now Jamie watched Springer carefully. "So who was really behind it? Who grabbed Chen?"

"That's been the sixty-four dollar question since it happened."

"You're shitting me, right?" Jamie couldn't stop her voice from rising. "Four months later and it's still a fucking mystery?"

"That's why there are two ongoing investiga—"

"Yeah? Must be some damn fat VIP asses hanging out there if they need four months to find cover."

"You want to hear the rest of this or what?"

"Oh yeah." Jamie motioned a small circle with one hand. "Can't wait."

"Two days after Chen was grabbed, on the ninth, a sixty-second video of him showed up online. He was alive, flanked by three men claiming to be part of—"

"The splinter group—Muslim, secessionist, anti-truce." Jamie shook her head. "I remember hearing that when I was in the hospital and thinking even then how it whiffed big time."

"Well, it shaped how the rest of us saw things. The idea of an obscure splinter group seemed quite viable, especially since after that one video it all went black. Nothing about Chen. Nothing about Lynn. Nobody knew if either of them were alive or what. Finally, the day after Lynn and the rest of you were rescued, a special ops team retrieved Chen, very much alive, from this ragtag crew of six guys. Supposedly the entire splinter group. All killed, of course."

"So somebody had intel about where he was and who grabbed him."

"Word is the intel was, uh, 'derived' only the day before, when Lynn was—when you and Lynn were—"

"It was *derived*." Jamie snorted. "From where? And who the hell did the deriving?"

"That's been classified. Only the Select Committee chairman and vice chairman are privy to—"

"Oh come on, Springer—no hints?"

"Dammit, Jamie—"

"Take as long as you like." Jamie folded her arms across her chest and pretended a smile. "I don't have to report to Quantico 'til the third of February."

Springer made a sound somewhere between a grunt and a groan. "Okay, okay. I've heard—a couple times removed, you understand, which means there's bound to be some, uh—"

"Swamp gas. Yeah, I get that. Go on."

"I've heard that it came from one of the contractors' spotters—"

"Which contractor?"

"Columbia Aegis."

"Archer's gang. What a shock. And the splinter group? Who were these six guys really?"

"Videoke buddies from Isabela City on Basilan Island."

Jamie pulled off her eyewraps. "Don't mess with me, Springer."

"I'm not. It's true. Six slum kids who grew up together. Seems they bullied their way into a shack in a shantytown along the Aguada River after one of their grandmothers died. Had an intermittent trickle of money, probably from petty theft. The neighbors said they were loud, drunk, and stupid for the year or so they were around. Distinctly unpious for supposed Islamists—though there's one unconfirmed report about two of them showing up now and then for prayers at the Timpul Mosque. Then one day the whole bunch of them evaporated."

"When?"

"Late April. About two weeks after Lynn first proposed sending somebody from each side to accompany the Red Cross teams."

"Okay, let's see if I understand this," Jamie said. "We're supposed to believe a posse of six impoverished, drunken, videoke-addicted squatters has a kind of group epiphany and decides one day to launch their very own version of the Philippine Muslim secessionist movement. Their commitment is so profound that they find the means to disappear from Isabela City and somehow pop up two months later on a whole other island more than five hundred klicks away—all without attracting the notice of anyone anywhere. Despite the drone surveillance and monitoring of all inter-island air and sea transport. Despite the foot patrols constantly checking people's IDs on every street and cowpath and mountain trail around El Nido. Despite all the so-called spotters desperate for the meager pesos they get from figuring out what crap will inspire a hard-on at those merc intel outfits the generals think are so damn valuable. Also, somehow, these six crooners from Isabela City manage to acquire automatic rifles plus at least one grenade launcher. Whose weapons, by the way? Zhong or ours?"

"Both."

"Right, just like good little surrogates should. Not to mention that they came upon such accurate and thorough knowledge of what no doubt was the secret itinerary of an important Chinese official that they were able fuck up the roads he was supposed to travel so they could intercept him and kidnap him. What's more, even though they were being hunted with every resource the U.S. and Filipino militaries could muster in a small area our people know very well, these six slum kids and their prisoner avoided capture for two weeks."

"Fifteen days."

"And after more than four months of investigation, this fairy tale is believed by the Pentagon and the Senate Select Committee on Intelligence?"

"No. But it's the only tale anyone's been willing to talk about."

"Until you heard something from this Intelligence Committee staff guy." Jamie leaned forward. "What something?"

Abruptly, Springer stood. "I shouldn't have said as much as I already have—"

"Mmm hmm." Jamie eased back and waited.

"All right," Springer grumped after a few seconds. "Fasten your seat belt."

Jamie set aside the textbook and repositioned on the bed to sit cross-legged facing Springer.

"This started last summer, but I didn't hear about it until a month ago," Springer said as she began to pace. "In July, a man in Chicago named Bacani contacted his senator because his son, who was a marine, had died over there, on one of the Palawan islands, and he didn't believe the Marine Corps's explanation. The best way I can lay it out for you is to have you listen to what this man said."

"You have a recording."

"Yes."

"Which you wheedled out of your staffer friend."

"Yes."

"And he got it how, exactly?"

"John Jakowski—that's Bacani's senator—brought the matter, and the recording, to Everett Harris—"

"Yeah, I remember Lynn mentioning him."

"He's chairman of the Senate Select Committee on Intelligence." Springer pulled a pocketcom from her jacket, which she placed on the bed. "The other voice you'll hear is one of Jakowski's people. Ready?"

"Oh yeah," said Jamie.

Bacani spoke quickly, nervously. "My son, Nimuel Bacani, served in Palawan with First Battalion, Ninth Marines, part of the Second Marine Division based at Camp Lejeune. He was assigned to Alpha Company's CLIC—that stands for company-level intelligence cell. Nimuel spoke Tagalog and was good at reading people, so his job was to go out with the rifle squads on their patrols. His commanders wanted whatever he could suss out, and also specific types of information that they'd tell him to snoop around for."

"Did your son talk to you specifically about what he did?" asked the aide.

"No, except for that one time the day before he died. He was very upset, said he felt backed into a corner and had to talk to somebody outside of it all.

"And when was this?"

"The eighth of June, about eight in the morning, from someplace off-base," said Bacani, his voice tightening as he spoke. "Said he didn't want to use Marine Corps comlinks. He sounded close to tears, which is—was—very out of character."

Bacani seemed breathless; he halted and coughed, then apologized before he continued. "Nimuel talked about getting reamed by some Ninth Regiment intel officer—a major, I think Nim said—for 'overreacting.' This was right after his company got sent to El Nido and he ended up on patrols that didn't really do anything. Nim called it 'worse than half-assed,' said the squaddies just picked a place to hang out a mile or so from the observation post—a roadside joint where they could drink beer and mess with some local girls."

"Your son reported this?" asked Jakowski's aide.

"He did," Bacani said firmly. "And this major told him his report had been DD'd—that means Deleted and Destroyed—and that he should be grateful, 'cuz a report like that could slam his Marine Corps career. Said Nim should just go with the flow."

"I see," said Jakowski's aide in a tone that managed to convey carefully noncommittal sympathy. "As I remember, when you first called our office, you mentioned two incidents."

"Yeah. The other one went down a week after Nim's run-in with that major. He ended up on a patrol with a new-guy squad leader come over from another company, and this guy didn't know to jack off. So they conducted a real patrol, moving along a dirt path a couple miles off the main road, and they encountered two guys who tried to take off on them. The squad got 'em, though, detained 'em. They had no IDs and their Tagalog was terrible. Nim said they spoke Tausug, and figured solid odds they were insurgents."

Bacani's effort to breathe grew audible on the recording as he continued. "Nimuel separated the detainees and got them both to talk a little, and they independently told my son, 'Hey, we're actually all on the same side. Please let us go and don't tell anyone about this because we'll get in big trouble if we don't do our part when this Chinese dude comes through here in two hours.' These guys looked scruffy, but they were well-armed, carrying comlinks, so Nimuel took them seriously and called it in. He was ordered to click up everything he had—images of the detainees and their weapons, his notes and audio, the detainees' biometrics, the stuff in their comlinks. So he did. Stand by, his squad leader was told, and they stood by for half an hour."

Now Bacani paused; judging by the sounds coming from Springer's pocketcom, he gulped something liquid before he went on. "Then comes new orders: The guys you grabbed are okay. They work for some contractor. Don't remember if Nim even said which one.

Anyway, the squad leader was told to let them go and quick-time it to—I forget what Nim called it. Someplace on a different road where they were supposed to help repair a washout."

After a moment's hush, Bacani said very softly, "That bothered Nimuel. But, y'know, they obeyed their orders and zigzagged around to where the road had washed away and started helping the contractor guys working on it. In the process, Nim ended up on a nearby hilltop where one side of the hill had been clear-cut so he could see all the way back to where they'd detained those two guys earlier. And right close by to that spot he saw three civilian vehicles get stopped by at least ten men.

"That's what your son said? At least ten?" asked Jakowski's aide.

"Nim said he counted eight visible to him and assumed at least two more because others were firing from the woods—y'know, the jungle—from two different places."

"And then what happened?"

"Nim said three people from the middle vehicle got dragged away. Then the vehicle got hit by a rocket grenade and blown all to hell. He used a high-res zoom lens to record the whole thing from three hundred meters away. And he spotted the two guys they'd detained earlier."

"He called this in, to his command?"

"Yes, sir, he sure did. Clicked up the video, too," Bacani declared, his voice finally beginning to betray anger. "Just about the time the rest of the squad made it to Nim's position, they were ordered back to the FOB. Command said special ops teams in the area would deal with 'the issue.' Back at the FOB, Nim was ordered to turn in his mission comlink. That night, he found all the data in his personal comlink account had been wiped. The next morning he was shipped to a new unit. Sent to a different island that very day—to Busuanga."

"And that's when…"

"Yes, sir," replied Bacani. "That's when he called me—when he got to Busuanga. He told me what I just told you. A-And he said he'd made a copy of the video from that last patrol, when he was up on the hill, even though it violated all kinds of regs. He did it on the way back to the FOB, copied it to one of his own datacards. Said he was gonna send it to me."

"And did you receive it?"

"No," said Bacani, sounding breathless again. "I don't know if he had second thoughts and never sent it or if he screwed up the address or if it got intercepted. I don't know. But—" Bacani's voice choked. "But he died the next day. They said it was an accident. That he drowned. But I-I just don't buy it, because even a decent swimmer wouldn't have gone down like that, like the way the report describes—and Nimuel was a very strong swimmer, a long-distance swimmer."

"I'm sorry, Mr. Bacani," said Jakowski's aide. "We're all so very sorry."

"Something's wrong here," Bacani brayed after an extended pause, and then his voice went formal; this part he had rehearsed. "So I-I'm respectfully asking Senator Jakowski to find out what really happened. Maybe if the senator can get that stuff from Nim's last patrol, then we—I—could find out the real story. Because I believe the answer to his death is hidden right there, in what he clicked up to his commanders. I'm hoping you can help me find the truth. I have a right to know what really happened to my son."

❖

"Christ," Jamie muttered as Springer clicked off the pocketcom. "Nim shoulda known better."

"Copying that video to his own datacard, you mean," said Springer.

Jamie nodded. "The Powers That Be were on to him the nanosecond he pressed COPY. Unless somebody showed him the workaround—"

"There's a workaround?" Springer appeared genuinely shocked.

"Oh yeah. Serious pain in the ass, but yeah."

"How many people know about it?"

"Anybody's guess. I learned it when I was a corporal, but I had an especially gifted teacher."

"Jeezus."

"You do realize the language Nim said those two detainees spoke—Tausug—is common in Malaysia and the southern Philippine islands. Like the southern part of Palawan—which was enemy territory last June. And like Basilan Island."

"Basilan…" Springer's face blanched.

"Where those six videoke buddies hailed from."

"Shit. I didn't know that."

"Mmm. Your friend on the Intelligence Committee gave you Nim's patrol data, too, right?"

"It's worthless."

"So no video. No detainee images or biometrics."

"Nope. He said the Ninth Regiment database had none of that and it's not at the Pentagon either. Nobody has it because it doesn't exist. Of course he was lying. I can always tell when he's lying—and when he's scared." Springer's voice had gone flat. "Anyway, the official version now is that Nimuel Bacani freaked out and most of what he told his father never happened. The stuff I did manage to get is useless crap."

"Can I see it?"

"Be my guest." Springer pointed her pocketcom at the room's videoscreen, and a second later a short list of files appeared on it. "Take your pick. How long do you want?"

"I want a copy."

"No fucking way, sweetheart. I'll give you half an hour, then this all fries, and if you try to copy it—"

"Two hours."

Springer laughed. "An hour. And my goddamn tablet. Right now."

"Second-from-the-bottom right-hand drawer of the built-in. Taped to the underside."

"Cute."

"And good-bye to you, too," Jamie called to Springer's unceremoniously departing back.

CHAPTER FOURTEEN
WHOA

"Cute. Real cute."
This Jamie muttered more than once as she clicked through the notes she'd taken on Nim Bacani's last patrol files, on Rafael Vicario, on Jonathan Armstrong Archer, on Oscar Zanella and Richard Lambert, on everything Springer showed her.

Fragments of fact and rumor and speculation, snatches of videos, photos, maps, recollections of things said, phantasms from the Palawan—they all floated randomly, weightlessly in her head and, finally, impelled her to her feet. Somehow, these fragments hid significance, harbored unrecognized patterns; now and then, a wisp of meaning teased for a second or two before it drifted beyond the meager gravity of her grasp.

Frustrated, nagged by the promise she'd made to herself to finish the Physics I course by her birthday, she paced her bedroom. The physics textbook and the course icon in a corner of her eyewraps shadowscreen beckoned. Completing the course meant she could attempt to make contact with Adele. It also meant she had to face the risk of Adele's silence.

"Okay, okay," Jamie grumbled. "Soon as I do the what-ifs again."

What if Bacani wasn't crazy?

What if everything he told his father was true?

What if Chen was abducted not by a handful of Isabela City videoke buddies but by someone who wanted to keep the war going? Someone like Jonathan Armstrong Archer, who'd probably already goosed the brass into conducting the assault on Narra. 'Cuz what does he care if some stupid grunt blows the head off a six-year-old Filipino? He wanted his platforms back, by god, and hell, easy enough to use his own merc outfit to help make it happen. Sure as shit explains why Columbia Aegis's name keeps popping up in all the wrong places.

And what if the whole point of abducting Chen was to provoke the Zhong into detaining Lynn? Because whoever had Chen abducted damn well knew the Zhong would hand Lynn over to their insurgent surrogates, damn well knew the insurgents didn't take prisoners, only hostages—and they killed their hostages. Nothing like beheading a kidnapped U.S. senator to goose Operation Palawan Liberation one more time...

Jamie clicked up the list she'd made of all the ex-generals and ex-politicians on the boards of directors of those defense contractors whose CEOs Springer's document profiled—nineteen names in all. Now she placed four names at the top of the list: Archer, Vicario, Zanella, Lambert. Suspects all, and each one with tentacles to elected officials, serving military commanders, more CEOs...

She stared at the list. *So now what?*

Now nothing. *The intel I'm after has long since been Deleted and Destroyed.*

For a fleeting moment, she considered talking to Adele about it. *Nope. Can't risk it. 'Cuz what if all Adele hears is the combat talking, sees only the mad sniper imagining monsters in the bushes?*

Adele's voice echoed. "You're stalling."

Jamie returned to her study position on the bed, balanced the physics textbook across her thighs, and clicked up the next course module.

"Nope. Still stalling."

Yeah. I know.

Don't think about it, don't think about it...

This became Jamie's mantra as she struggled distractedly through Module Eighteen/Collision Theory—and remembered nothing when she tried to answer the review questions.

"C'mon, pay attention," she chided aloud. How many times had she read the same damn sentences? How long had she been gritting her teeth?

Do. Not. Think. About. It.

She began collision theory for a third time—and had made it to the second section when a message appeared in her shadowscreen's lower left corner. Immediately, it got tangled up with relative inertial reference frames.

Say what?

DO YOU LIKE THE VIOLIN, TOO?
JUST DISCOVERED THIS RECORDING
KEPT THINKING ABOUT YOU WHILE I LISTENED
—ADELE

Whoa.

Jamie yanked off her eyewraps and flung her gaze to the physics textbook laying open in her lap, where Newton's First Law lay crisp and motionless on its paper page: "Every body continues in its state of rest...unless it is compelled to change...by forces impressed upon it."

Adele. *I saw that, right?*

She slipped her eyewraps back on and read Adele's message again. It came with an attachment—a concerto by Brahms, according to the filename. Gut tightening, heartbeat achieving a state of absolute acceleration, Jamie started the music and listened—listened hard—for Adele's intent.

She listened to it twice over, trying to understand. What what *what* did Adele mean?

There were so many possibilities, some good, some not so good. Too many not so good.

The music might be Adele's implicit kiss-off: Here's why, after due consideration, I realize, I feel, I *know* with every wave and particle of my being that, yes, okay, you play a melody here and there, but you're too shadowed, too grim, too doomed to isolation—your wasteland is altogether too damn much to take.

Just ask *her, for chrissake. Just send her a message saying... saying what's true, no bullshit—and try not to sound like the village idiot...*

For the next forty-plus minutes—the entirety of the third time Jamie listened—she crafted and re-crafted her reply to Adele, which eventually shrank to eight words unable to ask anything:

NOW I LIKE THE VIOLIN, TOO
A LOT

The instant she sent the message she groaned her regret—hadn't honesty just cornered her into confessing her preference for the shadow, the grimness, the isolation? Yet her fingers remained paralyzed for another eternal minute before they broke free and took unhesitating command. For eight more words:

AND I THINK ABOUT YOU
ALL THE TIME

Oh god. Jamie stared at her right index finger, the one that had so impetuously punctured the SEND plane. How could it have done that? *Maybe I'll just never communicate anything to anyone ever again.*

With fumbling fingers, Jamie clicked off her comlink, ripped off the wristband, and shoved it and her eyewraps into the bedside drawer as fast as she could—because Adele might reply. Because Adele might not reply. Not ever.

For days, she didn't dare retrieve her comlink from the drawer. She couldn't study; she couldn't read at all. She couldn't think about physics or Newton's Laws or Nim Bacani or Archer or Vicario's ginger group or Lambert or Zanella—and she ran from Adele's shimmering image, Adele's unattainable possibility.

Oh how she ran. Jamie's world clenched into endless slogs along Great Hill's trails, arduous bouts of weight training, dozens and dozens of laps in the pool, timed stumbles though her own makeshift version of a Marine Corps combat fitness course, manic off-trail gallops through the woods, preferably as darkness descended and she was likelier to trip.

Whatever it took not to think about clicking up her comlink… or about Springer's goddamn intel…or the number of days 'til The Brunch…or what the hell she'd do if they really did decide to give her a Blue Max…or about squinting through a rifle scope's crosshairs as her breathing slowed and eased and she slipped into the forever between exhale and inhale that would seduce her finger's deadly twitch on her rifle's trigger…

❖

"Here." Marching down the second-floor hallway toward Jamie, Lily held out a pocketcom at arm's length, her expression both impatient and amused, her head swinging slowly back and forth, back and forth. "Take this," she ordered, shoving the pocketcom within an inch of Jamie's nose. "And speak."

"Uh." Pocketcom to her ear, Jamie cringed. "Hello?"

"…and dammit, Lily, wait!"

"Uh…Lily's, uh—" Jamie swallowed hard as she watched Lily snap an about-face and stride away. "Lily's left you with me."

Silence. Then: "Okay. So let me start by apologizing."

"No, no, *I'm* sorry," Jamie burbled. "I should've—I wasn't sure how you'd feel about what I wrote—" Jamie turned toward the hallway's wall, pushed her forehead against it, and tried to breathe. *Just breathe.*

"I initiated," said Adele. "Why would you think I wouldn't want to keep communicating with you?"

"Because—" Now Jamie swung around and pressed her back hard at the wall; knees bending, she slowly slid toward the floor as she spoke. "Sometimes I just don't know when to—I shouldn't have—I said too much. Presumed too much."

"You wrote sixteen words. And I liked every one of them."

Jamie thumped the last few inches onto the floor, gluteus maximi leading the way. "You did?"

"I did." Adele went quiet for several seconds, then added, "But it wasn't my intention to chase you down. I called Lily to make sure nothing else—I mean, you just vanished and I thought maybe you'd—"

"No, I've managed to behave myself. Well, mostly. I shouldn't have shut down on you like that. I figured I'd overdone it. And I didn't want to know that yet."

"Your silence would preclude you suffering mine."

Jamie curled forward and lowered her head onto her raised knees. "Yes." Her stomach hurt. "I'm sorry."

"Does that mean we're, uh, talking?"

"Yeah."

"Good. I was hoping you'd say that."

"Can I start with a question?"

"Please do."

"Why did it make you think about me?"

"The Brahms."

"Yeah. The Brahms. It's so…serious."

"Oh. So you *don't* like it."

"I do, actually. I think it's beautiful. But it's—it's—" Jamie interrupted herself when she heard the concerto start. "You're playing it now?"

"So I can answer your question. Do you hear it?"

"Yes."

"Good…" Adele whispered, stretching the word into a hush. "It's a story, really…" For a while, they said nothing else while violin and orchestra began their tale.

When Adele spoke again, her words emerged slowly, softly out of a husky simmer. "Sometimes surviving is much more of an accomplishment than it feels like while you're busy doing it."

Jamie waited for a sense of accomplishment to overtake her. And waited.

"The Brahms isn't the only music that makes me think of you," Adele said. Jamie imagined her with a small, lopsided smile on her face.

"It isn't?"

"I'll show you. But only if you promise not to disappear on me again."

"I promise." Eyes closed, Jamie leaned back against the wall, her legs splaying out in front of her across the hallway floor as she whooshed into weightlessness. *I promise I promise I promise…*

"First I want to look at you." Adele went quiet again, waiting for a reply, probably. "Where are you?" she finally asked.

"Uh—" Jamie cleared her throat again. "In the hall…upstairs…"

"Near your room. Where there's a nice, big videoscreen on the wall."

"How do you know that?"

"It's the room where I usually stay when I visit."

"Oh. Right."

"And if you go into your room and click up the videoscreen, you can also click up the videocam and log into Café." Adele paused. "So we can see each other." Another pause. "Unless you…don't want to see me. Or be seen."

"I do," Jamie said quickly, wincing as she thudded back to earth like she weighed a thousand pounds—because she'd have to admit it. "But I—I don't, uh, have a Callithump Café account." She might as well have admitted to ignorance of indoor plumbing.

"You're kidding."

"Never had a reason."

"Until now."

"Yeah." Mercifully light again, Jamie stood and walked toward her room. "Until now."

CHAPTER FIFTEEN
SURVIVAL OF THE FITTEST

*W*hat was that?

In the three months Jamie had lived in the house at Great Hill, she'd grown accustomed to its sounds, yet she'd never heard anything like this dull thunk that interrupted her work on the last of Physics I Classical Mechanics. She looked over the rim of her eyewraps, listened carefully, and perceived...absence.

Where was the weird, icy prickle at the small of her back that should be needling up her spine by now to warn all hell was about to break loose?

Maybe she'd heard a small, distant kick from the heating system only recently turned on as October waned. Yep, a reasonable explanation, good enough to keep her in studying position. After all, she assured herself, it had been the sort of sound that would tend to get lost in the ordinary bustle of Great Hill—and hell, six days before the mid-term elections, eighteen days before The Brunch, nothing at Great Hill remained ordinary.

"We'll all be ad-libbing for the duration," Mary had quipped earlier when she headed out to spend the afternoon picking late apples with Edgar.

Jamie's own ad-lib had inspired the comment because she decided at the last minute not to go off with them as planned. No, she'd sacrifice end-of-season apples for a clear shot at completing the damned physics course, which she'd pledged to have done by her twentieth birthday— tomorrow!—and which she should've wrapped up a week ago.

Here, now, stood her chance to get back on schedule.

She was close. Only one more chunk—and the whole of the afternoon to do it. Then the final exam. *I can just pull it off, since nobody'll be around tomorrow, either—not even Mary. And Adele will still be out of comlink range...*

Already, Jamie missed Adele's image on her videoscreen. They hadn't explicitly formed anything habitual during the last five days, instead sticking with a semi-vague "talk to you soon." But "soon" turned into the next day, and the next—and each day they made contact earlier than the day before, each day they hung out together longer than the day before. Afterward, Adele's music always echoed, Adele's image shimmered on the blank screen, behind Jamie's eyelids, and last night, in her dreams, too.

Which meant Physics I didn't have a chance. Not until Adele accepted that invitation to join some old friends at the Provincetown Center for Marine Studies on a trip to their Georges Bank monitoring stations. Jamie's goal now was to finish up the course before Adele returned.

How nicely that would work out, since no one had indicated the slightest awareness of her birthday, hidden there behind the luster of Halloween. She'd commemorate this one after she submitted her final—a little party of one in her room with a chocolate bar, perhaps, or one of Kizzy's cookies, to salute both Halloween and completion of her first-ever college course on the very same day she'd scraped through twenty years of playing survival of the fittest on Planet Earth.

Hell, I might even get a passing grade.

Jamie refocused on the words of Physics I Module 28 filling her shadowscreen: Recall Newton's Third Law of Motion...

She recited aloud her own version, formulated long ago during scout/sniper training. "If you press a clit with your finger, your finger is also pressed by the clit. Because forces always come in pairs and exert themselves upon each other."

Certainly she and Adele had been exerting force upon each other, and oh yeah, Adele's force pressed upon her, a flare of arousal that refused to ebb, that damn well paralyzed her in front of the videoscreen as she listened to Adele's music, gazed at Adele's splendidly animated image.

She expected to pay dearly for that; Shoo Juh's meticulous conditioning had been relentless. Oh, it was classic. Pavlovian. And she was a pathetic, drooling dog. Turn her on and it was all instantly, starkly real again: There she kneeled, naked and shackled, Shoo Juh's glacial sneer looming over her, the fiery sting of a thick strap hard across her backside, The Bastard's grating metallic treble ringing dissonant in her ears as she watched a buzzing electric baton or sometimes a power drill coming closer, closer...

But—

Jamie felt a smile crease her face. *But not this time.*

She had girded, expecting the worst. Yet the phantasms only roiled indistinctly at the far edges of her vision, unable to close in, somehow held at bay. For five days, it had continued like that. Almost like being…*y'know, normal.*

She'd managed something similar the first time she and Adele spoke to each other out there on the trail, but only because she repressed—no, she bloody well suffocated—her budding lust.

But not this time. This time, she had walked doomed right into the inescapable, irresistible turn-on of Adele Sabellius and emerged almost unscathed not once but five times.

Now everyone around her, at least everyone female, seemed lightly erotic, their sensuality made palpable by her hyperawareness of that animate impulse between their legs, sometimes soft and tentative, sometimes galvanically insistent. It was her own impulse, of course, between her own legs, forever affected by spending more and more time being acted upon by Adele's force, Adele's spectacular force…

For the first three days, they communicated by music. Brahms, then a tender, lilting piece with a flute and a harp. On the fourth day, their conversation upstaged the music. Adele talked smoothly, easily of the pleasures of returning to the wooded dunes of Truro. Jamie stumbled over descriptions of her escalating exercise regimen, how much it helped her tolerate even an hour or two sitting still enough to study physics; she did not mention ghosts, but she saw recognition in Adele's eyes.

"After you escaped," Jamie asked, "did you ever want to find out more about what happened? About why? And who was responsible?"

"Yes. It took a while, but I ended up obsessed with all the layers and layers of Why. It was like peeling an onion." Adele's eyes gazed intently over Jamie's left shoulder, at what Jamie knew was her own image on Adele's screen. "I've never found an Ultimate Truth or an Ultimate Solution, but I suppose I'm kind of there now for good—in the realm of Why."

On the fifth day, Adele wanted to know what Jamie would study in school "in a perfect world where you could do whatever you wanted." Jamie said that it'll never be a perfect world and asked Adele to play the Brahms again.

Adele's eyes fixed on Jamie then, and for the first time during their videoscreen convos, Jamie's sense of being 225 kilometers away from her evaporated. "I think I'm gonna go back to school. Next year."

"A doctorate."

"Yeah. I need to know a lot more about a lot of things. I thought good environmental resource management would be the best way to stop the kind of degradation that was at the root of the last pandemic. That it could be enough to prevent the next pandemic, among others things. But it doesn't address the problem of growth itself."

"So what will?"

"Decoupling."

"Decoupling..." Jamie had to dig for that one. "Something about sustainable development—how to have economic growth without wrecking the environment, right?"

Adele's grin returned. "Close enough."

"Good luck with that." Jamie shook her head. "I mean, who's going to volunteer for decoupling?"

"Ha. I'm not that naïve. Policies need to *require* decoupling."

Jamie shook her head again. "I'd say that's a pipedream."

"It's an imperative. Ever hear of the tragedy of the commons?"

"Nope. But I bet when you're done telling me, I'll be thinking about Murphy's Law and the unintended consequences of attempting to fix the effects of unintended consequences."

That made Adele laugh. "Slick, Gwynmorgan. Very slick."

"I'm an atheist, too," Jamie said. *And behold,* she didn't say, *the difference between someone who joined the Red Cross and someone who joined the Marines.*

Adele obviously wanted to keep talking, a miracle for which Jamie felt deep gratitude, but she'd promised to take Luce and Biz out to dinner and had yet to pack for the trip to Georges Bank. After she clicked off, her image still glowed on Jamie's blank videoscreen when a question— The Question—struck sharp as a slap across the face: *Why the hell is someone like Adele Sabellius slumming around with the likes of me?*

Oh yeah: She's decided I'm brave.

And how long could that illusion last?

Never mind about how the Brahms makes her think of me, all heavy like that, radiating strength. Truth is, I am whizzing through the air like the little stone she kicked that day out there on the trail. "Gotta try to land on my feet," Jamie muttered to the wind turbines more visible than ever since the oak trees had begun to shed their leaves.

The Physics I course was a start, she'd told herself over and over— the way to begin turning her future into something with sufficient mass, sufficient force that she could bear to live in it. A future that might, just might, include the possibility of Adele. She didn't dare look at it head-on, of course; the phantasms would figure out what she was up to, and they were also a force.

So she must skitter sideways, peeking up only rarely from the immediate moment.

And in *this* immediate moment, dammit, that meant sitting still in a huge, empty house with a clunky heating system and paying fucking attention as her shadowscreen explained how the motion of two bodies interacting via a gravitational force is mathematically equivalent to the motion of a single body with a reduced mass that is acted on by an external gravitational force—

Hey!

There it was again—that odd thunk. Every muscle in Jamie's body leapt into high alert as icy slivers zinged up her back.

What the fuck was that?

Crouching a little, yearning for a sidearm, Jamie crept down the back stairs quickly, quietly in stockinged feet. She needed only a second or two to check the family room, breakfast area, and kitchen at the back of the house. No one there. She slipped next into Lynn and Rebecca's room. It was empty, too. But through the doorway to Lynn's small adjoining office she saw a stranger half-turned away from her, bent over the desk with its array of videoscreens, one hand reaching for Lynn's comlink rack.

She hesitated when she saw him. Sleek, darkened eyewraps notwithstanding, his profile had a regular-guy look to it; from four meters away, he seemed almost innocuous in his faded hunter's camo hoodie and tired, baggy jeans. If he'd looked up, smiled at her, and said something about fixing a system screw-up, she might have believed him.

But any doubt about his right to be there vanished when he noticed her—and bolted fast and frictionless through the far doorway between the office and the study. She knew immediately, as much from the nanosecond when the surprise on this face hardened into hostility as from how he moved: Military.

She tore after him automatically, her agitated, distinctly civilian *what the fuck!* commandeered by an angry hyperdrive so thoroughly adrenalizing that all the world seemed to slide into slow-motion, giving Jamie the time she needed for analysis as she pursued him out the front door and westward across the wide pebbled driveway.

Didn't expect anyone to be here 'cuz he was working off obsolete intel. Which wasn't obsolete 'til a couple hours ago. So who? Who helped him? And where's his helper now? She arced her gaze about 270 degrees from the second garage on her right to the western edge of the south meadow on her left: Nobody else in sight. And especially nobody coming out of the security center at the far end of the second garage. *Shit. Either he's taken out whoever's in the security center or whoever's in the security center is his accomplice.*

Briefly, she wished she'd put on some kind of shoes. The driveway would be getting rougher soon, and her feet would pay for those larger, sharper stones. Even so, by the time they streaked past the security center door, she was gaining on him.

A little past your prime, huh? Forty-something ex-special ops merc probably. Infiltrated when? Last night? Yesterday? Awake all night, weren't you? And it was cold, too…

In Jamie's estimation, his best escape route lay to the northeast through a klick's worth of unpopulated woods, then onto Pipeline Road, where, if he had a brain, he'd left a vehicle near the westbound on-ramp to Route 128, maybe even a vehicle with a getaway driver.

But he kept running west, not north, which surprised her. *You're experienced, wouldn't sidle in here without solid situational awareness…So what's the plan, dude? And why're you sacrificing momentum to turn around and grab a visual on me?* Jamie's stomach gnarled as she saw his right arm swing toward his waist and stay there. Prepping. *Ooh. Shit. You got a weapon—and you're figuring out when you're gonna use it…*

She watched him flick his head rightward more than once as he ran. *Okay, so not 'til you hang your right into the woods. Not 'til you get to…where?*

Fifty meters ahead, she knew, the driveway split—main driveway to the left, west driveway to the right. And looming on his right, to the north where she believed he had to go—lay Great Hill itself, the highest terrain on the whole property, some fifteen meters higher in elevation than the driveway down which she chased him. *All that between you and your best exit. Gonna have to pump those tired legs, 'cuz you gotta go either over the hill or around it. And oh yeah, dude, you know it, too…*

Then the rest explained itself to her in a low, calm voice almost like her own: *If he could've, he would've left through the back of the house, shunted a little east first, then north, and avoided the hill altogether—a shorter distance by twenty percent anyway. So this is Plan B. He's got this scouted already, has his Plan B spot picked out, the place where he'll have the quickest, easiest climb over the hill, then northeast to Pipeline Road.*

And she knew precisely where that place was. Thirty meters in front of him, almost forty in front of her, the rugged, jack-hammered cut in the granite on the right side of the driveway relaxed for a few meters into a gentle natural fold in the land where a smooth, much lower-angle reverse curve eased the first crucial ten or twelve meters up the hill. Damn slippery in the rain—but the day was dry and sunny and autumn-crisp. *That's where he'll hang his right—there, before the driveway splits…*

He glanced back at her again, and his gait changed.

Shit. He's slowing down. Just slightly. 'Cuz why, 'cuz why? 'Cuz he wants me closer, no more than a couple meters behind him, so I'm a nice big target. 'Cuz he means to take me soon as we're both climbing, while I'm still a few steps lower...

That's when she decided. *Max it now and I can catch him before he gets off the driveway.*

She made her body do it. No words, no grunty exhortations. Already, she'd moved to the right edge of the driveway where her feet found more grass than stones and she made less noise as she stretched, stretched her stride. She sprinted as hard as on that last day in the Palawan, obeying the old rule: When you mess with Caprice, don't stay in one place any longer than you must.

Lungs and throat on fire, legs and feet shrieking, she caught the infiltrator at the base of the smooth granite fold and plowed her right shoulder into the back of his thighs, clapping her arms around his legs. She squeezed, hoping to hug his legs tightly enough to force them together. It worked and he slammed against the granite crunchingly hard, taking her with him while he yelled something she didn't understand.

Her plan, such as it was, centered on acquiring his weapon. But he had swiveled rightward as she tackled his left side, so his body didn't buffer her fall as much as she'd hoped, and she lost her grip too soon.

Fortunately, he couldn't grab his weapon, now trapped between his belly and the rock on which they struggled. He kicked wildly to liberate his legs and roll onto his back, catching her right shoulder once and twice narrowly missing her head—moves that gave her both a glimpse of a holstered .45 tucked at the left side of his waistband and belated enlightenment. Finally, she understood that her obstinate pursuit of this guy had been a really dumbass thing to do. One more kick and he'd have the leverage he needed to grip his weapon, turn it on her, and...

Shit. I'm gonna die right here. Shit. This is last thing I'm ever gonna think.

Desperate, she pumped her legs one final what-the-hell time, taking a long-shot chance at crawling up his half-turned body just enough to grab his weapon before he could. It didn't work. He had the inestimable advantage of raw male strength. But he chose—no, no, he *needed* in an almost squeamish, freaked out way—to shove her off of him, away from him. And this he did instead of pulling out the .45, pointing it at her, and snapping a round into her face from a centimeter away.

Maybe he can't stand bloody brain matter spattered all over him anymore. Requires a little distance now. Whatever his motivations,

Jamie saw opportunity and dove for it, managing to slip her left arm around his ankle as he lifted away from her. He splatted face-first again with a cry of pain and tumbled sideways off the granite back to the edge of the driveway, once more taking her with him.

His boot grazed the side of her head as they rolled, but she got her thighs clamped around his shins. From her position alongside his right leg, she lunged, planted her right hand on his .45, and tried to pull the weapon from its holster. *This is fucking suicide...shouldn't even be possible.* Then she realized why he hadn't clobbered her yet. Something was wrong with his left arm.

Beneath her, the ground vibrated almost imperceptibly. *It's a car,* the low, calm voice informed her; *if you could look up, you'd see it coming.* The infiltrator must have felt it, too, or seen it, because for an instant, his body froze. The car, they both understood, was a game-changer. *Goddamn. Maybe I* won't *die today.*

"*Yaybem* tee mahter!" the infiltrator growled as the car's horn starting honking.

Jamie had exploited his rattled focus to claw further up his body, cornering his right forearm under her shoulder as she tightened her grip on his weapon and yanked on it. But he recovered quickly, using only his trapped right arm to lift her entire torso in cadence with his grunted, "Yaybem tee *mahter!*"

He was plenty strong enough, she knew, to toss her aside. Which would've been okay if she could take his .45 with her. But the weapon didn't budge, and he was hoisting her higher, higher...

High enough to give her left arm new leverage; she managed to grab his genitals with her left hand and twist violently.

He screamed and his right arm collapsed underneath her while he pounded her back with his weakly fisted left hand, then landed a chop into the side of her neck at the moment she finally snatched the .45 from its holster. If his arm had been okay, if he'd had a better angle, his chop would have broken her neck; instead, it cost Jamie her grip on the weapon, which skidded to the far side of the driveway.

And then she made a bad mistake, worse than deciding to chase him in the first place: She went for the weapon.

It lay within her line of sight but not his, and it seemed so close. A mere pounce away. But getting it meant letting go of him, and the instant she did, his liberated right arm whacked her to the ground.

"Pizda!" he screamed, already on his feet, his booted foot swinging into her solar plexus. She saw it coming, tensed her abs the best she could, and thought, oh so fleetingly, that he looked like he was kicking a field goal, his right arm flung wide, his head down, all his power concentrated in the leg, the heavy boot zooming toward her belly. And then, as the car horn blared closer, she felt herself rise off the ground and thud spread-eagled flat on her back across the middle of the driveway. "Pizda!" he screamed again.

Okay, yeah, it did hurt. Jamie blinked at the blue sky visible through the pine and oak branches bowing over the driveway; her body seemed to insist on that. Then she demanded to look around for the infiltrator, who stood over her, less than a meter away, his head whipping back and forth as he searched for his weapon.

Gotta get him before he picks it up…

She expected her body to do what she saw as her best next move: Sweep her legs up and rightward into the strongest, quickest, two-footed kick she had, aimed at his nuts. But nothing happened. She heard the car horn sound louder, much louder, an enormous trumpet somewhere above her head. Slowly, slowly, the infiltrator's head swung pendulum-like toward the sounds, more sounds, the long, scraping crunches and squeals of tires suddenly braking on gravel and someone shouting, a woman shouting.

Now. Get him…now…

Jamie raised her legs, bending her knees as she brought them together. *Yes*, she thought, even though everything seemed much heavier than it should, *that's it—*

And then she couldn't breathe. At all.

Keep going…

But the infiltrator saw what she was trying to do. "Yaybem tee mahter!" he roared, curving a furious kick into her right side. "Uhdee ya pizda mahter-ayno!"

What? What'd he say? The light above her dimmed and tunneled; she could no longer see him. An inferno began to rage across her chest, and she coiled into the torment of it, frantic for air. With the last of her strength, her volition, Jamie tried to grab the infiltrator's leg, not only to keep him from retrieving his weapon but to know what he said. She had to know what he said.

"Pizda!" he bellowed from far, far away. And then something detonated in Jamie's right side and all the world flashed hot and bright before it condensed into blackness.

CHAPTER SIXTEEN

PIZDA

O h god, please, Jamie."
      Where and when. Why did it always have to be so damn hard to wake up knowing where and when?

Jamie was tempted to try opening her eyes like a regular person. Because she hadn't registered the usual signs—none of the swamp stench or the virulent humidity or the piercing, implacable trepidation...

On the other hand, if she stirred even her eyelids she'd probably throw up. Because pain engulfed her—siren-blast strangle-pummel-stab-burn pain that makes you flail and beg and promise Caprice anything, anything to get it to stop.

Yet she didn't move. All the air had been sucked out of her; she was empty. So the pain just heaved through her, and down there at the deflated middle of her, nausea burbled the contents of her stomach toward her throat.

This suggested danger, certainly, with malevolence a likely collaborator. Not to mention that voice...how could that voice even be possible?

A dream maybe. Or a feint, pretending to sound like—

Doesn't matter, 'cuz if this keeps up...

But it began to ebb. The siren-blast pitched lower as it Dopplered away from her, the inferno consuming her chest cooled some, and Jamie realized she could breathe. Sort of. Oh god, how she wanted to suck the air back into herself, a huge, deep breath, the hugest, deepest breath ever...

"Jamie?"

There she is again.

Eagerly, reflexively, Jamie blinked her eyes and they opened—to sunlight twinkling through branches of white pine and bare oak framed in luminous blue. *Oh.* Great Hill's driveway. Splattered flat on her back by that guy. The infiltrator. *Oh shit.* Where was he? *Coulda found his weapon, could be aiming it right now...*

She swung her eyes rightward to where she'd last seen him and tried to lift her head.

"No, no, Jamie, don't move yet."

Adele's face, smoother than buttersoft suede, floated in from her left. Adele's eyes, obsidian aflame, came closer, closer. Adele's voice repeated her name. She heard Adele's fear and anger in the sound of her name.

What. The fuck. Hey, she wanted to say, you're supposed to be a hundred klicks out to sea. She wanted to ask why how when, so she started to pull in the hugest, deepest breath ever—

But she wanted too much; her ability to sort of breathe abandoned her. She stared at Adele, reached for Adele. She dug her heels into the ground, convinced that if she could shift onto her side then the air would come back. But only the pain came back...

"Shh now," Adele soothed, her palm warm on Jamie's cheek. "Stay still and take small, shallow breaths."

Stay still? Jamie felt her eyes widen at the prospect. *How can I fucking stay still? I can't breathe!*

"Shh. Look at me," Adele commanded, her gaze worried and gentle and firm. "Stay still."

Once upon a time, stillness had been Jamie's specialty, her expertise. Transfixed by Adele's eyes, she tried to remember. You get into your zone, a Marine Corps instructor told her long ago, and the rest is easy.

Her zone. Always, Jamie remembered, getting into her zone started with breathing. Slow breathing. Calm, easy breathing...*Doesn't mean I have to actually take the shot, or even use a weapon. 'Cuz, hell, I can focus, aim, follow through on whatever I want...*

Adele's diligent eyes waited for her. *Focus on whatever I want...*

More than anything, Jamie wanted to smile at Adele. Slowly, her nostrils filled with the boundless comfort of Adele's honey scent, and she focused, aimed...smiled.

Adele smiled back relief, and tears conflagrated in her eyes. "We have to stop meeting like this," she said.

❖

It took way too long to shake off the distractions of the pain, of Adele's hypnotic eyes, too long to grasp how Lynn and ET in one car, Adele and Lily and the baby in the other, coming one behind the other up the west driveway, witnessed her foolish, entirely unsat fight with the infiltrator.

Jamie refused to merely lie there while the driveway's stones poked into her back, while the infiltrator remained so close—yet only her head had salvaged any mobility. So she could do nothing more than watch…while ET conducted a scrupulous three-sixty sweep of their surroundings from behind a nine-mil, all the while barking commands into a wristcom…while Lynn ignored ET's plea to stay in the vehicle and ran instead toward her and Adele…while Lily scrambled several meters from the first car to grab the infiltrator's .45, then dashed back to the crying baby.

Sitting ducks, every one of them. And they had no clue what was going on and she couldn't just blurt it because she couldn't get a decent breath of air in her lungs and what the hell does she say first? She needed to say it all first…

Get back in the cars, it's not safe!

Adele, what're you doing here?

Lynn, I caught that SOB messing at your desk!

ET, something's fucked in the security center!

Omigod, omigod, what he said! It's the same! Same as what The Bastard said! Uh dee yapizz dahmah terayno. Uhdee ya pizda mahter-ayno.

It jumbled out of her, finally, on a succession of thin wheezes, her ragged fragments punctuated by ET's shouts to take cover in the AV and keep the doors and windows locked.

"It's armored," Lynn said to Adele.

Adele nodded. "Armored vehicle. Got it."

A heartbeat later, they had Jamie upright between them, interrupting her attempt to speak the thoughts careening wildly in her head…"Heard it, part of it, somewhere else, too…" *Just once, somewhere in the dark. But where who when what the* fuck *is going on?*

Neither her words nor her feet could keep pace as Adele and Lynn half-carried, half-dragged her to the second car and lowered her groaning onto the back seat. On the other side of the car, Lily clambered in with Evvie.

"You'll drive," Lynn told Adele before darting around the car and into the front passenger seat. "Everyone okay?" she asked as the last car door slammed; already, she'd clicked up ET on her pocketcom. "Channel me in," she told ET, her eyes lingering on Jamie.

Then Fitzgerald showed up, loping toward them from the direction of the house and the security center, his eyes too often darting northward as he approached too slowly—burdened, Jamie suspected, by way too much explaining to do.

"Ask him…where…was he?" Jamie said as he looked at the car, then averted his eyes.

"Good question," Lynn said. "We'll know soon."

But Lynn switched her pocketcom's sound to a headpiece she tweaked into her ear. Jamie could only watch ET buttonhole Fitzgerald, talking low and fast, watch how he seemed relieved to keep his gaze away from the car while he endured ET's in-his-face interrogation.

As two other security people arrived, Lynn listened mostly, said okay a couple times, then relayed ET's confidence that any imminent danger from the infiltrator had passed. "But ET wants the house and the grounds thoroughly inspected before we go in, and I concur," Lynn explained. "They'll need some time, so we'll wait at ET's place—and she wants us to go in through the garage. Pilar's already got a team there." Lynn swiveled to look at Lily. "And Dana's en route."

Jamie didn't want to leave, even though her chest hurt, even though they were headed only to the end of the west driveway, where ET's house was. Some kind of truth—*the* truth—held fast to this spot, and if she left now she might lose its thread forever. *Focus, dammit, focus.*

"You heard what he said?" Jamie beseeched them. "'Uhdee ya pizda mahter-ayno'?"

"Yes." From the driver's seat, Adele replied a little shakily, her eyes finding Jamie's in the rearview mirror while she started the car's engine. "He was swearing at you."

Jamie gaped. "You understood him?"

"More or less. It's a pretty common Croatian epithet."

"Croatian?"

"Mmm. 'Odi u pizda materinu.' Means 'go to your mother's cunt.'" Adele turned around to glance sheepishly at Evvie at last happily working a bottle, then at Lily. "Oops. Bad word. She's not going to remember that, is she?"

Lily's attempt at a smile appeared a little thin. "I think bad words are the least of our worries."

"The Bastard is Croatian," Jamie whispered, unable to draw enough breath to speak louder. Lynn threw her a look but said nothing.

"Or maybe Serbian," said Adele, calmer now as she supervised the dashboard while the car backed down the driveway. "The two languages are very similar. This guy just now, though, if I had to guess, I'd say he was probably Croatian."

"Why?" asked Lynn.

"Something else he hollered," Adele said.

"'Yaybem?'" Jamie tried.

"Yeah. 'Jebem ti mater,' which means 'fuck your mother.' My understanding is that a Serb would be likelier to go for 'serem ti se mater.' 'I shit on your mother.'"

"They're connected," Jamie muttered, her nausea returning. "The Bastard and this guy who broke in—"

"Could be coincidence," said Adele, her eyes catching Jamie's in the rearview mirror. "There are Croatians all over, and they certainly swear. It's considered an art form." She angled the car into a modest turnout alongside the driveway, starting the back-and-forth of reversing the car's direction. "Or I could be entirely wrong, Jamie. Maybe he isn't even Croatian."

Jamie stared back up the driveway, where several security people now scuttled about. "Wait." *That's not all…there's more…c'mon* think, *dammit*. "He said something else, too."

"Pizda," Lily replied. "Screamed it twice right after you got this pistol away from him." She tilted her head toward the infiltrator's .45 now lying at her feet. "And when he kicked you that last time."

In the front seats, Jamie noticed, Lynn and Adele winced; for an inflated second, nobody said anything. And then Adele and Lynn spoke nearly simultaneously.

"Pizda," repeated Adele, her voice darkening while she ratcheted up the car's speed. "An especially derogatory version of 'cunt.' Gives 'odi u pizda materinu' its punch."

"Christ," said Lynn, turning around, "I forgot about the gun. You made sure the safety's on, right?"

But Jamie didn't hear Lily's reply. She heard another voice altogether, from another time when everything hurt like hell. "Tell him his pizda skedaddled…"

Stacy.

For a moment, just a moment, Jamie found herself back there—cowering naked in the dark beneath the sharp, unfriendly branches of an indifferent row of shrubs, her backside on fire, listening to Stacy taking orders from—who? An accomplice? A boss?

Stacy's angry, frustrated voice echoed…*I did exactly what you wanted…stretched it as far as it'll go without committing a fucking felony…tell him his pizda skedaddled…*

For days after she'd made it back to Great Hill, Jamie heard those words and realized she'd fallen for a quintessential scam, and, wallowing in impotence and gloom, *she'd* done exactly what *Stacy* wanted.

Because, oh yeah, Stacy was shit accomplished at exactly. Exactly the right squint, exactly the right words spoken with exactly the right tone, exactly the right edginess. Everything Jamie could see, hear, smell, feel about Stacy had attested to the gruff, guarded empathy of a fellow traveler, one experienced at treading adeptly on darker paths. And it was all a lie. Stacy had been bird dogging, professionally and with a collaborator—bird dogging for a customer who craved a certain kind of sexual sacrifice, and Jamie had exactly matched the guy's order.

For a pizda.

"Oh god," Jamie muttered, closing her eyes. *I thought it was random...*

❖

"C'mon," said Adele, half-holding Jamie up while Lynn closed the door behind them. "Your blood pressure's tanked. Let's get you—ah, there."

Adele angled her onto ET's sofa and helped her ease into the cushions, first her upper body, then her head—and then, with wonderfully understated delicacy, Adele sat beside her, an unexpected gift.

In any moment but this one, Jamie would be bouncing with questions for Adele, figuring out the earliest opportunity to talk alone with Adele. But in this supremely ugly moment, she thought only about Stacy.

Because nothing about Stacy—not when she showed up, not what she said or how she said it, not her casual take-it-or-leave-it invitation—nothing, nothing, nothing was the least fucking bit random. And now—

Now Jamie faced having to talk about it again. And Adele would hear every word.

"How're you feeling?" Adele asked.

Jamie hadn't realized she'd closed her eyes; she opened them to Adele and Lynn studying her, their faces crunched into nearly identical frowns. Her chest ached and she had yet to pull in a decent breath, but the nausea had passed and she picked up a trace of Adele's scent. "Better."

"You're awfully pale," said Lynn, who held a pocketcom in one hand and couple of cold packs in the other. "I'm not sure where we should put these first."

A woman's voice buzzed from Lynn's pocketcom. *Uh-oh. Rebecca.*

"I'm fine," Jamie said quickly, attempting to head them off.

Too late. Abetted by Rebecca, they now discussed internal bleeding and Lynn said something about an ambulance to drag her off to the hospital.

"I'm fine," Jamie repeated. Goddamn, she was going to have to try to talk them out of this, but talking required breath, and breathing took such effort. "Really," she insisted while Lynn stood a meter away pointing the pocketcom lens at her so Rebecca could see her. "I'm fine."

"Oh god, give me a break," Rebecca's voice crackled through Lynn's pocketcom. "Lynnie, I want her here ay-sap."

"No. I'm fine." Jamie dropped her eyes, but they snuck rightward to stare at Adele's knees next to hers. The warmth of Adele's gaze on her cheek, her neck oozed down, down into a hungry, humid swirl deep in her gut. *Just wanna stay here a little while, right here, like this.*

Then Adele leaned into Jamie's view. "I want to touch you," she said very softly, almost in a whisper. "But I don't dare. First you get drop-kicked in the celiac plexus—"

"You saw that?" Jamie glanced into eyes now bottomless and velvet soft.

"From a distance." Adele leaned just a little closer, her voice still low. "And then he tries to chop your head off—"

"Didn't want him to shoot me. Or anyone el—"

"I know, Jamie. I was driving the first car. Had an unobstructed view of the whole thing. Including the liver shots you took after the pistol went flying. I was stepping out of the car by then and, I swear—that second time he kicked you? I heard a rib crack."

So Adele noticed. Jamie was pretty sure at least one, maybe two ribs on her right side had indeed cracked. But, hell, all Rebecca would do was order assorted scans to reveal what she already knew, then get in her face about resting and taking painkillers. "I *am* okay," she said.

"Well," responded Lynn, who now stood over her. "We're not. So humor us, Jamie. Please."

Jamie looked up into Lynn's anxious eyes. No matter how brief, she loved those moments when the energy of Lynn's entire, undivided attention came at her, swept through her. She loved the opportunity to say yes to Lynn.

But, Jamie comprehended with shrill, new clarity, she hated, hated, *hated* hospitals.

"Will it help if I come with you?" Adele asked quietly.

CHAPTER SEVENTEEN
PLEASE DON'T GO

W hy is she here?
Not that Jamie objected. Hell no.
Adele had stuck with her through tedious hours of hospital shit, getting her to drink water, chatting up the techs during test after test to glean the results then flash a quick thumbs-up signaling that yet another of Rebecca's well-okay-you-can-go-back-to-Great-Hill-tonight criteria had been met.

Adele had shushed her rasping, winded attempts to explain how That Word threaded through everything, from the infiltrator to Stacy to The Bastard—and no way can so much pizda pizda pizda be coincidence, no fucking way...

There'll be plenty of time to talk after all this, at the house, Adele had assured her over and over. And please, Adele said later, take this pill, please, "Because you need a painkiller so you can breathe properly. Otherwise, you'll end up with pneumonia, and then god knows when you'll be able to finish a sentence."

Just what Rebecca would say, only Adele actually managed to make popping a mind-altering narcotic sound like a good idea. Even though Jamie knew from miserable experience how rapaciously the phantasms feasted on pharma, how all reason and coherence would pervert into a tangled, disorienting buzz of fallacy and dread. Maybe the fear of it quivered there for a second on her face; what else accounted for the sudden soft concern in Adele's eyes, the way Adele took her hand and said, "I'll stay right here with you, don't worry"?

Pretty soon, Jamie didn't worry. The phantasms retreated with a mere glance at Adele, and, of course, Jamie's glances lingered. By the time the two FBI guys showed up with their questions about what happened, all her joints seemed slightly disarticulated as some jiggly invisible force tugged on a gazillion tiny, invisible strings to lift her; she hovered a centimeter or two above the gurney breathlessly babbling everything she could think of about the break-in. Afterward, she recalled only the way Adele's face swung between polite smile, wide-eyed worry, and a slitty-eyed, angular frown. Yet by the time Lynn and Adele helped her don sweatpants and zippered hoodie for the ride home, Adele's face had relaxed again. And now, back at Great Hill, Adele sat next to her on one of the family room sofas, warmly asking about her appetite while the rest of the clan assembled odds and ends from pantry and refrigerators into a late evening potluck that spread quickly across the breakfast table.

"Why are you—" Jamie clamped her mouth shut; her mouth could not be trusted yet. The pharma's more pronounced effects were in blessed retreat, but whatever wandered across her brain continued to roll warped and shambled right off her tongue unless she tackled it and held it down.

"Here? Me?" Adele responded casually after a second's pause in which a year of Jamie's life crawled...slowly...by...while she waited, waited, waited for Adele to say the rest. An infinite heartbeat later, Adele winked. "Just thought I'd come around for a couple days to play that piano."

"Oh." Jamie's stomach plunged. "Ri—" Suddenly, Adele leaned in close, closer, and kissed her full on her lips, a resolute kiss as fervent as it was gentle.

Beyond words, beyond thought, her pulse pounding out raw and ravenous from the core of her indigence, Jamie syncopated with Adele's incandescent rhythm and surrendered everything.

❖

"What's so funn—" From the far end of the kitchen, Springer's voice jounced upward with curiosity and mild protest at being left out of something—until Lynn's murmurs cut her off.

"Where's the honey mustard?" asked Lily too loudly while the murmurs blossomed into a classic Great Hill greeting of Springer that filled the kitchen and spilled across the breakfast area into the family room.

"I think that's our cue," Adele mumbled into Jamie's mouth.

"Nnnnn..." Jamie opened her eyes as Adele's lips withdrew. "Have to?"

Adele's nose caressed Jamie's cheek. "Mmm hmm...ready or not."

"Not."

Lifting herself off the sofa, Adele traced a lone finger softly along Jamie's jaw. "Later?" she whispered.

Jamie tried not to squirm. "Oh yeah."

"Aah, I get it." Springer now stood grinning at Jamie from the far side of the breakfast area. "Kinda makes up for a really crappy afternoon, huh?" she said, then swung back toward Lynn. "You didn't tell me."

But Lynn had responded to a comlink call. "Okay," she told her pocketcom with obvious reluctance, her gaze swerving from Jamie to Rebecca and back again. "FBI wants a few more minutes with you," she said to Jamie. "ET's bringing them up now."

"Got a question or two myself," Jamie said. She clamped her right arm against her side to make her lift-off from the sofa a bit less uncomfortable, but pain girdled her chest anyway, eliciting minor profanity while she blundered determinedly upward—and right into a slow-motion overbalance.

"Stay," Adele commanded, hastily retracing her steps in time to keep Jamie from pitching forward like a felled tree. "The FBI can come to you."

And the FBI did. Two government-issue agents followed close behind a drained, ashen ET. Jamie thought maybe she recognized one of them from the hospital. She could tell they'd have preferred to talk to her alone, but Senator Hillinger was having none of it.

"Oh please, just call me Lynn…How about some coffee, it's decaf at this hour, I'm afraid, or perhaps you'd like some tea or lemonade, and we're also having sandwiches, so join us, there's plenty…You don't mind, do you, if I record this conversation. I want to make sure no detail is lost, and if it's all right with Jamie—Lieutenant Gwynmorgan—now that she's feeling better, we'd *all* like to hear about the afternoon's events…Yes, Jamie?…Oh, excellent, then let's get settled with something to eat and proceed, shall we?"

They didn't have a chance, not even the older one Jamie didn't recognize—a big shot Assistant Special Agent in Charge, sent to assuage a senator. He got as far as, "Well, ma'am, we'd rather…" before he noticed Dana and Lily hunkering with Evvie into the near end of the larger family room sofa while Mary and Edgar claimed the far end. ET and Springer carried in a couple of breakfast table chairs and placed them a few feet from the smaller sofa where Jamie and Adele sat, then plunked themselves into two cushy leather swivel chairs across the room. And while Lynn leaned against the sofa arm next to Jamie, Rebecca prowled behind the agents.

Taking advantage of Lynn's momentum, Jamie barraged them with questions: Did the security cams grab a decent image of the infiltrator? Why didn't Fitzgerald come out of the security center in time to help catch him? Any streetcams along Pipeline Road? Because if there's one within a hundred meters of the westbound on-ramp to

Route 128, odds are it'll show his exfil to a waiting ride. And you guys got his weapon, right? That should tell you something, that and his Croatian swear words…

They waited her out, politely repeating the same prevarication about pursuing several lines of inquiry. Her answers to their questions soon had them suppressing yawns; her answers must've been the same as what she'd said during the hospital interview she could recall only in haphazard scraps. But what about pizda? They didn't seem to give a shit about pizda…

She'd have to do it again, talk about the way pizda connected the infiltrator to The Bastard and to Stacy—and make them listen this time, understand this time that pizda meant something, dammit.

The two agents lowered their heads with the effort of sustaining their patience as she stuttered from one euphemism to another until the cringe that had been building finally overwhelmed her and she shut up, staring at the floor, girding for their follow-up questions. But they asked nothing. Instead, the Assistant Special Agent in Charge showed her a composite facial image of the infiltrator.

Defeated, Jamie stared at the image. Maybe a little paler, but yes, it was him. Odd that she didn't remember anything at all about describing his face. "How'd you put this together?" she asked.

The Assistant Special Agent in Charge nodded toward Adele. "Ms. Sabellius helped us."

Jamie tried to smile at Adele. "Ms. Sabellius did a damn good job." The agents left a minute later without finishing their sandwiches.

"Jamie, you haven't eaten anything, either," said Adele.

"Not hungry," Jamie mumbled. The scorch in her chest had broiled into her throat and liquefied; tears threatened now, demanding escape. *Shit.* She closed her eyes. *Shit shit* shit.

"Try anyway, okay?" Adele's voice, hoarse and tired.

Eyes still closed, Jamie murmured assent. Orneriness would not help her now. When she opened her eyes, Rebecca stood in front of her, hand extended palm up to display a small pill.

"After you get something in your stomach," Rebecca said. "Then to sleep with ye."

"I'm pleased to say we found the makings for a cheesesteak sub," said Mary, placing a tray on Jamie's lap. "Although I don't know if it's still considered a sub when it's on one of Kizzy's mini baguettes."

Dana showed up a second later with a glass of lemonade; now mother, daughter, and grandmother stood aside each other gazing down at her, waiting. Worrying. Behind them, Lynn pulled away from a whispered confab with Springer and ET to slip a hand around Rebecca's waist, and Lily came over with the baby to nuzzle Dana's shoulder. Jamie wondered why she hadn't understood sooner: All of them at Great Hill had been worrying about her the whole time, for three long months.

"Thank you," she said to them and to Adele, who sat beside her still. "For taking care of me."

She wanted to say more, a lot more; the feeling of it heated her eyes, pressed against her temples and the bridge of her nose, tightened her throat. As inadequate words jumbled into nonsense before she could say them, she bowed her head and blinked at the food Mary had made and brought to her—until Adele's hand glided onto her forearm and gave it a tiny squeeze. Jamie nodded, then picked up the cheesesteak-filled mini baguette and bit into it.

❖

She didn't remember falling asleep. She didn't even remember getting up from the sofa. Or climbing the stairs to her room. Or undressing.

Jamie didn't wake up, either; she sloshed gradually onto a shore of awareness like a castaway, the right side of her chest dully throbbing in time with her heartbeat while the dream on which she'd been floating disintegrated into countless red and black shards.

Around her, the dream throbbed, too, as it continued to fracture like tempered glass into smaller and smaller fragments: A boot camp drill instructor's guttural insult...On her belly, crawling, her rifle slung across her back...Stacy's snarl—"Running out of nerve, are we, Lieutenant Pizda?"...A power drill revving louder, coming closer... The Bastard's galling, grating snigger...Shoo Juh's low reminder in her ear—"I own you, hong mao"...

Hong mao, hong mao cannonaded Jamie's pulse in her ears. Hong mao, hong mao echoed her unhappy ribs, until at last she realized what she heard was only her own heartbeat. She blinked open her eyes and beheld the ceiling of her room at Great Hill streaked in morning light.

Goddamn. Nightmare had snaked into memory: Stacy *did* call her lieutenant that night. How in hell would Stacy know her rank—unless Stacy already knew who she was?

She'd dreamed about the power drill again, too, closer than ever. Goddamn, it had been too real...

Stop that. It's over.

Over.

Carefully, gingerly, reminding herself to breathe with her diaphragm, Jamie inhaled, exhaled. She commanded her eyes to swing left, down, right. Yep, all alone.

And yet...

Had she done this? Propped herself up with a platoon of pillows, neatly aligned herself with the edge of the mattress rather than sprawling diagonally across it as usual? Slept buck naked between the sheets in Lynn's house for the first time in her three months there?

And next to her, the other half of the bed was—wrong. Rumpled wrong—

"Good morning."

Jamie saw her legs first. Adele's legs, adorned in blue-striped pajama bottoms. A soft Callithump T-shirt snugged her Venus de Milo breasts, and she smiled—oh god, that smile. With relaxed, gravity-defying grace, she carried a tray on which she'd managed to arrange... *Let's see...orange juice...coffee...two bowls of something...mmm, that's yogurt...couple of bananas...toast...and I smell bacon...*

"I hope you're hungry," Adele said, setting the tray on the room's small desk.

"I am." Jamie glanced at the bathroom door. "And I gotta—" She'd started to move her legs over the edge of the mattress—until she remembered about being nude. And that the bedcovers had slipped to her waist. She halted, unaccustomed to the flush of physical self-consciousness sweeping her—and embarrassed at being embarrassed. Because, hey, she was a marine, she'd long ago learned to shower in bunches, she'd spent months naked in a cell; hell, The Bastard probably never once saw her clothed, so why should she get all squiggly now about Adele?

And yet...

"Let me give you a hand." Adele grinned. "And maybe a robe?"

"I, uh—" Jamie forced herself not to pull the covers over her breasts. "I guess I'm at your mercy."

"Are you?" Adele's eyes glinted as she turned away. Yet not to search for Jamie's robe, which had mysteriously migrated from the closet to the desk chair. Adele picked it up and turned back to Jamie, her eyes sparking like firecrackers as she approached. And then her breath heated Jamie's neck and her lips grazed Jamie's lips, prelude to the ripe, protracted kiss that followed.

But they were not alone. Hong mao, pulsed Jamie's clit, and horror-dread-misery clenched her belly. In an instant, her time with Adele free from Shoo Juh's power over her had ended. No liberation after all, merely a few days' respite. She struggled not to fidget as Shoo Juh whispered again, "I own you, hong mao."

"Mmm, sorry," Adele said upon pulling slowly away. "It's just that you're so—tempting."

Damn. She saw it. Jamie tried to return Adele's smile. "Gotta pee."

A moment later, Adele had Jamie sitting upright on the bed, feet on the floor, the robe slipped smoothly on, right arm first, then left. "Ready?" she asked, wrapping her hand around Jamie's left forearm.

"Yeah."

And then Jamie was on her feet, shuffling stiffly to the bathroom.

"You're okay?" Adele asked. "To, uh..."

Forcing a smile, Jamie avoided meeting Adele's gaze. "I can handle it."

As she slid the bathroom door out of its pocket in the wall, she heard Adele click up the flute and harp music that had staved off Shoo Juh only days earlier. Hand on the door, Jamie waited for the music to help her again. But no, not this time. She left a three-inch gap anyway, instead of shutting the door entirely—to aid the illusion that all was well.

But Jamie couldn't stop staring at the person in the mirror, who, in her opinion, looked like shit. *Tell me one more time...*Why would Adele be interested in kissing someone who looked like shit? A high school dropout whose past was mired in shit, whose future guaranteed years and years of slogging through plenty more shit.

And if Adele kept kissing her like that...

Then what?

Then she'd have to play the odds—a kind of Russian roulette where losing meant her rocketing arousal would pull a one-eighty on her and explode into full-blown flashback. And she already knew: Her respite was over, she had no hope of winning—so it would be Shoo Juh touching her, not Adele...

Doomed.

Jamie squinched at her reflection as she turned on the tap, placed her hands into a stream of hot water, and left them there. *Correction: Still doomed. Forever fucking doomed. Only way I'll probably ever come again is if I'm getting the shit beat out of me.*

A stick of bacon held by two fingers undulated through the doorway's three-inch gap. "If you stay in there much longer," Adele singsonged from the other side, "I'm gonna end up eating *all* of this."

Jamie slid the bathroom door back into its pocket to face her.

"What's wrong?" Adele asked immediately, her face and voice abruptly darkening.

"I can't do this."

"Pardon me?"

"I'm—" Jamie shook her head. "I'm too fucked up for—for—"

"For what?"

"For you to play around with." Jamie eyed the closet door, access to which Adele inadvertently blocked; if she could reach her clothes, she could put something on and get out of the room, out of the house, out of her skin, out of her head—

"Play around with," Adele repeated. A crease formed above her nose and she planted her feet, arms akimbo, while she glared up at Jamie with eyes black and dangerous. "You mean diddle you, then blow you off."

Jamie opened her mouth to speak, but didn't, because yes, that was exactly what she meant. She lowered her head, watching Adele's legs, contemplating which way would best get her past them and to the closet.

"So this is why you decided you're at my mercy," Adele pressed. "And why that freaks you out."

"Oh." Jamie glanced at her, and then couldn't look away. "So it—"

"Showed?" Adele's head moved down, up, down; her eyes bored into Jamie's. "Yes. It did."

Jamie repelled an inclination to duck. "Never been known for my subtlety."

"But you're damned accomplished at stalling. Or maybe I should say evading."

No, Jamie thought, this is still survival; evasion, resistance, and escape come later. But she said only, "Sorry."

"Sorry for what exactly?" Adele didn't budge—or hide her anger. "Oh, yeah—for being too fucked up, right? Well, before you try any more of your evasion techniques, I want to know what the hell you're really talking about."

"I'm just not ready—"

"I do not diddle, Jamie."

"But you don't mind slumming, huh?"

For a moment, Adele could only stare; then her eyes swept Jamie's face, searching for explanation. "What are you doing?" she asked, her voice low and near to breaking.

Jamie had to look away; she was betraying that unspoken bond which had formed and already strengthened between them, the implicit promise to allow one's inside underside to be seen, safe in the knowledge that the other would not flinch.

And yet...

She hadn't told Adele about Awa or Shoo Juh, or even the non-euphemized story of Stacy. And there had to be limits, right? Limits to understanding and tolerance. To acceptance. So she made her move, forward through the bathroom doorway to edge Adele back a couple of feet, then she'd shift rightward toward the closet door and clothes and no, not escape, dammit—this was survival. "Excuse m—"

But Adele refused to move. They stood toe to toe, chest to chest, Adele's chin lifting defiantly. Yet her eyes...Jamie had to look away from her eyes. "For god's sake, Jamie—"

Jamie stepped right. Adele stepped left to block her way.

"Excuse me," Jamie said again, louder this time as she dragged her gaze back to meet Adele's.

Adele held her ground, her voice determinedly steady. "What are you so afraid of?" She reached up to place her hands on Jamie's arms but stopped short of contact; her hands hovered an inch or two away as her eyes probed Jamie's. "My god," she panted, suddenly breathless with new understanding. "You're afraid of *me?*" Adele retreated backward, the impeccable sculpture of her face slumped into disappointment and sorrow. "Jamie, why? What did I do?"

The path to the closet was open, unimpeded, its door but three meters away. Four steps max. Quickly, Jamie took one step, another. Adele didn't stir, except for her watching eyes, now liquid and aching.

But each step fostered its own eternity, and after the second one Jamie could not continue, even though she'd ripped her gaze from Adele's face, Adele's pain, to concentrate on the closet doorknob. "You didn't do anything," she managed to say. "It's not you. It's me. I—I can't do what regular people do." The effort of saying it stole her breath; when she tried to inhale, her ribs rebelled and she teetered into dizziness. "No, I'm okay," she wheezed when Adele moved toward her to help, "and I'm sorry...I'm...so...sorry..."

Adele steadied her before she toppled backward, then steered her toward the bed. "Uh-uh," she objected. "Going for a walk."

"Uh-uh yourself," Adele replied. "Bed rest for you today. Doctor's orders."

Jamie bowed her head; she was out of fight. Soon she'd returned to bed, assisted by Adele, who inserted a stick of bacon in her mouth to plug her stream of apologies.

Twenty minutes and two slowly consumed bowls of granola later, during which they talked little and only about what they were eating, Jamie eased against the bed's pillows while Adele leaned back in the desk chair where she'd been sitting. "I'm not slumming," she said quietly.

"Then why?" asked Jamie.

"Why you?"

Jamie nodded.

"I like you," said Adele. "A whole lot. Which, uh, doesn't happen to me very often."

"You could have anybody—"

"Tried that, actually. But I'm lousy at shallow diving." Adele's head dipped almost shyly, and her small laugh struck Jamie as self-deprecating, relief and fatalism in counterpoint. "Turns out I'm also way too picky. Just anybody won't do. Hell, it takes just anybody about three days to wish I'd never been born."

"But—"

"If I'm…" Adele paused. Maybe this wasn't as easy as she made it look. "If I've misread how you feel and I'm out here all by myself, tell me now. Please."

Jamie shook her head. "I just don't understand why—"

"Do you want me to leave, Jamie?"

"No."

"Do you want to try? With me?"

To Jamie, it seemed that years went by before she could speak. Years and thousands of words, exclamations of doubt, of disbelief, of fear. Of course, always fear.

Adele saw it all—all those years and words condensed into an instant—yet she never wavered, never flinched before the terrible risk of being left out there alone. She simply sat in the desk chair, graceful in her strength—oh so lightly, unselfconsciously graceful while she watched Jamie, waiting.

"I think I've been in love with you since the moment you found me that morning beneath the wind turbines," Jamie said. She trembled now at a very high frequency.

An evanescent tremor seemed to ripple through Adele, too. "So that's a yes, then."

"Yes." Jamie exhaled. *If this is a dream, I want to stay right here, right now, just like this, and never wake up.* "It's a yes."

"Okay." Adele moved from the desk chair to lie on her side across the foot of the bed facing Jamie, head propped up on a hand. "So what's going on?"

And now we go Gwynmorgan diving? Just like that? "There's a lot I haven't talked about," Jamie murmured. "And if I tell you—"

"You think I'll run screaming away."

"Pretty much."

"So what, exactly, have you got to lose?"

"Are you kidding?" Jamie protested. "I have everything to lose."

"But if you don't talk to me—don't tell me what's messing you up—then sooner or later either you'll push me away or I'll stomp off in a pissy huff. Which suggests to me that if you don't talk you lose everything anyway. *We* lose everything anyway."

"We could just not, uh…"

One of Adele's eyebrows arched while she waited for Jamie to finish. And waited. "Not?" she said finally. "Mmm, not deal with it? Not ever talk about anything that matters? Not care what happens when I..." She reached out to run a finger along Jamie's bare foot, tracing a tingling loop from big toe to ankle and back again—and inducing a needy, undeniably noticeable quiver in Jamie's pelvis. "How will that work, do you think?"

"Uh...not too well, I guess."

Slowly, Adele withdrew her hand. "What's a guh shyah?"

Jamie gawked. "Where did you—" Nope, no good, she'd have to gulp a breath. "Hear that?"

"You said it in your sleep."

"In my—you were—"

"Here. Yes. All night." Adele's face tensed almost imperceptibly. "You asked me to."

Oh.

Right.

Jamie blinked at the memory suddenly engulfing her like a rogue wave risen unanticipated out of a calm morning sea. Please don't go...

"Do I snore?"

"Jamie." Adele poked the bottom of her foot. "What does it mean?"

*Breathe first. Slow, careful, from the diaphragm...*In, two three four...out, two three four... "It's a title." Jamie forced out the words. "An honorific. Literally, 'beneath your pavilion'—because you're so important and I'm shit on your shoes." *Breathe. Breathe.* "I learned it in Saint Eh Mo's, the place where I was—" *Breathe...*

"A prisoner of war," Adele said softly.

Jamie lifted, then lowered her head. "I try not to think about it."

"I'm really sorry, I didn't mean to—"

"No, don't apologize. Especially since I, uh, brought it up, so to speak. It was—" Jamie girded. "Guh shyah was something I was made to say by my—by the person who interrogated me. She called me hong mao—'red fur'—to indicate that I was an animal, less than human."

"She," Adele repeated in a hush, eyes wide.

"Never knew her name. I called her Shoo Juh. Not to her face, of course. Had to call her g-guh—ah, sorry, sometimes it's hard to say it without all kinda crap getting stirred up." Jamie inhaled as deeply as her ribs permitted. "Guh shyah," she declared, keeping her eyes on Adele to anchor herself. "Had to say guh shyah, the more groveling, the better. I, um, didn't say it as much as Shoo Juh wanted."

"Why?"

Crooking her head, Jamie half-smiled at Adele. "I was stalling. Any time Shoo Juh spent hassling me about my disrespect—well, it kept her from asking questions about my unit, or our missions, or intel. Had to make it through thirty-nine days before I, uh…"

"Said anything."

"Yeah, well, you should be told, since you believe I'm so wicked brave: I didn't pull it off."

Adele's eyes had ceased normal blinking. "What happened?"

"I wilted. The guh shyah shit was just a mindfuck. An excuse for shing—punishment, which was always separate. Once Shoo Juh said it—" Jamie had to halt again. *Breathe…*

"What did she say?"

"Pretty much the same thing every time. 'You are punished because you do not respect your superiors, hong mao.' Which meant there'd be no stopping it. Didn't matter if you screamed guh shyah a thousand times or begged to tell her every secret you'd ever heard in your life. Once shing started, it went on 'til…'til…" Jamie let her head slip back onto the pillows. She didn't dare close her eyes. No doubt Shoo Juh waited there, behind her eyelids, so she stared at the ceiling.

Adele's hand stroked her calf. "It's okay, we don't have to—"

"I do have to." Jamie turned to look at Adele. "Unless you're leaving right now, I need to say it and you need to hear it."

"I'm not leaving unless you kick me out." Adele seemed to hold her breath for several seconds. "So tell me—shing went on until?"

"Until I came."

"As in—"

"Yes." Jamie cleared her throat. "Shoo Juh would—" Jamie cleared her throat again. "Would ease up just enough to remind me what relief felt like. Then *zap!* and she'd take the relief away. Back and forth until I'd lose it, spill into—into—"

"You'd come."

"Yeah. Always got a good laugh. Sometimes that would be the end of it and she'd leave me alone for a little while. But other times she'd get pissed off, like she didn't really want to win at all, and she'd ramp it up, just keep on going…"

"'Til you passed out."

"A lot of it blurred, so I can't say when exactly I started babbling. I know I made twenty-three days—barely. But the next sixteen? I had no sense of time because of where I was, but I wilted way before that. I only realized it when she started asking me questions about things I must've told her. Stuff I'd made up to misdirect them." Jamie didn't look at Adele. Not yet. "Shoo Juh got it all. She was real expert at what she did…"

"No sense of time, you said." Adele spoke in a whisper. "She kept you isolated."

"And in the dark. About five months altogether, I think, maybe six. For part of it—a long time, it felt like a long, *long* time—I didn't see or talk to another living soul. And I kinda lost it." Suddenly, Jamie needed to move; she repositioned herself on the bed, stretched her shoulders as best she could; it had been such a small space. "While it was happening and right after, I remembered the interrogations and shing as different each time—the pacing of it, the mindfuck du jour, the techniques and implements. Now I'm remembering more, dreaming about it a lot, and I can see the pattern in what Shoo Juh did, how she kept on escalating. It was—she was—very calculated." At last, Jamie looked at Adele. "And she didn't do it just for intel."

Adele's eyes caught fire. "You mean—"

"She got off on it."

"Oh god, Jamie."

"So maybe you should reconsider asking me to, y'know…"

"Because now anything sexual…"

"Takes me right back there." Jamie twitched. "Into a flashback, reliving it. Whenever I…"

"Whenever you feel pleasure," said Adele. "Sexual pleasure."

"Yes." Jamie swung her eyes to the window and searched out the wind turbine's lazily spinning blades. Thursday, October 31 would be a bright, sunny day. "I thought for a while I was getting past it, but I was wrong. Thing is, all that time, Shoo Juh was the only person who ever looked me in the eye. She was my only real link with the human race. I believed her when she told me I deserved to be punished. 'Cuz it's true. I do deserve it."

"No—"

"Yes." The turbines' blades spun faster, as if they'd heard Jamie say it. She nodded, shaking loose the tears that had filled her eyes. "I might be able to talk myself out of the other shit, how much responsibility I had or didn't have. But not Awa." Gut seizing, she paused to drag air into her lungs. "No way around that one. A six-year-old kid, and I blew her head off."

Yep, there it was: Adele flinched. "An accident."

Jamie tried to shrug. "Doesn't matter. Awa's just as dead…"

"Shoo Juh knew?"

"Don't remember telling her. But she emptied me, so I must have."

"And the punishment—" Adele lowered her head; Jamie couldn't see her face, but her voice seethed with compressed fury. "Shoo Juh used it to—to—"

"Sometimes when she touched me, she wasn't cruel, a-and it felt good. Relief like that, it washes over you, and it feels wicked good. And now I can't seem to stop seeing her." Jamie tapped her temple. "In here."

"So." Adele raised her head and rubbed her index finger across her lips very much the way Lynn did. "You're still Shoo Juh's prisoner, enduring her punishments."

"She always said she owned me. That it'll never be over."

"Well, she's not here," Adele declared, her gaze never leaving Jamie's face. "And I am."

"Yeah," Jamie said admiringly. "You sure are."

"So I have to figure out…" Adele ran her hand along Jamie's foot again. "How to touch you in a way that you know it's me, that you feel *me*, not Shoo Juh." Abruptly, Adele lifted her hand so it hovered above Jamie's foot. "If that's okay with you."

"Y-Yeah," Jamie managed eventually, once the siren melt of Adele's touch faded and cooled. "I want you to touch me." Adele's hand returned to her foot, and behind her eyes, Shoo Juh's ice-smile flashed, a beacon signaling a swarm of black- and red-tinged phantasms to descend and claim her.

Breathe, Jamie commanded herself, *and resist*. She kept her eyes on Adele's face, lit now with the same ineffable compassion she'd seen that morning beneath the turbines and had seen so many times since, on the trail the first time they talked, on the videoscreen, as she lay busted up on the driveway, in the hospital.

"Should I ask?" Adele asked. "Before I touch you, I mean."

"Sometimes."

"Should I ask now?"

"No. Not now."

Adele moved herself closer to Jamie until they were side by side. Jamie squirmed as their legs made contact, then their hips, but relaxed when Adele merely snugged in close. "I won't let that woman keep you there, Jamie. I will help you let Awa go and I will help you get Shoo Juh and Saint Eh Mo's out of your brain if it takes me the next twenty years."

"You can't say that."

"I just did."

"But what if I never—"

"I have faith."

"When you can't stand me anymore," Jamie said, shifting so she could catch Adele's gaze, "promise you won't stay just because in this moment you made a ridiculously brash declaration."

"A ridiculously brash declaration, huh?" Adele lifted her head and looked at Jamie for a long moment, her dark eyes velvet opaque. "You mean you're worried we'll turn out to be sexually incompatible." Before Jamie could reply, she grinned, which set off sparks in her eyes and a clarion trill in Jamie's clit. "Okay, I promise," she said, then snugged close once more.

Jamie waited for the phantasms to penetrate the edges of her vision, of her awareness, but they only churned vaguely on the other side of some force field. Adele's force field. Jamie nestled her cheek against the top of Adele's head, closed her eyes, and inhaled Adele's scent, richer now, a milky, honeyed warmth. "You smell so good," she whispered. *Please, please don't let this be* too *good to be true.* "But I still don't get the part about why you want me."

"That's all right. You will."

"Can we listen to the flute and harp music again?"

"Sure. Give me a second." Adele clicked awake the room's sound system. "There we go. And one more thing—" She hiked herself up to kiss Jamie's forehead. "Happy birthday."

CHAPTER EIGHTEEN
TRICK OR TREAT

She knew it was my birthday...wow...she knew...that's why she's here...

"I'm sure they want to check on you," Adele said as the last of the flute and harp concerto waned. "But nobody's going to knock until we leave the door ajar."

"Oh. Yeah." Sensing Adele about to move, Jamie inhaled her scent one more time. *She knew and that's why she came to see me...*

Adele snuggled a quick kiss into Jamie's neck beneath her ear, then sprang off the bed, heading for the closed bedroom door. A sneak kiss, Jamie thought—deliciously, meltingly electric, already eliciting its soft almost-moan before she could worry about what it might make her feel.

Lynn showed up first and only briefly. She was dressed for the cameras, but her face attested to her fatigue and worry. "You're okay?" she repeated as she scrutinized Jamie, clearly needing to hear Jamie say it—yes—watch Jamie say it—yes—three separate times. Yes.

Jamie sought updates, but Lynn replied only that the situation was "evolving" and offered a small, so-it-goes smile—nothing like the famous grin that lit her eyes and made you eager to follow her anywhere. When her suit jacket pocket pinged, she sighed. "I suppose I should be grateful there actually are candidates who want me to say nice things about them right before an election. Which is what I have to go do now. Again. At least I only need to travel as far as the teleconference setup in the study."

Jamie lasted for perhaps a minute after Lynn left.

"Pit stop?" Adele asked when Jamie started inching off the bed.

"Gonna go find ET. She'll be able to tell us something."

Adele groaned. "I knew it. Are you always like this?"

"Like what?"

"It's not fair, you know."

"Huh?"

"I'm trying to set an example here. By hanging out in bed with you. In a prone position. The way *you* should be. But this instinct you have—" Adele scooted smoothly, lightly off the bed where, still in T-shirt and pajama bottoms, she'd stretched on her side. "To rebel, to push and worm your way out of whatever's restraining you. It's sexy. Makes me want to tease it instead of calm it down."

"Mmm." Jamie grinned. "That could work. You could tease it now by giving me a hand."

A knock at the door cut off Adele's reply, and in strode Dana, who skipped the niceties and got right to the point. "Pretty clear now our intruder had help."

"Inside help," Adele said.

"Yep."

"Fitzgerald," Jamie muttered. The only one on Great Hill's security staff who hadn't treated her like a suspect for the first two months after she arrived.

Dana's eyes narrowed. "How'd you know?"

"His body language yesterday, the look on his face—when he finally found the nerve to show up. I'm betting they cornered him. A hostile recruitment."

"So he's told the Feds." Dana's tone did not suggest sympathy. "But then he would, wouldn't he?" She glanced at Adele first, then took in Jamie, whose feet had now reached the floor. "Aren't you supposed to stay in bed today?"

"She's stuck," Adele said, addressing Dana but moving to Jamie's side of the bed. "Can't stand or get her feet back up without it hurting like hell. Which means *we* decide which way she goes. Pick up her feet while I help her relax back into the pillows."

Jamie rolled her eyes, but this only provoked a resistance-is-futile snicker from Adele. "Okay, okay, I surrender—*if* you tell me…" She caught Dana's eye. "What else Fitzgerald had to say."

"Claims it began months ago. His brother's in trouble in Florida, and someone who wanted to get into Lynn's office squeezed him with a blackmail-bribery combo."

"Months ago?" Jamie echoed.

"According to Fitzgerald, it should've been over in a couple weeks, but things got out of hand." Dana placed Jamie's feet on the mattress and plunked into the desk chair. "He met the guy he dealt with in a bar in Saugus. Gave the guy info about our security and received instructions about what to sabotage in order to create blind spots. So they could break in without being detected. Fitzgerald assumed they wanted access to Lynn's comlinks, maybe also to plant a bug or two in her office, the study, her bedroom. Says he was told it was imperative that the break-in not be detected."

"Yeah," Jamie snarled. "I bet."

"They planned to do it on an evening when the house was empty. Fitzgerald was supposed to keep them apprised of our schedules, then make sure he got himself assigned to the security center for the duration—trade shifts if necessary. For a long time, the scenario they needed happened at least once a week. But by the time they hooked Fitzgerald, Evvie had arrived." Dana dipped her head toward Jamie. "Then you. Suddenly, everyone was around more. Fitzgerald also said the paths they managed to create that bypassed the security sensors kept getting noticed, so they had to retreat several times and start over."

A chill shivered up Jamie's spine. "Paths?"

"They had Fitzgerald screw up certain sensors and cams. Disable them, misdirect them. So they could approach the house and leave again—"

"Undetected," Jamie rasped. How many times had she been out there, spotted something anomalous, and decided she'd seen nothing more than another Palawan haunt? How many times? "Shit."

"You caught 'em once that we know of—the night after your, uh—" Dana paused, no doubt to search for an adequate euphemism.

"Stacy," Jamie said.

A quick nod and Dana kept going. "Fitzgerald never had a chance to undo his changes to the sensors, so we found their path even though a couple days had passed. After that, they got desperate. And reckless. Altogether, Fitzgerald says, they were at it for four months." Dana leaned forward, elbows resting on her thighs. "God, we've been lucky. Even with Fitzgerald. We're redoing protocols now based on what he's told us—"

"You've talked to him yourself?" asked Adele, who still stood at the foot of the bed.

"I have. I'm not sure how much I believe his story about being totally cornered into this fiasco. I suspect the filthy lucre tempted him more than he admits, but I think he really disliked the actual doing of it. And he seems genuinely contrite. Says he thought the house was empty. Jamie wasn't supposed to be here. Acts quite upset that she got hurt, and he's scared witless that the people he did this for will not treat him kindly."

"You said four months?" Another chill scurried along Jamie's back. "That puts it right after we got our asses out of Saint Eh Mo's."

Dana nodded. "Right after it was clear that Lynn hadn't been killed. And judging from what they already knew when they approached

Fitzgerald, they'd been watching us well before that. May also have taken a crack earlier at Lynn's place in Washington."

"Who *are* 'they'?" Adele asked; she sat now at the foot of the bed, her hand unobtrusively positioned so that her forearm touched Jamie's right calf.

"He doesn't have a clue," said Dana. "He described the guy he dealt with. No kid—maybe forty years old. Clearly not the same person who actually broke in—assuming, of course, we believe his description of his contact. The FBI should have a facial image based on his input by tonight, but both these guys sound about as average as a person can be. Which means we can't count on finding them anytime soon, if ever."

"Did his contact speak with any kind of accent?" Jamie asked.

"American. Like they talk in New Jersey, Fitzgerald said. And he thought the guy was ex-military."

"Why'd he say that?" Jamie blurted. "Did you ask?"

"Demeanor. And the guy had a tattoo." Dana rubbed her temples. "Couple of numbers and something about 'the walking dead'—"

"Circular, yellow, figure of death in a purple robe carrying a scythe," said Jamie in a monotone.

Eyebrows hiking, Dana nodded.

"Marine Corps. The One-Nine, out of Lejeune." Jamie gulped back a rising tide of nausea. "Lynn needs to know that, Dana. It's the same unit as—"

"The dead corporal whose video of Chen's abduction is supposed to never have existed," Dana said, surprise tickling her tone. "You're exceptionally well informed."

"His *name*," Jamie said, "was Bacani."

"Yes," Dana nearly whispered, head lowered. "Thank you for reminding me. Nimuel Bacani."

"Who very likely died for that video," said Jamie, because hell, they all might as well know right now what she really believed.

Adele almost asked it then: Who is Nimuel Bacani and *what* video, dammit? Her face had become eloquent with the question, but Dana spoke first.

"Think it could be somewhere out there, official denials notwithstanding?"

"Yep."

"Me too."

"And what about the guy who broke in here yesterday, the Croatian?" Jamie pressed. "Also military. I'd bet my life on that."

"Please don't. Once was enough," said Adele without a glimmer of a smile.

"The guy's biometrics are all over that pistol. Fingerprints. DNA." Dana straightened herself and stood. "But they match nothing. Not a damn thing anywhere. He's the invisible man."

"The Croatian invisible man," Jamie mused. "Question is, who'd be able to disappear his records like that? Same crew who disappeared Nim's video?"

"Can't rule out the possibility." Already, Dana had started tapping on her pocketcom. "Duty calls," she announced, then squinted at Jamie. "You take it easy. We're supposed to help you heal, not make it worse." And she was out of sight, her voice trailing behind her as she launched a comlink conversation.

Jamie had pretty much explained to Adele who Nim Bacani was by the time Rebecca arrived carrying a briefcase. "You're damn lucky for someone who's so accomplished at finding trouble," she observed cheerily after poking around a bit and using the device built into the briefcase to complete several scans.

"Yeah, I agree." Jamie held Rebecca's gaze—and comprehended she'd never quite done that before; she'd always let her eyes leap away, or slink away. Now, oddly, looking right at Rebecca, having Rebecca look right back at her, just wasn't hard anymore. "I *am* damn lucky. And you've been damn tolerant. Thank you."

"Uh—" Rebecca blinked. "You're welcome." She smiled then, a kind smile, and her eyes twinkled. "You earned it, kiddo. You really did."

That was when Jamie understood. *She's been waiting for me. This whole time. Waiting for me to see her.*

Jamie returned Rebecca's smile, and then a question—*the* question—popped out of its own accord. "Who's after her?"

Rebecca drew in her chin; the conversation had just skipped a half-dozen steps. "I don't know," she said after a moment, her eyes fixed on Jamie's as tears began to fill them.

"I'm gonna find out, Rebecca," Jamie said.

Maybe Rebecca actually believed it, because she seemed to almost nod. A knock at the door interrupted whatever she'd intended to say, however, and Mary and Lily appeared, laden with food.

"Luncheon is served," Mary announced. "You, too," she said to Rebecca, who had risen and begun to edge toward the door.

"Mum, I have to—"

"Not for another hour you don't, and Lynn is busy waxing poetic about the achievements of Congressman Somebody-Or-Other, so sit. And eat. We've brought up plenty."

"It's a wonder we're not all twenty pounds overweight," Rebecca grumbled. But she sat down precisely where her mother had patted a hand on the bed to indicate her spot.

❖

"How are you possibly going to find out who's after Lynn?" demanded Adele approximately four seconds after Mary, Lily, and Rebecca left.

Jamie began to inch off the bed. "Pit stop," she explained.

Adele went slitty-eyed. "Yeah?"

"And, well, I feel pretty good so I thought we could go for a short walk, too," Jamie tried. "A little way down one of the paths, or maybe the driveway...."

"Oh, *su-ure*," Adele drawled as she helped Jamie upright. "And we'll just happen to find ourselves ambling along the *west* driveway, huh? Exactly where you chased that guy yesterday. So you can check for something, you know not what, that someone might have missed."

"I just need to—"

"Rest. You just need to rest. In that bed. Maybe I ought to leave for a while so you can take a nap."

"No." Jamie reached for Adele's arm. "Please don't go."

Adele's eyes transmuted from glinting deep brown to unfathomable black. "Oh baby, the way you do that," she murmured, stroking Jamie's cheek. "And yes, I'll stay with you. I'll even take a nap with you. *If* you come straight back to bed."

Jamie sighed her relief. "'Kay. Thank you."

She couldn't sleep, however, couldn't stop brooding about the way pizda connected the infiltrator, Stacy, The Bastard. Adele had suggested coincidence. No denying the possibility, of course.

But in the last six months, three very nasty strangers on two separate continents called me pizda. What're the odds of that being coincidence when less than one tenth of one percent of the world's population has ever even heard the word?

Jamie peeked at Adele lying next to her, eyes shut, breathing already slow and even. Given the chance, Adele probably would remind her that coincidence is all about unlikely odds, then start concocting equations to compute the likelihood of encountering a Croatian word in any given locale under a variety of possible conditions.

None of which would make a damn bit of difference...

Because merely thinking about pizda sent a frenzy of icy pinpricks stampeding their alarm up and down her spine. This was instinct she'd trusted for years, instinct that had saved her more than once in the Palawan. Instinct she'd ignored more than once since coming to Great Hill—and one of those times had been that night with Stacy. Jamie would not ignore it again.

*Pizda, pizda. Follow it back…starting with yesterday's infiltrator—
very likely a merc, connected enough to be invisible, obviously targeting
Lynn.*

*Then back further to That Bitch Stacy, who until yesterday had me
believing our encounter was random. I know better now. And that slip
she made, calling me lieutenant—means they gave her enough intel
to understand how to psych me out. Also means they followed me all
afternoon, from the moment I left the house, because I ended up in that
bar by sheer accident.*

*What're the odds they've compartmentalized all this, each player
aware of only a little piece? So the guy infiltrating yesterday probably
never heard of Stacy. And odds are not only that Stacy never heard of
him, she probably didn't even know that targeting me was really about
targeting Lynn. Which is why they told her not to search me. If she
searched me, she might've figured out too much.*

*Ah, but they got sloppy, didn't they? Whoever "they" are. Because
pizda seeped into at least three of their compartments. Goddamn, if
the source of pizda isn't The Bastard, then sure as shit it goes back to
The Bastard's organization—the organization that Shoo Juh once said
serves many masters…*

Jamie swallowed hard. She had loosed the phantasms, and now the
sounds and smells of Saint Eh Mo's came for her. "Pizda," sneered The
Bastard as a sultry whiff of habagat, the Palawan's seasonal monsoon,
goaded her back, back to the cell so small she couldn't stand up in it,
and she recalled the thought she'd clung to once in that steamy, gritty,
horrific place: *Could be May by now…*

And if not May, then late in April.

April…

*When someone—an enemy with clout—hears Lynn will be going
to the Palawan, recognizes an opportunity. Six weeks later, Chen
Dongfeng gets grabbed in what has to be a quick-reaction mission. A
mission that had only six weeks to go from zero to a hundred. Easy to
fuck up in such a fluid situation, especially when you have to stay in the
shadows, invisible.*

*So a patrol in the wrong place at the wrong time clunks into
the middle of it all with a videocam. Means you're stuck cleaning up
afterward. Not just the six suckers from Isabela City, but Nim, too.
Because of what's on his patrol video.*

This Jamie mulled for quite a while, attempting to soothe the
prickling along her spine. To no avail. What was she missing? What?

Think, dammit…

*If all Nim had managed to record was those six suckers in the act
of grabbing Chen, the video would've made it to Vivian Velty or some*

other media hotshot in a heartbeat—and Nim would've made sergeant. Because a video like that would back up the absurd idea that those six suckers worked alone. But, according to his father, Nim recorded eight abductors and assumed at least two more, since fire was coming from the woods.

So why would "they" take on the immense hassle of eliminating Nim and his video rather than simply adapt their window dressing to accommodate what he recorded? Why, dammit?

"Because the wrong someone must've shown up on that video," Jamie muttered before she realized she'd said it aloud. Next to her, though, Adele didn't move. Adele's breathing—slow, deep, impossibly sexy—didn't change. She watched Adele's breasts rise, fall, yearning to touch them, kiss them. Soon her own breathing followed Adele's hypnotic rhythm, and though she tried not to move, she couldn't quite keep still.

"That's better," Adele said quietly, eyes still shut.

"Sorry. Didn't mean to wake you."

Adele opened her eyes. "Uh-oh," she said when she saw Jamie's expression. "It's worse than I thought. Must've fallen asleep. Which, I'm guessing, you did not."

"No."

Adele rolled onto her side and faced Jamie; she reached to touch Jamie's leg but refrained, her fingers coming to rest a centimeter from Jamie's thigh. "So. On the one to ten stir-crazy scale, where would you put yourself right now?"

"Fourteen." Jamie's eyes closed involuntarily, and behind her eyelids another moment, another world blossomed—a world where Adele's hand caressed her leg, slid past the impediments of her robe to massage her taut inner thigh, to seek with strong, knowing fingers, to delicately unfold her and discover the slick of arousal begging *find me…*

"I'll make a deal with you."

Jamie's eyes quivered open to see Adele sit up. "Shower," Adele said, "then get dressed in something simple like sweats, go downstairs for a little while—"

"Yes!" Thank god, because the phantasms had started writhing at the periphery of Jamie's vision, their grays darkening, reddening.

"Using the elevator. Down *and* back up."

"Yes!" Anxious to move as much and as far as possible, Jamie began to edge herself off the bed. "I bet I can stand by myself."

"And no lobbying for outside."

"How 'bout just—" Jamie swallowed the rest when Adele's face threatened a scowl. "Okay. No lobbying for outside. But later on, soon as I can, will you walk up to the top of the hill with me—at night, to look at the stars?" Without help, allowing herself a minor wince, Jamie stood. "There's this spot I found…" *Where I can try to explain what I'm gonna have to do…*

"Yes," said Adele, her eyes lit by *that smile.* "I'm looking forward to it already." Then the light in her eyes flared. "In the interim, would you like someone to join you in the shower and wash your back?"

❖

The first hint came at the end of the second floor hallway, on the landing between the front stairs and the elevator: Somebody had left a backpack on the steps heading to Robin's room on the third floor.

"That yours?" Jamie asked.

"Uh, yeah," Adele answered quickly as she ushered Jamie into the elevator. "I'll get it later."

The second hint showed up on the first floor soon after they exited the elevator: The house seemed way too quiet.

"Where is everyone?" Jamie asked.

"Dunno," Adele answered with a shrug as she steered Jamie toward the family room at the rear of the house.

"Will you play the piano?" Jamie asked a moment later. "I've never seen you play."

Next to her, Adele smiled and bounced onto her toes to kiss Jamie's cheek. "I sure will, baby."

"Ahh, I really like when you call me th—" Jamie froze, except for the arm she thrust in front of Adele's chest. "Shh!" *What the fuck? How can this be happening* again?

"What?" Adele said much too loudly.

Jamie pointed toward the family room a few feet ahead of them and whispered as softly as she could, "Someone's in there. Near the piano."

"Uh-oh." Too damn loud again—and now Adele grinned like a fool. Then a rich, rollicking belly laugh peeled out of her and her eyes fired as she pirouetted in front of Jamie.

"Del!" Jamie yelled, reaching for her—and missing.

From the piano in the family room came a chord, loud and grand, and then another. A meter in front of Jamie, eyes alight, body cheerfully defying gravity, Adele beckoned with outstretched arms as a chorus of female voices launched a ragged rendition of a familiar song…*Happy birthday to yoooou…*

One step, two, and through the balusters of the back stairs Jamie saw them—the entire household, including Robin, gathered around

Mary at the piano, belting out their birthday greeting. On a silver platter atop the piano they'd placed a cake covered in chocolate frosting, smartly decorated, festooned with twenty diminutive yellow candles whose determined little flames trembled in time with the piano's energetic extravagance.

Jamie couldn't speak. She couldn't move. The scene before her wavered liquidly as her eyes filled with tears she couldn't brush away. "C'mon, baby," Adele said gently, taking her by the hand and leading her the rest of the way into the family room.

❖

One by one, they gave Jamie hugs, which slowly drew her out of a dazed amazement, and they gave her presents, too.

From Robin she received "the Cam-Killer," an upscale boonie hat that used solar power to interfere with surveillance cams' ability to get a clear facial image. Mary's gift, a khaki-colored parka, was Jamie's first ever store-bought winter jacket. Lynn gave her the next physics course she planned to take, along with a two-part analytic geometry/calculus course—both from MIT—and Rebecca presented her with "the very best mathematics tutorial and reference tool ever created— the animations bring real clarity to it all."

Lily and Dana came next with new eyewraps. "Resilient as hell," said Dana, "military-grade multi-sensor detection, best resolution and magnification capabilities, super secure, lots of interface options, plenty enough memory and storage that you can dump everything else if you want—"

"And she'll go on and on if we let her, but you're better off checking out the documentation," teased Lily. "Not 'til you insert these, though." She opened her hand to reveal two tiny earbuds. "Concert hall quality amplification and playback." Lily tilted her head toward Adele. "For a reason."

Adele approached almost shyly holding a memory card between thumb and forefinger. "Music," she nearly whispered. "All sorts, performed by a variety of musicians. Including me."

"You?" Jamie repeated. "You have recordings of *you*?"

"Just promise me you won't click any on when I can hear them."

"Why?"

"Because all I hear are my mistakes."

They'd noticed so much more about her than she would ever have believed possible. Then they gathered it up and made this, the only birthday party Jamie'd ever had, into a collection of what they'd concluded were her favorites—and they nailed it pretty damn well, too…

Eating informally in the family room rather than at a table. Lemonade and cheesesteak subs and veggie-potato salad and butter cake with a thick layer of soft dark chocolate frosting and real cherry filling on a plate with a fat scoop of vanilla ice cream—and no one saying anything at all about trick or treat.

Conversation laced with laughter that would unexpectedly teach you something, make you think about the world a bit differently than you had before—and the whole time the people showing you what they see, how they see, have a warmth in their eyes, in their voices, their touch, and you feel embraced, cared about, and yes, safe. And there's such unspeakable release in that.

Then, just when you think it can't get any better, Adele seating herself at Mary's piano, her fingers skimming the raised fallboard before taking their position above the keys…Adele closing her eyes, and as you decide she's the most exquisite human being you've ever seen in your whole life, her fingers start dancing, her body curves forward to stoke powerful, sinewed forearms, her face sublimely rapt as she phrases the music into an achingly beautiful story all her own.

CHAPTER NINETEEN
OCCAM'S RAZOR

P lease don't do it."
    Adele's voice had gone husky and her profile, ethereal in the moonlight, warned of a glower as she perched on the smooth granite mound near the top of Great Hill.

Damn. This isn't working. At all.

The northerly breeze that seemed playful when Jamie showed her the spot now had its dander up, but this hadn't spawned Adele's stubborn irritation as she hunkered into her jacket and folded her arms around those legs of hers, sleek and strong beneath her faded jeans.

Once more, Jamie almost relented. Almost. The words formed but stuck in her throat. No, she would not, could not relent. She had to know, dammit. "I *gotta* do it," she said.

The three-quarter moon disappeared behind clouds rolling southward, and Adele's profile nearly disappeared, too, into the momentary moon shadow. Jamie waited for her to say something else, but she didn't.

What was there to say, anyway? They'd talked about it on and off since late morning. Ever since the docs at the hospital said her ribs were doing well and she told Adele her plan on the way home. "After I vote tomorrow, I'm going back to that bar in Boston—Demeter. To see if Stacy shows up to take another crack at me."

Of course, Adele got all slitty-eyed again. And then came an artillery barrage of questions.

You really believe there's a connection between Stacy and the break-in?

And that guy back in the POW camp? Really?

And what're you gonna do if you actually run into this Stacy person? Ask her who taught her the pizda word? Punch her out? Go with her so she'll have another chance to beat you up and play out her fucked up scene with whoever the hell she's procuring for now?

The questions turned out to be rhetorical—surprise!—and Adele provided her own answers.

A coincidence does not prove a relationship.

Correlation does not imply causation.

Occam's razor tells us the more complex your hypothesis, the lower its probability of explaining any given observation.

From Adele she learned about the index of coincidence and confirmation bias and false equivalence. Lengthy, polished, uncomfortably logical arguments all—and every one of them designed to impugn what Adele eventually called, in a moment of eye-rolling exasperation, "this ill-conceived notion of yours." Then, finally, came the topper: Lynn does not need your help anymore.

Jamie tried to defend this ill-conceived notion of hers, but she lacked Adele's Weapons of Algebraic Rationality. No razors for her, only compulsion sharpened by instinct.

So much for telling Adele everything. Or at least telling Adele every thought and idea as it coalesced in that woolly space between her ears. *Shoulda waited 'til the very last minute. Or maybe not said anything at all 'til it was over. One way or the other.*

"It's cold out here," Adele announced, and got to her feet. "I'm going in." She stood over Jamie, pausing, her eyes and expression masked by shadow and the night. They had walked up from the house together; if they were to return the same way, the moment would be now.

Anyway, that's what Adele's posture implied, chiefly because of the way she'd tossed most of her weight onto one leg and thrust her hands into her jacket pockets.

Fuck you, Jamie thought. "I'll be down in a few minutes," she said, and raised the zipper on her new parka while squinting at her best estimate of where Adele's eyes ought to be. Just to emphasize the point: I'll go back when *I'm* damn well ready—which isn't right now.

Adele's outline nodded, but for a moment, she didn't move. "I like your spot up here," she said at last. "Thanks for showing it to me."

Ah, a partial peace offering. Which would be partially accepted. "Be careful on the path. You got the flashlight, right?"

"Yeah, but what about you?"

"I'll be fine. It'll be like a greenish high noon as soon as I click these new eyewraps into night vision mode."

"Okay," Adele mumbled, her disappointment evident. She flipped on the flashlight and started her trek back to the house.

Jamie watched her black outline quickly meld with the trees, watched the flashlight beam flare erratically before it diminished into a halo fading behind the hill's granite topography.

Goddammit.

Adele was so smart. So generous. "Nothing'll help you heal faster than rest, heat, and ice," she'd said on Saturday morning, "so I better stick around to keep you honest." This she did for three incomparable days without a trace of hesitation or boredom. Her mere presence enchanted the simple acts of eating and napping. Her kisses instantly tamed Jamie's restlessness. And when she helped Jamie complete the Physics I course, which had blurred considerably since the break-in, she revived the topic so adroitly, so memorably that Jamie realized she was also a sparklingly charismatic teacher.

But she was fucking infuriating. *Because whatever else you are, Adele Sabellius, you are* not *the boss of me.*

Cantankerousness for its own sake had limits, especially when one was sitting alone in the dark on cold granite in air temperatures only a few degrees above freezing. Thus Jamie didn't wait long to stand up, click on her new eyewraps' night vision, and begin the trek back to the house.

By the time she reached one of the steeper sections of the path west of the second garage, she'd already slowed some to look around with the eyewraps, which delivered a clarity and detail unlike any night vision gear she ever used in the Palawan.

Jamie halted mid-step. Off to her right, she recognized the gnarled scrub oak where a couple of months ago she'd discovered what seemed like a hide. She looked leftward at the house forty meters away, then back at the oak, remembering.

It had been Fitzgerald she mentioned it to that August day. And he played her. Oh christ, how he played her, acting all concerned, promising to check it out. When she heard nothing more about it, she figured he didn't want to embarrass her by telling her she'd hallucinated it all. And, sure as hell, once she retraced her steps later to check it out again for herself, she'd been grateful that he'd said nothing, because she saw no hide anymore, either…

Maybe I should go into the city right the fuck now. March straight from here down the east driveway and onto Walker Road, then Pine Street. Lots of streetlights on Pine Street, real easy for The Bastard's spotter to confirm it's me. Already got a warm coat, gloves, this hotshot boonie hat from Robin. And, let's see—yeah, here's my ID and credit shit, too, still in the same pocket from this morning's appointment at the hospital. I can load maps on the way, pick up cash at the station.

Okay. If I hump I can just make the nine fifteen train, which'll put me at Demeter's door by 2300 hours. Okay.

❖

"Where are you going?" Adele asked from behind the wheel of a dark sedan as it drew alongside Jamie about halfway down Walker Road.

"Out." Jamie didn't turn her head or slow down.

"Want a ride?"

"No."

"Please get in the car."

"No."

Adele didn't speak again, but the sedan continued down Walker Road next to Jamie, who refused to look at either the car or its driver. She tried to walk faster, but her ribs objected, and her mission had hardly begun. A six-and-a-half-klick-an-hour pace it would have to be, like it or not.

Goddamn, I should never have said anything about this. Because one wrong word in a public place burns it. So how do I get her to—

Suddenly, the car stopped. No screech of brakes. No snide remark from behind the wheel. The car just stopped. Jamie walked on for several more meters, but then she, too, stopped. Because a troop of tiny, cold needles now clamored up her spine. Something was wrong.

As Jamie turned around, the car pulled next to her and Adele spoke barely above a whisper. "You gotta get in."

Jamie leaned toward the car window. "What is it?" she whispered back.

"Please, Jamie. Get in now."

Quickly, Jamie got in. Adele gripped the steering wheel tightly and stared at Jamie, fear flicking across her shadowed face.

"Lily just called me. Fitzgerald's dead. Somebody slit his throat."

Chapter Twenty
Rules of Engagement

This would be *so* much easier if you would just say out loud what you're feeling instead of traipsing off without a word." From the middle of the low-lit family room, Lily pointed a finger at Jamie's chest. "Yes, you. I mean you." Before Jamie could respond, her finger swerved to Adele a few feet away. "And *you*—" Lily glared, but her voice cracked. "You need to—"

"I know." Adele bowed her head. "Shut up and listen. I know."

"So give it a try—both of you. Inside this time, yes?" Lily's poise seemed restored when they nodded, yet she continued to exude a kind of low-grade disquiet—fear kindled by the shock of hearing about what happened to Fitzgerald, no doubt, only partly salved by the knowledge that everyone who mattered to her was okay. "God, it's almost nine and I haven't nursed Evvie yet," she fretted, already taking the back stairs two at a time.

Jamie and Adele watched her disappear down the upstairs hallway, and then, as if the smaller family room sofa had been permanently assigned to them, they sat next to each other on it, though they kept half a meter of space between them. They'd spoken little during the short, numbed ride back to the house, and now, alone again, they glanced mutely at each other.

Finally, Adele said, "I'm listening."

Jamie exhaled. Slipping away to catch the late train was out of the question now. Even veering into the comparative safety of wondering aloud about when the rest of the clan would return or the particulars of Fitzgerald's death was out of the question. "Shit."

"Oh, well, that explains everything."

Jamie exhaled again. "About tomorrow—"

"You mean when you'll go to that bar on the off chance you find that woman—"

"On the real chance she finds me. Because she's connected to the break-in. And The Bastard. And now to Fitzgerald's killer. Or is that also coincidence?"

Adele scowled at her hands fiddling nervously with each other in her lap. "All connected, you think, by one word." She'd chosen to ignore Jamie's jab, but skepticism still tinged her words. "Pizda."

Jamie rubbed her face. "I need to go to that bar again because—" She leaned back, let her head plop onto the sofa cushion, and addressed the ceiling. She would do what Lily wanted, but she refused to watch Adele's reaction, thank you very much. "Because it's the only way I can find out how crazy I really am."

"You're not crazy."

"Oh yeah? For three months, I've been seeing things, hearing things that weren't real. Movement in the corner of my eye, rustling in the woods around the house, a hide on the path up to the turbines, The Bastard's laugh during a party on the south meadow." Jamie closed her eyes. *C'mon, dammit*, she silently taunted the phantasms, *come and fuckin' get me*. But they had retreated into shadow. Biding their time, probably. "I get lots of flashbacks. Even full-blown hallucinations. Which fit right in with the nightmares. Ask your sister; she'll tell you. I require saintly forbearance even when I haven't been kicked in the ribs."

Jamie could no longer sit still; gripping her chest, she pushed herself off the sofa, keeping Adele to her right, forcing her eyes straight ahead. "Truth is, I'm a fucking disaster area. Hell, the night I met Stacy, I had whole conversations with Shoo Juh. It's like the ground I'm standing on cracks and breaks off and I fall away, and I can't tell the difference anymore between what's real and the shit messing around in my head. Except now—" Jamie turned to face Adele. "Now I find out maybe the reason some of that shit seemed so real is because it *was* real."

Adele rose from the sofa to stand in front of Jamie, her hands hovering near Jamie's forearms, her eyes imploring. "I know you're not crazy."

"Del, listen to me. If Stacy was no more than coincidence, then I don't dare trust my perceptions of anyone or anything—not you, not Lynn, not the goddamn time of day—because I sure as hell didn't come anywhere close to perceiving the truth of her. If Stacy was no more than coincidence, I'm unbalanced. Maybe too unbalanced to ever get my balance back. But if somebody who knew—" Jamie squeezed her eyes shut and shook her head. "Ah, god…if Stacy got coached by somebody who had intel about how to play me—well, I can live with that. I can work with that."

"Because if she was coached…"

"Then the battle space had different parameters than I thought. And different rules of engagement. Way different."

"The battle space…" Adele's voice hitched. "To which you'll have adapted accordingly next time."

"Oh yeah." Jamie opened her eyes to Adele's face much nearer than she expected, and tense with worry.

"What if Stacy doesn't show up? What if you discover there's no connection, only coincidence?"

"I—" Jamie dropped her gaze. "I don't know."

"You're doing it again," Adele murmured.

"What?"

Adele closed in; the warmth of her breath, then her lips glided along Jamie's jaw, firing every nerve in Jamie's body. "Will you come upstairs with me?" she whispered.

"What?" Jamie bleated, heart suddenly racing, a chaos of images and impressions tumbling in her head. Not even a kiss this time, and her inflamed crotch surged involuntarily into Adele's hip. And stayed there. Begging.

"Mmm." Adele's hip returned the greeting as her eyes, smiling now, scooted downward. "Is that a yes?"

"Del," Jamie panted, reaching for her ribs even though it was her clit that throbbed, wet-hot and hard and still cleaving to the soft, succulent oscillation of Adele's hip. "We haven't resolved anything."

"Hey, we're only just getting started."

"I'm walking wounded in so many ways." *Breathe*, Jamie urged her aching chest. *Breathe…* "I can't promise anything."

"I can." Adele's eyes, bottomless black, held Jamie's while her hands slid delicately along Jamie's hips and together they rocked slowly back and forth in cadence with her words. "I promise to have your permission before I initiate anything with you, for as long as you need that, for forever if you need that. I promise I will stop the instant you say stop. I promise to tell you the truth always."

Caught in a whirl of arousal and alarm, Jamie stood in the middle of the bedroom as if she'd never seen it before.

"I would like to undress you," said Adele.

Jamie's heartbeat hiccupped. Shouldn't this be considered for a moment? The hows, the what-ifs, the then-whats…Yet someone said "Okay," and Jamie knew she'd heard her own voice. *Oh god, what am I doing?*

The clothes Adele began removing, however, were her own. Slippers and socks went first with unceremonied grace. In an easy, dancelike flow that unveiled her breasts, she swept shirt and bra over her head, igniting in Jamie another knee-weakening rush. Around Adele's feet, jeans and boyshorts fell into a pile—and there she stood for an eternal, mesmerizing moment, muscle and tendon poised beneath smooth skin. Then she stepped forth strong and confident and luminous to squat, legs wide apart, and slide a hand down Jamie's jean-covered calf to a sock-swathed ankle.

"May I?" she asked, glancing up with a small, crooked smile.

A light electric current flowed up Jamie's leg. "Yes."

By the time Jamie's eyes had ceased blinking, her feet were bare and Adele stood before her, hands hovering at the third button of her shirt.

"May I?"

"Yes." Jamie fumbled with the fourth button, but Adele's hands stopped her.

"Let me," Adele said. "Please."

What about this simple request made Jamie tremble as she nodded? It started in her chest at such a high frequency that she could almost hear it—a hum whirring outward to constrict her throat, fill her head, zing into her shoulders, down her arms, though her belly, firing the hypertender tissues between her quaking legs.

She should never have said yes to any of this. She should never even have come upstairs—because the phantasms could always smell turn-on that lasted too long. They smelled it now as they churned in her peripheral vision, mustering, multiplying, reconnoitering for Shoo Juh. Goddamn—Jamie despised their unpredictability. One minute, she'd kiss Adele and amp right up, able like a regular person to just get off on it—and then out of the fucking blue the phantasms and their mistress race in, not just to ride along but to mangle the whole thing.

"You look tired." Adele's voice, close and low. "Why don't you sit down?"

Jamie opened eyes she hadn't realized were shut. "I'm—" Fine, she'd been about to say in her usual don't-mess-with-me way. Until she noticed she, too, was naked.

Naked...*how the hell did that happen?*

"Here," said Adele, and pulled the desk chair nearer.

The chair. Built for just one—a perfect refuge. Carefully, right arm clamped around sore ribs, Jamie eased herself into it and exhaled.

"Are you comfortable?" Adele seemed to speak the words lazily, in slow motion. Jamie looked up to find her sitting a meter away at the corner of the bed, legs blithely crossed, big toe teasing the edge of the chair seat. Adele leaned back on one arm; her free hand stole Jamie's breath as it traced a small loop around the hollow at the base of her neck, then slipped between ripe breasts to descend through lithe abdominal topography and come to rest at the base of her pubic mound.

Jamie tried not to squirm while her simmering need oozed out of her and competing instincts clamored in her head.

If she stayed, she'd end up at the tips of Adele's fingers and the phantasms would strike and Shoo Juh would seize her turn-on, shove into the space that should be Adele's and rule it.

So take off, dammit. Babble excuses, grab your clothes, and go. Tell her you need to be alone. She'll respect that. And then double-time your swollen sorry twat downstairs and swim laps, get on the goddamn treadmill and count Fibonacci numbers. Hell, do it backward and count negafibonacci numbers. That'll bore Shoo Juh enough to leave you the fuck alone…

But Jamie didn't budge.

"I can see your leg twitching," Adele said, lowering her head, shifting her weight as her free hand snaked lower to stroke her inner thigh. "Perhaps you ought to try holding on to that chair."

"W-What?"

"One hand gripping each side of the seat. So you stabilize your ribs and keep inhaling those good deep breaths…"

"What?"

"I want to show you something. Will you let me?"

"Do I have a choice?" Jamie's hands gripped the chair seat just as Adele had suggested, though it seemed more like a command.

"You always have a choice. You know that."

Jamie ripped her gaze from Adele's crotch and compelled it upward along the same path Adele's hand had descended, climbing Adele's abs to taut nipples crowning breasts somehow even riper now, all the way to that small hollow at the base of Adele's neck. And there her eyes stayed, hypnotized by the hollow's tiny pulse, by Adele's invitation.

"Will you let me show you?"

"Is it gonna hurt?" Jamie asked the tiny pulse.

"Oh god." Adele's soft laugh resonated. "I hope not."

"Can't you just tell me?"

Adele laughed again. "Loses too much in translation."

Jamie inhaled. Jamie exhaled. Way more than her leg twitched now. "Okay. Show me."

"Close your eyes."

Instead, Jamie's eyes snapped wide and she stared at Adele, who stared back silently, eyes opaque. Waiting. "Okay," Jamie whispered, and closed her eyes.

"Is she there?"

Jamie half grunted, half groaned her protest as Shoo Juh's shimmering visage sneered emphatically, daring her to challenge its power. No, she wanted to shout, no, no, no. She tried to force Shoo Juh's image away, into the red-tinged black blur out of which it had so quickly materialized. But Shoo Juh was unmovable...*I own you, hong mao*...

"Is she there?" Adele repeated. "You see her, don't you?"

"Yes."

"Open your eyes then."

"She'll follow me..."

"Shoo Juh is a ghost who cannot own you unless you want her to."

Jamie's eyes popped open. "I *don't* want—" Still reclined on the bed, Adele smiled at her, eyes ablaze. "Oh," Jamie wheezed as a new wave of arousal claimed her. "Oh..."

Legs parted wide to accommodate long, nimble fingers that slowly, slowly circled the glistening pink between labial folds, Adele thrust her hips tantalizingly upward. "What do you see now, Jamie?"

"Y-You. I see you." Jamie leaned forward in her chair prison. "You're beautiful." Avid to break out, she shifted hands that still gripped the sides of the chair so she could stand up—

"No, no," Adele crooned. "Stay right there. And hold on to the chair. Hold on."

"*Why?*" But Jamie obeyed.

Adele's hips heaved and pitched to the voluptuous rhythm of her fingers. "So I can show you."

"God, Del..." Jamie rolled her pelvis forward, trying to push her crotch against the chair seat's lightly pommeled center contour, but the seat only taunted her. "You're driving me nuts."

"Hold on," Adele murmured, darkening eyes riveted on Jamie. "And tell me what else you see."

"Please..." Beyond measure Jamie didn't want it to be true, but she couldn't deny it. Shoo Juh's sneer flickered before her, too, a kind of semi-transparent veil between her and the world, between her and Adele, and at the corners of the veil, Shoo Juh's phantasms seethed their threat.

"Focus through it, Jamie." Adele's rhythm accelerated as her fingers parted her labia to deepen their spiral around her clit. "And look at *me*." Her breasts rose, fell, rose again with her breathing, and the muscles in her belly went taut. She stretched her legs so the toes of her extended feet grazed Jamie's knees, persuading them apart, and she objected when Jamie's grip on the chair seat loosened. "Uh-uh. Stay there. And hold on."

Moaning frustration and need, Jamie rocked against the seat's pathetically inadequate pommel as Adele's motion syncopated and escalated toward climax, but Jamie remained in her prison, hands clutching the sides of the chair.

"Close your eyes," Adele said.

Jamie closed her eyes. "Unnhh," she whimpered, quivering now from head to foot. Because Shoo Juh had retreated. Behind her eyelids, she beheld Adele's exquisite body in supple undulation, and Adele's bonfire eyes fixed on her, claimed her, overshadowed everything.

And then warm hands slithered along the insides of her thighs. "Hold on, baby," Adele purred from only inches away. "Hold on." Hands caressed her legs further apart, coaxed her hips higher—and soon a finger, then another entered her.

She curled upward toward hot breath and a fervent tongue that quickly found her clit, and suddenly she bucked, wide-open eyes unable to prevent the blind, mindless alarm from automatically coursing through her as Shoo Juh cackled, as the phantasms attacked, all of them all at once in a chaos of malevolence that threw Adele's image into darkness. "Uhh-*UNHH!*"

"You're safe, my sweet." Adele lifted off the chair to stroke Jamie's cheek, kiss her hesitant mouth once, twice. "No one here but you and me."

"Scared." Still gripping the chair seat, Jamie stared into the chaos, searching for Adele's face.

"I know, baby." Adele's voice consoled her. "Nothing wrong with being scared."

"Don't wanna be scared…" Oh god, Adele had brought her so, so close… "Help me," she begged.

"Look at *me*, Jamie. *I'm* what's real. Right here, right now."

Jamie searched for the warm, enveloping protection of Adele's rich brown eyes—to no avail at first. But Adele's hand kept stroking her cheek, Adele's soft, honeyed scent surrounded her, and after a while, she could no longer see what terrified her—though it twisted in her belly, frothed hysterically in her head.

"For this little bit of time while it's just us, the ghosts cannot have you," Adele said when at last Jamie managed a small I-see-you smile. Then, with consummate gentleness, Adele kissed her mouth. "Is that all right?"

"Yes."

"Come on," Adele said, rising to her feet and taking Jamie's trembling hands from the chair seat. It felt like freedom, like the joy of breathing clean, clear, fresh air after believing you were forever doomed to the fetid dankness of a prison cell. Is this what Adele wanted to show her? That her own mind had imprisoned her, that her own mind had the power to release her?

Adele led her to the bed, lay down on it next to her.

"Stay with me?" Jamie beseeched. "Right here, all touching me? Just for a minute? Please?"

"Yes, baby, I will. For as long as you want."

Adele had not given up on her, would not surrender her to Shoo Juh…

And right then, something adamantine and merciless—something that had always been there, even before Saint Eh Mo's, deep in Jamie's gut, clutching it, enslaving it, and always hurting her, always—began to yield.

"I didn't know," Jamie murmured some time later, maybe minutes, maybe hours, maybe rousing from sleep, "that I was so…so…"

"Chained." Adele skated a finger down Jamie's abs, then lifted her eyes to catch Jamie's gaze. "I can help you with that. When you're ready."

"I, uh, might be ready now."

"Yeah? Let's see, shall we?" One of Adele's eyebrows fluttered upward; she was asking permission, like she'd promised.

"What do you have in mind?"

"Would you like me to show you?"

From the shadows at the edge of her vision, Shoo Juh smirked.

No, I will not cower before you anymore—I will not…Jamie focused on Adele's face. "Yes," she said. "Show me."

Adele levitated over her. Up her neck, along her jaw glided Adele's mouth, ardent and yet careful, almost deferential until their lips, their tongues tentatively greeted each other. Stay with me, pleaded Adele's kiss, stay…

What does it take, a moment like this?

More than rootless desire, unkempt and unaware. More than ambitious desire forced through the narrow, methodical channels of stratagem. For Jamie it took nothing-left-to-lose desire, bitter and blind, stumbling through a rutted labyrinth of pain and fear and penetrating need in pursuit of what had been glimpsed once here, a moment there—a point of light deep in the shadows that not even Shoo Juh could entirely obscure. All she had to do was keep looking at Adele…

"Okay?" Adele asked as her legs straddled Jamie, as they met crotch to crotch and began rocking together.

"Oh…my…god…yes…."

Yes yes *yes*…Adele above her, arching, head flung back, riding her, grinding into her—and overshadowing Shoo Juh again…This didn't just electrify Jamie's clit. It changed *everything*.

"You okay?" Adele hummed, at last leaning forward onto her arms, swinging her legs inside Jamie's. "Don't want you to be hurting…"

"I'm…good." Jamie wanted to smile, tried to smile. Her desire had delivered unto Shoo Juh the insistent pain in her ribs, and now she reveled in the heroic effort of withstanding that pain, Shoo Juh's pain, to reach for Adele, to bathe in Adele's resplendent presence, above her now, lowering to anoint her body with a kiss that extended from mouth to pubic mound and back again.

"So you like being on top," Jamie panted, breathless, pelvis rising in search of Adele's, which now hovered millimeters above hers, teasing.

"Sometimes." And Adele slithered downward once more, her tongue flicking along Jamie's torso while she swooped lower, lower.

"Now for those chains," Adele mumbled into Jamie's labia. And soon Jamie's chains began to melt away on Adele's tongue. When at last she was entirely molten, she came in long, abyssal waves. Waves of pain endured. Waves of freedom won. Waves of glory. Waves of joy.

As her last wave ebbed, Jamie reached down to Adele's head nuzzled firmly between her legs and wriggled her fingers through Adele's hair. "You have all the gifts, Adele Sabellius. Except for the one I haven't given you yet."

Adele rose again to position herself alongside Jamie. "After your ribs heal, I'll make sure you have plenty of opportunity to give me whatever you think I deserve. But for right now…" She curled on her left side and placed Jamie's right hand between her legs. "Just please hold on to me."

CHAPTER TWENTY-ONE
EMOTION RECOLLECTED IN TRANQUILITY

A lmost ten o'clock, Jamie. Wake up and smell the morning."
Adele sounded downright bubbly, but sometime in the
night, Jamie had finally discovered an excellent sleeping position on
her right side and her ribs weren't nearly ready to give it up yet. She
grunted, pulled a pillow over her head, and soon snuggled into a dream
in which she was surrounded by the light, friendly chatter of women's
voices.

"We'll have to be really careful not to overstep," one of them said.

"It doesn't seem fair," said another. "How do you possibly protect
yourself?"

"With a honeypot and pixie dust," replied the first voice, which
had started to sound like Dana's. "The honeypot looks and acts like the
real thing so as to lure the attack, but really it's all fake. Meanwhile, the
pixie dust rubs off on the bad guys' attack bot and sticks with it after
that, wherever it goes."

"Namely, all the way back to its source." Hmm, now a third voice,
which sounded like Lily. "But you know damn well if our pixie dust
sends back anything useful—like bad guy identities—we'll end up out
of bounds legally."

"Even if the bad guys initiate everything?" Okay, that was Adele.
Definitely Adele.

Jamie yanked the pillow off her head, whereupon a hand descended
from above to tousle her hair. "Ah," said Adele, who leaned in to kiss
her forehead. "She awakens at last."

"Hi." Jamie rubbed her eyes. "I just had the weirdest—Hey," she
said to Adele. "You're dressed already?"

Adele wore a breast-caressing black sweater and faded jeans that
perfectly accentuated her curves. "Busy morning," she explained.

"I'm sorry," said Lily from the foot of the bed, "I'm just not sure
this is a good idea. We're only in early beta and there are bound to be
bugs."

"So I wasn't dreaming," Jamie mumbled.

"We need to do real-world testing," said Dana, whom Jamie found sprawled on the desk chair. "Why not this way? If we cross any legal lines, we'll use the 'oops, sorry, it's only beta' defense and dutifully trash the errant data."

"Anything's better than sending Captain Courageous here into a situation where she's tempted to go off with some stranger," said Adele.

"Stop right there," Jamie demanded, erratically pushing herself upright. The covers slid to her waist, exposing bare breasts, but she didn't care. "What's going on?"

"Well." Next to Jamie, Adele straightened her back, squared her shoulders almost formally. "Since you're determined to go to Demeter and see if that Stacy person turns up, I thought it might be useful to consider what she'd really expect to get from you, and—"

"Does this mean you're okay with me doing it?"

"It means I know I can't stop you. Not again. So I'm stuck with what I still think is a supremely shitty idea—"

"And no doubt your colleagues concur," Jamie muttered, eyeing Lily and Dana.

"Not if you do it right," said Dana. "Has its risks, of course. I mean, we have to consider whether anyone—including you—who saw that intruder might be targeted the way Fitzgerald was." Dana smiled a little ruefully and shook her head when she saw Jamie's expression. "Ha. Didn't think of that, didja?"

"Uh, no. I didn't."

"Well, since you weren't the only one who can visually ID him, the guy's better off skipping out than killing five people—" Dana put up a hand, anticipating Adele, who verged on interrupting her. "Okay, okay, five *more* people, one of them a United States senator. So I'm from the school of thought that says we can back-burner that possibility. But if you're going to try this, my view is that you should use the right tools—and use them someplace where there are plenty of other people around."

"*And* give up on the automatic assumption that you'll encounter Stacy again," Adele added. "Disappointing as that may be."

Jamie opened her mouth to reply—and shut it again. Because in fact she *did* want to confront Stacy. "I just figured…"

One of Adele's eyebrows popped upward as her glare blossomed into unspoken eloquence: You figured what, exactly? That Stacy humiliated you, emotionally and physically—and, by god, you want to avenge yourself, right? And along the way, you think you'll somehow force Stacy to tell you everything about "pizda," right? Even though you damn well know it's utterly impossible because you can't even

really, truly make love to me yet since broken ribs just...do...not...
heal...in only six days.

"Anyway," said Dana, braving the silence, "we've agreed that after
what's just happened around here, the idea that there's a connection
back to, uh, Jamie's night on the town isn't so farfetched."

"Mmm hmm." Adele folded her arms across her chest and stared
straight ahead. "Just unlikely."

Jamie bit off a smile as the realization dawned: Adele's quest for
reinforcements had backfired.

"But it's worth testing," Lily said to Adele with the sort of mildly
exaggerated patience that comes from having repeated something one
too many times. Her eyes then swung to Jamie and stuck. "As long as
we keep everyone completely safe."

"So," declared Dana, sitting erect in the desk chair, "If there's
anything to this, you'll be approached, Jamie. Maybe at the bar, maybe
on the way there or back. Based on what's just happened here, we can
assume they're more interested in spying on us—Lynn or Callithump
or both—than in trying to grab you a second time."

"*If* that's even what happened the first time," Adele insisted.

Dana nodded acknowledgement but kept on going. "We know
they're desperate to get us under close surveillance. Fitzgerald told us
that. And untraceability obviously matters a lot to them. Otherwise I'd
be talking to Fitzgerald today as planned. Which means their interests
are best served by an attempt to zap spyware onto your comlink in the
hope that it'll infect anything and everything you contact. Like Lynn's
comlinks, the house systems, Callithump systems."

Adele turned to face Jamie. "It also means you don't have to go
off with Stacy or anyone else, because we've got a countermove to a
spyware zap."

"Something to do with pixie dust, right?" Now Jamie grinned.
"Tell me more."

Lily sighed. "Okay, okay, I surrender. I'll go along with trying it
out."

"Yes!" Dana pumped her fist, then spoke to Jamie. "I won't bore
you with the techy details, but in essence, the comlink you'll take with
you to the bar is a special kind of honeypot. Special because it has what
we call pixies in all the right places. This comlink will replicate your
apps, and we'll insert fake versions of your contact and message data,
put in a few things from your actual library. It'll perform a charade of
your typical activities, like send messages, navigate, shop, pull stuff
from your library. And all that will continue after the spyware infects
it—so the spyware will be fooled into snooping around as usual for
ways to infect other devices and networks via your contacts."

"But none of it's really my contacts, right? Because the spyware's in an entirely fake environment?" Jamie asked.

"Yep. The spyware actually ends up in a honeypot—a great big simulation." Dana offered a sly smile. "And as the spyware does its thing, our pixies, which the spyware can't perceive, attach a tiny, hidden chunk of code—the pixie dust—onto any data the spyware transmits out of the honeypot simulation to the attacker's command-and-control device or network."

"And then," Lily added, "our pixie dust sends information about the attacker back to a gullypot we'll set up. The smaller the amount of pixie dust, the harder it'll be to detect, so the data on the attacker we instruct it to collect must necessarily remain limited. We have a bunch of options, each one made into a separate pixie dust module, but we should control ourselves and restrict which ones we deploy. We want the pixie dust to be able to protect itself from discovery by the attacker's defenses, which means we deploy stealth and zero-day patch avoidance capabilities, plus a kill switch. After that, I suggest—"

"We need to know who's doing this," Jamie reminded them.

"Ah, well," replied Lily, "no doubt they'll thoroughly disguise themselves. But we can use the pixie dust to track the data transmitted by the spyware, trace its path through subnets and device locations, and we can examine the attacker's use of things like encryption techniques."

"That doesn't get us very far." Jamie shook her head. "I'd be better off—"

"Actually," Lily said quickly, "it can tell us quite a lot. For instance, we can instruct the pixie dust to stick itself onto any other devices, systems, and subnets the attacker communicates with. We'll be able to map what's probably an entire previously unknown surveillance and data theft darknet. And if we bring in the Feds and get permission to collect private data, we'll eventually connect that darknet to specific organizations and people."

"Because this pixie dust of yours sends enough data back to the gullypot that you're able to analyze it all and spot patterns," Jamie said. "Yeah. I like that. How long will it take for us to learn anything?"

"Sorry, can't say," Lily admitted. "Remember, the payloads come back to us in encrypted fragments that piggyback on packets generated by the targets. Also, as the pixie dust sticks onto more and more subnets, systems, and devices, the payloads will end up scattered and out of sync, since each one latches opportunistically onto other packets traveling through the network universe until it encounters a 'friendly' packet that takes it to an address from which it can hop onto our ephem darknet—"

"As in ephemeral, yes? So our end is anonymous?" asked Jamie.

"Oh yeah," said Dana with a smile. "Invisible to the public Internet. Layers of encryption, layers of routing, layers of anonymity—all ending in an isolated, quarantined gullypot. The data coming back from the pixie dust is currently impossible for anyone to follow home to us. So even if someone discovers the pixie dust code on a device, its source remains untraceable."

Jamie shook her head. "Wait a minute. If the bad guys are also using an anonymous darknet, why should your pixie dust have any more ability to track down who they are than they have to track down who we are?"

Now Lily laughed. "Our pixie dust is designed to bring back data about its path through even the most encrypted, onion-routed, anonymous darknet. Although it may not, since we're only in early beta—which is why I've been reluctant to use it. Fact is, this is an arms race, and while we can't know everything our enemies are doing, we have a pretty good idea based on both our research into what's even possible and our analyses of known offensive and defensive strategies and weapons. Our pixie dust is, as far as we can determine, further out there on the bleeding edge than anything else in existence. It certainly won't be bleeding edge for long, but right now it is. Which means the only folks who currently have defenses against it or anything like it are—" Lily spread her arms inclusively. "Us."

Dana extended one leg and poked Lily with her toe. "A long way of saying we think our pixie dust will produce results, but we can't promise that and we can't predict how long it'll take. So plan on having to be patient. Very patient."

"*If* anyone shows up with spyware to be patient about," Adele grumped.

❖

"Meet the Callithump Security Research Center's newest toy," said Dana, proffering an ordinary pocketcom.

Jamie took it and turned it over in her hands. "This doesn't look like much."

And it hadn't come for free, either. She'd waited for three days during which Adele alternately attempted to talk her out of the whole thing, retreated to finish graduate school applications, and vented anger, frustration, and worry on the piano, generally in that order and especially after Dana and Lily agreed that yes, Jamie should go alone.

She had to promise to stay in areas where plenty of people were on the street. She had to promise to go to Demeter just once. And she had to agree, as Dana put it, to talk about it to Lynn—and Rebecca and Mary and Springer and anyone else on the planet—only after the fact. Emotion recollected in tranquility, Dana said. Better for everyone, Dana said, though Jamie had her doubts about that.

"A good honeypot *shouldn't* look like much." Dana winked. "This one's been set up with above-average security. Don't want to make things too easy for an attacker or they'll suspect what we're doing. Remember—it doesn't have to be clicked up for a spyware zap to work, but it does have to be connected to its power source. For an attack to succeed, the attacker has to physically touch it with a device of their own—though that device can be small and disguised. Like, say, a ring or a coin. Four seconds of contact is plenty if their spyware is top-tier."

"Okay. And the gullypot?"

"We've set up two, actually. One gathers the data we anticipate will include personal private information, and we'll share it with the Feds. The other gathers data we reasonably expect will not include personal private information—and that one we keep and analyze the bejeezus out of."

"You'll get reports, right? I want to see those reports."

Dana shrugged. "They'll come with a wicked high gobbledegeek quotient. I'll see what I can do about having some translations made for you. It'll all be super-encrypted and available through a three-factor-authenticated darknet account."

"And the people you have working on this should be compartmentalized enough that nobody sees the whole picture—"

"Relax, kid. It's already done."

1654 hours. Sixteen minutes to mount-out. One last time, Jamie checked the long mirror on the back of the bedroom door. She wore her usual: Jeans, two-pocket bush shirt, black this time, boots, leather jacket, plus a vest to fend off what would be a chilly night. No eyewraps. Not even Robin's boonie hat. Money and ID, sure, but only the honeypot pocketcom Dana had given her earlier.

She pulled the pocketcom from her jeans and stared at it. "This is a good idea, dammit," she muttered. "This needs to be done."

Downstairs, as if in reply, Adele began a new piece on the piano that Jamie didn't recognize. Delicately, ethereally melodic—and sad.

Jamie glanced at the mirror. She could call it off right now and nobody would think any worse of her. Dana would probably find someone to play her part and launch some version of this little mission within a week, so no harm, no foul. She would avoid having to look

Lynn in the eye when she returned and admit to what was, by any measure, a crafted, premeditated deception. And Adele…Adele would probably dance on top of the piano with relief.

Why then? Why should doing this matter at all, much less have become something she found herself clinging to with such tenacity? Adele had spent three days trying to get her to "think forward, not back." Let it go, leave it behind, move on, your future beckons…etcetera.

She listened, she really did—and she tried. Started the first of the analytic geometry/calculus courses Lynn had given her, talked with Adele about what going to college was like day-to-day, minute-to-minute, even blurted something about studying structural engineering and then architecture…maybe someday, in a perfect world…

Most of all, Jamie let Adele love her and did her best, despite her miserable ribs, to love Adele back. In a perfect world, it would have been just like the first time all over again, when she and Adele had managed to relegate Shoo Juh to the shadows…But unlike Adele, Shoo Juh did not seek permission. Shoo Juh filched, hijacked, seized, usurped. Each time Adele touched her, Shoo Juh wriggled more intently in the shadows, intangibly nearer, intangibly clearer.

No, no, she was too vulnerable, too exposed. To the view through her rifle's crosshairs as her finger's tug on the trigger blew bodies apart. To the unrelenting flashes of chains and electric batons and power drills. To memories that refused to stay forgotten, memories of Shoo Juh's cruel insistence on guh shyah, of The Bastard's cackling contempt for pizda.

How do you leave that behind when it won't let you go? When it's out there, real in the world, toying with you, mindfucking you because you stand between it and its target?

"You damn well stop acting like a ghost in your own life," Jamie said to the mirror. "That's how."

The hardest part was saying good-bye to Adele, who rose from the piano, held Jamie's face with both hands, and kissed her with a fervent, open mouth.

"Not fair," Jamie rasped, fire raking her clit.

"All's fair," said Adele. "Be careful."

❖

Thanks to her ribs, a thump of discomfort accompanied each step of Jamie's three-klick trek down Walker Road onto Pine Street and through the center of Manchester. Just as well; the distraction kept her from obsessing about Adele's kiss, which had altogether too much good-bye in it, or sneaking too many glances around her to scout for watching eyes as the last of twilight faded.

She moved as quickly as her squawking ribs permitted. The plan called for her to have little time to make the 5:44 train, so that this journey into the city, like the last one, would appear spontaneous, erratic even. No doubt her stiff, slightly lopsided gait reinforced that impression. Certainly by the time she slouched into a seat as far back in the train's rearmost car as she could get, she looked the part of someone beset.

Once in the city, she was to stay on major streets. "Causeway to Stanford to Cambridge to Joy to Beacon Street," Dana insisted. "Friday after work, so plenty of people out and about, even though it'll be dark. But don't go through the Common. Beacon to Dartmouth, understand? So you get all the way to Demeter on streets full of people. Because making this look authentic means you're out there alone. On your own. Do it this way so we get you back in one piece."

Jamie walked through Demeter's green-and-gold door at 1918 hours to be greeted—and recognized with a satisfied smile—by the same big woman who'd checked her ID the first time. "Welcome back, Lieutenant. No cover." Jamie chose the same spot as before, way at the back of the bar, ordered the same food and drink, then waited.

She expected to wait for a while. And for the first half of her hamburger, she wanted the person who showed up to be Stacy—despite what Dana had told her: "You can't give away what you know, or they'll figure out you're part of a honeypot and back off." Too bad. Jamie had thoroughly juiced herself with thoughts of confronting Stacy—as in "I know what the hell you're up to, bitch. Now tell me where you heard that word."

And maybe such friction between what she'd have to do and what she wanted to do had fueled her so far. Now, however, sitting at the bar, ribs aching as she adjusted to the pounding bass of the music, she recognized the light quiver in her shoulders, her thighs, recognized the mildly buzzy lightheadedness. Adele and Lily were right—she'd done this too soon. She could taste her fatigue. And what if another damn BDSM parade sauntered by like the last time? What if Shoo Juh lay waiting in the shadows, in the dogged bass that shook the floor?

Breathe, dammit, breathe…

Jamie decided to avoid watching the throngs of women who'd soon begin to show up strutting stuff she maybe couldn't yet handle after all. She'd intended to stay until either Stacy or an obvious surrogate appeared and found a way to touch the pocketcom she'd be holding in plain sight—or until the place closed. But not even half an hour at Demeter and she wanted to bolt.

No!

No, you gotta give it a chance—just hope to christ you don't *see Stacy tonight...*

The first encounter occurred moments later when a woman who sauntered up to the nearest barstool hitched one buttock onto it in what was probably supposed to be her sexiest move and ordered a beer. Spiked hair, built like a wrestler, thick hands adorned with several chunky rings, dressed head to foot in motorcycle leather, the woman worked hard to come off like someone in charge. Hard enough that Jamie couldn't be sure she was really anything like her costume. But she damn well might be a spyware zapper.

So Jamie pulled out her pocketcom and clicked it up with what she hoped was a classic checking-for-messages flourish—just as the woman completed a long swig of beer and asked through a squint, "How's the food here?"

Thus began a stilted conversation during which Jamie casually rested her pocketcom-holding hand on the bar within inches of the woman's arm, making sure the small, bright screen displayed a list of recent messages from "Lynn."

The conversation ended about two minutes later, after the woman placed a hand over Jamie's and asked, "Can I offer you dessert?" Jamie tried to count to ten, made it to six, then declined and withdrew her hand. As her pocketcom's display flipped from 2021 to 2022 hours, she asked the bartender for another seltzer water and kept her eyes on her hands now folding protectively over the device. However, she focused her attention, all of it, to her peripheral vision, where Spiked Hair gestured frustration and departed.

Ah, could it really be that blessedly simple? She had no way of finding out until she got back to Great Hill and handed over the pocketcom for analysis. And if Spiked Hair turned out to be, well, just Spiked Hair, then she'd have blown her only shot. So she stayed.

Over the next eighty minutes, several others circled, sniffing, but none came nearer than about eighteen inches to her left hand, which continued to fidget with the pocketcom. Jamie'd thought about this; it had, she hoped, the two-pronged effect of making her look like a jilted lover worriedly waiting for a message, and therefore less likely to respond to a come-on...yet for someone interested in zapping spyware onto the device she held—well, there it was, already clicked on, easy to touch for a few seconds with even the lamest pickup routine.

At 2143 hours, the second encounter squeezed next to Jamie at what had become a crowded bar. Cute, blond, and effervescent, she burbled inane questions she quickly answered herself, apparently to get a laugh, which Jamie obligingly provided. Soon she nuzzled up too close, though with a certain whiskey-infused panache. "I *like* you," she announced, resting her head on Jamie's shoulder and wrapping both hands around Jamie's pocketcom. "Just forget—" She grabbed the pocketcom from Jamie's hand and brought it close to her face. "L-Lynn? Whaddaya care about Lynn, huh? Ya got *me* now, hon."

This time Jamie didn't bother counting. She snatched back her pocketcom, said "No thanks," and abandoned both the blonde and the barstool for a vacancy along the wall several meters away.

Now her gaze had nowhere to go but the narrow, elbow-height shelf attached to the wall behind her—or the floor. So she watched lesbian feet—sneaker-clad, sandal-clad, fuck-me-five-inch-heel-clad… until she realized a pair of black engineer boots had halted dead in front of her.

"Hey, marine."

Before Jamie could look up, strong hands grabbed both of her wrists and pinned them to the shelf behind her, jostling several nearby bottles and glasses.

"You," Stacy barked as she shoved herself roughly into Jamie's right side, "owe me an apology."

"Screw you, bitch," Jamie growled between clenched teeth as she struggled to keep the pain from showing. *Count it…two…three… four…*Then she made one of the few moves left to her: She tried to bite Stacy's face off. And nearly succeeded.

As it was, Stacy drew back just fast enough. She also held down Jamie's left hand—and the pocketcom it clutched—for a few more seconds before letting go. "Too bad about you, marine," she muttered.

It was an invitation, and it hinted of what sounded almost like regret.

Jamie stared at her. Goddamn, they were *that* desperate…

Now another hand slid sinuously over Jamie's, and for a nanosecond, she functioned like an entangled photon simultaneously experiencing two distinctly separate moments. For she'd have sworn she never took her eyes from the lurid dare on Stacy's face, and yet in slow, slow motion, her head turned and she watched long, graceful fingers pluck the pocketcom from her hand, click it off, then place it in her jacket's inside pocket and neatly zip the pocket shut.

Smiling her own invitation, Adele Sabellius slithered in front of Stacy. "Dance with me," she said, and led Jamie toward the music.

"You were gonna go with her, weren't you?"
"No."
"*Weren't* you." Adele was not asking.

"I—" Jamie peeked leftward at Adele's profile crisp against the haze of light pollution from Boston's industrial outskirts as the car sped northward. "I dunno."

Adele glanced over from the driver's seat but didn't speak.

"I'm sorry," Jamie said.

"That I stopped you?"

"That I ever considered it in the first place." Easing her head back, Jamie watched the lights of the city slip behind them on their right as they crossed the Tobin Bridge. "And, um…thank you for dancing with my two left feet."

"I like dancing with you. You're sexy, even with broken ribs. Next time, we close the place."

Jamie turned her head to look at Adele. "Next time? Seriously?"

"I'll teach you the cha-cha. And salsa dancing."

"Thank you," Jamie said. She put her hand on Adele's seat so the edge of her fingers brushed Adele's thigh. "For…for…all of it."

Smiling, Adele picked up Jamie's hand and rested it on her thigh with a small squeeze that meant Jamie's hand should stay right where she'd put it.

For the rest of the ride, Jamie watched Adele drive…home. Yes, she had to admit it, wanted to admit it: Great Hill and the people who lived there had become her home. The thought sent a shiver through her. Because, after all, how long could such a thing last, really?

"She knows," Dana murmured, taking the pocketcom from Jamie and quickly departing the low-lit kitchen for the offices over the second garage.

"How?" Jamie asked. Behind her, Adele stood mute, head shifting back and forth—the signal that Jamie was on her own for this part.

"How do you *think?*" Lynn's voice came from the family room, sounding weary. And maybe angry. But mostly it sounded sad.

"I'm not going to apologize," said Jamie as she spotted Lynn sitting alone on a large ottoman in front of the hearth, prodding the embers of a dying fire that provided the room's only light. "It was a good idea and I wasn't in any danger—"

"I understand that. Dana had you covered better than you know." Lynn patted the space next to her on the ottoman. "I expect you're pretty sore and tired, but take a minute. Please."

The space next to Lynn was small and Lynn shifted aside only slightly, so they sat shoulder to shoulder, and for several moments they said nothing.

Finally, Jamie spoke. "I'm okay, Lynn."

Lynn nodded and continued to poke the remains of the burning logs. "I didn't mean for it to be like this."

"But it *is* like this. You and I met at Saint Eh Mo's—we needed each other to survive Saint Eh Mo's—because we had the same enemy. And, obviously, the fight's not over yet."

"Your fight *is* over, Jamie. You're here to recover and—"

"And move on? How do I do that while the enemy—your enemy and my enemy—is actively engaged in trying to hurt you?"

Lynn shook her head. "Even if what you say is true, this doesn't have to be your fight anymore."

"Or yours. You can walk away the same as you're saying I should. Christ, Lynn, why not? You sure as hell don't need to prove anything to anyone. You have more money than god, so you can protect yourself and everyone you love and generations of their progeny. You can spend the rest of your life having fun. So why give a shit about what or who gets destroyed or the kind of world we end up with because of a bunch of sociopath power gluttons? Let them take what they're so greedy for. Step aside and let them win and they'll leave you be."

Lynn didn't move. Lynn didn't speak. Finally, she shook her head. "No," she said as though she'd considered Jamie's suggestion and decided against it. "I can't."

"Me either."

CHAPTER TWENTY-TWO
THOSE PEOPLE

It sounded like a shout. And it seemed to come from so nearby that Jamie sprang awake and tried to fling herself to her feet before she'd untangled them from the bedcovers. This sent her careening face-first into Dana, who had ignored Great Hill protocol and bounded into the bedroom without bothering to knock. Or flip on a light.

"It got zapped twice last night," Dana repeated breathlessly as she caught Jamie's shoulders. "Twice."

"Uhh...god," Jamie groaned, the pain in her ribs overtaking her. She clutched the sleeve of Dana's sweatshirt for balance and began to comprehend. "You mean...it worked?" she gasped through a grimace.

"Sure as hell did—"

"What the *fuck*?" Adele protested sleepily from the far side of the bed, then made a grab for sheets and blankets yanked off her by Jamie's stumble. "What time is it?"

"Twice," mumbled Jamie, easing herself back onto the bed. "What does that mean?"

"Two different people zapped the pocketcom," Dana said. "First one at nine fifty-four—"

A humph came from Adele as she turned on the lamp next to her side of the bed. "The little blonde."

Jamie's head whipped around. "You were there already?"

Adele winked. "When was the second one?" she asked Dana.

"Ten thirty-eight."

"Stacy," Jamie growled, teeth grinding.

"So." Adele gestured impatiently at Dana. "What else do you know?"

"Ah, well..." Dana sat on the bed. "We've never seen either of these codesets before, but they're related. Similar injection techniques and structures, though the first one is simpler. Also, they exploit the same vulnerabilities, and they use similar approaches to file naming and the same string decryption algorithm. We're trying to decrypt the payloads, but that'll take some time."

"Encrypted payloads." Jamie rubbed the muscles along her jaw. "So you don't know what they're after yet, right?"

"Well, we know some things from watching what they've been doing in our honeypot environment." Dana paused, looking very tired. "The first zap steals data. It harvested contact and system configuration data as well as content on the pocketcom and what it thinks is your service provider network, so it can move on and harvest the same sort of stuff from other devices it infects."

Adele leaned forward, her eyes intent. "And the second zap?"

"Stacy's," confirmed Jamie.

"More complex than the first one. It installed a module that's remotely controlled. When it's turned on, it inserts content onto the system it infects, complete with credentials and authentication that appear entirely genuine." Suddenly, Dana's energy returned. "Within a few minutes of the zap, it put a small, innocuous message on the pocketcom—completely credentialed, dated five weeks ago, and entirely fictitious. We think they're testing, letting a fake message sit there a while to see if the usual counterfeit recognition software spots it. Which it has not."

"So one's a copycat of the other?" Jamie asked.

"Uh-uh." Dana shook her head. "More like two teams working off the same basic framework of modules."

Adele slid a forefinger across her lower lip. "What about the pixie dust? Did it get picked up and has it been able to, uh—"

"Phone home?" Dana smiled weary victory. "Yes and yes again. Very short messages so far. We got pixie dust from both zaps sending back payloads from the same darknet server—probably the attackers' command-and-control server. Don't know whose it is yet. Our cryppies are the best, but they can work only so fast. Sure as hell confirms that the two zaps last night were connected, though. In a few days, we'll know more." Dana stretched her shoulders, rolled her head, and stood. "Right now, however, I am going to bed."

"Thanks, Dana," said Jamie.

"Thank *you.*" Dana offered a tired, disheveled salute. "This code is damn nasty high-end stuff that took somebody a shitload of money to create. You've saved a lot of people a lot of headaches by sucking it into a honeypot so we can analyze it, counter-hack it, and neutralize it. Nice work. Now go back to sleep. And the next time you give me a counter-hacker's gold mine, I'll remember to knock."

Jamie pulled up the covers and edged herself into the pillows while Adele turned off the light. Dawn was still forty minutes away, according to the time display on the videoscreen. But sleep would be impossible.

Adele snuggled close. "Good one, Gwynmorgan. I am truly impressed. Now shut your eyes."

"Can't."

"Sure you can." Adele snuggled closer, and soon her hand slid slowly up Jamie's inner thigh. "'Cuz I have an app for that."

Saturday mornings had always been Jamie's favorite time at Great Hill—everyone around, everyone relaxed—but Saturday, November ninth was special. They were all there, even Robin, and they gave the day to each other, talking, eating, walking the property's trails together. This, Jamie decided as she watched them, reveled in them, is what home is. *And this is the best day ever...*

Later, Adele slid her hands along Jamie's hips and took possession, steering the smoothly rounded abundance between Jamie's legs into her own. Her lips parted and eager, she hoisted herself up to Jamie's mouth, where her tongue played delicately, then voraciously. "I love them all, too, I really do, but I want you to myself for a while," she murmured.

"Uhhh." Jamie was dizzy now, on fire now. A little moan quivered out of her when Adele withdrew to tug on her jeans and underwear until they lumped around her ankles. "You're getting wicked good at this," she managed huskily as the cotton of Adele's leggings teased her naked hips, her naked, swelling genitals.

"I'm inspired," crooned Adele, now removing her own clothes.

Seconds later, Adele had them both horizontal. She crawled up Jamie's leg and, arriving at Jamie's shirt, unbuttoned it and swept it wide, mock-trapping Jamie's spread-eagled arms.

"You like me this way, don't you?" Jamie quipped, squirming her defiance of the autonomic urge to free herself from Adele's hold.

"Yeah, maybe I do." Adele grinned and tightened her grip on Jamie's arms. "Could be the best way to keep you out of trouble."

Adele descended then, circling deliberately, her tongue taunting as it advanced, retreated, advanced...

Oh yeah, Jamie thought, *the very best day ever...*

"I have to go back to Truro tomorrow," said Adele as they lazed in bed on Sunday morning watching the wind turbines' restive spin.

"Oh." Jamie's stomach cramped. The moment she'd been dreading had arrived. "Yeah."

"Come with me," Adele said. "Luce and Biz are going to Arizona for a couple weeks, so it'll be just us. We can have the place to ourselves pretty much right up to Thanksgiving."

"On November twenty-fifth, I gotta report to the Navy Clinic in Newport for a medical evaluation—"

"The Monday before Thanksgiving, right?"

"Yeah."

"Great. I gotta bring Luce and Biz's car back here anyway, so we can head over to Newport first and then—"

"Well, uh—" Jamie began talking too fast. "I think maybe I should stick around for—" An insistent knock on the bedroom door and the menacing scowl that suddenly claimed Adele's face were all Jamie needed to halt mid-sentence. "Come in," she nearly shouted, eager to fling her gaze toward the doorway.

"Is this a bad time?" Dana asked, glancing twice at Adele.

"No. It's fine." Jamie clamped her eyes on Dana. "What've you got?"

"Couple things. First, the credentialing you'll need to access the reports on Blondie and Butch." Dana chuckled. "That's what we're calling the two zaps."

"Very amusing," Adele groused.

Dana's eyebrows hiked, but she soldiered on. "Plus, we made our first breakthrough. Not on the zap code—we'll be duking it out with that for quite a while. But we've gotten some pixie dust payloads carrying data from a comlink with, believe it or not, a fifth-order link to the attackers' command-and-control server—"

"Fifth-order," Jamie repeated. "You mean—"

"She *means*," snapped Adele, "it's the fifth device in a chain. Command-and-control server relays dusted data to comlink one, comlink one sends dusted data to comlink two, and so on until you get to comlink five."

"Uh, right." Dana's gaze skittered back and forth between Jamie and Adele. "And that fifth comlink sent pixie-dusted data back to comlink four. Encrypted, of course. But they, whoever 'they' are, used a poor-quality pseudorandom number generator to produce the encryption key. Overstretched entropy, y'know?"

Jamie didn't, but she nodded anyway.

"Remember when I said our cryppies are good?" Dana folded her arms across her chest and proudly pumped out her breasts. "Well, they're awe*some*. Because in less than thirty-six hours they deciphered the encrypted data that fifth comlink sent to the fourth comlink. They're working on retrodicting past encryption keys now, so we'll be able to read the comlink's earlier messages, too."

Jamie bounced on the bed, causing her ribs to bitch, but she didn't care. "What've you deciphered so far?"

"A hundred and five zeroes and ones. Could represent any number of things, but the most interesting possibility we've found so far comes from hypothesizing that the zeroes and ones are Morse code. Zeroes as dots, ones as dashes. After a lot of coffee and trial and error, we arranged them in groups of five. Which gives us a twenty-one-digit number."

Adele moved her legs—curiosity overcoming pique, probably. "And what kind of number do you think it is?" she asked, her voice cool with counterfeit indifference.

Grinning slyly, Dana swung an arm toward the room's videoscreen and clicked it on. Another click brought up a satellite view of the Earth. "I think it's date, time, latitude, and longitude—in that order. Nothing in the number about which hemispheres, but even so, we end up with only four possibilities."

Dana began to click through them. The globe spun, zoomed, and a small arrow appeared, pointing to a remote, uninhabited part of Kazakhstan. Another spin and zoom, and the arrow reappeared at a spot in the south Indian Ocean far from any land. Then the imagery shifted to an uninhabited region of northern Patagonia, and finally—

"Hey," Jamie said while the videoscreen, which had sped northward, began its next zoom-in. "It's going to Cape Cod."

"What the *hell?*" Adele's voice pitched upward as the zoom slowed. "That's Truro." When the arrow appeared, she actually gasped. "Jeezus, this too bizarre." She grabbed Jamie's forearm, her voice jittery. "It's—It's pointing right at Aunt Zerviah's house."

"Who?" chorused Jamie and Dana.

"Zerviah Endicott. An old lady who's been dead for, I dunno, five or six years. I met her when I was in high school. She was related to a couple of friends of mine who lived—" Adele gestured at Dana. "Take us a little southward—yeah, there. That's Long Nook Road, where my friends—they were cousins—lived across the street from each other. There, in those two houses. About a mile down the road from Aunt Zerviah's. Sometimes we'd tag along when she went berry or mushroom picking."

"Oooh." Jamie snickered. "This must screw up your index of coincidence pretty good, huh?"

Adele pinched Jamie's backside.

"Ow!"

"Dana, didn't you say date and time, too?" Adele asked while she scooted beyond the reach of Jamie's retaliating right thumb and forefinger.

"Today. Eleven o'clock." Dana glanced at the videoscreen's time display. "But the numbers don't tell us if that's local time—which is to say, in about thirty-five minutes—or universal time."

"Which would mean four hours and twenty-five minutes ago," said Jamie. "Damn. Either way, it's too late for us to do squat."

"Luce and Biz might be willing to drive over and look around before they leave this afternoon," Adele said. "It's Sunday, so no hunting. They'd be just a couple of old ladies taking a little walk down a National Seashore trail near Long Nook Beach."

Dana's head edged side to side. "I don't like the sound of that."

"Dana's right, Del." Jamie didn't try to hide the real trepidation Adele's suggestion stirred up in her. "Odds are they'd be spotted before they'd see anything. And they might attract attention that could be dangerous if those people connect them back to Lily, then Callithump, then Lynn. Which wouldn't be difficult."

Adele stared at Jamie, her eyes narrowing with comprehension. "Those people…" she repeated in a whisper that seemed to struggle for air.

❖

Silence descended after Dana quietly closed the bedroom door, and something about the way Adele sat there clutching the covers to her breasts, unmoving, unblinking as she stared straight ahead, kept Jamie frozen in a state of uh-oh.

"I rescind my invitation," Adele finally announced without looking at Jamie, her voice raw but steady. "I don't want you coming to Truro with me."

"Del…"

"I mean it." Adele tossed aside the bedcovers, stood, and pulled on a robe. "And I think I should leave today. Immediately, in fact."

"Del, please."

"What's the matter?" Adele wheeled around; her eyes blazed. "Oh, right. You've decided that *now* you want to come with me, huh? So you can sniff around Aunt Zerviah's. Well, it's a free country, sort of, so go right ahead, Lieutenant. You sure as hell don't need *me* to help you find your way."

Lieutenant. Jamie never wanted the rank, and she hated when a Marine grunt called her that, replete with the required deference, occasionally tinged with a special resentment reserved for officers. But it had never felt like an outright insult until now.

Chapter Twenty-three
Hell-Bent

W hat happened?"
Inside the parka that had been her birthday present from
Mary, Jamie shrugged. Hardly an answer, but it was all she had to offer
Lynn, who now approached the smooth granite mound near the top of
Great Hill where she sat. As Lynn got closer, Jamie pulled away her
blinking eyes to stare southeastward again, at the distant riled waters of
outer Massachusetts Bay.

"Well." Lynn plunked down on the granite. "She left about fifteen
minutes ago."

Jamie nodded.

"C'mon, sweetie," Lynn said. "Time to talk."

"I don't have anything to say."

"You always have something to say."

Jamie fiddled with the parka's zipper for a long minute, then
sighed. "She left because I…I hesitated."

"About going to Truro with her."

"How'd you—"

"She told Lily."

"And Lily told you."

"Mmm." Lynn offered a semi-apologetic smile. "It's the worst
thing and the best thing about four generations under one roof."

"Mostly the best thing, I think. The way you guys stick together,
ready to help each other. Being around it is…addictive."

"Yeah. I know what you mean."

"Del wanted…she expected me to say yes right then, and I didn't
think I should just assume…I-I wasn't sure. It didn't seem like a good
time to go…and besides…" Jamie shook her head. "Shit. I'm not ready
for this. I am *so* out of my league."

"And besides…" Lynn prompted her.

"I don't know what to do…" Jamie gestured frustration.

"Depends on what you want. Your starting point is here, now. The strategic question is: What do you want? Once you know that—"

"Yeah, the tactical options become obvious. But what's it matter, anyway? I can't get there from here."

Lynn leaned forward into Jamie's view, her face hinting the smile to come. "This from the woman who got me out of Saint Eh Mo's." She sighed, and Jamie knew she exaggerated the sigh. Just a little. "So you have to take the long way 'round. Wouldn't be the first time. The only question is: What do you *want?* And to answer that, you're going to have to be honest with yourself."

"To be honest, I want these shadows—Shoo Juh's shadow, The Bastard's shadow—to stop creeping along the edges of everything I see. To stop turning into nightmares every time I shut my eyes." The acidic burn in Jamie's belly sizzled up the center of her chest. "I know it's supposed to just be the haunts of war, but I could never shake the feeling there was a real threat. Every instinct or intuition or whatever that I had kept going nuts, and for a long time I figured I really was insane. Figured I had a life sentence—crazy, disoriented, freaked out to the very end. But now I know the threat was—*is*—real. That's what the shadows mean."

"Something real, like the song says."

"What song?"

"An old ballad. Before your time." Softly, Lynn sang a wistful melody.

"What be our dreams
"But trickster schemes
"When sleights of mind reveal
"Shadows of something real
"That wink away in waking's glare—
"Like war and love, in dreams all's fair."

"Yeah," Jamie said. "The break-in and pizda and Fitzgerald's murder and Stacy and what went down with Nim Bacani and his video—they're all shadows of the *same* something real. So was the trap you walked into at Saint Eh Mo's. I've got to know whose shadow I'm seeing."

"Jamie—"

"Del says you don't need my help anymore. And maybe you don't. But it's hard to watch you under siege for having the guts to keep people like Jonathan Armstrong Archer and Rafael Vicario and Oscar Zanella and that FDL guy Lambert from corrupting you out of doing your job. And—" Jamie tried to stop, but the words kept rolling out of her. "And I hate having to go back to the Marine Corps and spend every fucking minute wondering how long Del will be able to stand it while I fester in a mudhole and she writes a PhD dissertation I'll be too dumbshit stupid to ever understand. And I don't know if I've got what it takes to get enough of an education so maybe I really could be—" Jamie lifted her arms into a sweep that included Lynn, the woods, the house, the faraway sea and sky. "Be part of this for real."

"You're already part of this for real, sweetie. And I think you've become part of Adele for real, too."

Jamie snorted her skepticism.

"I have a news flash for you." Lynn wrapped an arm across Jamie's hunched back. "Although Adele Sabellius is very bright, very charming and attractive, and has a heart of gold, she is *not* perfect. For instance, she's wrong about my not needing your help anymore."

"Yeah?"

"Like all of us, Adele has her weak spots. One is that when she jumps in, it tends to be unhesitating, hell-bent even—the flip side of which can be that she'll sometimes end up mulishly headstrong. Perhaps you've noticed."

"Yeah, well, she can be persuaded...I think..."

"I've always thought she jumps in like that because she's on a kind of quest. She follows an intuition, an insight she deeply trusts, usually based on what she perceives in somebody she's dealing with. So she can *seem* to trust others easily, maybe too easily. But she does not. And because she does not in fact trust easily, when she decides her intuition or insight was wrong, she also ends up feeling that her trust has been violated. So she withdraws, suddenly and significantly. Restoring her trust takes work. Perseverance."

"I didn't—I mean, I never meant to—"

"Remember, Jamie. This is someone whose world ended utterly and without warning when she was eleven years old. She never got that world back. I wonder sometimes if she can't stop searching for it. Or at least some key part of it—"

"Safe," Jamie murmured. "That's the key part she's after. Safe."

"You said a minute ago you liked the way we stick together, ready to help each other."

"Yeah. A lot."

"Part of how we do it is to honestly let each other know, situation by situation, what kind of help will make a difference. Keeps us from slamming into each other like bumper cars at an amusement park."

"Okay." Jamie straightened up. "What kind of help do you—"

"No, sweetie. I mean you."

"Me? I-I don't know..."

"Well, would it help if you understand you'll really upset all of us if you do *not* think of us and this place as your home?" Lynn stroked

Jamie's back as she spoke. "Would it help if I tell you I sincerely believe you're more than smart enough to catch up educationally in a field you care about rather than what the Marine Corps might pressure you into?"

"Yeah." Jamie exhaled and a tiny shiver fluttered outward from her solar plexus. "It does help."

"And when it comes to those Palawan demons, I can tell you that you're winning. Because I can see it. You're so much stronger than you were even a month ago. And now, as you said, you know you're not crazy. That knowledge is your ultimate weapon. The rest is just details."

"I like your faith in me."

"It's justified. I'm not suggesting you'll find it easy, but I think you can deal with the shadows and nightmares without having to parse this chain of events that may or may not stretch back to the truce talks and my going to Saint Eh Mo's, that may or may not still be playing out with the break-in and this spyware Dana's so amped about. And that may or may not involve Lambert, Zanella, Archer, and Vicario. Very astute of you, by the way, to pick them—Archer, Vicario, and Zanella, I mean—out of that brief Springer showed you, then add Richard Lambert to your list. And you got her to tell you about Nimuel Bacani, too. Springer may finally have met her match."

Jamie gulped. "Please don't be mad at Springer. She thought maybe—I mean, I was poking at her about your new legislation and helping at the brunch next Sunday. She was only trying to keep me in the loop. Just in case."

"I know." A smile teased the corners of Lynn's mouth. "Don't worry. It's not the first time Springer's pushed the boundaries. And it won't be the last. But you need to embrace a couple of things. First, you no longer have to doubt yourself—or prove anything to yourself or anyone else. You *can* tell the difference between what's for real and what's only in your head. You *can* trust your perceptions, your intuition to spot a mindfuck."

Hearing it from someone else, and especially hearing it from Lynn, had a kind of cleansing effect on Jamie, as though she'd stepped from a mud fight into a cascade of sparkling, warm water. "Yeah," she said. "Yeah."

"And second, your help has already made an enormous difference. In important ways and more than once. You interrupted a break-in before any damage was done. You're almost single-handedly responsible for a complete overhaul of all our security—mine, Great Hill's, even Callithump's. Your so-called 'second night on the town' last Friday will be paying off for months, perhaps years. You've given us a real edge. And I thank you. Again. I am so indescribably grateful for you." Lynn took up Jamie's hand in hers and gave it a squeeze. "And since you're one of us, I'm going to let you know what kind of help I need that'll make a difference."

"Good." Jamie held on to Lynn's hand. "Please tell me."

"I need you to stand down for a while. Walk away from all the stuff with the break-in and pizda and Nimuel Bacani and those four sordid men. I know you won't forget about it—can't forget about it—but you can push it into the background and pay attention to the foreground, to the reality that's right in front of you. If you do that, you'll get even stronger, more balanced—and you'll help me get the running room I need. Do you understand?"

"Yes." But Jamie couldn't stop a frown from taking her face.

"I promise I will tell you what I learn. And I will call you when I need you, Jamie. I promise."

"I could just—"

"I've *got* this one, understand? And right now I need you to do something else."

"What?" Jamie straightened up again as a small squad of pinpricks raced up her spine.

Lynn handed her a sheet of paper, a printout that showed a flight reservation marked PAID and CONFIRMED.

"Are you sure?" Jamie asked.

"Oh yes, sweetie, I certainly am."

"But what if—"

"Won't know if you don't try." Lynn's smile lit her face. "And I want you to try very hard, okay? I want you to persevere."

"Okay." Jamie let the nourishment of Lynn's smile flow through her and managed to respond with a nervous smile of her own that seemed to quiver in rhythm with her accelerating heartbeat.

From the moonlit street thirty meters away, the house struck Jamie as the seed from which Great Hill must have sprouted. A generation older and much smaller, it nevertheless exhibited the same determined loyalty to classic New England architectural form and materials, and the same need to hunker into a south-facing hillside and surround itself with woods.

No cars in the driveway, but a few windows glowed and a floodlight illuminated the space in front of the house's two ground-level doors, one for a garage, another a few feet away for people. Pulling the hood of her parka over her head for protection against a rising northwest wind, Jamie stared at the windows' warm light. The place itself seemed inviting, but she didn't—couldn't—take those first steps down the shell driveway, eerie bluish-white beneath the almost-full moon. Her invitation had been rescinded.

On the other hand, it's friggin' cold out here. So either call and get that cab to come back or knock on the goddamn door.

"Ah shit," she said, shoving the toe of her boot into the driveway's shells. Retreat sorely tempted her. Might this not be better done in daylight? Launched from a place of her own, even if it was only a rented room at an inn a few miles down the road in Provincetown?

*I mean, what about perseverance says you have to leave your ass hanging out here at—*Jamie checked her eyewraps' time display—*at 1954 hours in a November gale after a roller-coaster ride in an unpressurized ten-seat plane trying to figure the odds of ending up with the door slammed in your face?*

The answer came a mere second later when a gust of wind smacked her sideways and threw the trees on either side of the driveway into a frenzy.

"Okay, okay," Jamie grumbled. She always could recognize a nudge from Caprice.

A few moments later, she rang the bell, then knocked. But no one answered. She climbed a granite-landscaped walkway dug into the hillside to knock at what she figured was the formal front door on the first floor. But still no one answered.

❖

"And here *I* was thinking you were a light sleeper."

Jamie's eyes opened to Adele standing over her. Huddled at the bottom of the walkway near the ground-level door because it offered a bit of shelter from the wind, she'd used her small backpack to cushion her ribs and, yes, okay, she'd rested her hood-covered head against the granite halfwall—but she'd have sworn she never shut her eyes. On the contrary, she'd been keeping her eyes vigilantly wide, waiting for the headlights of an approaching car, Adele's approaching car. From her position, which afforded a view of the entire driveway, any approaching car would be impossible to miss.

Except...

Except Adele loomed above her, feet wide apart and arms akimbo, while the headlights of Adele's car nearly blinded her.

"Hi," Jamie said, wishing she could see Adele's face. But it was backlit by the headlights' glare, shadowed by the night.

"Hi yourself." Adele's voice gave nothing away. Not a good sign. Then Jamie noticed she swayed ever so slightly.

"I-I don't want to fight with you." Chilled and stiff, Jamie stood. "I hate the way I feel right now. And I'm sorry for—for being hell-bent."

"Hell-bent. Yeah. You are." Adele took a deep breath and forcefully exhaled it. "An' you were right. Spec—" She swung her head back and forth, as if to shake off an impediment. "Spectacularly right. An' I'm mad at you."

"For being hell-bent or being right?"

"Yes." Pivoting, Adele clicked her pocketcom at the garage door, which obediently began to lift. Clearly, she intended to return to the car and steer it into the garage, but she stumbled and would've fallen if Jamie hadn't stepped forward to catch her arm from behind. "I'm fine, thanks," she humphed.

"You smell like scotch. You stagger like scotch."

"Well, then." Adele pulled her arm from Jamie's grip to walk unsteadily into the brightly lit garage. "*You* put the damn thing away," she said, one hand gesturing dismissively, the other opening a door that led from the garage into the basement of the house. "Keys're in it," she called out and disappeared.

❖

Jamie would've considered spending the night in the car but for the possibility that on the other side of the door, Adele might lay unconscious on the floor.

Thanks to an earlier peek through one of those glowing windows, Jamie already knew the area had been finished—tiled floor, painted walls and ceiling—into what appeared to be a decent sized den and, behind it, a small bedroom visible through open double doors. And yeah, she could go outside and peek through the window again. But that just didn't seem much like perseverance. So in she went.

Adele had made it to the edge of the bed in the room behind the den, where she sat unmoving, head down, hands slumped in her lap.

"Del?"

No answer.

Jamie came close enough to smell scotch again. "Del."

"Oh god," Adele mumbled. "I feel like shit."

"Maybe you should lie down. Let me take off your shoes."

"You." Adele raised a hand in an attempt to point, but it promptly collapsed onto her thigh. "I'm pissed at you. Really...pissed..." Then, with a moan, she flopped straight back onto the mattress and didn't budge or open her eyes, not even when Jamie slipped her shoes from her feet.

Well, okay, not exactly an invitation to stay. But Adele hadn't kicked her out either. Jamie removed her parka, her boots, and went in search of a bathroom, which she found nearby down a hallway.

Coaxing Adele all the way onto the mattress turned out to be fairly easy, though she roused only enough to curl up in the middle of the bed. After putting a pillow under her head and sweeping the covers over her, Jamie stretched out a few inches away and gazed at her, stroking her cheek, her hair, realizing that although they'd spent nearly every moment of the last ten days together, the sight of Adele in repose, eyes closed, was a new experience.

"Forty-five days since I laid eyes on you, Del," Jamie murmured. "I know it's way too soon to say I love you. But I do. I love you. And I'm so sorry I did anything to make you doubt that."

For the first time since they'd started spending nights together, Jamie roused before Adele did. She had dreamed of imprisonment and pain, as usual, and helplessness too; unable to distract an unseen interrogator's interest in Adele, she screamed and cursed to no avail. But she woke to exactly the same position on the bed in which she'd fallen asleep—except now Adele nestled against her, one arm flung across her belly so that long, graceful pianist's fingers possessively cupped her jean-clad crotch.

Finally, a good sign. At least the insensible Adele wanted her, still wanted her.

Determined not to jeopardize it, Jamie lay motionless except for exhaling the dream out of herself. And, of course, she couldn't ignore Adele's hand. Acutely thankful at how quickly Adele's fierce grip weakened her recollection of the dream, she reveled in the hot flow of arousal, and soon her crotch rotated oh-just-a-little upward, her clit flicking against the center seam of her jeans, toward Adele's unconscious resolve.

At the tips of Adele's fingers, all the energy she ever was or ever would be compressed into an infinitesimal space of infinite density, an incomprehensibly small point that pulled everything into itself—time and gravity and fear and hopelessness and all the light and sound and fury of the world. Beneath Adele's fingers, ending and beginning converged, indistinguishable, then turned inside out and catapulted into a whole new, untried universe.

If she kept going, she could have a life here, with this woman who held her, with the women of Great Hill. She'd be able to learn what she needed to, use it to make a decent living doing something she could sink her teeth into. And yeah, the phantasms would be there, she knew that now. The phantasms had become part of her life's landscape. But, by god, they didn't have to *rule* her life's landscape. At least not all the time.

Minutes passed. Jamie closed her eyes…until whenever it was that Adele's hand suddenly doubled down on the flesh between her legs, stealing her breath.

"Hell-bent." Adele growled into her shoulder. "If I didn't feel like such crap, I'd hell-bend you right now."

Jamie grinned at the ceiling. "I might like that."

CHAPTER TWENTY-FOUR
HOMEBODY

A dele didn't recover until late Monday afternoon from what had been her first—and, she swore repeatedly, her last— foray into scotch.

"You make great French toast," she declared that evening. "Though I never considered having it for dinner."

"You don't mind?" Jamie asked. "Having it for dinner, I mean?" French toast drenched in maple syrup was as close as Jamie could bring herself to offering up hair of the dog.

"Mind? Oh no, it's delicious. 'Specially with all this bacon." Adele put down her fork and studied Jamie across the simple wooden dining room table.

"What?"

"You're a real homebody, aren't you?"

"Dunno. I never really—"

"That's why you didn't want to come with me." Adele's head bobbed slowly up and down. "Mmm. I get it. Lynn sent you."

Adele didn't seem angry. On the contrary, her voice, her expression, were entirely neutral. She might as well have been reading a list of ingredients off a cereal box.

But right then, Jamie wanted to cry. She lowered her head to hide the tears overspilling her eyes. She dropped her hands to her lap to steady her shoulders. She held her gut tight, tight, because even a small breath and all the parts of her would dissociate, disintegrate, disappear...

Close...your...eyes...yes...like that...

"Jamie?"

And don't move...don't move...not yet...

"Jamie?"

"Lynn...an' you..." Jamie wheezed, "all I have...there's...nothing else..." She was sinking inward, into the blackness of nothing else, which was never very far away, which could pull her beyond feeling or thought or need or caring, because in this blackness there could be no more trying, no more hoping...

Around her, things started to jumble, yet it was all far away, already far away, farther than sight or sound or touch could reach, and soon the jumbling would be gone and she would be gone, too. Not into the blue like the first time...that had been a lie the first time, Caprice's tease. But this time...*this time it's easy, so easy...*

Except for that honey scent, warm and close...

"It's okay, baby, it's okay. I understand. I do." Adele's kisses, urgent yet gentle, abundant with possibility as they interspersed with her words, gathered Jamie out of the blackness piece by piece. "Who you are—right here, right now—gives me hope. You shine a light into my darkness. I can't imagine a life without you."

Jamie opened her eyes to Adele inches away. "Oh god, Del, I will fail you."

"No. You won't." Adele kissed her again. "As long as you stay true to yourself, you can't fail me."

After that, so much got said in small moments. In the mornings while they made love before breakfast. In the afternoons when they took long walks along the Outer Cape's beaches, Truro's back roads, Provincetown's sleepy streets. Through homebody evenings in front of Luce and Biz's old-fashioned woodstove.

On their very first walk, Adele led the way to an antique lighthouse maybe two klicks down the road—a fifteen- or sixteen-meter truncated cone of white-painted brick capped by a glassed lantern room with a still-working beam that cycled every few seconds out over the North Atlantic, then across the hills of Truro to wink at the northern end of Cape Cod Bay and Provincetown visible in the distance. "Built in the eighteen-fifties," Adele said admiringly. "Moved back once because the cliffs had eroded so much. A few more years like the last few and it'll have to be moved again."

"How high up are we?"

"A hundred and nineteen feet above sea level, which, as you can see, is right down there."

When Jamie took a step toward the cliff edge about six meters away, Adele grabbed her arm. "No, don't go any closer. It's incredibly unstable."

"Looks okay."

"From up here, sure. But wait 'til you see it from down there." Adele slipped her arm through Jamie's and steered away from the cliff. "C'mon, tide's starting to ebb. We'll take the road to the beach and I'll show you."

"How far?"

Adele smiled; she was more relaxed than Jamie had ever seen her. "You tell me when we get there."

"Two klicks, give or take," Jamie announced twenty minutes later as they stood in the small, sand-swept parking lot at the end of the road. Forty or fifty meters of beach stretched before them in both directions as far as the eye could see, every inch accosted by the large, thundering North Atlantic surf they'd been able to hear the whole way down the road. Now Jamie understood why: Wave after enormous wave crested and crashed and slithered up the beach. The wind had calmed during the night, but the ocean still rolled in, austerely, remorselessly beautiful.

"Gods on the march," Adele intoned in what struck Jamie as a ritual acknowledgement. She took Jamie's hand and began the gradual five-meter descent from the blacktop to the beach along a well-trodden path through meager tufts of beach grass. "This way," she said when they reached the beach, nodding toward the dunes on their right, which soon loomed raggedly above them.

"I see what you mean." Jamie had to shout over the relentless roar of the waves. "It's getting undermined from below by the constant wave action."

"Yep. And when it's sufficiently gouged out, whole chunks of clifftop break away, grass and trees and all." Adele pointed. "Like there. And there. Eventually, they slide all the way down and the waves chew up what's left of any vegetation. A single strong nor'easter can rip away forty feet of dune in places. Grind everything up like a garbage disposal. Some years we lose more than a hundred feet. Sometimes way more."

Jamie walked over to a shape mostly buried in sand that looked manmade. "Concrete blocks."

"Part of the old Ellison cottage, probably." Adele shaded her eyes to peer at the top of the cliff. "It was taken a few years ago." She nodded leftward to a twisted wood remnant. "There's still a bit of their stairway left. Higher up, you'll notice a pipe sticking out of the cliffside. A few feet below the top. See it?"

"The water line that used to go to the house?"

"Mmm hmm. Several of those along here."

A few minutes later, Jamie pointed upward. "Jeez. That looks exactly like a snow cornice. Least little bit of vibration or weight and down it'll come. Same as an avalanche."

"You do backcountry skiing?" Adele didn't hide her surprise.

"Nah." Jamie avoided her gaze. "Used to read lots of survival stories, that's all."

"Hey." Adele slid her arm through Jamie's. "My kinda girl."

"Really?"

"Oh yeah. Stories like that help keep things in perspective."

They walked on, arm in arm, shoulder to shoulder. "I like it around here," Jamie said after a while.

"Excellent. Around here is my favorite place on earth. As least so far."

"A refuge."

"Yeah. Exactly. As free as it is safe. Until the sea eventually takes it, anyway."

Jamie squinted at Adele as they continued southward down the beach. Free and safe—she'd have to think about that, about how much freedom a person needed to be Safe. *Just another word for nothing left to—*

"Jeez." Jamie halted where the cliffside had become dark bluish gray, its upper reaches hardened into huge, ropey claws reaching toward the water. "That looks like clay." She shoved her heel against a nearby mound of it, expecting it to be hard, but it gave way beneath her boot. "Soft. Unstable as hell."

"Yep. Runs for about a quarter-mile pretty much directly under the lighthouse."

"So right up there where I see that cornice—"

"Yes, ma'am." Adele's eyes opaqued. "It's almost precisely where you were going to ignore the warning sign and poke around the edge of the cliff."

"Until you saved me." And then Jamie drew her close and kissed her—an electric, soaring kiss that defied the phantasms, that deserved to last forever.

"Five klicks," Jamie said on a cloudy afternoon during what had become their longest walk yet. "Maybe we should head back."

"Shit. Your ribs." Adele stopped. "I'm sorry. Let me call a cab to come out from—"

"I can walk." But Jamie stopped, too, and stared up the road where it curved westward as it made its way down into Provincetown. She was sure now: This *was* where it happened.

"What is it?" Adele stepped closer, examining Jamie as her hand began a typical click-up motion with her comlink.

"I'm okay." Jamie brushed her hand over Adele's and tried to smile. "Don't call a cab. It's just—" She glanced westward again. "Up ahead, where there's that real nice view of Provincetown, that's where my mother died."

Adele opened her mouth to speak, but no words came out. Her eyes, dark and liquid, probed Jamie's and her hands cradled Jamie's face. When she found words, she spoke them in a hush. "I will do whatever you want."

Jamie blinked. *What* do *I* want?

"Would you like me to stay with you?"

"Yes."

"Are you..." Adele paused, the creases around her abyssal eyes subtly shifting as she concentrated, comprehended, and then offered Jamie her hand. "Ready to show me where it happened?"

"Yes." Jamie took Adele's hand. "I'm ready."

Dana's call came during breakfast. "I'm sorry," she said, though Jamie didn't think she sounded terribly regretful. "No way around it. The data coming back from the pixie dust is clearly carrying private personal information."

"About people who are spies," Jamie said.

"Very probably. So we're handing it all off to the Feds."

"Without looking at it?"

"Well, *we* see it because we're doing the decryption—"

"But you can't show it to so-called third parties. Like me. Which is why I haven't gotten anything except those first hundred and five zeroes and ones."

Silence.

"So that's it? The end of the story?"

"The end of your chapter, I'm afraid," said Dana. "I can give you informal updates concerning what we're learning about the spyware—"

"But not the spies," Jamie grumped.

"Them's the rules," Dana reminded her, "and it behooves us to play by them."

Behooves you, maybe. Doesn't behoove me a whole lot. And yet...

For a week, she'd done exactly what Lynn wanted. She stood down. She shoved her ruminations about pizda and the break-in and Nim Bacani and those four sordid men into the background. Just for a little while, she figured—a brief R and R while she waited for more results from the pixie dust.

And it had been magical, this time with Adele. Sure, the phantasms skulked at the edges still, and sometimes they'd work their way closer and rush her and lower their veil over her. But not every few minutes anymore, not even every few hours anymore, and fighting them off took less and less time. It just wasn't as scary, now that she knew she wasn't crazy.

So maybe Lynn was right. Knowing she wasn't crazy was her ultimate weapon, and maybe she could leave the rest, the details to others. Like Dana. Like the Feds.

"Okay," she said to Dana, surprised at her own calm. "Thanks for the heads-up." For a nanosecond, as the words spoke themselves, a wave of doubt shuddered through her: How safe was it really to give up watching, worrying? *Just to know whether it's The Bastard who's behind all this pizda stuff...that would be enough...*

Jamie left the table and began pacing the living room. *What if I never find out? Does it really matter? Because I already believe it, every instinct I have tells me it's true, and I'm not crazy. So fuck you, lee-eh huaw. I know what I need to know. Which is that if you ever mess with me again, I will kill you or die trying. Without hesitation. Without regret.*

Adele's hands slipped around her waist from behind. "It's Sunday. No hunting on Sundays. Let's go for a walk in the woods. We can pick up the path right behind the house."

Soon they tromped southeastward along a sandy, little-used road through a forest of pitch pine and scrub oak made miniature and idiosyncratic by poor soil and dogged, salt-saturated wind. They passed no houses as they traversed the treed dunes; the area was entirely free of human habitation.

"We're on the Old King's Highway, believe it or not," Adele said. "Part of the National Seashore now."

"Ah, take a breath." And Jamie did. "Not a cam in sight."

"This way." Adele pointed leftward when they came to an intersecting path. A bit more than half a klick later, they encountered another intersection. When Adele turned right onto it, Jamie got suspicious.

"We have an actual destination, don't we?"

Adele smiled and walked on. About a klick later, she stopped and pointed to a hill southeast of them. "We're heading there. See it?"

Through the tangle of small, bare oaks, Jamie discerned a structure. "What am I looking at?"

"Aunt Zerviah's house."

"Shit, Del." Jamie shivered, but perhaps Adele didn't notice.

"Like a closer look?"

Jamie gaped. "Now?"

"It's empty."

"How do you know?"

"Because last Sunday I drank way too much scotch with one of the owners. Fiona. I let her think I might show up at our ten-year high school reunion, which she's helping to plan, and that made her *quite* talkative."

"Shit, Del. How'd you find her?"

"Bumped into her. Happens all the time when the tourists finally go home. And when I saw her I was extra special nice to her." Adele's hip ricocheted off of Jamie's. "For your sake."

"To find out about Aunt Zerviah's."

"For the last four years, some hunters have rented it. Always in November, before Thanksgiving.

"Who are they?"

"Couple of guys from New York. Ned and Sid. 'Never any wives in tow,' as Fiona put it. They pay in cash, arrive Friday afternoon, and leave the place on Monday neater and cleaner than they find it. Very reliable, according to Fiona. Always remember to put the house key back under the flower pot by the kitchen door."

"Wow."

"So do you want to have a closer look or what?"

As the days passed into a second week, Adele checked her comlink more and more frequently.

"What's up?" Jamie asked finally.

"I'm—" The way Adele looked down and shuffled a foot gave it away. *She's unsure, makes her shy.* "I've decided where I want to go to school—Henry Yount's environmental economics program at MIT. It's not just that he's a really good teacher in a really good doctoral program. He also runs a nonprofit consulting group that does reclamation and sustainability projects all over the world. And he picks a few of his graduate students to work on those projects, which takes care of a lot of tuition and food bills. I got into one of his courses when I was doing my master's degree and ended up with decent feedback from him. Gives me hope I have a chance at getting accepted. But I haven't heard anything yet."

"When'd you submit the application?"

"Eight days ago."

Jamie nudged Adele's shoulder. "Give the man some time."

"What about you?"

"Me?" Jamie tried to keep her cringe from showing.

"Yes, you. And the Marine Corps. The next two years of your life. The twenty years after that."

"Dunno. The Corps has six prioritized criteria it applies to officer assignments, and individual preference is way down at the bottom of the list. So I haven't given it a whole lot of thought."

Which was half the story, actually; the other half was that she hated thinking about what would come next for her, much less discuss it, since—

"Since you figure you gotta swallow twenty-one months of shit." Adele's tone, oddly lilting and hopeful, seemed out of whack with her words.

"But only twenty-one months."

Adele pounced, wrapping her arms around Jamie's, trapping them, inadvertently squeezing still-tender ribs. "So you've decided. Oh thank god, thank god." She spun Jamie around in an excited circle. "So then what? School? Structural engineering and architecture after that, right? Because, how'd you put it? 'Since the nature of materials and environment defines the limits of design, it makes sense to deeply understand that nature before designing anything.'"

"Wow, you remembered that…"

But Adele refused to be distracted. "Tell me. Say it."

"Yeah," Jamie said to herself as much as to Adele. "I guess I *have* decided." She must have grimaced at Adele's exuberant embrace, because quite abruptly Adele let her go and started chattering apologies, but she drew Adele's arms around her again. "Hey, I'm good. In fact, Adele Sabellius, I have never been better."

"Please." Unable to pull her gaze from Adele's breasts, tight and firm and teasing against the soft yellow knit, Jamie tugged at Adele's sweater as they reclined on a pair of large floor pillows near the woodstove. "I'm fine. Please."

Adele rumbled skepticism. "It's too soon."

"It's not." Wriggling closer, Jamie began to nibble along Adele's neck. "And I can prove it."

"Oh yeah? And how do you propose to—" But Adele's question succumbed to Jamie's kiss. She tried again with her next breath, but Jamie kissed away that attempt, too. Three more breaths, three more kisses, while Jamie's hands caressed her breasts, Jamie's hipbone sinuated between her legs, persuading her onto her back and seducing her into a horizontal crotch dance. Until, finally, she intervened on the next kiss with a forefinger delicate upon Jamie's parted lips. "All right, then. Show me your proof."

"Yes, ma'am!" Jamie rose onto her knees, exhilarating in her own lightness, her resilience, aware of Adele's hips beneath her, circling, calling. She yanked her sweatshirt over her head and twirled it across the room. "Now yours."

Eyes fluttering closed, hips rollicking involuntarily upward, Adele allowed Jamie to liberate her from the rest of her clothes even as her hands slipped down, down, undoing the buttons on Jamie's jeans, squirming into the slick melt inside.

"Uhh…god…" Jamie shuddered as she descended into Adele's touch, its keen sureness familiar now, yet always utterly revelatory. Exquisitely, magnificently revelatory…

Then, somehow, Jamie found herself flat on her back and Adele was removing her jeans, her underwear, taunting wet, engorged flesh with dancing fingers. Beneath Adele's sparkling gaze, Jamie shuddered again as Adele straddled her.

"Oh my, look at you…" Adele whispered, eyes blazing now. Her rhythm slowed, she skimmed a fingertip lightly along the base of Jamie's throat to encircle one breast, then the other, her eyebrows quivering minutely as Jamie quivered, too, beneath her touch.

Never mind who started this; the tension that always kept something in Jamie rigid and, yes, afraid, had been taken by surprise. Its fist-clench of her gut, its grip on her throat relaxed, and the phantasms that had lurked dimly at the far, shadowed edges of herself fluttered away, leaving her trembling, groaning, surrendered.

Once, twice, again, Adele rode her to the brink of orgasm, and she vaulted upward, pulling Adele close to kiss her, rolling them both sideways until Adele lay beneath her once more, looking up at her, laughing.

Jamie began the slow, deliberate swoop down Adele's beautiful body, from a spot just behind Adele's ear along her jaw to kiss her, kiss her, kiss her before nipping and licking down her neck to her firmly rounded breasts, full and rosy-nippled, and onward across the leanly furrowed frontier of her abdominals to plunge with utter abandon into her labial folds.

Jamie knew she'd taken Adele beyond words as small sounds became less and less intelligible, less and less controlled. Her tongue flicked and spiraled, syncopating with Adele's rhythmic thrusts and groans. She loved the taste of Adele's hunger, she loved the pulsing resilience of Adele's engorged clit. And she loved riding Adele's bucking bronco orgasm so much that she came right along with it.

CHAPTER TWENTY-FIVE
COMPLETELY SELF-CONTAINED

If we don't go now, you could be late," Adele called from the bottom of the stairs.

"On my way." Having only just realized how much she didn't want to leave, Jamie cast her gaze around Adele's bright, comfortable bedroom one last time and picked up her backpack. "Bye," she whispered as she clicked off the lights.

The morning ahead had ugly written all over it: Long, mostly pre-dawn drive to the Navy clinic in Newport, then hours of the medical work-up's prodding and needles and assembly line hurry-up-and-wait that provided plenty of time to contemplate what one was being assembled for.

Adele attempted conversation, but right from the start Jamie couldn't do any better than monosyllables. Eventually, Adele gave up and simply reached for Jamie's hand, which she placed on her thigh, her own hand wordlessly commanding *hold on to me.* So Jamie held on.

Just a medcheck, Jamie reminded herself as she studied Adele's profile. Been through the drill before.

And yet...something about this time around had her downright frosty, that adrenalized alertness encapsuled in a steady, smooth calm. Poised and ready. Expecting the worst.

Maybe it was because for the first time since starting her conleave she'd be scrutinized in a real, live Navy facility by real, live Navy people. This had already resulted in a regulation haircut that had Adele sneaking peeks at her for hours afterward.

Or maybe it was the terse order she'd received only two days ago that shifted her appointment from early afternoon to the crack-ass of dawn. What if her comlink had still been clicked off and she'd missed the message? She saw herself standing at attention while some irate Navy twit chewed her out; then, depending on the asshole quotient of the clinic commander, she might even face non-judicial punishment. At least her officerness meant any NJP would have to come from her commanding officer...

Though god only knows who the hell my commanding officer is these days. Of course, a few comlink clicks would tell her, but she didn't want to know. Not yet. She had sixty-nine days of conleave left. At sixty days out and not one day sooner, she'd decided weeks ago—then and only then would she deal with all things Marine Corps. Which left nine more precious days. So she should be babbling away now, making every moment with Adele count.

And yet…only when the car passed a highway sign more than two hours later and Jamie saw NEWPORT 4 MI did she suddenly find words. "I dreamt about Awa last night."

Adele threw her a glance. "Do you remember it?"

"A little. Like a videoclip. We were someplace green. Trees, bushes, grasses. I'd been walking, I think, and off to my left the ground sloped upward away from the road, and I saw Awa standing there, maybe three meters away. Because of the slope, we were at eye level, and god, how she stared at me. I wanted to tell her I was sorry, that I didn't mean to hurt her, but I couldn't talk. So we just looked at each other."

"Did she seem angry or upset?"

"No. She was…blank." Jamie sucked in air. Why did she always seem to end up breathless when she talked about Awa? "I had the feeling it was because I didn't deserve to see any emotion from her. But…at least…"

"Try exhaling first," Adele suggested quietly. She waited while Jamie exhaled, inhaled. And then…"You were saying: 'At least…'"

"At least she didn't run away from me."

Adele swung her gaze from the highway to Jamie. "Just so you know: Neither will I."

"I'm scared, Del."

"Of going back."

Jamie shrugged. "It's like way, way inside I can't stop shaking. I don't know when it started. While I was still in the Palawan. God, maybe before that even…I don't know. But after the Palawan, when I finally woke up in the hospital, it had a life of its own. And it had built a direct line to—" Jamie held out her right hand, palm down. A very slight, high-frequency tremor was unmistakable. "Doesn't go away."

"I've noticed it."

"Yeah?"

"And I figured—" Adele squinted briefly at Jamie's hand. "Well, so much for marksmanship, and that might work out for the best."

"When it comes to the Marine Corps, I—" Jamie flexed, then fisted her right hand. "I'm not sure I can really get a grip on much of anything again."

They had exited the highway, and now Adele pulled the car into a strip mall parking lot, clicked off the engine, and swiveled to face Jamie. "I read somewhere about how snipers are accustomed to being completely self-contained. From what I can tell, that was true for you for a long time. Pretty much your whole life."

Jamie shrugged. "I guess."

"Well, I think there's a limit to how long a human being can do that. Because we're not supposed to be self-contained." Adele took up both of Jamie's hands in hers. "To survive, we need to love each other and help each other. And maybe the part of you who understands that is refusing to be self-contained anymore."

Another shrug. "I guess."

Adele leaned forward, her honey scent filling Jamie's nostrils, her lips caressing their heat across Jamie's lips. And then, as it had every time during every day for the last twenty-three days, Adele's slow, deep kiss melted into Jamie's chest, Jamie's belly, Jamie's clit. "You're not alone anymore, my sweet."

"Oh god, Del, I want to live every second I can with you, I want to make love with you, dream with you, work with you, play with you, dance with you. I want to spend every night of my life with you."

"Mmm." Adele's smile ignited her eyes. "Sounds like my kinda plan."

❖

"That's it, sir? I'm done?" Jamie asked the mildly officious, white-coated lieutenant commander who'd just finished plowing a couple of gloved, lubricated fingers into her rectum.

"You can get dressed, Lieutenant," he replied as he peeled off the gloves and left the exam room without bothering to look at her.

Alone, Jamie let her head rest against the wall next to the exam table and fully inhaled for the first time in four hours and fifteen minutes. The medcheck was over; she'd get a copy of the report in a few days. She dressed to Adele's words echoing…*Sounds like my kinda plan*…

Thus the cursory knock on the exam room door that came as she tied her bootlaces took her by surprise. So did the vague, unplaceable familiarity of the man whose head appeared for roughly three seconds to request she report ay-sap to room 219 at the end of the hall.

"Come in, Lieutenant," called out a male voice a moment later when she tapped a knuckle on room 219's door.

Jamie's stomach backflipped; she recognized the voice—and understood now why the face she'd just glimpsed seemed familiar. *Oh. Shit.*

She didn't move. Wiser to take just a second to consider the possibility that she'd lost her mind. Not a phantasm. But a stroke maybe, affecting whatever part of the brain creates hallucinations—and, who knows, maybe big stroke means big hallucination…

"Sooner rather than later if you don't mind, Jamie."

Jeezus, it's really him.

Jamie turned the doorknob, stepped into a spare office with one window, two doors, and, three meters in front of her, Ben Embry, major general, United States Marine Corps. The man who promoted her from staff sergeant to first lieutenant with a frigging comcall, the man who snuck a Navy Cross onto her pillow when she couldn't stop him because she was fucking unconscious, the man who started all these idiot shenanigans with the Blue Max. Behind him, his sergeant, whom Jamie had met on the Palawan mission that turned her into the Corps's most reluctant officer, put a pitcher of water and two glasses on the desk. Both men were out of uniform, as was Jamie, but she snapped to attention anyway, careful to peer unblinking over the general's left shoulder.

Embry nodded at the sergeant, who immediately departed using the door across the room from Jamie. "Have a seat, Lieutenant. I'm, uh, undercover here and we don't have much time."

Twenty minutes later, he'd laid it all out, shaken her hand, yanked a civilian boonie hat low over his brow, and left using the same door his sergeant had. "Convenient that all the cams between here and my car have crapped out," he said with a wink as he disappeared.

Dumbstruck, Jamie watched the door slip shut behind him and wondered: How in hell am I gonna explain *this* to Del?

"Sorry that took so long." Jamie tried to smile at Adele when they met up in the clinic's lobby, but the corners of her mouth resisted.

"What happened? You look…odd."

"Let's get out of here."

"Tell me," said Adele a few minutes later as she started the car.

Jamie surveyed the parking garage, half-expecting to see Embry skulk into a black sedan with darkened windows. "Let's get a little farther out of here. And how about some music?"

Adele clicked up the Brahms violin concerto. "Just a guess," she said.

"A good guess." Jamie pulled in as deep a breath as possible. "After the medcheck, I ended up in a meeting." She needed another breath. "I've been given my next billet. Office of the Inspector General of the

Marine Corps. What's called a special temporary assistant inspector general, in my case specialized in HUMINT—human intelligence. Technically, I've volunteered to be a short-term individual augmentee, but that's only to avoid becoming a longer-term involuntary recruitment robot."

"And you just happened to spontaneously decide this somewhere between the blood test and the eye exam?"

"It was suggested."

"One of those offers you can't refuse."

"Yeah. Pretty much."

Adele said nothing for perhaps fifteen seconds, then: "Wait. Don't you have to pass fitness tests before you can go back to—to—"

"Active duty."

"Right. Well, while I was waiting for you I walked around—as far as the fences and the sentries allowed. And I didn't see a single place that could be used for combat fitness testing."

"I didn't do any fitness tests. Which brings me to the interesting part."

"Uh-oh."

"He—" Jamie halted and started over. "Uh, the person I met with—"

"Whose name you cannot divulge…"

"I've made a kind of deal with him. The good part is that the doc I saw will indicate in his medical report that I'm not fully fit, which is certainly true. But he'll say I can handle limited duty."

"And how true is that?"

"True enough for me to do this special temporary assistant inspector general gig. For eight months. By then I'll have accrued thirty days' leave. Which will take me a little past my next birthday and put me at less than a year on my contract. And because they want the one-lite slot I'm occupying—"

"Excuse me—what's a one-lite?"

"Slang for first lieutenant. Only so many of those in the Marine Corps, and since I won't be staying in, they'll terminate my contract early so they can get themselves another one-lite. Happens often enough when time left on the contract is less than a year and when the officer exhibits some kind of disability—in my case, nerve damage in my right hand that keeps causing me to fail the marksmanship qualification."

"Am I hearing this right? You'll end up discharged a year early?"

"Yep."

"That *is* good. So what's the bad part?"

Jamie's shoulders drooped. "I gotta do a month's training first. Starting December thirtieth."

"So I lose you a month early."

"I'm sorry."

When Adele turned to look at Jamie, tears had filled her eyes. "So am I," she said softly.

"At least I'm done at the beginning of next October."

"And you got this in writing?"

"I signed some stuff."

Adele's head shifted back and forth as her gaze swung between the road and Jamie. "I'm smelling another bad part."

"It's gonna play out in stages—"

"Oh christ. Why don't you just fuck up the fitness tests as soon as possible?"

"Because if I do, they'll toss me into a Physical Conditioning Platoon until I either pass the tests or my contract expires."

"Instead of discharging you. Why?"

Jamie sighed. "The Blue Max. It's been a while since an officer's gotten one, much less an active duty officer who's still alive and might be planning a military career."

"But you're *not* planning a military career. So just decline it. It's what you said you wanted to do."

"Yes, it is what I want to do. *If* I do, though, I'll spend nearly two years getting pounded. Retribution, basically, because one does *not* decline a Blue Max." Jamie paused. "As it happens, I figured on that. Been trying to prepare myself for it." She tapped her head. "Y'know— up here."

"God, Jamie, that's—that's awful," Adele sputtered, anger cracking her voice.

"It's my own damn fault, since I signed a five-year contract. Also, there's more to it—something I didn't know until today. Turns out I'm not the only one who's up for the Blue Max. There were four of us on that ridge, including a guy who didn't make it, and all four of us have been nominated. Approval's in the bag, apparently. The person I met with made it crystal clear: If I decline the medal, no matter my reasons, I will demean what the others did."

"You believe the others deserve the medal."

"Oh yeah."

Adele's eyes stayed focused on the road; she said nothing. Finally, her head dipped into a minimal nod, which Jamie hoped might signal her acceptance. "So what are these stages you mentioned?"

"As long as I'm on temporary limited duty, I'm considered unfit to apply to The Basic School for officer training, which is what I'd be itching to do if I was gonna stay in the Corps. I'm told the manpower management people will expect me to be fit enough to submit an application next spring—so the first stage happens when they notice I haven't. That'll take 'til June. Then Em—" Jamie cleared her throat. "Then over the next couple of months I'll be encouraged to stay, culminating with my being informed sometime during the fall that I'm to receive the Blue Max."

"Their bribe. Which you will accept."

"Yes, but only if it's quid pro quo for an early discharge on medical grounds, which they can turn into a story about how I wanted to stay in the Corps but could not. And about six weeks after the public announcement comes the worst part of the whole thing—"

"The medal ceremony." Adele smiled. "Of course. You *would* think that's the worst part."

"At least by then I'll be on terminal leave or maybe even discharged, assuming it all goes down as described."

"Ohh-kaay…" Adele's skepticism stretched the word as her eyes left the road again to squint at Jamie. "In summary, then: This guy you cannot name just so happens to bump into you at the Navy Clinic in Newport—ah, wait. He intentionally intercepted you—" Adele's hand pounded the steering wheel as she fully comprehended. "No, no, it's more than that. He's powerful enough to rearrange your appointment for the *purpose* of intercepting you. So he could present you this so-called opportunity to 'volunteer' in exchange for an early discharge, while letting you know in gruesome detail how unappealing your alternative is. Special temporary assistant inspector general specializing in HUMINT must be some seriously important job. Curious that such a big shot couldn't just order you to—"

"Stop."

"Stop talking about it or stop thinking about it?"

"Yes."

"Where will you be going at the end of December?"

"Virginia. A satellite office of the Inspector General of the Marine Corps. Then lots of travel from there. Doing inspections."

"How long will I have to wait to see you again?"

"I don't know."

Once more, Adele went silent while her forefinger rubbed her lower lip. "Okay, so that's the tip of the iceberg," she said after several excruciating seconds. "Will you ever tell me about the eighty-nine percent hidden below the waterline?"

"Yeah, someday. Even if I'm not supposed to."

Adele reached for Jamie's hand, placed it on her thigh, and lightly stroked it with those fingers Jamie loved to watch. Yet Adele's body, Adele's voice seemed a little farther away than before Jamie had walked into the clinic. The Corps, Jamie realized, had already begun to take custody.

"I want to touch you all I can for the next…" Adele paused. "Thirty-five days." Her voice had remained steady, but her fingers fidgeted her agitation until…"How dangerous is doing inspections?"

Jamie snorted. "The boredom might kill me."

"That bad?" Adele asked, relief billowing in her small but genuine laugh.

"Sure as hell sounds like it."

And it sure as hell did.

Embry had actually ordered her to look bored, act bored. Feel free to half-ass the IG training, he'd said. Don't stress out about all the preparatory research that goes into each inspection—you'll follow people around and observe as they do their jobs, but you'll still just be asking questions off a standard checklist.

"Hell, I hope you *will* be bored," the general declared, "since bored leads to sloppy and sloppy invites exploitation."

"So my job is to act the fool."

"No. Nobody'll buy that from someone with a rep like yours. I want to finesse a meme—the classic combat hero who struggles in garrison. And, in this case, a wounded hero who's still limping, as it were. I want you to come off as ready to leave the Corps but the Corps won't relinquish you. Let people notice that tremor in your hand." Embry's small smile verged on apologetic. "Oh yeah, Jamie, it shows. I want you to come off as tired, uncomfortable, lonely, just starting to get disillusioned and disgruntled."

Jamie squinted at him. "That shouldn't be difficult."

"Good."

"Why me?"

"Because you're not just any one-lite." Embry's smile grew crooked, which made his roughhewn features appear impish. "You have ongoing communication with a senator on the Armed Services Committee who's likely to be sitting on the Intelligence Committee come January and is driving legislation that could have enormous impact on how the Pentagon operates, not to mention who operates it. Ensconcing you in this billet will raise suspicion that you're scouting for her. And that's our bait. *You* are our bait. So all I care about is that no matter the fuck what, you make damn sure your comlinks are on when you're doing the job. The rest you'll leave to my people."

As Embry paused and leaned back in his chair, Jamie knew what she'd hear next. He wanted her to reprise her performance with a pixie dust-toting honeypot. She sprang out of her chair then, not yet re-acclimated to the rigid military decorum that required she stay put because a general had told her to sit.

"How the hell did *you*—" she demanded before she halted, remembering who he was, who she was.

"Sit down, Lieutenant, and wrap your head around the fact that I found out about your most recent escapade quite by accident." Embry's crooked smile deepened. "I contacted Dana Westbrook because I had reason to believe Callithump Security was developing something like the pixie dust code. Which is a capability I need. How convenient that, of all the people on the planet, *you* should be this capability's first in-the-wild beta tester."

"So you've been hatching this plan for a while." Jamie sat down. "Sir."

"Ever since I talked my way into my next billet—director of Marine Corps intelligence."

"Intel? I thought you said you wanted me in the Inspector General's office."

"I do. You'll report to Sarah Zachary. She's got her eagles now and she's just moved to the Inspector General's office as the new director of the Intelligence Oversight Division."

Jamie remembered Zachary. She'd been a lieutenant colonel working as Embry's intelligence chief the day Jamie gaped at the one-lite rank insignia resting atop the palm of her hand. A combat appointment, Zachary had called it—a dizzying, envy-inducing promotion that flung a dropout with nothing more than a GED across god knows how many pay grades into a solid career in the Corps. A career the dropout didn't want—and somehow Embry had realized it.

He talked on while Jamie pondered how he knew when she'd only just decided herself and the only person to whom she'd said the words—I am going to separate from the Marine Corps as soon as possible—was Adele.

She managed to pick up Embry's thread again as he said something about a new kind of inspection to be conducted by smaller teams working out of rented civilian digs down in Norfolk, "where you can travel to and from inspections using three different military bases within thirty klicks of each other. I want this op well beyond the Beltway, far from that hotbed of leaks and gossip over there in Arlington. Sarah's designing flash intel inspections that unit commanders find out about only when the inspectors show up on their doorsteps ready to follow them around. None of this no-notice crap that really means 'oh, gee, you get just three or four days' warning.'"

"So Colonel Zachary will assign me to—"

"To do flash inspections, yes. You'll be part of a Special Projects pilot program. And you'll carry a honeypot comlink—well, two actually. One Marine Corps issue. The other your personal comlink. And we'll see who the hell wants in on your commo and your data."

"Then these comlinks I'll carry will be tethered to your ops center, not Colonel Zachary's." Jamie stared at him. "Because you think—"

Embry's black-eyed glare shut her up, but he quickly relented; she had, after all, merely inquired about the commander's intent. "We've always had to deal with narrow business and political interests influencing military strategy and posture," he said. "It's the dark underside of a mercantile democracy. But attempts to manipulate strategy and drive tactics using intel that's intentionally misleading or even outright fraudulent—well, that crosses a line. It gets people needlessly killed. It makes a mockery of our intel establishment. And when it's well organized enough, when it infiltrates deep enough, it becomes a rogue shadow intel infrastructure that can take our foreign policy off a damn cliff. You're going to help us find out how big our problem really is."

And that was it. Within a minute, their meeting had ended.

Jamie focused on Adele's graceful fingers now possessively entwined with hers while they drove toward Great Hill.

Breathe in…two…three…four…

Just thirty-five days left to once again become completely self-contained.

CHAPTER TWENTY-SIX
THE RABBIT HOLE

Only Mary was home when Jamie and Adele arrived at Great Hill just ahead of sunset. Barely into her greeting, hands lightly clasping Jamie's forearms, Mary halted, ever-vigilant. "What happened?" she asked as her grip tightened and the many lines in her face transmuted from cheerful to worried.

Jamie attempted a no-big-deal smile; she didn't look forward to communicating her half-story over and over again. But Adele ran interference for her, first telling Mary, then one by one as they came home over the next three hours, telling each of the others about "the meeting."

This prompted extended eye contact and an unspoken are-you-okay? in their eyes. Jamie replied with some version of, "Yeah, quicker this way," thinking all the while it smacked of what you'd say when the time had come to put down the family dog.

Still, she got many warm hugs, plus kisses from Mary, Lily, and yes, Lynn too—all of which made breathing easier. Soon she entered a kind of altered state in which some portion of her awareness pulled up, up, out of her and slightly sideways to behold each moment of the countdown to the end of her conleave.

Jamie wanted to remember it all—needed to remember. All the sights, sounds, smells, smiles. Every piano note, every laugh, every touch, every orgasm. So she could weave it all into a glimmering thread of recollection she could hold on to because yes, yes, it had all been *real*. And if she clutched it tight, the thread might lead her back out of the lightless labyrinth into which she must venture on December thirtieth, back to these people, this place, this budding life.

Thus did Thanksgiving come and go. The best one ever, Jamie confided to Adele, not quite revealing it was really the only one ever, except for that strange meal during boot camp where every move—even lifting a fork to her mouth—had to be accomplished at strict right angles and without speaking, except for the occasional bellow of "Sir! Yes, sir!"

As the countdown continued, she began collecting the basics she'd need to return to active duty, since little of what she'd had in the Palawan made it home with her in usable condition. It all fascinated Adele, who sniffed it, rubbed it between curious fingers, glowered suspiciously at it like it harbored some sort of sinister intent, then looked up at her, eyes black with dark imaginings that Jamie tried to hug away. "Don't ever doubt the importance of bluster in any military organization." she'd remind Adele between kisses. "That's why we all stomp around in unison."

She spent her days with Adele, who worked out alongside her. She listened raptly, watched intently while Adele played Mary's piano. They focused on the future, sitting shoulder to shoulder while she worked on her analytic geometry/calculus course and Adele plowed through Henry Yount's most recent tome on the economics of sustainability.

At twenty-five days to go, Jamie said something about wishing time would stop and recognized that Adele's response—a quip about the arrow of time that blossomed into a small, strangely sexy dissertation on cosmology and the second law of thermodynamics and entropy and the physics of information and quantum chaos—was actually a way of fending off the grief and the loneliness she knew lay in wait for her. "All actual physical processes are to some degree irreversible," she said, then pulled Jamie into a long, inflaming kiss that melted Jamie's legs. "See?"

"I think I need more examples, professor."

And for the rest of the afternoon, Adele obliged.

That night, Jamie dreamed of wearing the camouflage uniforms she'd already folded and packed into a new duffel bag, of snapping an ammo pack into a sleek new rifle, then hunkering with it against her shoulder, caressing its trigger with her gloved finger while she squinted through its smartscope to see in its crosshairs the profile of a little girl—and in the same instant her finger pressed, the child turned to stare at her and the instant petrified…this final instant of a child's awareness…

For the next four nights, Jamie dreamed the same dream.

At twenty days to go, a distinctive message-received beep emanated from Jamie's wristcom.

CAN YOU COME SEE ME BY YOURSELF, EARLIEST CONVENIENCE?

Ten minutes later, Jamie knocked softly at the door to Lynn's little office sandwiched between the study and the bedroom Lynn shared with Rebecca. After a smile that couldn't quite erase the crease between her eyebrows, Lynn led the way into the much larger study and shut the heavy, soundproofed double doors that separated it from the front hallway.

"I so look forward to the day when I can stop apologizing to you," she said even before she let go of the doorknobs.

"So Embry explained."

Lynn nodded. "And I'm afraid there's not much that can be done about it. At least not by me. I seem to inspire a certain circling of the wagons these days in some portions of the so-called Pentagon Establishment. You, meanwhile, have become something of a prize."

"Because of the Blue Max, Embry said."

"Also, I regret to say, because of blowback that's really directed at me."

"Your legislation."

"And I'm seen as having 'stolen' one of their marines. Some of the senior Pentagon leadership—notably the commandant of the Marine Corps and his close aides—have become quite possessive of you." Lynn sat on one of the room's sofas and patted the seat next to her. "Quite clever of Ben to persuade you to volunteer for this inspector general thing he's got Sarah Zachary doing. He always was a master at exploiting the terrain."

Jamie sat where Lynn indicated. "Seems like it's not a bad idea, really. Though I admit I'd like it a lot better if someone else could do it. Because I'm—" She exhaled, rotated her shoulders. "I'm—"

"Yeah. I know. You're used up. And you're not really fit yet. And you shouldn't be doing it. All of which I told Ben. But you've been caught in a political crosswind—or maybe I should say whirlwind. The regulations can be used either way in your circumstances—to allow you to separate from the Marine Corps, or to hold you to your contract and toss you into a bureaucratic maze of rehab and fitness programs while parading you around for recruitment and public affairs events. I applaud Ben's motives, I appreciate his plan, but I'm not sure *you* wouldn't be better off giving speeches—"

Jamie shook her head vigorously. "Uh-uh. Nine months of people treating me with kid gloves because I'm an inspector versus twenty-one months of being pawed and yanked on to answer questions about what it feels like to shoot someone—it's a no-brainer."

"I'm not so sure about that." Lynn grabbed Jamie's hand, urgency in her face, her voice, her grip. "Ben has to get a lot done before—" She lowered her head, which moved side to side almost imperceptibly. "Before people with more clout than he has figure out what he's up to and sabotage it. He's going to move hard and fast, so for nine months, we'll hardly see you. You'll have truly earned that last thirty days of terminal leave. And then some."

A kind of hollow formed in the middle of Jamie's chest where Lynn's words echoed. *We'll hardly ever see you.* "I don't have any good options. But at least with this one I'm done twelve months earlier."

"That's not all. Some of those inspections will be conducted in field conditions—maybe combat conditions. You'll have to carry a firearm, Jamie. You might even have to use a firearm."

Jamie blinked. She hadn't quite allowed herself to think about that. "Just for a few days," she assured Lynn—and herself. "In and out. Helps a lot when you know you won't be staying."

Lynn tried again. "Those forms Ben talked you into signing—I can get them unsigned. And I can show you a few tricks to make dealing with public situations easier—"

Again, Jamie shook her head. "I'll be okay." She let her eyes drift to the study's large south-facing window and peered at the distant sea. Nope, one way or the other a bunch of her stress triggers were going to get pulled, ready or not; returning to any sort of active duty would resurrect the shadows, reinvigorate the nightmares. How much or when? Well, that was beyond knowing. But maybe talking some now, with one of the people she trusted most in all the world and the only person at Great Hill who understood what she faced, would keep her strong. "Besides, if Embry's idea works—"

"A damn big if."

"I've adjusted to never finding out what results the pixie dust produce. But I like to think it'll have some worth. More worth than becoming a poster child for cannon fodder. Like maybe it'll help you get your legislation passed. Y'know, indirectly, by bringing to light problems that your bill fixes. It might even help nail Archer."

"Archer? You mean Walker-Monroe's CEO?"

"Yeah, the same Archer who talked the brass into screwing the Singapore truce talks so we could push farther south into Narra. And whose Columbia Aegis crew pulled all kinda shit over there. Like kidnapping Chen and all the rest that's spilled since—right up to the guy breaking in here and what happened to Fitzgerald."

Lynn winced, something everyone at Great Hill did whenever Fitzgerald's name came up. "So your bet's on Archer, is it?" she asked.

"Yours isn't?"

"Springer grumbles about Rafael Vicario, how Machiavellian he is. ET suspects about twenty percent of the Congress." Lynn's shoulders gestured doubt. "I'm not prepared to speculate. I have a bias that makes my speculation inherently untrustworthy."

That took Jamie a minute. "Oh," she said finally. "You mean Lambert, don't you? You think Lambert and FDL are behind all this?"

"I always think Richard's up to something. Like what happens when you've had a run in with a venomous spider. Afterward, you keep thinking you see it squiggling around at the edge of things—only to turn and see it's something innocent. Or nothing at all. Which means I can't afford to speculate. But I believe we've got serious issues in our intelligence community that need investigating by professionals, not amateurs. No matter how gifted those amateurs may be."

"I guess amateurs can make good bait though, huh?"

"Jamie, unless I intervene now, you're going to get a fragmentary order tomorrow that changes your report date to next Monday."

Jamie couldn't move. "What?"

"This coming Monday. Before Christmas. The order will say something about your having to be interviewed for your new billet. But actually you'll be getting off-the-books training in handling the pixie dust code, social engineering techniques, operations security strategies, how to communicate with Ben's people."

"Since I'm an amateur."

"Like I said, he's driving hard and fast. Eleven days' training, right through Christmas. Then a three-day weekend pass. Then—"

"Then it's December thirtieth and my IG training starts."

"Let me stop it all right now. Giving speeches isn't so bad."

"No, Lynn. I can't. I'm all outta ooh-rah. And I want those twelve months."

Sunday, December 15, and the good-byes were classic Great Hill. For Jamie, they blurred even as they happened. Just as well, maybe, that all those tears stuck inside her kind of fogged everything up; blurry memories were tougher to dwell on, tougher for one's doubt to pervert into a final parade of permanent good-byes.

The very last good-bye, murmured in the middle of Boston's South Station a few minutes before Jamie's train departed, was the hardest. Her tears came unstuck then, slipping silently down her cheeks while she hugged Adele, her mind screaming *Don't go*, her words forming promises and more promises…We'll do a facecall every day and be able to see each other, I'll come home whenever I get a pass and oh god I miss you already and it'll be over soon, I promise, I promise…

Finally, reluctantly aboard the crowded train, Jamie fingered the bracelet now circling her right wrist. Black matte, half an inch wide, engraved with three names, three dates, three locations—an honor bracelet, authorized for wear in uniform, even cammies, even during ops.

Adele had given it to her the evening before all those good-byes and all those stuck tears—when the two of them had lingered near the piano after the rest of the household began to casually wend toward the kitchen for a rare laid-back Saturday supper at home. Nobody had said the words "good-bye" and "supper" in the same sentence, but since Robin had forsaken studying for finals to come home, it was pretty obvious.

"I-I know the names are—difficult to look at," Adele said when she put the bracelet in Jamie's hand. "But I thought if we did it this way, nobody could ever order you to take it off."

Jamie tried not to tremble as she peered at the names etched into the bracelet. FJ Arnoldt, her boot camp buddy whose body she'd found, his throat slit. A Bulanadi, the child who stepped in front of her bullet. WT Sherman, the only Saint Eh Mo's POW who didn't survive their escape. "In the spirit of remembrance," Jamie whispered.

"More than that," Adele said. "It's not just an honor bracelet. It's a comlink with a built-in darknet flume."

"A what?"

"It's how you can access a very special Callithump darknet." Lynn's voice, approaching behind Jamie. "It doesn't have a name, but it's how you can communicate with any of us at any time in complete, untraceable privacy from just about anywhere."

Lily piped up from the breakfast table where she and Robin were setting out dishes. "Made of a new electromagnetic-shielding nanocomposite, very rugged, solar- and kinetic-powered. It's even waterproof down to a hundred feet."

"Comes with every one of Callithump's security and counter-surveillance goodies, too," Dana added. "We've put everything into these. Super-processors, memory, storage, full interface suite—user-gyroscopic virtual shadowscreen and keypad, built-in mic, an extendible gyro microcamera lens so you can do two-way facecalls. Even wearable shielded mini-cords that'll hardwire it into eyewraps or a wristcom so you have the option of avoiding radio interfaces."

Jamie's eyes had found Lynn. "Who else has one?"

But it was Dana who answered. "All of us," she said, lifting her wrist to reveal a silver bracelet. "Like I said, new-generation. Best connectivity, security, and privacy we've ever had, not least because we've used our pixie dust technology to enable it to exploit every network in the world to send and receive data, regardless of firewalls and restrictions."

From the breakfast table, Robin and Mary waved their own silver bracelets.

Jamie's eyes returned to Adele. "You have one, too?"

Nodding, Adele opened her hand to reveal a bracelet identical to Jamie's but with a different engraving: SEMPER TECUM. "'Always with you,'" she translated. "I, uh, also had that inscribed on yours. On the inside. I hope that's okay."

Jamie kissed her full on the mouth then, to tell her yes. A possessive, voracious kiss that tentacled deep as her entire body cohered to Adele's.

Closing her eyes against the others on the train, Jamie remembered that kiss.

❖

TRAIN JUST ARRIVED, THE RABBIT HOLE BECKONS, SO HERE I GO.

WISH ME LUCK, DEL.

GOD, HOW I LOVE YOU...

WILL CALL ASAP

Already, the isolation and constraint of this new billet made the world gray, foreboding, and something gnawed relentlessly at Jamie's belly from the inside out, seeking escape.

She stepped off the train pissed and edgy, still pondering the implications of the fragmentary orders she'd received from a major named Ossado, leader of Special Projects Team Charlie, to whom she now belonged. Ready or not.

Wear civvies, including a full-brim cover, Ossado's FRAGO said. Well, jeezus, she'd planned to do that anyway rather than travel in service alphas, which would no doubt induce people to stare, maybe even recognize her. More curious was the next instruction: Except for your ID, do not pack anything that indicates you are a member of the Marine Corps. Bring no uniforms.

But it was the last part that sent an icy sting racing up her spine: Do not bring a comlink. Your command will supply all commo gear, including what you will need for personal use.

Then, that morning, came another FRAGO informing her that Ossado had upended her housing arrangements, so as she walked down the platform toward the main hall in Philadelphia's 30th Street Station, she had no clue where she'd be sleeping that night.

Twenty meters before she reached the end of the platform, Jamie noticed him. He'd dressed in civvies, too, but even at that distance, she could tell he matched up with the image of Ossado carried in the orders she'd received from him—dark, not-quite-civilian-cut hair, lopsided smile, weary eyes, mid-thirties, about the right age for a major. When she got within ten meters of him, he grinned and started waving.

Okay, I'll play. She grinned back and gave a wave.

"Hey, sis, 'bout friggin' time," he called out when she neared the gate, then bear-hugged her as soon as she walked through it. "God, it's good to see you! Merry Christmas!"

Jamie laughed, hugged him back, and muttered in his ear, "In exactly three seconds, I will scream bloody fucking murder and do my damnedest to kick your balls into your throat if you don't prove to me who the fuck you are."

"And before we take another step," he declared brightly, "Mom wants to say hi. You know the address, right? Here, take my pocketcom and click her up so we can say hi together."

"Uh-uh." She shook her head, then tilted it toward a bank of public comlinks. "Let's use one of those. Bigger screen. Bro."

She led the way, picked out one of the comlinks, then used her body to block the view of this man who appeared to be Ossado and tapped in the address Embry had given her back in Newport. A moment later, Colonel Sarah Zachary's face and shoulders appeared on the comlink's screen—and on a large display behind Zachary, Jamie saw herself in distorted close-up, Ossado right behind her, the station's neoclassic main hall stretching behind them both. It was the view from Ossado's pocketcom lens, which he held just in front of her as she spoke with Zachary.

"Lieutenant Gwynmorgan," said the colonel, offering a satisfied smile. "You look well. Much better than the last time I saw you. Safe journey, I hope."

"So far."

"Zoom out, Major," Zachary ordered, and the image on the display behind her zoomed out. "That'll do, Major. Got it, Lieutenant?"

"Not really, Colonel."

"Then pay attention to what the major tells you."

❖

Having said it aloud, Jamie couldn't get it out of her head; the idea of kicking Ossado's smarmy balls into his throat held great appeal.

He had donned eyewraps after their strange greeting and his right hand kept working his pocketcom, suggesting that he continued to communicate with someone while they walked in silence to the train station's parking garage, where he unlocked a dark sedan and motioned her to get in.

As he maneuvered the car out of the garage, he said, "Looks like you had no ground tails. And best we can tell, no eyes in the sky, either."

"So I'm what? Undercover or something?"

He tossed her a look, probably because she had yet to call him sir. "'Or something' is close enough, Lieutenant."

She didn't reply. She just might swear at him if she opened her mouth.

Ossado didn't drive far, but it took a while, thanks to the traffic. When he halted the car in front of an especially innocuous OdysseyLodge, he handed her a keycard.

"You're already checked in. Room three twenty-nine." He turned to face her full on. "And let's get one thing straight right now: I don't give a damn how much you backhand the IG training or the IG work you'll do between now and next October. Make of that whatever the hell you want. But you sure as shit will spend the next eleven days devoting your full, focused attention to what my colleagues and I will be teaching you. Or I will rip you a new one. Are we clear?"

"Yes, we're clear."

"I will knock on your door at zero seven hundred sharp. Your room will be our classroom, so make sure it's shipshape."

Jamie exited the car without another word—a very uncool way for a lieutenant to treat a major. Had anyone asked her about it, she'd have said she didn't give a damn. In truth, however, she wanted to pick a fight. A fight she'd lose, of course. But a fight that would end her Marine Corps career a lot quicker than what she faced as long as she delivered up those yessirs.

She waited for his voice to order her to halt, turn around, get back in the car so he could begin the work of ripping her a new one. Instead, she heard his car pull away.

❖

The hotel room was minimalist, old, worn out, and its thin walls did little to absorb noise from adjacent spaces. But it seemed clean enough. Jamie clicked on the scratched videoscreen to a program full of talking heads, found a volume she hoped would obscure the sound of her voice, and fiddled with the still-unfamiliar inside of her honor bracelet until her finger found the tiny bump at the edge of a small, nearly invisible hatchway.

If she hadn't been half-convinced that Adele would be too busy elsewhere to answer her call, she might have had less trouble with the subtle press-slide motion that shifted the hatch cover aside to expose the controls hidden beneath. She needed three attempts before she got it open—whereupon she froze.

Ossado had ordered her to carry no comlink. Ossado had placed her in a space of his choosing, not hers—

Why would he do that? The place she'd picked was below the federal employee per diem rate, so why change it?

Could be innocent. Maybe he's got a room down the hall. Maybe I'm not the only eleven-day wonder and he wants us clustered, even though it seems like the training will go down one-on-one.

Or maybe he's got microcams all over this room. To see if I obeyed orders and left my comlink at home. To see who I'll contact with the hotel comlink.

Jamie stood in the middle of the room, tempted to begin looking for cams. If there were any, maybe she'd find them, maybe not. But either way, Ossado would realize she'd gotten suspicious. *And I'm supposed to be a honeypot. A tired, disgruntled honeypot. Okay, major, consider it done.*

Jamie scooped up the room's keycard from the top of the tattered dresser and left, closing the door firmly behind her.

Once outside on 12th Street, she soon found a Chinese diner still open and serving at 2200 hours on a Sunday night. She settled into a booth at the back, ordered something with chicken, and waited to see who'd walk in behind her. *This might be paranoia but for Ossado's comment that no one followed me to Philadelphia. Only one way he could know that: Someone working for him* did *follow me to Philadelphia.*

God, she was tempted to use the honor bracelet's screen and audio interfaces so she could see Adele's face, hear Adele's voice. She'd promised that. Promised a facecall every day. How much would anyone notice if she held her hands low in her lap and spoke softly? Should she worry about directional audio surveillance, which can pick up human voices from hundreds of meters away?

Maybe if no one else had come into the joint, she'd have chanced it. People did come in, though—a couple, followed a few minutes later by a guy alone. They sat well away from her, but she didn't like the way the guy glanced over. So no audio. She decided to contact Lynn first.

SORRY THIS IS TEXT

SEEMS LIKE THE FIRST 'LESSON' HAS COMMENCED & I'M TAKING
    NO CHANCES

EATING MOO GOO GAI PAN WITH LEFT HAND, TEXTING WITH RIGHT

NEVER EXPECTED TO FIND CONCEALMENT IN ANYPLACE CHINESE

They texted back and forth for several minutes until Jamie finally asked the question that would put the Callithump darknet to the test; if it was anything less than Dana said it was, she'd likely be in handcuffs by morning.

PLEASE, PLEASE TELL DEL AS MUCH ABOUT WHAT I'M REALLY DOING
    AS YOU THINK IS OK
IF I SAY ANYTHING, I'LL BE DISOBEYING ORDERS
——BUT NOT YOU
YOU CAN TELL HER
EXPLAIN IT
PLEASE

A moment later, Lynn replied:

I *WILL* EXPLAIN AND SHE'LL UNDERSTAND WHY YOU COULD NOT
GIVE ME 10 MINUTES, THEN TEXT ADELE
LOVE YOU…

Jamie counted those ten minutes down to the second and finally, fingers trembling, clicked in Adele's address.
Adele was waiting for her:

OH BABY, THANK YOU FOR FINDING A WAY TO LET ME KNOW
IT'S SUCH A RELIEF TO UNDERSTAND
AND IT'S OK THAT I CAN'T SEE YOU, HEAR YOU

Only when the people working the restaurant started hovering did she click off, which was agony. Adele made her go first—

SO YOU CAN IMAGINE ME HERE WAITING FOR YOU
WHICH I AM

Once back in her room, Jamie got undressed and tried to sleep in her skivvies. The sounds from beyond the room's walls had receded, but she remained wide-eyed and skittish anyway.

She wanted an automatic weapon and plenty of ammo. She wanted to control a vantage point from which she could see everything without being visible to anyone. *God, how the hell do civilians do it? No weapons, walls too damn meager to stop even a BB pellet…and where the hell are Ossado's cams?*

Only after she put on her jeans and shirt again and stretched out atop the bedcovers would her eyes close. And only when the room's alarm jangled her eyes open did she understand the furious hand-to-hand combat that left her gasping and exhausted had been a dream. Just a dream.

It might as well have been real. She rose stiff and sore, her shirt soaked through with the sweat of battle. Zero-five-hundred hours, according to the readout on the room's videoscreen. *Hell, for all I know, Ossado moved me to this hotel to avoid whoever he thought might've followed me on the train…'course, that doesn't mean he didn't install cams to watch over me.* She blew off the workout she'd planned to help fortify her for the first day with Ossado and shuffled into the bathroom to turn on the shower.

Truth is, I have no friggin' clue what the truth is. All I know is I'm gonna have to do this alone, completely self-contained. For the next two hundred and ninety-two days, starting right the fuck now.

Jamie stood at parade rest in the middle of her hotel room, feet twelve inches apart, left hand clasping her right behind her back just below her belt and fingering her honor bracelet, her lifeline. Maybe, just maybe its darknet flume had passed the first test, because Ossado had yet to brandish handcuffs.

Instead, he paced before her and made official what she already knew from Lynn: Over the next eleven days, she'd receive instruction in the finer points of handling pixie dust, identifying and using social engineering techniques, how to maintain operations security, the codes she'd use to communicate about any "special" matters. "Because I'm the conduit between General Embry and you. What you want to say to him goes through me. And vice versa."

After a pause, he added two things Lynn never mentioned—how eyewrap-cams would be used to record anyone trying to infect her comlinks and how to behave when she believed she was under surveillance.

"We're doing this training well away from Norfolk because officially it's not happening and you're not here. You're still on leave. Except for me and Colonel Zachary, we don't want anyone you'll be working with to know you're being trained as—"

"Bait."

Ossado squinted at her. "Mmm. The IG training will be conducted in Arlington, out of the Marine Corps Inspector General's office there, and we'll assign you housing for that, too." He glanced around the plain room. "Not unlike this palace. During those fifteen days, you'll have time to arrange your housing in Norfolk—within certain bounds."

"What does that mean?"

"Off-base rentals close to the team's office. We're ensuring team members live in situations where someone reliable is always around while they're at work or out of town. We've been able to line up several duplexes where we can rent both units. All close to the office and within an hour's drive to two Naval Air Stations and an Air Force base with regular flights to all over hell and gone."

"Our very own buddy system."

Ossado's squint, now apparently permanent, contracted even further. "Mmm." He pulled a wristcom and a pair of eyewraps from the leather briefcase he'd walked in with and laid them on the room's bed, then pointed to the eyewraps. "Put them on."

Jamie examined them as she obeyed. "One of my honeypots, I presume."

"Officially Corps-issued for active duty only. Two comcards built into them."

"Two?" Jamie took off the eyewraps and looked at them again.

"One's the honeypot with the pixie dust," Ossado said. "You'll keep it clicked up every single second you're on duty or commuting to and from a team activity. The other comcard is clean, and by default it's off and disconnected from its power source so it can't be infected. It will not connect or turn on unless the honeypots are off and disconnected from power. When you need to communicate with me, use the clean comcard, and only in secure circumstances. Understand?"

"Yes."

"Now take a gander at the temple arms, front and sides. See those very small black dots? Those are fisheye cams, on by default so we have a visual record of everyone who comes near you. You'll train with these eyewraps for the next eleven days, then return them to me on the morning of December twenty-seven before your liberty commences. They'll be formally issued to you on December thirtieth when all team member comlinks are issued."

Jamie glanced at the wristcom on the bed—a nice model, what one might expect a young officer to wear. "And that's the other honeypot— my fake personal comlink?"

"It is. We picked a wristcom instead of eyewraps because a wristcom's easier for a bad guy to attack by touching it for a few seconds."

"So what about a clean personal comlink?" Jamie asked. "Can I use my own?"

Shaking his head, Ossado picked up the wristcom and handed it to her. "This is also a two-fer. Has a second personal comcard that's clean. Works the same as your eyewraps—off and disconnected from power by default, won't function unless both your honeypots are off and disconnected. The wristcom you keep for the duration, starting now."

Jamie donned the eyewraps, strapped on the wristcom, and resumed the position of parade rest while she planned her first active-duty purchase: A Faraday cage booster bag large enough to hold eyewraps and wristcom, small enough to occupy a cargo pocket, strong enough to block all electromagnetic signals from escaping or reaching whatever the bag contained. Because, commanding officer or not, she just couldn't bring herself to trust the man standing before her.

Three days' liberty sounds great when you have none at all. But when you're actually liberated, it becomes cruel. Because if you're trying to get home to Adele, it's really only one day. Most of each of the other two are consumed by the ever longer journey, 560 kilometers from Philadelphia, 800 kilometers from Arlington, 970 from the exile of Norfolk.

Nine hundred klicks away for 260 days. And anytime you want to travel beyond the 400-klick liberty limit, you have to go begging for permission—unless you decide in your frenzied despair to risk discovery of your unauthorized absence and spend a small fortune on a plane ticket for a chance to touch her again, kiss her again. But when you do that, she flips out because she's terrified you'll get caught and end up in the brig and your meager time with her withers into misery.

It's far better when she comes to you, especially when she can arrive in time to celebrate the moment your liberty starts and stay right 'til your liberty's snuffed out. That's what keeps you sane—when you find someplace to stay, down by the beach maybe, away from the goddamn Team, and finally her warm honey scent enfolds you, her hands and mouth and exquisite eyes embrace you, and you wrap yourself around her and you can breathe and let go and immerse in her presence, her presence that lights your days of liberty and holds the nightmares at bay and you can actually get some decent sleep.

God, how you try to savor that kind of liberty. You make love three or four times each day you have with her, you focus on details, make mental videoclips of simple, mundane moments—a smile, a laugh you'll replay many, many times. To carry you 'til you once again get a liberty worth having.

In between, you shove a pillow over your head at night so your bad dreams don't keep waking your roommate, who's only read about the Palawan and obviously finds you a tad unnerving. During the interminable days, you make sure you appear to be playing by the rules, but you continue your surreptitious search for commo workarounds.

Because the rules are out-fucking-rageous. The rules claim not only the ten or eleven hours you spend working, they take the rest, too. After all, a honeypot has to be ever ready with its seduction, so the rules say those damn Marine Corps comlinks are all you're allowed to carry, and they have to be on your person at all times unless you're in your quarters. Where you can just turn them off and have all the privacy a one-lite could want.

Yet there's that chill again, those icicles prickling up your spine every time you recall Ossado's heh-heh wink the day after Adele's visit for those eighty-six magnificent hours.

So, finally, you get it.

The problem hasn't been that you're too damn paranoid. The problem has been that you're still not paranoid enough.

No matter what command tells you, don't ever doubt that those comlinks and especially those eyewrap-cams are *watching*. Twenty-four seven. Even in your quarters.

Hell no, that shit never sleeps. "Forget" to bring along your Corps-issued comlinks when you go for a morning run? Command will know. Command will fry your ass. Try using that booster bag you finally managed to sneak off and buy? Command will send a tech to take care of "a remotely detected glitch."

You try to convince yourself it doesn't matter that they're watching, doesn't matter that you might as well be living naked in a glass cage. But it does matter.

So, finally, you, the hunted, decide to hunt.

Deception serves as your primary weapon. Ironic that so much of what you need to pull off this two-step gets taught to you by the very people who insist on your constant surveillance.

First you "lose" the handheld electronic probe-and-jam gear they issue before you go off to execute an inspection—can't turn it back in if it rolled out of the helicopter, right? Now you have your very own P&J, which you use to sweep your quarters and discover two multisensor cams mysteriously affixed to one of the light fixtures. No sweat. Select a range from fifty megahertz well into gamma ray exahertz and randomly press SPOTJAM until you decide on the best way to eliminate them.

Simultaneously, you "accidentally" blindfold those damn eyewrap-cams with a pile of dirty underwear as soon as you close the door to your room. Add audio and a garble of electromagnetic waves—from your so-called personal comlink, from the videoscreen in your room, from the satellite radio and the building utility system—and see how long it takes for someone to "just happen" to drop by. Repeat this daily, too, so it becomes part of your pattern and they stop checking up on you because every time they do they find you immersed in multiple videogames, listening to music, and eating popcorn.

All the while, you're introducing commo from your honor bracelet's darknet flume in small increments, so the tiny corresponding signal changes go unnoticed as the flume piggybacks its payload onto a random selection of the packets bouncing on and off the public networks that surround you.

Here's where you allow yourself a teensy smile. Because the commo signals coming from your little corner of the world are a chaos of indecipherable noise, and those in Special Projects Team Charlie's ops center, wherever the hell it's hidden, are now unable to get a decent read on your quarters.

Finally, you're ready for the payoff: On the floor of your closet, wrapped in a nanocamouflage tarp that acts like a great big booster bag, only the wrist of your trembling right hand protruding slightly, you can do a real facecall…

CHAPTER TWENTY-SEVEN
CLOSE

Eighteen days on, three days off. The inspection cycle never varied.

Initially, Jamie believed she was stuck on the wrong side of Ossado's OCD. Ten uninterrupted days of preparatory research about the unit to be inspected—always starting on a Friday, ending on a Sunday. Always followed by five weekdays on the road, three to execute the inspection, bookended by a travel day to, a travel day from. Then three days to write up the inspection report. And, at last, three days' leave, always Tuesday through Thursday. No. Matter. What.

Jamie went through it four times before she appreciated the extent to which the cycle itself might be part of the social engineering of the honeypot. As in make a big frigging deal—but strictly in whispers—about this mysterious Special Projects Team Charlie working in civvies out of some crappy, leftover office building 320 klicks from the Corps's IG headquarters. Low-key security but stringent. Military bureaucracy's equivalent of a cloak of invisibility. And then put someone in charge who has a thing about order and schedules and symmetry. Someone predictable, the embodiment of a classic opsec vulnerability easily overlooked by people with a penchant for right angles in their haircuts.

Intentional or not?

For weeks and weeks, Jamie didn't give any of this a passing thought. Instead, she fretted about the thread back to her conleave life stretching thinner as she tangled in the byzantine arcanities of the Marine Corps.

How much thinner could the thread get before it snapped?

A world away in Washington, Lynn had introduced her bill and was the talk of the chattering classes as debate over it revved. She always responded to Jamie's texts and occasionally initiated one of her own, but inevitably they were brief. Jamie yearned to simply be in the same room with her.

And Adele…Adele had been accepted by Henry Yount into both the program at MIT and into a paid gig at his consulting group. Adele was working now, living in Lily's old apartment in Belmont; she had an upcoming project of her own in Cuba, not to mention a dissertation to plan, research, and write. No way could she take every third week to traipse down to Norfolk just because that's when Ossado decided to grant a breath of liberty to her grunt girlfriend.

She did, however, manage to meet Jamie in Washington, at Lynn's place in Georgetown, which lay within the liberty limit, and Lynn was around then a little, too.

The thread felt stronger after that. Jamie had real faith in it after that. Plus her deception of Ossado's surveillance produced no fallout, no sign it had been discovered. So either her techniques were still working or he'd ceased snooping. Jamie just didn't buy the third possibility—that the surveillance somehow continued but Ossado had become transformatively better at suppressing his leer.

Though she remained beneath her nanocam tarp, slowly she and Adele relaxed a little, allowing themselves the luxury of trivia—Adele gave her a virtual tour of the Belmont apartment, she made a joke about being forever doomed to repeat "a three-week-long Groundhog Day where nothing ever happens."

"How do you know?" Adele asked. "If anything's happened, I mean. It's not like the honeypot's gonna shoot off fireworks when it's zapped."

A rhetorical question, but it got Jamie pondering.

How many times during twelve inspections over the course of 260 days would somebody, anybody actually zap her comlink? Once for each bad guy? Twice, like at Demeter? If so, how many bad guys did Embry think were out there, and how many of those had the wherewithal to engineer an encounter with her?

She'd been told during honeypot training not to bother even thinking about that. "Don't go in with expectations or judgment," Ossado had said. "You won't be able to read intent, much less guilt. Hell, for all we know, someone who infects your comlink may not even know they're doing it. Certainly, you'll never know and you won't be getting any feedback, either—not along the way, not ever. You just do the damn inspections."

So Jamie did, counting each Day to Terminal Leave. Only during her morning run on DTL176, which would begin a new inspection cycle, her fifth, did she finally begin to reflect on those first four inspections: A ground combat element at Twenty-nine Palms, the military liaison office at the embassy in Jamaica, a forward operations location in Guatemala, another in Colombia.

All four had two things in common: Nobody had ever heard of flash inspections before, much less been subjected to them, and sure as hell *nobody* liked them. "We're here to tag along and observe as you go about your mission," the inspection team leader invariably told the balking commander of the unit to be inspected. "We'll ask simple questions strictly about your HUMINT recordkeeping if and only if our interactions with your personnel do not disrupt their activities."

All four inspected units also had the same sorts of gaps in their HUMINT recordkeeping. Exactly the sorts of gaps Lynn's new, improved legislation targeted—and exactly the sorts of gaps the Marine Corps wanted to argue it could prevent with self-regulation.

Yet no one Jamie dealt with before, during, or after any of these four inspections seemed suspicious. Officious, yes. Most definitely irritated at the sudden presence of three inspectors with impeccable credentials they had to honor. But nothing more—and nobody touched her wristcom.

As Jamie trudged into the start of DTL176 and another inspection cycle, she wondered if Embry had sent her, honeypots in hand, on what amounted to a wild goose chase.

Until she clicked through the startup authentications at her desk and saw what rolled onto her screens. The next inspection would be a real drilldown, to one battalion's company-level intelligence cells. The Ninth Regiment's First Battalion.

❖

Holy fucking shit. Nim Bacani's unit.

Jamie stared at her center screen. The One-Nine had been back from the Palawan for almost eight months and was now some three months into its next deployment cycle, smack in the middle of pre-deployment training at Lejeune.

What else did she want to know? Excitement trilled up and down her breastbone. Everything there was to know about the One-Nine's HUMINT-related activities lay at her fingertips.

A once-only limited-time offer, ladies and gentlemen. For the next eighteen days, you can access mission files, CLIC personnel files, any battalion staff analyses and reports where HUMINT comes into play, going back as many as three deployments. And what will this extraordinary deal cost you, ladies and gentlemen? Well, now…well, now…

Jamie's fingers hesitated above the keyboard, tremoring. How paranoid was she to worry about autotrackers on the One-Nine mission data from last 7 June, when that squad from First Battalion's Alpha Company had patrolled the mountains around El Nido as Chen Dongfeng travelled by road to the El Nido airstrip?

On the other hand, she'd reviewed previous deployment data in three of her four inspections to date. Reviewing the One-Nine's data—including any ops last 7 June—would be protocol for this inspection, too.

Okay, okay…don't just jump for it. Proceed the way you always do. Last in, first examined. Get to it when you're supposed to. So you don't give away that you know anything about Nim Bacani…

❖

She worked fast, truly focused and alert for the first time since being sentenced to Norfolk. Not that she'd done a bad job so far on the research. Quite the contrary. Jamie knew she had a gift for sifting out the right details and using them to prepare drilldown questions for the "real" inspectors, the team's captain and sergeant.

This stood in marked contrast to what happened when the team executed an inspection.

For one thing, during three of the four previous inspections, she'd had to wear cammies. Definitely a trigger: Phantasms quickly overpopulated her peripheral vision.

And in Guatemala and Colombia, she'd carried both an assault rifle and a sidearm. It could've been worse, though. She never fired or even had to aim the weapons, and carrying them may actually have tamed the phantasms some, at least compared to walking around unarmed. But she avoided sleep; she didn't want to find out what sleep might have in store.

In the vicinity of other officers, she spoke as little as possible. She relaxed some when it was only grunts, however, and after a while she'd be able to talk with a few of them, those with a certain look in their eye, and then the rest would warm up, and as they bantered she'd briefly hear an echo of the old camaraderie.

She also heard a fair amount of new rumor and gossip—as well as accounts of what happened on ops. Shit that shouldn't have happened, that made her cringe, because she knew her goddamn eyewrap-cams were designed to record it all. More than once, she'd hear it coming in the way their voices went low, yank the eyewraps from her face like something was wrong with them, and thrust them into the booster bag in her cargo pocket—all to keep the hapless grunts from taking a fall for the brass.

Some of what she heard she reported to Ossado. Grunts getting orders to conduct real-world intel activities during what were supposed to be training missions, indications of contractors providing intel products without proper authorization. But Ossado always found a way to declare it out of mission scope. "Focus on your mission, Lieutenant," he told her. "And don't forget your goddamn comlinks."

After six days of research on the One-Nine, Jamie had worked her way into Alpha Company and back to 7 June. And there it was: A morning patrol in the hills a few klicks from the El Nido airstrip. Uneventful, according to the mission report, except for the squad hooking up with a couple of Columbia Aegis contractors to help repair a road washout. No mission commo audio files. No mention of two possible Tausug-speaking insurgents or a firefight involving three vehicles and at least ten men. But the patrol's roster was there—eight squaddies, one of them Nimuel Bacani.

Jamie pulled a pen and a small pad of paper from a pocket and wrote down the names. The squad leader's name—Sergeant RT Soto—she circled. She would start with him.

Soon she realized she would end with him, too. He'd gone absent without leave on 10 June, the day after Nim died, and nobody in the Marine Corps had seen him since. But that was the good news. It meant he could still be alive. The others—all seven of them—were dead.

❖

It didn't occur to Jamie that more than just her comlinks might be honeypots until long after DTL157, the day she'd tracked down Sergeant Soto's girlfriend using intel painstakingly acquired during three days at Lejeune among the One-Nine's grunts and NCOs.

The woman lived with her mother and her two-year-old in Baltimore, just inside the liberty limit, and to see her, Jamie decided the time had come to change.

Not an appealing prospect, because change attracted unwanted command attention. So Jamie figured it better be breakout change: She bought a car—an old clunk of a thing, too big, too blue. But as the most common model on the road, it granted a modicum of anonymity, and it worked fine, didn't cost a whole lot, and would provide the perfect pretense for a drive to Baltimore during her next liberty. Especially since she wouldn't be able to see or talk much with Adele anyway; Adele was off on the first of several trips with Yount to work on her Cuba project, a UN-funded environmental preservation venture in Havana.

Jamie planned and rehearsed for what she knew would be a one-off in Baltimore. Because a second attempt would betray that what was supposed to look like a chance encounter at the bar where Soto's girlfriend worked was no such thing. But the idea that dykey Lieutenant Gwynmorgan would haul her ass to a Purple Tulip concert in Baltimore?

No question Ossado and everyone else would believe it once they got a look at the band's lead singer.

She felt like she did okay. For an amateur. She'd managed to follow Soto's girlfriend into the restroom, click BARRAGEJAM on her P&J, and talk real fast for a few seconds. She got it all out, explaining to the wide-eyed woman who she was, what she knew, that she could give Soto a way to "do what his friend Nim wanted" and get out from under the AWOL charge. "I'll be in Washington on May twentieth. He can find me at a place on M Street in Georgetown called Slamdunk at seventeen hundred hours."

Yet she came away with a sense that, except for the concert, she'd probably wasted her time.

Twenty days later, Jamie sat unhopefully at Slamdunk's bar surrounded by a noisy, energetic after-work crowd and waited. And waited. At 1942 hours, she gave it up. Urgently needing to pee, she beelined to the restroom—and found Soto's girlfriend at the restroom sink when she emerged from the toilet stall.

Jamie nodded at the woman and clicked her P&J into short-range barragejam.

"He wants to know how you'll do it," said Soto's girlfriend.

"He's got the video?"

"Yeah. But he ain't givin' it to nobody in the Marine Corps."

"I don't blame him. Any way you twist it, he's been screwed. How about a senator?"

"The lesbo one all them stories say you're buddied up with. He said you'd say that." Soto's girlfriend shook her head. "No way. No one in government."

"How about a media person? Someone famous with a rep for changing the game *and* protecting their sources."

"Who?"

"Vivian Velty."

Silence.

"There's a joint on Seventh Street called Lorem Ipsum," Jamie said. "Vivian Velty will be there tomorrow, seventeen hundred hours, alone and ready to listen. I hope your boy works something out with her, but if not, he can go back underground. No harm, no foul, and sure as hell no turning him over to the Corps. Or anyone else. Whatever goes down between him and Vivian, I'm out of it now. So you tell the sergeant good luck from me."

Soto's girlfriend nodded and walked away.

❖

Well, okay, it was a pretty risky ad lib—maybe even illegal. Hell, probably illegal. Jamie headed back up to Lynn's place trying to remember the regs. As she recalled, they prohibited disclosure of internal documents or information that hadn't been officially released, "no matter how a marine comes into possession of a document." But what about a "document" the Marine Corps had declared nonexistent?

At least Jamie knew Vivian Velty was in town, due at the dinner party Lynn would be throwing three hours after the meeting with Soto she hoped Velty would agree to—and Soto would show up for. Getting Velty's attention was the easy part. Getting it to focus on Soto? Maybe not so easy.

"Hello, Lieutenant," Vivian Velty oozed, making Jamie's rank sound downright pornographic as she approached the crowded steps of the Lincoln Memorial where Jamie perched waiting for her. She had de-glammed with tailored gray slacks and a ponytail. Dark eyewraps made her difficult to recognize, and no less predatory than the first time Jamie met her, despite the come-hither way she crossed her long legs when she sat down. "I understand from our mutual friend that you'd like to have a confidential chat."

Jamie appreciated the lack of bullshit, since even short-range barrage jamming in public places around Washington tended to get noticed sooner rather than later, and Jamie had clicked on the P&J buried in her pants' cargo pocket when Velty got within three meters of her. "Our friend," she replied, "says you keep your promises."

"I do."

"If what I'm about to tell you comes to nothing, I want your promise not to disclose anything you learn about it from me—including *that* you learned it from me—to anyone."

One beat, two beats, then: "Yes. I'll promise you that."

"Have you ever heard of Nimuel Bacani?"

When Lynn first came to Washington, she bought three contiguous townhouses on one of the quieter streets in Georgetown. The largest of the three stood on the corner of Avon and Dent, its fifty feet of tree-shaded brick painted a cool and stately light gray that gave it a senatorial air. Around the corner on Dent Street, the second, much more modest place cheerfully nestled its sunny eighteen-foot yellow façade between the pale gray lady's narrow side and a red-painted twin occupied by the head of Lynn's Washington office.

In this little yellow townhouse, barely more than a thousand square feet on two floors, Lynn lived when she was in Washington. The dinner party, however, like all of her frequent Washington soirees, Lynn hosted in the gray house, and when it ended around 2300 hours, she returned to the yellow house through the heavy fire door she'd installed in the structures' common basement wall and came straight up to the guest room, where Jamie worked on her analytic geometry/calculus course.

"What did you do with Vivian?" Lynn asked uneasily. "She never showed up tonight."

"She—" Jamie shook her head. "She didn't call you?"

Head shifting minimally side to side, Lynn sat in a neighboring chair. "Leave anything out?"

"No, don't think so. I figured you'd hear from her before I do. For comment if I'm lucky. To let you know your stray's an asshole if I'm unlucky. I'll only hear from her if she keeps her promise and sends me a copy of the video."

"Hmm…" Lynn's finger traced her lower lip.

"Negotiations, maybe? Setting him up somewhere safe? That could take days. Even longer if his girlfriend and the kid and maybe his girlfriend's mother go with him."

"Or someone's managed to track you the whole way."

"You mean use me to grab Soto? That suggests somebody patterned my One-Nine research, which only happens if the data had autotrackers on it. And then whoever's doing that also has to spend a pile putting a team on me that, frankly, is wicked good."

"They would be wicked good, wouldn't they?" Lynn lowered her head, her gray eyes examining Jamie. She looked like she wanted to spit out something foul-tasting. "They're professionals."

"Well, I got a little bit of training on that last December—"

"Oh yes, three days a spy doth make."

It hit hard, a coldcock.

"Jeezus, Lynn." Jamie squeezed her eyes shut. *What the fuck have I done?* "I'm sorry. Oh god, I'm so—" *Breathe…breathe…* "I just had this—this feeling after I realized everyone from the June seventh patrol was dead except for the guy, the patrol leader for chrissake, who skipped out right after Nim died, before anything had happened to any of the other six." *Breathe…* "I figured Nim gave him the datacard with the video." *Breathe…*

"Jamie—"

"An' he fuckin' disappears from Busuanga, y'know? 'Cuz he's short, stocky, dark, got Indian blood in him. Good Spanish speaker. He can pass for Filipino…just. And he gets his ass to Manila. Then slowly—it takes him months—he works his way back to Baltimore. On ships, I'm betting. Crew. Because Sergeant Soto is in love. He wants his

life back. So I—so I figured I could, y'know, as an inspector I could…
oh jeezus, Lynn, is she—"

"Stop. Vivian is no fool. And you brought her a beaut. If anyone
can reel it in, Vivian can."

"He wouldn't deal with you or me."

"Oh, he dealt with you. He's trusted you, Jamie. And I confess
I'm not sure you could have found any other path through this jungle
than the one you're on now. Given the position you're in, I think you're
doing great. The person I want to throttle is Ben Embry."

"So you think Vel—Vivian might be doing okay?"

"I'll give her 'til one a.m."

"And then?"

"Then I go looking for her. Carefully."

"Stealthily."

"Mmm. Click on GNN, will you?"

Jamie wondered if Lynn and Vivian Velty had done this routine
before. Something about the way Lynn clicked up her pocketcom when
it beeped at 0043 hours gave it away. "Well?" said Lynn, then twice
murmured "Interesting" before concluding the call.

"Good or bad?" Jamie asked.

"Amazing what that woman can do in twelve hours." Lynn clicked
off the GNN talking head on the videoscreen and turned to Jamie.
"Here's what I can tell you so far…" Another beep interrupted her and
she spoke into her pocketcom again, then clicked off. "Dana says hi.
Where was I?" But she went mute, staring at the floor.

"Lynn?"

"Oh, sorry. I haven't had much time to think about this…" She
straightened up in the chair. "Here's where we are—some of this from
Vivian, some from Dana. And don't look so surprised. I said I'd keep
you in the loop."

"What about the video?"

"Patience, kiddo. Patience. First of all, Vivian said her five o'clock
meeting 'went very well' and everyone's in transit to safety. If I say
more than that and you do not report it to your commanding officer, you
could end up in trouble. It wouldn't stick, but it would be a hassle. As it
stands, we can make a convincing argument that your communication
with me about Sergeant Soto was lawful and therefore protected."

"But—"

"And that Vivian acted on information from me, perhaps even as
my agent."

"But—"

"Vivian doesn't believe you were followed, or if you were, you managed to slip them. But it looks like your research *was* patterned, as you suggested."

"How do you know?"

"A new, high-profile warrant was issued for Soto early this afternoon, though nobody's yet thought to go sniffing around his girlfriend. From which Vivian infers—and I agree with her—that they followed your research but not your conversations with the One-Nine's lower ranks."

"Soto's buddies belong to Bravo Company, not Alpha."

"Ah." Lynn smiled. "Of course. When the moment's right, I'll be asking some pointed questions about the timing of that warrant. And about the seven other people on Alpha Company's June seventh patrol."

"When you have the video, you mean."

Lynn's smile remained on her lips but no longer reached her eyes. "Dana just told me one of those honeypots Ben has you parading around—the wristcom—was zapped with a variant of the Blondie spyware. On April twenty-fourth. But it was dormant—and unnoticed—until yesterday. Dana's in quite a dither about it getting by the first layer of the honeypot's sentry software."

"April twenty-fourth was Lejeune. Last day inspecting the One-Nine." Who? Who had touched her left wrist long enough to—"Wait. You said a variant of the Blondie spyware? The same as what the woman at Demeter had?"

Lynn nodded. "That's not all. The pixie dust from the wristcom honeypot Ben has you wearing came back with payloads from the same comlink that sent the poorly encrypted message last November—"

"The fifth-order comlink. The one that sent the message with a hundred and five zeroes and ones." Jamie rubbed her cramping belly as icicles stampeded up her spine. "Which pointed to Aunt Zerviah's house."

"Dana said the command-and-control server from the November attack went silent a while ago, as did the comlinks traced from it." Lynn's smile was gone. "Except for the fifth one. That fifth-order comlink is still active."

"And its tentacles reach all the way to the One-Nine," Jamie rasped. "Which means all the way back to the Palawan."

"Not yet irrefutably," said Lynn. "But close."

CHAPTER TWENTY-EIGHT
FEEL HOW I GOT YOU NOW

I have comp time coming," Adele announced on DTL118. "Can you drive to Georgetown tomorrow night after your liberty starts? Lynn will be gone all week. She told me we're welcomed to use her place."

Jamie couldn't say yes fast enough. Her seventh inspection—of a CI/HUMINT unit stationed in Djibouti—had been rough. The unit did interrogations and they were very good at it. Jamie didn't sleep for five nights. Not one wink. She caught up some during her three days of report writing, but the price was ferocious nightmares. She needed to hold Adele. Needed it bad.

At 2214 hours on DTL117—fifty-eight days, eighteen hours, and thirty two minutes since the last time she'd breathed in Adele's scent, burrowed against the warmth of Adele's skin—Jamie parked her car in front of Lynn's little yellow Georgetown house, hurried toward the front door, saw it opening as she approached.

Almost there, almost…Jamie shut the door, dropped her duffel on the floor, placed Ossado's wretched comlinks into separate small Faraday cage drawers in a chest near the door, leaned against the nearest wall—and just stared at Adele, unable to move, unable to speak.

"Oh, baby," Adele whispered, her worried eyes studying Jamie's face as her hands caressed it. Adorned only in a robe, Adele lifted onto tiptoes and wrapped her arms hard around Jamie. "Show me everything."

After a hypnotically endless kiss that seemed to last a mere nanosecond, Jamie mutely followed Adele up the stairs to the guest room, shedding her clothes as she went.

With wordless grunts and moans, she reached, reached for Adele, reached for the feeling of her face nuzzling into Adele's flawless breasts, of her ardent need snaking up Adele's writhing leg, of the eager ride on Adele's untamed hips. Their rhythms syncopated, a counterpoint of tongue and lips and anointed clefts, until Adele's eight thousand fervid clitoral nerve-ends igniting in tumultuous wave after wave after wave.

And still Jamie could not speak. But Adele understood the language of her hunger, her isolation as she curled quivering into Adele's shoulder.

"You're okay," Adele soothed her, embracing her, pulling her close. "You're okay, baby." Adele kissed her head gently, nestled a hand between her jittery legs, and began to massage. "I got you now. You just stay right here with me and feel how I got you now…"

Clutching Adele, nourished by the softness of Adele's breast against her cheek, Jamie surrendered to the sounds of Adele's voice, the relief of Adele's touch, Adele's honey scent, and then her orgasm spilled out of her and into sobs that ebbed slowly, slowly into sleep.

Too early in the morning, Adele took a voicecall from Henry Yount during which she said little more than, "Yeah, okay." But she let the bedcovers slip from her shoulders as she sat up, and when she clicked off, her face had stiffened into a frown.

"What?"

"This Cuba thing is getting a little dicey."

Now Jamie sat up, too. "What does that mean?"

"There's a group there called Partido La Cuba Auténtico—LCA for short," said Adele. "They're rabidly opposed to the current Cuban government, which they regard as way too socialist and anti-growth. In Cuba, they're definitely a minority, but fairly powerful in the Oriente— that's the eastern provinces. They're the rich guys mostly—business people, some politicians, police chiefs, judges, the few who've benefited most from what Henry refers to as 'Cuba's cautious return to the capitalist fold.' They get support—and a great deal of money— from the nietos de exiliados in Florida."

"The descendants of those mid-twentieth-century Cuban exiles? I thought those guys had moved on. Assimilated."

"Not all of them. Some still expect to waltz in and instantly take back 'their' country once LCA comes to power. If they had their way, the prison at the Guantanamo Naval Base would reopen so they could lock up the current Cuban Council of State and Council of Ministers and throw the key into Guantanamo Bay."

"So what's got Henry calling you now?"

"This trade agreement our government's about to sign that expands economic and technical cooperation with Cuba. It emphasizes sustainable economic development and environmental protection, which means, among other things, our projects will probably expand beyond dealing with urban water pollution to include soil degradation and desertification."

"I bet LCA wants to stop it anyway, right?"

"Oh yeah, and one of the ways they're trying to do that is with accusations of ecoterrorism against the lead Cuban environmental group involved in the agreement—Tierra Verde."

"The same Tierra Verde you're working with in Havana?"

"Yep. LCA is blaming a so-called radical arm of Tierra Verde for a series of fires and bombings in the Moa semi-autonomous economic zone. Which is ridiculous. There *is* no radical arm. Tierra Verde doesn't do that sort of thing. And besides, it has a good relationship with Inseque—"

A chill tap-danced up Jamie's back. "Walker-Monroe's energy company? Jonathan Armstrong Archer's energy company?"

"Energy and assorted natural resources," Adele said. "Like nickel and cobalt. Inseque pretty much runs Moa, and they know they need to clean the place up, so—"

"Shit, Del." Jamie turned urgently to face her. "You're going there, aren't you? To Moa."

"That was the plan. For three days at the end of our next trip. Henry wants to get a look at what might well become a second project in Cuba, starting next year."

Jamie squinted at Adele. "But he's hesitating now, right? Worried about violence in Moa because…" Jamie closed her eyes—and saw it. "Because you'll be there with Tierra Verde people. Who might be targeted by LCA. Or maybe even the ecoterrorists."

A wave of nausea overtook Jamie when she saw Adele's minimal nod. *Don't go, don't go, don't go…* She wanted to scream it, wanted to grab Adele and demand it, beg for it.

"Though I question the notion of ecoterrorists," Adele said huffily. "Can't remember the last time it didn't turn out to be a scare tactic conjured up by people who want to keep raping the planet."

"A bomb'll kill you no matter who throws it."

"Which is why Henry won't decide about going to Moa until the last minute." Adele spoke matter-of-factly, and Jamie glimpsed the Red Cross worker in her—strong, determined, efficient, maybe a little too fearless for her own good. "That's what he called to tell me. And if he decides he's going, that's when I'll decide if I'm going along."

"Or you could all just stay home and wait for things to calm down." Jamie would have said more, something about how kill zones have a way of popping up when you least expect them, but a subtle vibration from the darknet flume in her honor bracelet got her to change the subject. "Were you able to bring down my Callithump eyewraps?"

"Bedside table. Behind you." Quickly, Adele leaned close for an electric kiss before Jamie had a chance to turn away from her. "I wanna spend the whole day with you right here," she murmured when she came up for air. "But not without a cup of coffee first." She bounced off the bed. "I shall return."

Three whole days, Jamie thought as she picked up the eyewraps. Regs be damned, she launched the relationship initialization routine: Put them on, click them up, start the meld sequence, take them off, rest the right temple arm against her honor bracelet, count to ten, and finally, with 116 Days to Terminal Leave, she had her own eyewraps again, secure-linked now with the darknet flume on her wrist.

Odd how this one little thing—eyewraps no one in the Corps knew she had, eyewraps she could count on not to betray her—made breathing so much easier. She lay back and eyeballed up a shadowscreen to find out who might be sending her a message at 0840 on a Tuesday morning.

"Del," she called a moment later, rising from the bed and already heading down the stairs to the tiny kitchen as she pulled on a robe. "Vivian Velty just sent me Nim Bacani's video."

They watched the thirteen-minute sequence over and over on the videoscreen in the living room, zooming in, stopping, replaying, zooming again.

"Once the camera settles down, the clarity of this is incredible," Adele said.

"Mmm, I figure he was seeking concealment, then found it, 'cuz nobody he recorded noticed him, and he wasn't all that far away." Jamie stopped the video once more. "See those two guys standing next to each other off to the left side?"

"Don't look much like Filipinos to me. You recognize either of them?"

"No." Jamie stared hard at one man, then the other. Caucasian, early thirties—the mercs in charge. "I never saw The Bastard's face."

"Someone's bound to ID these guys once the video's made public."

"Whenever the hell that will be."

"Well," said Adele, "I think Vivian's right to be concerned about getting Nim Bacani's family out of the line of fire." She glanced at the image of the men on the screen as she pulled Jamie against her. "Those people are dangerous. But for the next three days, we don't have to think about them." She clicked off the screen, stood, and scooped up Jamie's hands. "Come upstairs with me, woman. Time's a'wastin'."

❖

DTL113. The time display in the corner of the videoscreen in Lynn's darkened guest room tripped from 0238 to 0239 hours. At 0300, Jamie would rise from the bed, get dressed. By 0330, she'd leave the house, leave Adele to drive back to Norfolk.

She turned her head to gaze at Adele lying next to her, asleep now after what would be their last lovemaking for a while. Jamie had slept, too, briefly—until another garbled dream about The Bastard's hand revving a drill and Shoo Juh's sneer and Awa's bloody, headless body rattled her awake.

A moment later, Adele also woke. "'S okay, baby," she said even before her eyes opened.

"How do you do that?"

"What?"

"Know when I've had a nightmare."

"Mmm. I wake up with, I dunno…a feeling."

"Sorry."

"No apologies. I want to know. I want to hold you and—" Adele snuggled close, kissed Jamie's forehead. "And when this is over, I want you to come to Belmont, live with me in Belmont."

"Yeah? I-I'd like that."

"What's wrong?" Adele asked after only a few seconds. "You're all restless now."

"Can we go to Great Hill on the weekends?"

Adele laughed softly. "Where else? I go up most weekends now. To get my hit. I can still smell you on the pillows in our room."

CHAPTER TWENTY-NINE

ADIOS, PIZDA

D TL111, 1140 hours. A third of the way through the third day of research on the next unit she'd be inspecting, Jamie spaced out yet again, and this time the moments she cared about passed unrecognized—when Adele stepped aboard the plane at Logan Airport up in Boston, when the plane taxied to the runway, when its engines roared the beast forward and then shoved it skyward on its way to Havana.

Damn. Just when she dared to consider the possibility that it was almost sort of over—as over as maybe it ever could be—she had to worry about Adele. Adele who was supposed to be safe.

Jamie glanced around the determinedly drab Special Projects Team Charlie office, then at her center screen's time display. 1143 hours. The minutes would pass even more slowly than usual for the next two weeks until Adele got home again.

At least she had the victory of Nim Bacani's video. It should've made her smile more, that victory, since it seemed her role, which sure as shit made her *feel* like she'd diddled a regulation or two, really would remain secret. And once made public, the video would give Lynn's legislation some whomper impetus.

Also, she'd proved it again. Proved she wasn't the nutcase she'd come to believe she was. *Proved* it, by god.

Plus, she'd played the honeypot fool well enough that Callithump pixie dust introduced at two different times and places had found its way to the same comlink, and in both instances the dust on that comlink was five degrees of separation away from her honeypot. Suggesting a chain of command. Probably parallel subordinate structures reporting to the same commander using the same comlink. The enemy's comlink—she was damn sure of that.

But. But but but…

Can't get there from here.

She saw no way to nail this enemy. Or connect him to The Bastard. Although she *had* shown—hadn't she?—that whoever tried to disappear Nim's video also wanted to disappear Lynn, and this whoever had kept right on messing with Lynn. Jamie had no doubt somebody like that would relish another opportunity to take Lynn out.

She had her theory, of course. That The Bastard and a band of thugs worked for Jonathan Armstrong Archer on the sly. That Archer would act audaciously to achieve his grand goals, unhesitating in the sacrifice of marines, of six-year-old girls in schoolyards, of a senator, and even, once in a while, of his own Columbia Aegis mercs. Because for Archer, everyone was fodder.

Hell, maybe that fifth-order comlink belonged to Archer himself. But it would be up to the Callithump cryppies and geeks to prove that, not her. All that was left for her now was 111 days of her Norfolk sentence. And worrying about Adele.

1151 hours. Jamie dragged her gaze across the screens in front of her, each full of endless, excruciating detail about the HUMINT activities of the next unit on her inspection agenda: A counterterrorism training outfit stationed at Joint Task Force Foxtrot's base in Honduras. Something about this crew must have attracted Embry's interest, since she'd been issued new honeypot devices that very morning. But damned if she could see what it might be.

❖

DTL103. As soon as the plane landed at the Humuya Air Base where JTF Foxtrot was stationed, Jamie sensed something amiss.

No question everything would be abnormal anyway, since the base had already begun to prepare for a tropical low way out in the Atlantic forecast to evolve over the next eight days into Hurricane Guthrie. Not that the forecasters believed the storm would hit Honduras. Oh no, it would veer north to cross western Cuba's swampy Zapata National Park, then the Gulf of Batabano and come ashore for real less than sixty klicks south of Havana—slamming the city as a category three monster on 30 June. The day before Adele planned to leave.

When Jamie told Adele about the storm and its projected path, Adele replied that she and Henry would pick one of two options: Depart Havana by Thursday, the twenty-sixth, for home—or go to Moa, 800-and-something klicks to the east, well away from Guthrie's expected path of destruction. Long trip by car on poor roads bound to be crowded with people dodging the storm, Jamie complained. No sweat, Adele assured her. "We'll fly over on Inseque's plane."

Inseque's plane. Jonathan Armstrong Archer's plane! Every time Jamie thought about it, her stomach cramped. She actually had to find a head and throw up before stepping onto the first flight, the one that took her inspection team to Guantanamo Naval Base. By the time she'd boarded the flight from Guantanamo to Humuya, the captain and sergeant on her team, whom she hadn't worked with before, had become convinced whatever she had was contagious and were careful to sit several meters away from her.

She walked off the plane at Humuya—in the middle of fucking nowhere, air viscous-humid and hard to breathe and making her itchy and prickly just like the Palawan—with one hand gripping the bellyache she'd endured for ten hours and obsessing about where, oh where would Adele be when the hurricane arrived in seven days?

Jamie had another question, too: Why the hell hadn't Ossado canned this inspection? She'd started wondering about that when they landed at Leeward Point Field at Guantanamo on the more remote western side of the bay which split the base property in two. As she waited for the flight to Humuya, she could see the flurry of activity across the water at the base's other, secondary airfield. Troops with weapons, field gear, and transport were bivouacking just off the runway. Damned if it didn't look like the base had become an infantry staging area.

"Yeah, well," a Navy petty officer responded when she asked, "we're boosting our force protection capabilities, ma'am. In case we have to expand our protection perimeter."

Straight from the commander's mouth, no doubt. Precisely the sort of Pentagon double-speak that left room, if necessary, for offensive action as well as hurricane prep.

And now, at JTF Foxtrot in Humuya, Jamie found herself struggling to engage anyone in the kind of casual chatter she'd made her routine upon arriving to do a flash inspection. Her technique was simple: She'd obscure the rank insignia on the collar of her cammie blouse and wander around asking dumb questions about where was this or that, then keep on talking with whoever answered her. No introductions, no crap about I'm-here-to-conduct-an-inspection. Let the captain go find the unit commander and do that. Jamie was supposed to bumble, and she did it pretty well.

But this time no one would talk to her. There was something almost tribal about it. They were inside, she was outside. Either these people shut down on anybody they didn't know—bizarre behavior at an installation of JTF Foxtrot's size, where normally the new people who constantly came and went provoked curiosity—or they damn well knew who she was already.

DTL100. For three days, Jamie got nowhere. And not just because regular ops had been suspended as the hurricane approached Cuba. According to the commander of the training unit they'd come to inspect, all HUMINT training activity had also been suspended, so her team was assigned babysitters who begrudgingly kept them busy for two days. Getting nowhere.

Halfway through the third day, even that pretense evaporated. For the first time during her IG gig, she'd been blown off by people who were supposed to be cooperative. Grumpy, okay, but cooperative. Not these people, though, and it made Jamie uncomfortable. Blowing off inspectors had consequences. Why didn't these guys care?

At least JTF Foxtrot felt, well, unsurveilled. So right out in the open, at 1400 hours on DTL100, Jamie switched her Marine-issue eyewraps for her Callithumps, which looked almost exactly the same, and tried to click up Adele and beg: Please, please, please duck the hurricane and go home.

Too late. Jamie got only a message: Adele and Henry had left Havana for Moa around 0800 with some Tierra Verde guy named Tavio. They'd be staying at the lone real hotel in Moa, owned by Inseque and across the road from Inseque's offices.

Adele left a second message several hours later. "I've got a bunch of meetings tonight, but tomorrow night I'll hang out at the Inseque offices from around six or seven until, say, nine o'clock so I can use their wireline, because wireless signals around here are nonexistent. I'll keep my fingers crossed we can facecall." The hope in Adele's voice made Jamie's chest ache and roiled her already agitated gut.

Jeezus, Del, why the fuck aren't you going home? Getting outta Cuba after Guthrie hits will be a horror.

Scowling at the ground, muttering obscenities under her breath, Jamie now marched in helpless frustration toward nowhere in particular—until she nearly collided with one of the Army NCOs from JTF Foxtrot's Medical Element.

"Oh, excuse me, ma'am," he said, stopping briefly to salute. As she returned his salute, he quickly whispered, "Behind the Warriors Club, nineteen thirty," before they kept moving past each other.

He showed up three minutes late. His nametape read Avellar; he didn't waste time on introductions or mince words.

"Inspector general, right?"

Jamie nodded. Could this guy turn out to be her first ever whistleblower?

"Well, I have something to report. Something that doesn't seem right and I didn't sign up for. I don't trust the chain of command above my own unit, so I was gonna do this once I get back to CONUS, once I can duck. But since you're here, I'm doing it now. Confidentially. And anonymously until after July eleventh, which is when I'm out of here. You can record my voice but not my face. Agreed?"

"Yes. Agreed." Jamie pressed hard against a tiny bulge inside the left temple arm of her Callithump eyewraps to click up AUDIOREC but didn't put the eyewraps on. "Please continue."

"You need to compare JTF Foxtrot training unit records with the Medical Element immunization records, which I can vouch for. We've shot up hundreds of guys trained off the books. Some here, but mostly at El Caulote and El Aguacate—"

"Where?"

"Ha. So those four-star resorts are off the books, too. I figured. El Caulote and El Aguacate are Forward Operations Locations about halfway between here and Puerto Castillo on the coast. Great places to train 'em up and ship 'em out."

"Ship 'em out of Puerto Castillo? To where?"

"Wondered that myself 'til last Sunday, which is when we got called up to El Caulote to deal with some salmonellosis. A lot of sick boys moaning for their mamas. Panamanian mostly, working for Paladin, which is a Costa Rican outfit, and also a Peruvian company called Ferro. That first night, plenty of them just wanted to go home, so I heard them grousing about where the contractors were sending them."

"Where?"

"Santiago. Nuevitas. Santa Cruz del Sur. Manzanillo. Guayabel. Never heard of any of those, but I figure Panama. A quickie invasion. And damn soon, judging by the chaos around here right now. Hell, it's probably all lies about where that hurricane's headed. It's probably really making a beeline for right here, or a little south of here, and I bet Southern Command knows that and plans to use it as cover. And an excuse after the fact. For occupation. A few military personnel, lots and lots of mercs. Anyway, most of those guys've probably reached their destinations by now. They were bitching to a fare-thee-well about having to spend two or three days in a ship's hold. And all of them were out of El Caulote by Wednesday morning."

"How many people have been trained at El, uh—"

"El Caulote and El Aguacate." Avellar shrugged. "Hundreds in the last six months. A couple battalions' worth anyway. Maybe a regiment."

"How do you think all this training has been kept off the books?" Jamie asked.

"My guess, based on a few well-soused nights in the joint behind us here? Only way there's sufficient cover is if it comes from on high—Southern Command back in Miami. Which is why I wasn't going the IG route through this chain of command, I don't give a damn what the regs say. The contractor pays to use facilities and staff here to train with weapons their guys keep. They train at least twice as many as officially counted, and train 'em half-assed in half the time, which they figure'll be good enough. I actually saw cash exchange hands once—lots of it, between the ranking Paladin dude and some 'visitor' who showed up with a plane full of assault rifles and ammo. Thank god they didn't see me." Avellar sloughed off a small quiver that had nothing to do with the air temperature. "And then CERP covers the rest."

"CERP? You mean funds from the Commander's Emergency Response Program. Which is supposed to be for helping locals, but gets spent on stuff like immunizations for all those off-the-books mercs, right?"

"Smarter 'n you look. Ma'am."

"Any clue who the contractors' client is?"

"Not a one." Avellar glanced around, suddenly nervous. "I gotta go. Good luck, Lieutenant."

Jamie planned to pass on Avellar's information as soon as she returned to Norfolk. All that changed about an hour after their conversation—once she had a chance to use her honor bracelet's darknet flume to conduct a search on the names of those five places where he told her the contractors were sending their mercs.

Santiago, Nuevitas, Santa Cruz del Sur, Manzanillo, and Guayabel were coastal towns with harbors, all right. In eastern Cuba.

A hard sting so cold it burned charged relentlessly up Jamie's spine. Telling herself that Adele would be okay in Moa—under Inseque's protection in Moa—did nothing to calm the violent tremor that now claimed her hands. A quickie invasion all right, like Avellar said. But it would go down all around Adele in eastern Cuba, not in Panama. And it would jibe with a hurricane expected to make landfall near Havana in eighty-one hours.

*Oh god…oh god oh god oh god…*In her head, this soprano chorus of panic grew louder as she comprehended.

It's been planned for months, maybe years. LCA in cahoots with the nietos de exiliados, aided by Marine units engaged in perfectly legal so-called "special activities" that are, how's the wording go again? Oh yeah: "Planned and executed so the role of the U.S. government is not apparent or acknowledged publicly." In order to do something about all that ecoterrorism, they'll say.

And now...now they see an opportunity to pull it off faster and cleaner by exploiting this hurricane, which'll rip the hell out of Havana, cripple the Cuban federal government's ability to respond to what'll be an armed secession of the Oriente. Eighty-one hours to Guthrie's landfall, hours of hurricane-force winds before that and after that. Means they're putting assets in place now, will make their move a few hours after landfall—midday Monday.

Maybe Del will be okay in Moa. Or maybe her association with Tierra Verde means she'll be seen as giving aid and comfort to ecoterrorists. And god knows what LCA will do with someone they decide is an ecoterrorist...

Reporting Avellar's information to Ossado would likely irritate him in the usual way and elicit the usual response. "Beyond your mission scope, Lieutenant. Move on." But it would be well within regs.

Reporting Avellar's information to Lynn Hillinger would also be within regs, since Lynn was a member of Congress and such communication would be considered protected. Especially if the U.S. military's involvement broke the rule about how its "special activities" were not supposed to influence U.S. political processes or policies—such as a Congressional vote on a trade agreement.

But whatever she told Adele about Avellar's information would constitute an unlawful communication—disclosure of internal information that hadn't been officially released.

So it goes. Jamie donned her Callithump eyewraps again, double-checked the eyewraps' link to her honor bracelet, and sent a warning to Adele. Only then did she compose a report about what Avellar told her, attach the AUDIOREC file, and send it to Lynn. When she finished, she switched to her Marine-issue eyewraps and sent the same report to Ossado.

❖

DTL99. By 0500, Jamie knew Adele hadn't received any of her several warnings. Or messages from anyone else, either. All commo was down in Moa, even wireline and direct satellite, according to a text from Lynn.

Shit. This is not good...

At 0848, shortly before the flight from Humuya back to Guantanamo landed, it got worse. "New forecast," the pilot announced.

"Guthrie's picking up forward speed and projected to turn north sooner. Landfall is now expected a hundred and fifty klicks further east—at Cienfuegos—on Sunday around zero-four-hundred."

"Oh man," grumbled the captain of her inspection team. "We're gonna have a hell of a time getting our asses out of Guantanamo now."

That's when Jamie put maps of eastern Cuba on her eyewraps shadowscreen and began studying the topography between the base and Moa, ninety klicks away by air, almost twice that distance by road.

Probably better off in civvies. Definitely should get my hands on some kind of weapon…

At 1108, she said to the captain of her team, "Forecast's changed again, sir. Now they think Guthrie'll hit another sixty klicks east, at Playa Ancon, around zero-two-hundred on Sunday. Looks like we're here for the duration, so maybe we ought to volunteer to help these guys. Before we're dragooned into filling sandbags."

When he agreed, Jamie assumed the position of attention, saluted him, and took off before he could think of anything more to say.

It had already taken her two hours to find what she'd been looking for: A sergeant in one of the Army force protection units brought in to patrol beyond the base's boundary—which they'd be doing in civvies. The guy she targeted might've been special ops; since he was a bit old for the rank and his blouse carried no nametape, Jamie figured he certainly was special some-damn-thing.

This substantially escalated the risk in what she was about to attempt. Yet the base was in a state of full-dress clusterfuck—people running, shouting over the unremitting roar of aircraft taking off and landing at a frantic pace, orders given one moment, countermanded the next. *Just what you'd expect when two missions—one sub rosa and planned, the other an immediate, unanticipated emergency—have to duke it out for resources…*

Before Jamie tracked down the nameless sergeant again to try talking her way onto his crew, she changed into the only civilian clothes she'd packed, abandoned both of her Marine-issue comlinks, minimized the gear she carried, and crossed her fingers. Would he see her anxiety? Would he want to know her name? Would he recognize it?

"My commander says I can volunteer to—" she began when she spotted him.

"We're headed into and past the city of Guantanamo," Sergeant Nameless told her in that brusque way some men use so you know they'll like you well enough as long as you meet certain requirements. "To keep an eye on things."

"Expecting trouble, huh?" she asked, working hard to appear indifferent.

"Speak Spanish?" he countered.

Shit. "No. Sorry."

"Didn't catch your name."

To lie or not to lie? Not, Jamie decided. "Gwynmorgan," she said, able to time her answer with the rumbling takeoff of a cargo plane.

"Okay then, Morgan, our guys are hopelessly stacked up in Miami and I got nothing but cherries here, so welcome aboard, as the swabbies say."

Struggling to remain expressionless, Jamie nodded.

"We've had intel"—the sergeant made mocking quotation marks with his fingers—"'ecoterrorist threats to interests in the economic zone.'" From a small pile of weapons—mostly assault rifles, some grenades, a few crew-served machine guns—he selected a standard-issue pistol and several ammunition clips, which he handed to her. "We'll set up in Guantanamo City, scout out from there."

"Well, man, that's where I can help if you want. Did a fair amount of scouting in the Palawan not so long ago."

The sergeant squinted at her. "Yeah?" He wanted credentials.

"Second Marines, Eighth Regiment."

Could he hear her heart bass-drumming in her chest? Tha-*THUMP*. Tha-*THUMP*. Would he press for details? *Don't move, don't look away, don't the fuck smile...*

He nodded almost imperceptibly. "I got a hole maybe you can fill. On up Route Five Seventy-one, about ninety klicks north of Guantanamo City. Small town called Sagua de Tanamo. I need eyes ay-sap up there on the main road between Holguin and Moa."

"Watching for what exactly?"

"Movement of Cuban Fuerzas Armadas."

"Army troops, you mean."

"Green uniforms, gray camo uniforms are bad. Blue or coyote brown with orange armband—good. And I wanna know about groups larger than, say, five people."

"Shit going down in Moa, huh?"

The sergeant smirked. "You know what those evil ecoterrorists are like. Got a bead on that nickel mining outfit's office building up there."

For a moment, Jamie stood paralyzed. *He means the Inseque building. Where Adele will be.* Her world went thick and heavy, an immense weight too crushing to oppose, but she willed herself to turn and look at him. *Speak, dammit!* "Uh, right."

He didn't seem to notice her struggle. "Nobody'll hassle you for, like, another ten klicks beyond Guantanamo City. See anybody with those orange armbands—they'll have 'auxiliares' on 'em—you let 'em know you're Yanqui. Most of 'em aren't Cuban, so they're kinda skittish. Just show 'em your ID and all will be well. Clear?"

"Yep."

"Good. I'm giving you one of my cherries who speaks Spanish—" The sergeant nodded toward a guy nearby loading gear and supplies into a plain civilian utility vehicle, then produced a tiny pocketcom and handed it to her. "Barrage jamming all over up there—except for the frequency on this, pre-programmed. We'll peel off and set up at the Hotel Guantanamo on Thirteen Norte. You'll continue on to Sagua de Tanamo." He glanced at the pistol he'd given her. "No fireworks, understand? It's why you're going in so lightweight. This is strictly eyeballs only 'til I call you back or next Wednesday zero six hundred. Whichever comes first."

❖

The Spanish-speaking cherry wouldn't—couldn't—shut up, and his blather distracted Jamie from figuring out how to ditch him. Once they got past Guantanamo City, she almost pulled the vehicle off the road to switch seats with him, on the theory that he might talk less if he drove. Barely more than three klicks outside the city, however, he revealed his profound incompetence at navigation, and right then she saw what she'd do.

The latest hurricane forecast, which popped onto the sergeant's pocketcom at 1420, was another matter. More than any storm in decades, it refused to behave as forecasters expected. Guthrie now had a forward speed approaching thirty klicks per hour and would strike the southern coast of Cuba only 300 klicks west of the Guantanamo Naval Base—and in less than twenty-four hours.

The storm initially predicted to cripple Havana, thus giving LCA and the nietos de exiliados a unique chance to decisively grab the Cuban Oriente, was going the wrong damn way. Yet, Jamie knew, the coup, or whatever it was, couldn't be called off. *All those guys're here already. Armed, ready to pounce, but outnumbered. Without the element of surprise, they're toast.*

"Still a go?" asked the Spanish-speaking cherry with hollow, I-wanna-go-home regret.

"Nobody saying otherwise."

"So where the fuck are all these so-called auxiliaries we're supposed to be running into?"

"Got me." Jamie disliked what she was about to do to him. Hell of a way to first experience the difference between training and The Real Thing. *Sorry, kid.* She put a razor-edge in her voice. "But that storm's coming way faster and closer than they thought." Now for the lie. "I need you to find me a damn shortcut. Pronto, please."

Cherries aren't real good at detecting lies, and they're prone to mistakes. Within twenty minutes, Jamie estimated, this one would screw up his next attempt at navigation. Frantic to recover, he'd darken his eyewraps to get a better view of the topo maps on his shadowscreen—and that's when she'd slip the cards out of the sergeant's pocketcom, depriving the device of all capability except automatic GPS transmission. Then she'd trick him into going off on his own on foot. Somewhere relatively safe, with instructions to be nice to civilians and hold on tight to the sergeant's pocketcom. *Sorry, kid.*

By the time Jamie reached the desolate, ramshackle periphery of Moa at 1850 hours, the wind had begun to gust and she'd come as near to hysteria as she'd ever been in her life.

Maybe she should have kept the Spanish-speaking cherry. Because she sure as hell didn't look forward to entering the Inseque building alone.

So it goes…

At a little after 1900 hours, she should've seen at least one security person at the resolutely utilitarian structure as she drove around it, but the place appeared deserted, provoking another shiver along her spine.

Inseque security's already pulled out. Next'll come Southern Command's mercs to tear the place apart and blame it on phantom ecoterrorists. Shit. It's gonna go down any fucking minute now.

She drove around the building again, but saw no one. Yet she didn't dare take the time to reconnoiter. *Looks like I'm ahead of them. And Adele oughta be in there by now, so I'll intercept her in time…*

Jamie parked the vehicle on a nearby side road, pulled her pistol from her cargo pocket, clicked off the safety, and approached the building's main door. It was unlocked and opened without triggering any obvious alarms. She entered, silently traversed the edge of the green-toned lobby area, rounded a corner—and stopped cold when she saw the rough, red spray-painted scrawl on the wall before her: VIOLADORES DE LA TIERRA—

Oh shit—

To her left, a door opened. Too late, she sensed footfalls behind her. Too late, she saw the blur of motion at the edge of her vision, way too close. Something slammed heavy and hard against the right side of her neck and the rough red letters spun, her legs buckled…Slowly, slowly the tiled floor swooped in on her, thudded into her…

❖

A grating, dissonantly high-pitched laugh came from the heavens above, taunting, and it seemed to Jamie that laugh had been there for a long, long time. "Ye-botch-key! *You* again, pizda!"

As soon as she opened her eyes, a boot smushed her face into a wooden floor in a high-ceilinged office area, its desks and chairs and comscreens spray-painted and vandalized. The last of the day's sunlight crossed the space above her in thick, horizontal streams that gave the air's fine particulates a foggy orange hue.

The boot relented and a streak of white fire seared Jamie's back, a sonic crack shook her. The yelp she heard withered into her own whimper, the room went black. And she heard that sound again…the sound of rusty metal shrieking, scraping, tearing across the inside of her skull…

I wanna be dreaming, she decided as the pain of the kick to her kidney wreathed her and intensified. *None of this matters if I'm dreaming.* But she tried anyway, tried to crawl away from the pain, away from recognizing that awful metal-on-metal cackle…

"Ah, no, no." The Bastard's inescapable laugh pealed above her again and the same boot plowed into her belly, stealing her breath, stealing what little remained of her ability to see or think. Or hope. "You will be, how do you say? The candle on our cake. You and that Inseque moron downstairs."

Oh…my…god…oh…my…god…

She'd dreamt about him so many times. That ugly, atonal blare, that odd accent, that imperious enjoyment of implicit threat—but never once had she seen him, not once in all those nightmares. If she saw him now, this was no dream.

The boot so fond of kicking her stood less than a meter away, a starting point. Her gaze traveled upward, along green-clad legs, across a black guayabera shirt to stubby European features, arrogance teasing thin lips, mouse-brown hair cut military-short—a face Jamie had seen before. He was the Caucasian man on the left in Nim Bacani's video.

Another male voice—American, Jamie realized—tunneled toward her from far away, tinny and unsure. "Want me to check her for cams?"

"Why? Are we not jamming?"

"Yessir. No signals getting out. None."

"Our little fire will do the rest." The Bastard's laugh brayed again. "Hey, pizda, we will make you a star." A hard kick into Jamie's left shoulder shuddered through her and she flattened onto her back. One blow at a time, The Bastard was stealing her awareness of anything except pain. "Everything ready to go?"

"Yes, sir."

"Good. Time for the star to take her mark, then. Got the big ones?"

"And the hammer."

No. This can't be happening. Not again.

The Bastard chortled, but Jamie heard rage in the sound. "Because of you, the old man put me through hell last year. And now here you are, instead of those environmentalist do-gooders who should have been here half an hour ago. Why, pizda? Why are *you* here?"

"You…" Jamie gasped.

"An errand for that dyke bitch you worship? Or are you sniffing after that hot pussy my boys say they'd like a piece of?" He bent over her, and for the first time, Jamie got a real look at his eyes. Ice eyes that spotted her terror at the thought of him grabbing Adele. "Ah, that *is* temptation. Two cunt-suckers for the price of one." He smacked his thin lips. "What fun watching you watch her die screaming. Let's hope she's hurrying here right now."

Oh god oh god. Del's okay, still okay. Relief quaked through Jamie, disintegrating her, dissolving her. *He hasn't got her.*

A frigid smile ghosted in The Bastard's eyes, but he spoke to the other man. "Set it up close enough so plenty of that shrapnel hits home. Here." He straightened up and shoved his boot hard into Jamie's groin. "Right here. I want her to feel it for as long as possible before she bleeds out. And she must be recognizable. Sliced up, bloody, burned, but recognizable."

The Bastard smiled and kicked her again. For the fun of hearing her yelp, of watching her try to worm away from him. He didn't stop her as she rolled fetally, then attempted to get up; instead, he sniggered and stomped her to the floor again when she made it to her hands and knees. With his foot, he flipped her onto her back once more, then kept on talking. Bragging. But at least he didn't have Adele. Yet.

"You see, pizda, the old man wants this building, so we must minimize the damage. But we need some sacrifices. To make it believable. So: A circle of fire around that slob downstairs, another up here for you—" He nodded toward a cardboard box now about three meters away. "But no real structural damage. Sadly, among the dead was a heroic American captured by the evil ecoterrorists."

Between thumb and forefinger of each hand, he twirled a long, large nail as he stepped to her left side. Smiling, he glanced down so her eyes would follow, so she would contemplate the slow swing of his leg back, back. Helpless, Jamie watched the kick come for her, heard the immense crunching sound before a red tsunami of pain rolled her groaning into unconsciousness.

The sunlight had deserted her when she floated upward to awareness. She didn't open her eyes but she knew The Bastard was close by.

Had Adele shown up? Did The Bastard have her?

Jamie tried to stay still, but her eyes fluttered open to find him standing over her. In silence he knelt on her right while the other man's boot clamped her forearm to the floor.

No, Del's not here. He'd be making her watch…

The huge nail impaled the palm of Jamie's hand with one hammer blow that blasted a blinding shockwave through every cell of her body, and she would've screamed if she could've found breath. Then came the aftershocks as The Bastard pounded the nail deep into the floor, one after another until the blackness closed in on her.

"Wake up, pizda!" he demanded before repeating the ritual on her left hand. "Wake up!" A boot heel Jamie couldn't see prodded her crotch to the beat of his abrasive, penetrating shrill—"Wake up, pizda!"—and her eyes opened again to The Bastard looming over her. "Pay attention while I show you how a fool meets her fate." He held up a large, open-top glass jug partially stuffed with rags and nails and razors and nearly filled with clear liquid. "Part one—highly flammable juice, a few cups of black powder, many sharp objects, plentiful vapors swirling, and it's ready to *pop!*"

He set the jug down beyond where Jamie could see without raising her head. When he realized this, he stepped over her and roughly lifted her head by her hair. "Uh, uh, uh—we must have you see. *See?*"

Dimly, she saw. He had nestled the jug into a small debris pile of furniture and draperies a meter or so from her feet.

"Notice, please," he mocked, "our neat circle of rags all around you." He nodded to the American with him, then let go her hair, and her head thudded to the floor. "Douse her, too—except her face."

While the man began pouring what smelled like gasoline onto the debris and then on her, The Bastard held up a stun gun. "Oh, how I would love to play with you." He peered with exaggerated regret at the stunner, then her. "But alas, this is our detonator. Which I shall place—here, I think. A bit of a delay while the flames move about our circle, but I want you to see when it sparks so you may appreciate your final moments." He set the stun gun down on her left amidst the debris, then yanked her head leftward so she'd see it.

"It is, of course, already wired into—" He waved an old-fashioned electronic timer and cackled again. "Voila! We shall place this just out of your sight." Then he clapped his hands. "So primitive. So simple. So effective. Just what one might expect from a crazed ecoterrorist, no? Ah, but enough of this now. I see the wind getting angry. This storm will come closer than they think, damn fools. The old man expects me to wait for your environmentalist girlfriend and her professor. But, I regret to say, you will have to do. Fortunately, you will do nicely." He indulged in one last kick to Jamie's groin. "In fact, *you* will do far better. Adios, pizda."

The smallest movement caused so much pain it obliterated Jamie's ability to think. But if she lay very still, the omnipotent scalding, clawing screech of it would lag and falter into a thunderous throb that bludgeoned her at a frequency just low enough, a rhythm just slow enough...and in one of its ephemeral lulls she managed to muster a question—*the* question: *How much time before that stun gun sparks?*

Then, in the next lull, another question: *How far away from me is it?*

Gotta know soon...
Very soon...
Because...
Hey—there...
There it is...
Maybe I can tear my right hand free...
Somehow...
Then roll left...
C'mon, left...
Left...
I had a good job and I left...

CHAPTER THIRTY
THE VAST CONSPIRACY

Jamie didn't remember waking up. Didn't remember any dreams. And the whole world seemed to be grinning at her. She tried not to fidget in the bed, because Adele hadn't moved yet. So she looked around the room, Adele's room at Luce and Biz's house. It felt right, this room, especially when Adele was in it, lying next to her; Adele made the whole house feel right. She'd just started thinking about her own house someday with Adele in it when Adele nuzzled her.

Did this count as awake? Good enough, Jamie decided. "Maybe we can go for a walk again today on that National Seashore trail, the one that runs by Aunt Zerviah's."

Adele groaned and burrowed into the pillow. "Didn't we just go to bed?"

"Yeah." Jamie bounced a little. "Last night."

Adele opened one eye. Briefly. "The clock says four fifty-six. We've had five hours' sleep. And it's still dark out."

Another bounce. "Aren't you hungry?"

This time Adele opened both eyes. "Not for food."

Jamie stilled as Adele reached for her. "No walks just yet, Lieutenant. You have other, more pressing duties."

Lieutenant.

"Del…" *You never call me that unless you're pissed at me.*

More pressing duties. *Goddammit.*

Jamie realized her eyes were closed. *Goddammit. I'm dreaming. It's not over yet.*

She rocked her pelvis upward in protest as Adele slowly evaporated away from her. *Not over yet.* Reluctantly, her eyes opened to the same white sheet-paneled ceiling she'd awoken to for…

No, no, do it right. Hour and minute first.

Jamie shifted her gaze to the videoscreen on the white sheet-paneled wall at her feet and found the four small numbers in the lower right corner. 0458.

Her keepers would knock at 0500 sharp, but she could lie there for another ten minutes or so without getting hassled. She needed that time—to think about time. To remind herself about where...in time... right now was. Beginning with...*then*.

So breathe in...two...three...four...

And out...two...three...four...

Every time she remembered emerging that night in the Inseque building from the blur of pain and gasoline-stench, she comprehended more. And every time, what came first was Adele's voice.

"Oh my dear god."

Adele said it just once, her voice descending half an octave with each word, but Jamie heard it over and over.

"Oh my dear god."

It was only a sound; Jamie had half-turned, her right arm and right leg thrust leftward in her attempt to reach the stun gun, so she couldn't see Adele, but the horror in the sound carried its own image, of Adele's bottomless eyes gone opaque and wide, hands splayed across already paled cheeks, mouth agape, of Adele's body bending forward in its first desperate rush toward her.

"Oh my dear god."

Then came Adele's touch, and Jamie felt in it that single nanosecond when Adele assessed everything, decided everything, and mutely begged her forgiveness for what would happen next.

"Fire hazard," Jamie had tried to say—yes, she *did* say it, yes, and what remained of her right hand motioned toward the stun gun.

But Adele didn't move away. Instead, she shouted out something in Spanish, which was when Jamie grasped that she hadn't come into the building alone. "I'm sorry, baby, I'm sorry," she said between gritted teeth. With both hands, she grabbed the agony that had become Jamie's left hand and pulled—fast. "We gotta get you out of here right now."

"Someone...downstairs..." Jamie gasped as Adele worked her left hand's metacarpals around the oversized nail head, and then she slid out of consciousness again.

Thus began a twelve-hour roller-coaster ride in and out of the blackness, trying to tell Adele it was The Bastard. "He was here, he did this...He's the ecoterrorist...only it's a fake, a setup...Oh god, Del, are you okay?" Adele held on to her the whole time, Adele's face smiled at her, Adele's lips kissed her, Adele's voice soothed her.

When she came 'round really, she lay in what sure as hell looked like a cave. Part of the vast system of defensive tunnels built years ago by the Fuerzas Armadas, Adele told her. Tavio, the Tierra Verde guy, knew all about the place because he was a reservist.

"Good spot to ride out a hurricane." Adele's eyes swept upward as a wind gust whipped into the cave entrance, propelling spray deep inside. "I, for one, prefer this to the hotel, which was our other option."

"Any commo yet? Need to...talk to Lynn."

"What you need is medical attention. Henry, Tavio, and I are working on it."

"Had the finesse...of a friggin' rhinoceros," Jamie wheezed. "No wonder I ended up...nailed to a floor. Great job, huh?"

"The security guard they trussed up on top of that funeral pyre on the first floor isn't complaining. He had about ten seconds left before it was going to spark, and the only reason the guys got to him in time was you."

"Lynn was right. You have a...heart of gold."

"I suppose that means we have to skip the part about—" Eyes ablaze, Adele's face quickly closed in on Jamie's. "What the *hell* are you doing here?"

Jamie attempted a smile. "Long story."

❖

The storm didn't ease for another six hours. Three-and-a-half hours after that, at 2030 on Saturday, Adele finally established an audio-only satellite uplink to Great Hill using the darknet flume in her bracelet. A few minutes later, Tavio made his own contact with people in Havana. And suddenly they had news. Lots of news.

The eye of Hurricane Guthrie had passed right over the Guantanamo Naval Base as a category four storm, destroying most structures, damaging the rest. And it wasn't nearly done yet. In another twelve hours, it would make a second landfall just south of Miami Beach and plow up the Florida peninsula. Rescue and relief for Cuba would be slow in coming.

From Tavio's sources in Havana they learned that Guthrie's path disrupted—and drenched—the attempted breakaway of Cuba's eastern provinces. As it was, there had been brief but intense fighting at Guayabal and Manzanillo and an assortment of smaller skirmishes elsewhere.

"So," Jamie said, "Southern Command's mercs marched right into—"

Tavio muttered something in Spanish, which Adele translated as "our meat grinder." Before returning to her own comlink conversation, she translated the rest of what he said: In several eastern communities, the Fuerzas Armadas were rounding up small bands of armed "illegal immigrants" while assorted Oriente big shots adamantly denied knowledge of their presence or of anything resembling provincial police auxiliaries.

Tavio believed some of those big shots would get away with it. "But not all," he said in English with a satisfied smile. "Not all."

Jamie remembered how her stomach turned as she stared at his little smile, because she'd been hoping she'd just pick up where she left off. Return to the base at Guantanamo and fly back to Norfolk knowing Adele was unharmed, finish doing the damn inspections, go on terminal leave, and somehow the Blue Max would've been forgotten. And that would be it. Finally, finally over.

But shit, now she'd gotten herself into a whole new tangle.

When, at last, Adele said Lynn wanted to talk to her and handed her the darknet-linked pocketcom that had become their commo lifeline, Jamie couldn't blurt it fast enough. "The Bastard was here. H-He tried to kill me—would've killed me if Del hadn't showed up. And I recognized him. He's in Nim Bacani's video, Lynn. He's the Caucasian guy on the left."

For a moment, Lynn said nothing. "You're sure," she said eventually.

"Yes. And he knows who Del is, knew she was here."

"Adele described your hands and—the rest. He did that?"

"Yeah."

"In Moa. At the Inseque building."

"Yeah."

"My god." Then: "Okay. I know you're not in good shape, but try to tell me everything you remember."

Jamie did. "I'm not sure what to do next," she said when she finished. "I'm probably listed as AWOL by now."

"I doubt that. Guantanamo's in chaos. We have reports from first responders of loss of life, including among command. Adele says you need medical care now. You won't get it at the base. The hospital there is wrecked. You should go into Moa."

"But—"

"From what we're hearing, you'd have a very hard time even reaching the base," said Lynn. "Besides, I think you're better off avoiding Southern Command. They've been caught red-handed and their Guantanamo base top echelon is right in the middle of it. They're in a tizzy. God knows what they might be tempted to do with one of the people who helped expose their mess."

"Did I?"

"Yeah, sweetie, you did. I'll contact Sarah Zachary, let her know you had no means to contact your commanding officer but you were able to reach me. I expect they'll come get you in Moa sooner rather than later. And then…" Lynn paused again. "I'm afraid, you'll enter debriefing hell."

"Shit."

"Between what that fellow Avellar at JTF Foxtrot told you and what happened at the Inseque building, a long debrief is inevitable."

"What should I tell them?"

"The truth," said Lynn. "Answer their questions as narrowly as you can without lying or coming across as obstructive. It'll feel more like interrogation, especially in the beginning, when Southern Command will try to bluster its way out at your expense. So, as best you can, play dumb when they aggress on you with leading questions. If no one keeps them from threatening you with formal charges, shut down for good and demand an attorney. And don't sign anything except honorable discharge documents."

"It's gonna get that bad?" Jamie asked.

"It might. For a while. I'm sorry, kiddo. I'm afraid your honeypot days aren't quite done yet."

"I don't underst—" But then she *did* understand. "Oh, I see. You're getting closer. So what I'm asked, and who asks and when—that'll tell you something, huh?"

"Oh yes, it certainly will."

"How vulnerable am I to getting court-martialed?"

"It could happen. But remember: They have to prove a case against you with legitimately acquired evidence, which they know your attorneys can examine and challenge. So, for instance, if they've had you under illegal surveillance and let's say you slip that surveillance, they're going to want to learn where you were, what you did—but they have to be careful not to reveal their illegal surveillance. Rather than just come out and ask you, it's better for them—and worse for you—if they can indirectly wheedle information out of you about that time period. In effect, they'll try to get you to stumble into incriminating yourself."

"Okay. How long?"

"Weeks, months. They'll keep you isolated. The only people you'll see or talk to will be them. At first, that'll be about intimidating you. Then, as what you say gets corroborated by evidence and witnesses, it'll be about keeping you under wraps. Not so much to protect you as to protect the investigation. Eventually, the Pentagon will be eager to keep your name out of it entirely."

"I figured they'll want me hanging from the highest—"

"Oh no, you're much too valuable.

"Valuable? Me?"

"As a distraction. Soon the Pentagon will be in dire need of a distraction."

"Shit. The Blue Max. I was kinda hoping it would just go away."

"Hell no, it's going to help bring the Pentagon to its senses where you're concerned. Before that, though, you'll feel very alone and forgotten. So please, please believe me when I tell you that you are *not* alone, Jamie, not forgotten. Not for one single minute. And when this finally *is* over, promise me you'll come back to Great Hill for a bit before you go to Belmont."

"I will. I promise."

Lynn turned out to be right about all of it. Which was why Jamie preferred to hurry through parts of her recollection—the ride from Tavio's cave to Moa's small but surprisingly sophisticated hospital, the tense, painful days there—then slow her recollection down again when she got to the part where she had to say good-bye to Adele. The achingly beautiful part.

They exchanged reassurances and kisses and promises. And tears, which they quickly wiped away, because how do you remember her exquisite eyes wanting you, absorbing the details of you, if you can't see through your tears?

"Let's pick a time," Adele proposed. "At the same time every day, wherever we are, whatever we're doing, we stop and take a minute and pretend like it's a facecall where we look at each other and say I love you."

"Twenty-one hundred hours, Eastern Time," Jamie answered. "Every night. I promise."

And then Jamie gave Adele her honor bracelet—"so I don't have to explain it, too"—and they said I love you one last time. For the longest time, for 127 days, Jamie survived on that last I love you.

Survived was the word for it, too. Because they cheated.

Damn sneaky, the way they used pharma and shuttered the room's only window and called it fucking medical care.

Then, sufficiently healed to be functional, she endured a rigid, minimalist regimen. Thirteen hours every day answering questions— and, soon enough, the same questions over and over—posed by people whose cammies never bore rank insignia or nametapes. One hour of exercise in an outside space as bleak as the white metal containerized housing unit where she was confined, its gray steel desk and shelves empty except for a change of cammies and underwear and a few toiletries, its videoscreen blank but for a time display. And certainly no comlink.

Always, she kept her promise to Adele, and at 2100 every night, she closed her eyes and pretended she was facecalling Adele, looking at Adele and saying I love you. That helped. And she thought: *This could be worse. This could be Saint Eh Mo's.* That helped, too.

But there were shadows. And nightmares. She clenched into hyperawareness and played to cameras she couldn't see.

Always, she listened, listened hard. For what their words, their tone, their pauses implied. Amazing what you can figure out from people who don't want you to realize they regard you as expendable. When you're sacrificed, they won't give a shit, which makes them dangerous, malevolent, your enemy. But at least you're on to them. At least you understand they're laying a trap when they're nice to you.

For 127 days, she studied her enemy, watched her enemy gradually decide maybe she wasn't entirely expendable after all. Lucky for her. She wondered about nameless, countless others who were not so lucky.

Now, of course, being lucky, she knew all kinds of stuff. Now that they had backed off and accepted whatever Lynn and Dana and Embry and god knows who else had unearthed about what she called The Vast Conspiracy. That was when they really started to let stuff drop. Maybe to see how she'd react. Maybe because they didn't care anymore how she'd react.

So first fucking of all, she knew she'd been right about Ossado's surveillance of her during the temporary assistant IG gig. A question, asked only once by an interrogator who appeared only once, gave it away. "Why haven't you exchanged any messages with Senator Hillinger since last winter?" Even now, her entirely true answer—"The Senator and I communicate as much as we deem necessary"—made her smile whenever she remembered it.

She knew the four-star in charge of Southern Command and several of his subordinates had been relieved of duty for instigating a series of rogue operations leading to what was supposed to be a coup in Cuba—the Oriente first, then Havana would fall, blah, blah, blah.

She knew the merc contractors involved in the Cuba fiasco had been banned from doing business with the U.S. government and had already changed their names.

She knew Southern Command's Cuba scandal had ensnared a passel of pooh bah civilians—including Rafael Vicario, a closet nietos de exiliados now outed and accused of puppetmastering the whole damn thing in an effort to boost his power base, and Oscar Zanella, the Mundus Energy CEO who had designs on Cuba's oil and gas reserves.

She knew enough to pose a chicken or egg question: Did Vicario and a few of his Pentagon friends dream up The Vast Conspiracy and then recruit people like Zanella and a bunch of exiliados and probably Jonathan Armstrong Archer to fund the little merc army they'd need for the grabbing of Cuba? Or did Zanella and the exiliados and Archer and whoever else come up with the idea and seek out Vicario to enlist his Pentagon and merc connections to help them execute it?

She also knew Nim Bacani's video remained under wraps. Because in 127 days no one had asked anything about it. She suspected Lynn's hand in that—to prevent her court-martial for violating Article 134, which was damn well what she did when she sent Sergeant Soto to Vivian Velty.

So Lynn had sufficient clout with Vivian—and was using it— to bury Nim's video until it could be made public without involving Jamie Gwynmorgan. For which Jamie was grateful. Yet after all this, The Bastard seemed to have waltzed away, untouched by what he did in Cuba as well as what he did in the Palawan. And whoever he worked for was waltzing away with him.

Damn. It was enough to provoke a person out of the skinny cot and into pacing the tiny three-meter space yet again. But as Jamie swung her legs to the floor, a small contingent of pinpricks diddly-bopped up her back.

Because she'd noticed the four numbers at the bottom right corner of the videoscreen: 0527.

Say what?

For the first time in 128 days, no one had knocked at 0500.

Right then, Jamie knew one more thing. *They're gonna let me go today.*

Chapter Thirty-one

Half-Assed, On-The-Fly

For somebody who knew so damn much, November eighth—a Saturday—harbored its share of surprises.

"That's all I have to do?" Jamie asked after a short walk from her white metal box to one of the others nearby where she signed a series of documents. A major she'd never seen before nodded and gave her a Certificate of Honorable Discharge and a lapel pin. "Good luck, Lieutenant," he said, offering his hand, which she shook.

Earlier, a sergeant she'd never seen before had brought a familiar-looking duffel bag to her white metal box. "In case you'd like to leave here in civvies." Jamie opened it and peered at all the stuff from her Norfolk digs neatly packed inside.

"Thanks," she said to the sergeant, since she was damn happy to get out of cammies and had no desire to ever return to the Norfolk apartment.

Now the same sergeant carried her duffel as he escorted her through the labyrinth of high concrete blast walls that surrounded the remote part of the Norfolk Naval Base where she'd been squirreled away. They emerged next to a parking lot not ten meters from her old blue car. In 127 days, she never once left this prison that, as she gazed at it from the outside for the first time in daylight, she began to suspect had been assembled just for her. A world of unyielding gray and unforgiving white and sometimes an aloof blue sky above; not a tree or a friendly face in sight, though a few brave blades of grass survived and the seagulls watched over her—

And, oh god, it had numbed her way more than she'd realized…

She drove slowly, reacquainting herself with the exhilaration of autonomy, of controlling a vehicle's movement, suspicious that maybe a sentry would stop her at the naval base gate. But no, merely a quick wave of her Corps ID and—she was free.

Hands trembling on the wheel, Jamie drove toward the Chesapeake Bay Bridge repeating aloud, "I'm a civilian now. I can go anywhere, do anything I want."

She got across the bay and fifty miles up the Delmarva peninsula before she grasped the likelihood that no one but her knew she'd been discharged and liberated—not Adele, not Lynn—and she had no comlink with which to contact them. Easily solved: In an hour, the farmland around her would give way to Salisbury, where she could buy whatever she wanted.

Salisbury came and went, however. Jamie could not stop driving. She could not quite reach all the way to the edges herself. It struck her that she was operating herself by remote control. She didn't trust it. She didn't like it. But she didn't know how to stop it.

So just keep driving. It's okay to just keep driving for a while.

Which was what she did until she saw a sign for Lou's Groceries and General Store. She could see it up ahead in the middle of nowhere, her view unimpeded by the flat farmland. It was the kind of place that had few people, few cams. *Not perfect, but this joint I can do.*

She steered the car into a corner of Lou's parking lot and looked around. A cam by the service area, one at the main door, no doubt something inside covering the point-of-sale area. She parked far enough away that Lou's cams wouldn't record her car's presence, then rummaged in the duffel for Robin's civvie boonie hat, put it on, and, girding, stepped out of the car.

Now she knew something else: Six months in Ossado's crew and four months in stir, all under constant camera surveillance, had fucked with her head.

God, she wanted to believe she'd finally achieved anonymity again. That as long as she didn't do anything to attract the attention of the patterning software, she'd go unnoticed. *Almost as good as living in a place like Lou's here—or better yet, way out in Truro where there are hardly any cams at all and nobody has a clue where the hell anybody is.*

In that instant, while she carried an armful of snacks to Lou's camera-covered point-of-sale, it hit her, the way a thought does when you've encountered it before but it slipped away: *I know why those guys go to Aunt Zerviah's at such an odd time of year. So they can meet without any possibility of being recorded together by a cam. And what if the timing matters, too? Always three weekends before Thanksgiving. Which, if I remember right, is also the weekend before the start of the Bretton Woods International Security Conference.*

Besides groceries, Lou sold comlinks and hunters' eyewraps and fishing poles and binoculars and camping gear and long johns. And cameras. Jamie's plan bloomed suddenly, fully when she saw a small, ruggedized camouflage model perched on a flexible mini-tripod, a telephoto lens already attached. It even came with an extended power pack and an extra-large datacard that would record continuous very high-res video for six hours.

A ripe plan, perhaps, but not yet rationalized.

Well, uh…

Won't take long, and the evasion stuff I'll need is cheap, easy to get. Something to sweep the car, just to make sure it's clean, and one of those surplus P&Js…

And it'll maybe give me enough time to—to—

To get used to this again. To de-numb.

So when I see them I'll be able to feel them, to say something. And when they see me they won't want to throw me in a loony bin. It'll be over by, let's see—sometime tomorrow afternoon. One way or the other. Really truly finally over. And then—

Then I can go home.

Damn good thing she was a civilian now. Any sergeant worth his salt would have ripped her a new one for nodding off like that.

On the other hand, her half-assed, on-the-fly plan remained on track.

She managed to figure out where to stash her car reasonably nearby. She changed into Marine Corps cammies plus boonie hat and gloves that made her essentially invisible to visual, infrared, and even radar detection. She remembered to click on the dual-cams in the second-rate eyewraps from Lou's. So there'd be a record of her actions, as much for herself as anyone else—because even after nineteen hours of freedom, nothing seemed quite real yet.

With almost carefree detachment, she worked her way in the dark through two klicks of scrub oak and pitch pine, gathering hide materials along the way, and scouted out a spot less than forty meters from Aunt Zerviah's kitchen door, where everyone entered and exited the house.

It was a good location, at the top of a slight rise in the land southwest of the house, about three meters higher in elevation and surrounded by a small stand of young, bushy pitch pine. Behind the spot, the land sloped away, out of sight of the house—a viable exit route. After picking it out, Jamie approached cautiously by inches flat on her belly, the way a snipe's supposed to, and set up her new camera to capture whoever might come up the driveway to her right and enter the house dead in front of her. All before the first glimmer of Sunday morning's astronomical twilight.

At which point she had to wait. No moving. No snacking. No getting up to pee, though she did find a way to squiggle a she-pee between her legs so at least her own piss wouldn't soak her. Because she'd be there for quite a while, and in November's wind-chilled forty-degree temps, pee-drenched legs invited hypothermia. Much as she wanted to see who showed up, she didn't think it was worth dying for.

And hell, a brief snooze was, perhaps, forgivable. The house had been entirely dark when Jamie slithered into position around 0300. By 0410, at last prodded by doubt, she began to waver. *Tell me again: I'm here watching what's very likely an empty house* why *when I could be—when I should be—cuddled with Del in our room at Great Hill?*

By the time she dug down to *Admit it; you're shit scared Del has moved on*, she was too exhausted to keep her eyes open.

Nothing in particular woke her at what her eyewraps indicated was 0516. At 0517, as the eastern sky began to brighten, she concluded she was a moron. *Just stand up and—*

But she stayed glued to the ground, mouth suddenly desert-dry, heart frantically thwacking against her chest wall. Someone had clicked on Aunt Zerviah's kitchen lights.

At 0524, the kitchen door opened and a hulk of a man stepped onto the small porch, a shotgun cradled in his right arm, even though it was Sunday and Massachusetts banned hunting on Sundays. The man used binoculars—no doubt infrared-enabled—to broadly scan south of the house, gazing eastward first, away from Jamie, then arcing gradually toward her. She would know in seconds how much her skill at preserving stealth had or had not deteriorated.

What the fuck was I thinking? Her carefree detachment had brought her to a position perilously proximate to the house—within easy range of even the wimpiest shotgun aimed vaguely southwestward, not to mention easy earshot of the man on Aunt Zerviah's kitchen porch, given the distance even the smallest sound traveled in this quiet Outer Cape realm.

The man's binoculars swept past her without hesitating, finished their arc, and had begun to swing back again when a second shotgun-toting man appeared at the kitchen doorway. "Clear?" he asked the first man.

"Oh yeah." The fellow sounded weary as he lowered his binoculars. "Your guy on his way yet?"

"ETA zero-six-hundred. Right on time."

"So the usual drill, yeah? I'll head out back and do a north side perimeter check 'til you tell me your guy's inside, then we switch 'til my guy's inside—"

"I dunno what the big friggin' deal is about us not seein' their faces. I mean, who's kiddin' who?"

"Don't even go there, man. It is what it is."

At 0558, a large utility vehicle with darkened windows and its headlights turned off appeared on the dirt road below the house. As it pulled into Aunt Zerviah's driveway, Jamie clicked up her camera's VIDEOREC and waited to see who would emerge.

The Bastard emerged.

The sight of him made Jamie nauseous. *Woulda been easier to have been wrong...*

While she tried to silently suck air back into her lungs, he halted to talk to his man, his eyes darting to various spots around him, including where Jamie lay, but hurrying off again. "The old man will be on time?" he asked with obvious impatience.

"Yessir."

"Any coffee inside?"

"Yessir."

Without another word, The Bastard entered Aunt Zerviah's kitchen and shut the door. Maybe ten minutes later, another vehicle arrived. It parked on the far side of the first vehicle, which blocked Jamie's view of the driver. When he emerged, she and her camera could see only his wide-brimmed hat and his back as he, too, went inside.

So close...so fucking close...

From the time nearly a year earlier when she and Adele had checked out the place, Jamie knew Aunt Zerviah's kitchen table was easily visible from the window a few feet from the door. What, then, were the odds The Bastard now sat at that table drinking coffee with Jonathan Armstrong Archer? What were the odds she could pick up her camera, reach the kitchen window unseen, record at least a few seconds of video of The Bastard and Archer meeting, and scoot the hell away before the two lookouts saw anything?

She wanted her real-time high-res recording of this event GPS-certified from start to finish, so she'd kept VIDEOREC clicked on. Now she squinted at the distance to the kitchen window. *C'mon, not even forty meters, just pick up the cam...*

She might have tried it—if one of the lookouts hadn't jolted her back to sanity by appearing and proceeding to walk a mid-distance perimeter around the house that took him within three meters of where she lay. He didn't see her, but he'd traversed the underbrush behind her position with a professional's skill. Nope, she wasn't going anywhere for a while.

At 0752, the kitchen door opened. For several seconds no one appeared. Then The Bastard's abrasive laugh came scratching through the air and he stepped onto the porch, half turned toward the man behind him, who remained shadowed in the doorway.

And then there he was, this second man. It was not Jonathan Armstrong Archer. Jamie squeezed her eyes shut, snapped them open again. *My god, Lynn called it. That's Richard Lambert.*

"...only a small setback," Lambert was saying. "Oscar Zanella will not point to us. Hell, if he'd followed my advice, we would've been able to give him as much success in Cuba as we gave him in Palawan. No, he'll vacation in Brazil while they hang Vicario and Everett Harris and those morons at Southern Command with some raunchy sex scandals, maybe a bit of fraud or embezzlement. It'll be business as usual by next summer."

"But, this video you heard about—that the Velty woman found. Òtac, you told me your Columbia Aegis moles had taken care of—"

"Relax. No biometrics, only one image. And we eliminated the little corporal who recorded it a long time ago. Our people in Washington will raise plenty of doubt about the video's authenticity. And you, son— Lambert placed both hands on The Bastard's shoulders—You will take a vacation, too."

"So." The Bastard lowered his head. "It's delayed again."

"Another year, Nerad, maybe two, some plastic surgery along the way. Then I can acknowledge you publicly as well as privately."

"It's only fair, Òtac. I've done everything you asked."

"You have." Lambert extended his arms and the two men hugged—an almost overly hearty embrace. "These things take time. Two, three years. Four tops." Lambert slapped the Bastard's shoulder. "Then you come in."

A minute later, Lambert left. The Bastard lingered, though, clearly upset as he paced the small yard area at the front of the house. He muttered unintelligibly and he, too, came within a few meters of Jamie's position before stomping off.

Typically, a snipe exfiltrates as painstakingly as she infiltrates, but something about the sound of The Bastard's voice, the way he marched about the yard kicking at dead leaves and small stones—

Maybe she figured he was rooting around for something bigger to kick. Maybe she sensed his eyes glancing toward her position too often, penetrating too close. Maybe she comprehended that if Lambert heard Vivian Velty had Nim Bacani's video, then it either had been or was about to be made public—suggesting Lynn might know she'd been discharged…and the people at Great Hill, *her* people, were waiting for her, worried for her. Or hell, maybe she just panicked.

Shit. I gotta get outta here. Ay-sap.

As carefully and quietly as possible, Jamie clicked off VIDEOREC and extracted the camera's datacard, which she placed in a small waterproof safepack and snugged into her cammie blouse pocket. *Breathe…*She stowed the she-pee and the dissembled camera in her cargo pockets. *Breathe…and figure out where they're heading…*

Lookout One…down front on the dirt road, eighty or ninety meters, obscured by the oak trees, making sure he keeps his back to the house.

The Bastard—pacing on the east side, walking away from me now…

And Lookout Two…yep, also over on the east side. The Bastard's talking to him…

Jamie wriggled backward on her belly, feet leading her out from the pine undergrowth. Barely the margin to extract herself without being spotted, but she did it and turned to begin a crouched run westward down the slope.

For the first eighty meters, she pulled it off. Then she heard a shout and they were chasing her. She veered northwestward, tear-assing through pine and oak underbrush, leaping and dodging as she ran, making for a stand of young pines that would provide more concealment.

Almost a good idea that would've worked if one of the lookouts hadn't driven a vehicle up the nearest path to cut her off, forcing her north and then northeast, closer and closer to the cliff edge. Twice she lost her footing, the second time landing flat on her face. As she scrambled up again from this belly flop, she glimpsed two of them behind her—one of the lookouts, The Bastard right behind him, both closer than ever.

Yet as she regained her feet, everyone, everything except her began to move in slow motion…It meant her brain had sped up, giving her margin to recognize her only remaining advantages: The men chasing her had decided not to shoot at her, and they thundered as they ran because they outweighed her by twenty, thirty, forty pounds.

She focused now on how she must run—light on her feet and fast, fast, toes barely touching the ground as she pumped and stretched. She focused on where she must run—right at the very edge of the cliff, picking out each place where each foot would commit to its minimal contact. *Make it look easy…make it look safe…*

And so she ran within inches of the cliff edge. Once a wedge of ground fell away as she lifted off it, but she didn't slow down. A moment later, she heard a man's scream and over her right shoulder glimpsed the lookout's flailing arms and legs as he cartwheeled out of sight over the cliff.

That's when The Bastard recognized her.

"You!" he shrieked and charged after her with new strength.

About a hundred meters later, she slipped again, her right leg breaking off a sliver of cliff, her hands clinging to clumps of dune grass.

She held on, made it back to her feet. But The Bastard tackled her legs on her second step and they rolled. And rolled. And The Bastard kept screeching, "You!"

Jamie grabbed at whatever she could—grass, sprigs of pitch pine, sand, more sand, too much sand. She kicked and thrashed, but The Bastard wouldn't release her legs, not even after a slab of clifftop gave way beneath him, then beneath her. She scrabbled to get a grip on something, anything as his weight dragged her down, down. Her gloved hands found a chunk of concrete block, which came loose and fell away from her as she clawed at it. Then another concrete block, which she could not hold on to, then an old pipe, which bent with her weight and The Bastard's weight, for he clung to her still—until the pipe ripped out of the cliffside and she tumbled, colliding with the sand as she fell and kept on falling...

❖

Jamie's eyes opened to a cloudless, extravagantly blue sky. For a glimmering instant, she thought she must have dozed off on the smooth granite mound near the top of Great Hill, and she wondered if Adele had arrived yet.

A violent shiver interrupted her thought; she couldn't understand why she was so wet, so very cold. And this weight across her belly and hips and legs—heavy, like the world's largest water balloon...it was giving her the creeps now. It was too heavy, too squishily intractable. She lowered her eyes from the sky to her belly—and screamed.

The Bastard's head rested there. He stared at her, eyes wide, mouth wide.

But he didn't make a sound because he was quite dead.

The high tide still sweeping across her legs helped her wriggle free of him. She was drenched when she finally crawled to her feet, and shaking so uncontrollably that her teeth clattered. She needed to get warm and quick, but she took a minute to look at him. To let it sink in.

He's dead. The Bastard is dead.

Jamie glanced up and down the beach. Empty.

The beach didn't give a shit—not about The Bastard, not about her. The beach was indifferent. Numb.

She waited for a feeling to rise up or wash over her. A feeling of relief, or maybe a somber sense of victory. Or whatever she should feel now that The Bastard was dead.

Look, for chrissake. He's dead.

So she looked at him again. Nothing. Except she shivered.

A few meters away, nearer the base of the cliff, she noticed her eyewraps and her boonie hat—the only bits of her gear lost in her plunge from above—and picked them up. Around them, the sand had been disturbed. Signs of a struggle—her struggle with The Bastard. He had lost. She had won.

But no, she had no memory at all of fighting with him. She checked her gloved hands: waterlogged, unbloodied gloves. Had she managed to drown him?

She glanced up and down the beach again. Still empty.

Whereupon all her instincts popped at once. *Shit. I gotta get outta here ay-sap.*

To the cadence of *he's dead, The Bastard's dead,* Jamie waded into the water to avoid leaving a trail of footprints anywhere near his body, smudged the prints she did leave when she stepped out of the water well down the beach, and returned to her car through two klicks of wooded sand dunes without seeing anyone…

By the time she'd changed back into civvies, the cadence had become a reminder. *He's dead, The Bastard's dead.* Because already it seemed unreal, like one of her imaginings during her 127 days in the white metal box.

Shivering still, she started driving. And kept on driving until, five hours of back roads later, no longer shivering, she parked her old blue car in front of Great Hill's first garage.

By the time she stepped out of the car, there they stood, crowding the front porch—Lynn and Adele and Rebecca and Lily and Mary and Dana, even Robin. They formed a gaggle around her as she walked in, all of them talking at once, all of them touching her. Inside, one by one they all hugged her, all but Lynn and Adele.

Lynn approached first, a frown forming as those gray eyes examined her. She knew she had sand in her hair and grit under ragged fingernails and she didn't quite have words yet for some things.

Of course Lynn saw it. "Are you all right?" she asked, running her hands lightly along Jamie's arms.

"Yeah."

Lynn nodded slowly, their understanding formed. They'd talk about it all, by bits and pieces, in the fullness of time. Lynn hugged her, stroked her face and kissed her forehead, and a hint of Lynn's smile appeared. "I am so very glad to see you."

Jamie pulled the little safepack from her rumpled shirt pocket, gave it and her eyewraps to Lynn. "You called it."

"What?" Lynn asked.

But Jamie had already turned to Adele, who stood statue-still and mute a couple meters away. With bottomless black eyes, worried eyes, eyes that wondered if she was really real, Adele examined her.

"He's dead," Jamie said, afraid to move.

"The Bastard." Adele squinted at her. "You found him."

Jamie nodded. "I'm sorry…I-I don't know why I…went there…"

"I know why." Adele stepped toward her, reached out to touch her…her face first, a whisper of a touch with hesitant fingertips that lilted to her shoulders, then down her arms until Adele's hands took up hers, gently, carefully, and kissed them each in turn, anointing them with tears, too, each in turn.

And then, only then, Adele wrapped her arms around Jamie, buried her face in Jamie's shoulder, and sobbed.

"Del," Jamie murmured, nuzzling into the top of Adele's head, filling her nostrils, her brain with Adele's scent, immersing in Adele's imperceptible hum. "Oh god…Del…"

They rocked back and forth until Adele quieted, then sniffled. "You are *so* infuriating, Jamie Gwynmorgan." She grabbed a fistful of Jamie's shirt and yanked, then reached up and steered Jamie's face into a kiss.

Arms wrapping around Adele, the exoskeleton of numbness formed over the last 127 days beginning to dissolve, Jamie melted into that kiss, that peerlessly real, forgiving kiss.

When Jamie came downstairs the next morning, everyone except Robin and Evvie sat pale and subdued around the breakfast table, looking up at her.

Uh-oh.

"How much did the eyewraps catch?" she asked, stuck in a spot at the bottom of the back stairs.

They seemed to wait for Lynn to respond. "Until you got back to your car."

Ah…that includes going over the cliff. So let's toodle off to another topic. Carefully, Jamie did not look at Adele. "Anybody know what ohtahts means?"

"Òtac," said Adele, rising to steer her to a seat at the table. "It means father."

"Richard Lambert is The Bastard's father," Jamie mumbled as Adele sat next to her. "Holy crap."

"Certainly explains a few things," said Mary. "We were just talking about how to get your camera video into the public domain without involving you. Especially since—" Mary didn't finish but the sadness in her face said it all.

Had they all seen what the eyewraps recorded at the bottom of the cliff? Jamie studied her scarred hands while she asked it. "Did I kill him?"

"Yes," Adele said softly, her voice steady and strong as her hand clasped Jamie's.

"I thought maybe…" Jamie watched Adele's hand, felt its grip tighten. Why didn't Adele shrink away from her?

Rebecca leaned forward. "You don't remember?"

"No." Quickly, Jamie glanced at Adele, then Lynn, then the others; incredibly, they seemed unfazed. "Only falling, finding him on top of me."

"Well," said Lynn, "you had the foresight to stick to back roads ever since you left the highway on Saturday back in New Haven, which means your car can't be autotracked after that. And your eyewraps' video has been deleted and destroyed, as have the eyewraps themselves."

"Plus," said Dana, "our security center records indicate you arrived here around one in the morning on Sunday."

"So you're out of it now." Lynn's smile spread around the table. "It's over. Finally."

"What about my cam video?" Jamie asked. "About exposing Richard Lambert?"

"Underway," replied Lynn. "Thanks to Vivian's newest anonymous source. And this time Richard will not recover."

"Really?" Jamie asked.

"Really truly," said Adele.

❖

For thirty-nine days, as Jamie dared to believe what her senses perceived and returned by inches all the way to the edges of herself, she waited to remember what happened at the bottom of the cliff, but she didn't.

She stayed mostly at Great Hill to dodge the media until Afterward. And for thirty-nine days, she tried to convince them not to come to the White House, but they would have none of it. Even Evvie was there.

With the exception of Awa Bulanadi's family, it seemed like everyone she'd ever known or heard of stuffed themselves into the East Room.

Vargas and Tibay, whom she hadn't seen since that day on the ridge in the Palawan. Sherman's family, North Carolina and the other POWs from Saint Eh Mo's, even some of the snipes from her platoon were there. So was a whole regiment of general officers, pooh bah politicians whose faces seemed vaguely familiar from the news, and Vivian Velty and cameras and public affairs people running around saying go here, go there. Hell, she even saw Jonathan Armstrong Archer, visibly smug as he glad-handed his way across the room in business-as-usual comfort.

Before the ceremony—which she would forever after call The Blue Max Circus—she had to do some nodding and smiling, and she probably faux pas-ed the whole way, since nothing quite made sense. When they stood her near the doorway and all those eyes turned to look at her, she retreated from the edges herself, numb again; the world became hollow and remote, out there at the faraway end of a dark tunnel, like peeping the wrong way through binoculars.

And then Lynn was standing beside her again and one last time the public affairs officers steered her, reminded her where to stand, when to turn, and don't worry, you don't have to speak, just shake the president's hand and say "yes, sir," and when the president steps off the podium, you can too and walk straight out of the room the way you came in.

She wanted to keep on going—out of the room, out of the building, away. And that happened, in a bumpy, jostled fashion, because Adele did that—Adele and Robin, one on each side of her.

By then she could hear the hushed voice quite clearly, the voice that had been there the whole time, from the moment she stepped out of the car to enter the White House and become the circus's main act...*I'm sorry, Awa. I'm sorry*. And the sound of the voice, the constancy of it, soothed her.

Chapter Thirty-two

Excellent Fortune

Strains of Chopin lilted out of Jamie's dream to greet her waking. She woke slowly, still dreaming of...

Velvet. Deep, warm velvet that smells like honey.

"Good morning."

Del...Jamie meant to speak it, but wasn't sure she had.

Forty-six days since she went over the cliff, and still no memory of what happened at the bottom. Maybe she'd never remember.

Six days since the Blue Max Circus and not a single nightmare. Six days seemed like forever—and no more than the blink of an eye.

Honey-scented velvet warmth snuggled against her cheek, tender, gentle. And then, with a soft laugh, velvet began to nibble her ear.

Jamie nestled response, perceiving no need to open her eyes, no need to move. "Mmm, perfect," she mumbled, reveling in the sensation of her own smile.

"Almost," the velvet corrected delicately as a stroke caressed Jamie's jaw and wisped down her body, down, down onto her pubic fullness.

Her reply mingled a sigh and a breathy squeal. "Del..." And Jamie wriggled into the velvet, circling, centering, needing.

And afraid. As always, just a little bit afraid.

Because the Woman who illuminated the world behind Jamie's eyelids controlled everything. Every breath, every heartbeat, every fleeting tremor was for Her, ruled by Her, impossible without Her. Inside out, electric and raw, Jamie surrendered to Her fervid exploration, undulated to the commands of Her voice, Her touch, Her tongue as She claimed Jamie's orgasm, provoking its rhythms, evoking its cravings, invoking a molten eruption of joy that scattered the dark debris of the past, that scattered fear itself.

Afterward, Jamie simmered, unable to form words.

She had no words for the way safe felt, for the way home felt, for the way Adele felt. Jamie's eyes opened to find Adele lying next to her only inches away, grinning, looking just like velvet.

Later, at the party tonight, Jamie's eyes would feast on all her beloved people. Lighter than air, she would exult. She would weep, still, at the beauty that surrounded her while she danced with them one by one, one and all.

But now, right now...

"You," she murmured, already soaring. "Now you..."

"Wait a minute. You said we didn't give big-deal presents to each other." Jamie sat cross-legged on the family room floor next to the Christmas tree, shaking her head. "You said donate to a charity, maximum no more than—"

"Correct," Lynn replied with a wily smile. "Until you're twenty-one, though, we fogies are permitted to give Christmas presents to you."

"But I *am* twenty-one."

Now Lynn grinned unabashedly. "This is from last Christmas. When you were elsewhere. Look at the dates."

Frowning her suspicion, Jamie turned to Robin. "'Til you're twenty-one. Is that really true?"

"Hell, yes," Robin replied with a grin that matched her mother's. She waved an envelope. "Antarctica Youth Expedition, here I come."

"You knew about this, didn't you?" Jamie asked Adele.

Cross-legged next to her, a beaming Adele leaned over and kissed her just below her ear. "Yep."

"But, my god," said Jamie. "This—" She picked up the envelope balanced on her knee. "This is a whole education. I could go to school for ten years on this."

"That's the idea." Rebecca winked. "Whenever you're ready. However you want to do it. For as long as you want to take."

"You've been giving me that look all day," said Lynn. "What's up, kiddo?"

Jamie had retreated to the far end of the kitchen, near the hallway out to the garage, while Great Hill's Christmas night gathering— expanded now to include Edgar, Luce and Biz, Springer, ET and Pilar, and several others—meandered from the dining room into the family room.

Offering a smile, resisting an inclination to shrug, Jamie began to edge out of the kitchen altogether.

"C'mon," said Lynn. "It's a lovely night out there. Let's go check out the turbines."

Finding their way by flashlight, they climbed the path behind the house in silence. Near the top, Jamie finally spoke. "I can't let you do this."

"Ah, I see."

"It's too much, Lynn."

"Too much like charity—"

"Yes."

"'Which is reliable for neither the giver nor the receiver.'"

"Yeah, something like that."

They reached one of the eroded rock outcrops near the turbines, and Lynn stepped onto it. "Ten years in the house and I've stood on this spot exactly three times. All three times with you." Lynn lowered herself, wrapped her arms around bent knees, and gazed southward, toward the village lights and the dark ocean beyond. "I see why you like it."

Jamie sat beside her, turned off the flashlight, and waited.

"I've been really fortunate, Jamie. I had a good idea at just the right time. I got the dedication and loyalty and help I needed at just the right time. And because of that, I've made a ridiculous amount of money. Even after we decided to charge less, or nothing at all, Callithump made more than I ever imagined was even possible. And I don't think I've—" Lynn hunched forward, firmed her grip around her legs, and slowly lowered her head.

"Lynn?" asked Jamie. "What is it?"

"I've tried not to be a criminal. Which, as you know, isn't always as simple as obeying the law. And isn't always easy when there's someone who's irrationally determined to fry your ass."

"Lambert."

"It's my own damn fault. If I'd backed off years ago, just let him beat me, things would never have gotten so—" Lynn nudged Jamie's shoulder. "But, hey, I digress. My point is that there's a price for excellent fortune, and a responsibility. Part of the price is having to fend off people who want to fry your ass, but there's also a responsibility that's hard to do right by. You have to figure out how to keep enough, for now and the future, to protect yourself and your family and those to whom you owe loyalty. And then you have to figure out how to consign the rest of it in ways that'll produce some benefit and not backfire on you."

"Like pay for my education."

"Yes, paying for your education *is* part of the responsibility I feel for my excellent fortune." Lynn turned her head to look at Jamie, her features obscure in the moonless night. "The question is which part. And I can't answer that. Only you can answer that."

Jamie squinted at the deep and deeper shadows of Lynn's face. "I don't understand."

"Yes, you do. You're just afraid to believe it." Lynn's hand gently brushed Jamie's cheek. "What I do for my family, what my family does for me, is never about charity. It's about love."

"Lynn—" Jamie's voice rasped and broke over the single syllable.

"Please understand, Jamie. If you want this to be charity, then I encourage you to take my charity with my endless thanks for *your* charity—which saved me from orphaning Robin and widowing Rebecca, which brought down Richard Lambert, among deserving others, and helped give my bill the votes it needed. And I'll root for you as you go on with your life when you leave us behind. Because if this is truly charity, then there will come a moment when you will need to leave us behind for good. It may take a while, but despite what I want or what you want, with or without Adele, your heart will need to leave."

Lynn reached for Jamie's hand, which Jamie gave her. "However," she said, "if you can allow this to be about love—if you can bear to be loved, Jamie—then everything will change for you. Wherever you go, whoever you're with, whatever you do, your heart will also stay here, with us. With your family. And, as one of the family, you'll have to take on a share of the responsibility for our excellent fortune. Because if you don't take it on, you'll end up becoming a criminal."

"Charity would be easier, wouldn't it?"

"I expect so."

"I might really fuck up this…this responsibility."

"Yep."

"Will you forgive me if I fuck it up?"

"Always, sweetie."

About the Author

Sophia Kell Hagin's first novel, *Whatever Gods May Be*, published by Bold Strokes Books, won a 2010 Golden Crown Literary Society Award for Dramatic General Fiction and also was a 2010 Golden Crown Debut Author finalist. In addition, *Whatever Gods May Be* won a 2010 Lesbian Fiction Readers Choice Award in General Fiction and received a 2011 LGBT Rainbow Awards Honorable Mention for Best Lesbian Debut Novel.

Some of Sophia's orphaned early writings may be found at her website, sophiakellhagin.com.

Sophia lives with her longtime love, life, and business partner in the wooded dunes of Truro, Massachusetts.